## Praise for Lexi Blake and Masters and Mercenaries...

"I can always trust Lexi Blake's Dominants to leave me breathless...and in love. If you want sensual, exciting BDSM wrapped in an awesome love story, then look for a Lexi Blake book."
~Cherise Sinclair USA Today Bestselling author

"Lexi Blake's MASTERS AND MERCENARIES series is beautifully written and deliciously hot. She's got a real way with both action and sex. I also love the way Blake writes her gorgeous Dom heroes--they make me want to do bad, bad things. Her heroines are intelligent and gutsy ladies whose taste for submission definitely does not make them dish rags. Can't wait for the next book!"
~Angela Knight, New York Times Bestselling author

"A Dom is Forever is action packed, both in the bedroom and out. Expect agents, spies, guns, killing and lots of kink as Liam goes after the mysterious Mr. Black and finds his past and his future… The action and espionage keep this story moving along quickly while the sex and kink provides a totally different type of interest. Everything is very well balanced and flows together wonderfully."
~A Night Owl "Top Pick", Terri, Night Owl Erotica

"A Dom Is Forever is everything that is good in erotic romance. The story was fast-paced and suspenseful, the characters were flawed but made me root for them every step of the way, and the hotness factor was off the charts mostly due to a bad boy Dom with a penchant for dirty talk."
~Rho, The Romance Reviews

"A good read that kept me on my toes, guessing until the big reveal, and thinking survival skills should be a must for all men."
~Chris, Night Owl Reviews

"I can't get enough of the Masters and Mercenaries Series! Love and Let Die is Lexi Blake at her best! She writes erotic romantic suspense like no other, and I am always extremely excited when she has something new for us! Intense, heart pounding, and erotically fulfilling, I could not put this book down."

~ Shayna Renee, Shayna Renee's Spicy Reads

"Certain authors and series are on my auto-buy list. Lexi Blake and her Masters & Mercenaries series is at the top of that list... this book offered everything I love about a Masters & Mercenaries book – alpha men, hot sex and sweet loving... As long as Ms. Blake continues to offer such high quality books, I'll be right there, ready to read."

~ Robin, Sizzling Hot Books

"I have absolutely fallen in love with this series. Spies, espionage, and intrigue all packaged up in a hot dominant male package. All the men at McKay-Taggart are smoking hot and the women are amazingly strong sexy submissives."

~Kelley, Smut Book Junkie Book Reviews

# No More Spies

# Other Books by Lexi Blake

ROMANTIC SUSPENSE

**Masters and Mercenaries**
The Dom Who Loved Me
The Men With The Golden Cuffs
A Dom is Forever
On Her Master's Secret Service
Sanctum: A Masters and Mercenaries Novella
Love and Let Die
Unconditional: A Masters and Mercenaries Novella
Dungeon Royale
Dungeon Games: A Masters and Mercenaries Novella
A View to a Thrill
Cherished: A Masters and Mercenaries Novella
You Only Love Twice
Luscious: Masters and Mercenaries~Topped
Adored: A Masters and Mercenaries Novella
Master No
Just One Taste: Masters and Mercenaries~Topped 2
From Sanctum with Love
Devoted: A Masters and Mercenaries Novella
Dominance Never Dies
Submission is Not Enough
Master Bits and Mercenary Bites~The Secret Recipes of Topped
Perfectly Paired: Masters and Mercenaries~Topped 3
For His Eyes Only
Arranged: A Masters and Mercenaries Novella
Love Another Day
At Your Service: Masters and Mercenaries~Topped 4
Master Bits and Mercenary Bites~Girls Night
Nobody Does It Better
Close Cover
Protected: A Masters and Mercenaries Novella
Enchanted: A Masters and Mercenaries Novella
Charmed: A Masters and Mercenaries Novella
Taggart Family Values
Treasured: A Masters and Mercenaries Novella

Delighted: A Masters and Mercenaries Novella
Tempted: A Masters and Mercenaries Novella

### Masters and Mercenaries: The Forgotten
Lost Hearts (Memento Mori)
Lost and Found
Lost in You
Long Lost
No Love Lost

### Masters and Mercenaries: Reloaded
Submission Impossible
The Dom Identity
The Man from Sanctum
No Time to Lie
The Dom Who Came in from the Cold

### Masters and Mercenaries: New Recruits
Love the Way You Spy
Live, Love, Spy
Sweet Little Spies
The Bodyguard and the Bombshell: A Masters and Mercenaries New Recruits Novella
No More Spies
Spy With Me, Coming September 16, 2025

### Butterfly Bayou
Butterfly Bayou
Bayou Baby
Bayou Dreaming
Bayou Beauty
Bayou Sweetheart
Bayou Beloved

### Park Avenue Promise
Start Us Up
My Royal Showmance
Built to Last, Coming May 27, 2025

### Lawless
Ruthless

Satisfaction
Revenge

**Courting Justice**
Order of Protection
Evidence of Desire

**Masters Of Ménage** (by Shayla Black and Lexi Blake)
Their Virgin Captive
Their Virgin's Secret
Their Virgin Concubine
Their Virgin Princess
Their Virgin Hostage
Their Virgin Secretary
Their Virgin Mistress

**The Perfect Gentlemen** (by Shayla Black and Lexi Blake)
Scandal Never Sleeps
Seduction in Session
Big Easy Temptation
Smoke and Sin
At the Pleasure of the President

URBAN FANTASY

**Thieves**
Steal the Light
Steal the Day
Steal the Moon
Steal the Sun
Steal the Night
Ripper
Addict
Sleeper
Outcast
Stealing Summer
The Rebel Queen
The Rebel Guardian
The Rebel Witch
The Rebel Seer, Coming April 22, 2025

## LEXI BLAKE WRITING AS SOPHIE OAK

### Texas Sirens
Small Town Siren
Siren in the City
Siren Enslaved
Siren Beloved
Siren in Waiting
Siren in Bloom
Siren Unleashed
Siren Reborn
The Accidental Siren

### Nights in Bliss, Colorado
Three to Ride
Two to Love
One to Keep
Lost in Bliss
Found in Bliss
Pure Bliss
Chasing Bliss
Once Upon a Time in Bliss
Back in Bliss
Sirens in Bliss
Happily Ever After in Bliss
Far from Bliss
Unexpected Bliss
Wild Bliss

### A Faery Story
Bound
Beast
Beauty

### Standalone
Away From Me
Snowed In

# No More Spies

## Masters and Mercenaries: New Recruits, Book 4

### Lexi Blake

No More Spies
Masters and Mercenaries: New Recruits, Book 4
Lexi Blake

Published by DLZ Entertainment LLC
Copyright 2025 DLZ Entertainment LLC
Edited by Chloe Vale
ISBN: 978-1-963890-05-1

Masters and Mercenaries ® is registered in the U.S. Patent and Trademark Office.
Lexi Blake ® is registered in the U.S. Patent and Trademark Office.

All rights reserved. No part of this book may be reproduced, scanned, or distributed in any printed or electronic form without permission. Please do not participate in or encourage piracy of copyrighted materials in violation of the author's rights.

This is a work of fiction. Names, places, characters and incidents are the product of the author's imagination and are fictitious. Any resemblance to actual persons, living or dead, events or establishments is solely coincidental.

Sign up for Lexi Blake's newsletter
and be entered to win a $25 gift certificate
to the bookseller of your choice.

Join us for news, fun, and exclusive content
including free Thieves short stories.

There's a new contest every month!

Go to www.LexiBlake.net to subscribe.

# Family Trees

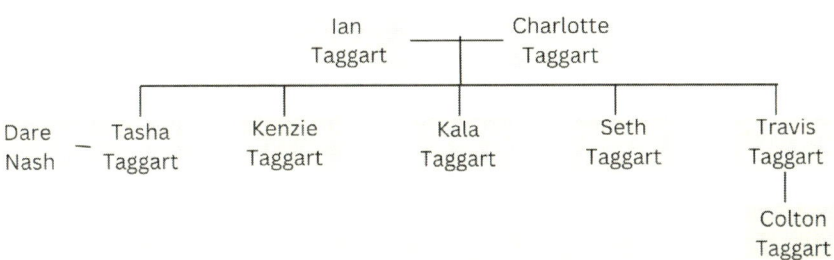

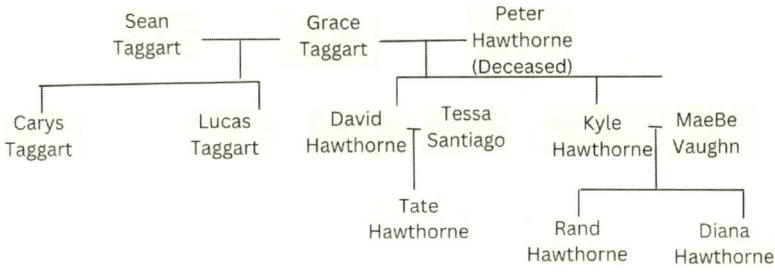

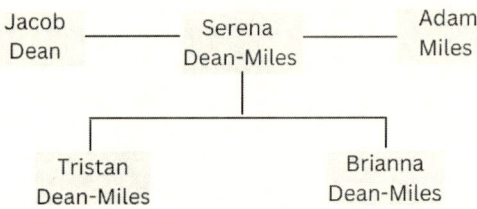
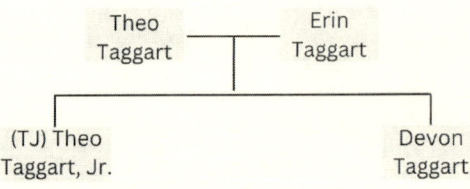
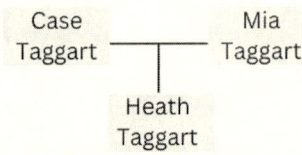
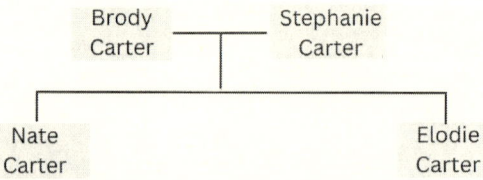
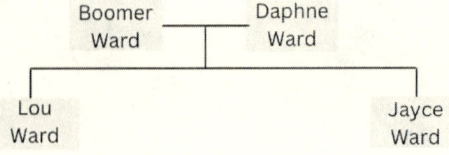

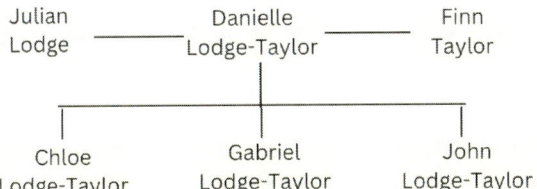

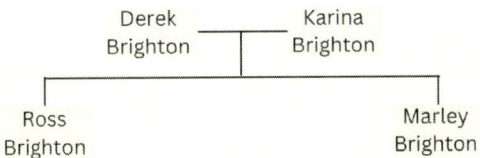

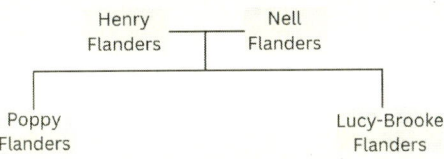

# Author's Note

So this is a hard one. As a writer there are always characters who come to mean something more to you, characters you connect with on a level you can't explain. Kala is one of those characters. There's a lot of me in her. I kind of view Tag's twins as two different parts of my personality. Kenzie is the one you'll most likely meet. She's happy and puts everyone at ease. She's the hostess and the "mom" of the group. But Kala is my darker side. The one my closest friends see from time to time. The one who worries and broods and falls into dark places. She's also the one who loves deeply and passionately. The one who takes on the weight of the world. When Chloe read No More Spies she told me it's the first time she ever thought I needed a trigger warning. That's saying something since I've put a bunch of characters through the wringer. So here's your warning. While there is no sexual assault on page, the idea hangs over the book. It is the shadow Kala can't seem to escape. Some of you will immediately understand, but some of you will scratch your head and wonder where I came up with it.

In order to explain Kala, I have to tell you my story. I was molested from the time I was eight until twelve when the man who assaulted me died. My uncle had a farm we would go to on the weekends and we would run kind of wild through the woods of East Texas, and this man was a neighbor. Memory is a tricky thing. What I remember is touching. Horrible and traumatizing, but so many have gone through worse. It wasn't until I returned to the farm years later that I saw a tent in the woods. It was in tatters as though it had been left behind for years. I froze at the sight. It made me physically ill to see it. And yet I cannot tell you why. To this day I don't know why I dream of red tents and wake crying. My logical brain tells me it doesn't matter, that I would remember. Of course I would remember if something horrible happened to me. But for a long time it was a shadow I couldn't escape.

There's a big difference between fifteen and fifty-four and I'm at peace with not knowing. I live in the space I do understand, the ones that are mapped out with love. But when I sat down to write Kala's book, all roads led me here again. I often process old wounds through my books and this is only different in that I think it's the most honest I've been. This book is steeped in trauma. It's about having all the opportunities for the best possible life and it still going wrong.

Now that I've made this sound like a light, happy read—yes, the sarcasm is all me, too—let me tell you what I hope you'll find in these pages. Hope. Love. The idea that we are put on this earth to lift each other up. I often have a song I consider inspirational to a story or a character. For Kala it's "Rainbow" by Kacey Musgraves. It's a song about life feeling like a storm but we always, always can find safe harbor. I hope you take my hand and let me lead you through this storm because there is love and light at the end.

It'll all be all right....

# Part One

## *That Night*

## Chapter One

Kala Taggart forced air into her lungs and tried to relax. Like this was a normal, everyday Saturday night. It was in some ways. She usually did sneak out of the house to spend time with Cooper, but tonight she was doing something different.

Tonight, she was going to make Cooper McKay hers. Her first. Her only because she was going to love Coop for the rest of her life. And she wasn't going to fake die on him like her mom had, so there would be no need for whatever the hell they did on Saturday nights.

She was pretty sure she knew what they did and it was gross because…parents…but what she was about to do with Cooper would be beautiful.

And it was a nice night for it. There was a full moon illuminating the path from her house to his. Only three blocks separated them, but it was too much. She lived for these nights.

"You're going to get caught one of these days, and Mom will ground you for life," her sister had said as she'd climbed out the window. She would give it to her dad. He knew how to lock down a house, but she'd figured out how to screw with the sensor in the window of the bathroom she shared with her sisters, and luckily it was big enough she could wriggle her way out and shimmy down the drain, avoid the cameras, and then she was free.

Honestly, she kind of enjoyed the exercise and was looking forward to the next time her dad redid the system. Getting one over on the old man was truly something to be proud of. She liked a challenge.

Cooper's house wasn't much of one. His dad wasn't as crazy paranoid as hers. It was easy to move around the sparsely placed motion detector lights. She crept around the back of the house, working her way toward the door leading to the kitchen. Cooper always left it open for her. She'd done it at least a hundred times since she realized she didn't actually have to listen to her parents when they told her to stay home. She had feet and they took her places.

Cooper was her favorite place.

"Hey."

She nearly started at the sound but managed to play it cool. Coop sat on one of the lawn chairs by the pool everyone joked about. Like *hey, do you remember the time we buried our enemies in your pool* jokes.

Her parents were weird.

Of course, they might not be joking since her dad used to work for the CIA and her mom counted assassin in her previous professions. "Hey."

She gave him the smile she only ever had for him. The truth of the matter was she had quite the reputation as a heinous bitch, and she was proud of it, mostly. But not with him. Never with him.

"You're late," he said, standing. He was tall and lanky, and she could remember a time when they were the same height, but the last few years had put a foot on him and she hadn't kept pace. "I was starting to get worried."

"It took forever to get Travis to go to sleep. Seth pays no attention whatsoever to what's going on around him, but Travis is more aware," she admitted. "And somehow he can tell me and Kenz apart."

Cooper's brows rose. It was his dumbass-said-what look. "Of course he can. I know you're twins, but you are unique. I hate it when people pretend they can't tell you apart. There's no one quite like you, Kala."

He was the only one who seemed to see her. Well, everyone saw her. He was the only one who didn't think she was a bitch who happened to have a saintly sweet twin. Like she and Kenzie were mirror images of each other, but Kala was the evil version. Not to Coop. Coop saw her for who she was. He always had. Ever since they were kids.

It was why she loved him. It was why tonight was going to be their night, and then they would go to the dance together and everyone would know they belonged to each other.

And those mean girls who hung around because Coop was gorgeous and popular and on all the sports ball teams could fuck themselves.

"Hey, I heard something about Kyle and MaeBe," Cooper said, worry in his tone. "Is that woman back?"

Ah, Julia Ennis. Kyle Hawthorne was her cousin. Technically not by blood since he and his brother David were her Aunt Grace's sons from her first marriage. But blood didn't mean a lot in her circles. When Grace had married Sean Taggart, those brothers had become family. Kyle had played with her and her siblings, babysat them, always got them ice cream when they were kids. He'd been gone for a couple of years and everyone pretended like he was in the military doing normal military things, but Kala was excellent at breaking into records and listening when she wasn't supposed to. She got grounded a lot, and it was her parents' fault because there wasn't much to do when she was grounded. Eavesdropping and spying were the only fun times to be had. "Yes. From what I heard this week, she's been causing all kinds of trouble. She wants to kill MaeBe because she thinks once Mae's dead, she can, like, move into her place or something. She's pretty psycho."

Julia Ennis had been Kyle's CIA partner. Because very few people in her family actually did real military time. Nope. They found out someone was connected to Ian Taggart and got the Agency invite real damn quick.

She was counting on it.

"I don't understand the connection. Is she an old girlfriend? I asked Dad and he said it was classified."

It was always good to have intel. Her parents had taught her information was a form of currency. Of course, she would never use it against Coop. She gave him everything for free. "He worked with her when he was with the Agency. From what I've pieced together she was actually a double agent for this group called The Consortium. They work for really rich people. Like an Illuminati organization.

Anyway, Kyle found out and tried to kill her, but he didn't do a great job. He also asked her to marry him, but that was before he found out she's a traitor."

"Shouldn't she be hiding?"

Kala shrugged. Who knew why psychos did the things they did? "I think she's doing what abusive shit men do. I think she believes Kyle belongs to her, and no one else can have him. Huh, when you think about it, it's kind of feminist."

Cooper's eyes rolled. "No, it's criminal. Kyle loves MaeBe. I think if he tried to kill this Julia person, she should want to break up. She sounds…intense. I feel bad for your cousin."

Something seemed to be making him anxious. "Our dads will take care of it. I'm pretty sure Kyle's moved Mae into the club. They'll be safe there while the 'rents work things out."

"Sometimes I think there's not a lot to work out," Coop said enigmatically. He looked over the pool, the ghostly lights making him seem oddly distant. "Sometimes it doesn't work and you have to make the choice to save yourself."

The last thing she wanted was distance between them. Distance wasn't what tonight was about. She moved into his space the way she'd seen her mom do to her dad a million times, putting a hand on his chest. "What's wrong? Did something happen today? We don't have to worry about my cousin and MaeBe. Dad won't let anything happen to them. He likes Mae and he always tells me no matter how dumbass a family member is, it's still our duty to ensure they don't die."

There was something grim about Cooper, but she could ease whatever was making him worry. She might think her parents going to a sex club every Saturday night was gross and unbecoming to persons of their advanced age, but they'd taught her how to take care of the people she loved.

He sighed, and his hand came up to cover hers. "Nothing really happened. I had practice and then I went to the movies with Mom and Hunter and Vivi. Dad was working on something at Sanctum. I'm pretty sure it's the Kyle/MaeBe problem."

Their dads had been close since they were kids. Alex McKay had been Ian Taggart's best friend for the majority of their long lives. It only made sense she and Cooper would form an attachment—different but every bit as meaningful.

He was so gorgeous. It made it hard for her to focus. But she was a woman on a mission. She stepped back, sitting on the chaise lounge and leaving room for him to join her. It was a breezy night, a hint of fall in the air. Homecoming was a couple of weeks away, and this year she wasn't going with him as a friend. "I'm sure the screwed-up Kyle situation is part of it, but my dad headed out with his tool kit, so something broke down. Dad likes to multitask when he can. I'm glad he has your dad since he's not actually great at fixing things."

Killing things was an entirely different story. Her dad was great at that, hence the possibility of the body under the pool.

One day she and Coop would have a place to bury their own bodies. Not their own own. The bodies of the people they were forced to take down in the course of their exciting careers as international superspies.

Unless, of course, Coop ended up playing pro sports, and then she would have to figure something out because she wasn't going to be apart from her husband for weeks at a time. He was the only person in the world she would give up her plans for. She'd come to accept he was the dream. Turned out for all her smarts and surly demeanor, she was just a girl who loved a boy.

Coop sank down beside her. "You don't want to go in?"

Usually they ended up in his room, playing video games and listening to music or watching movies on his laptop and making out. It was how they'd spent every Saturday night for the last three months. It had been perfect and she cherished it, but it was time to move the relationship forward. High school would be so much easier once she and Coop settled things between them. "I do, but I thought we should talk first."

There was the grimness again, like she'd brought something down on his head, something he couldn't avoid. "Yeah, we should."

Some of her confidence wavered, but she shoved the thought aside. "Good. I thought we should talk because homecoming is in a few weeks and we haven't made plans."

"I think we need to talk about Jimmy Roads first." He shook his head. "You promised you would stop."

She bit back a groan. She'd kind of hoped he hadn't heard about what had happened after the game. The fight—if one could call it a fight—had taken place yesterday, and she'd thought she'd gotten away with it. After all, the asshole probably didn't want it to get around he'd been taken down by a girl. "He hit you with an eighty-mile-an-hour fast ball."

She always tried to attend Coop's practices. While it wasn't baseball season, the team still got together to keep their skills sharp. They'd been playing a pick-up game Friday afternoon, and Jimmy was a dick.

Coop's jaw tightened. "And you broke his nose. Do you know how fast I had to talk to make sure you didn't get suspended? He wanted to go to the principal. Hell, they probably wouldn't even suspend you. They would send you to alternate ed or kick you out."

She'd thought the dude would at least have some dignity. She'd been wrong. Whiny-ass boy. "I didn't mean to break his nose. I meant to have a talk with him. He's the one who got handsy. I have the right to defend myself."

Jimmy had been condescending. He'd parroted all the things Coop's other "friends" said. She brought him down. Coop was just being nice letting her hang around. Their dads were best friends so Coop felt like he had to be friends with her. She was pathetic since she was chasing a guy who was far above her. Not that her patheticness had stopped the guy from putting a hand on her shoulder and offering to take her behind the bleachers and give her what Coop was never going to give her.

He was lucky it had been only his nose she'd broken. But she wasn't a whiny punk who was going to cry to Coop. She'd handled it.

"You wouldn't have to if you would just be…normal." He took a long breath, seeming to try to keep himself in control.

"It's normal to not want your boyfriend to get injured by a jackass." Maybe she'd been wrong. He'd used that word. The one she hated. Normal. She wasn't normal. She wasn't feminine. She wasn't easy to get along with. Why couldn't she be more like Kenzie? Or better. Why couldn't she be as perfect as her older sister, Tasha? Kenzie was still weird. If she hadn't had Kala around to give her cover, Kenz would have been considered super weird. But Tash was perfect.

*I don't know, Ian. I sometimes wish she was a little more like Tash. Life would be easier for her.*

Her mom hadn't meant the words unkindly—hadn't meant for her to hear them at all—but Kala had taken them to heart.

Coop was the one who liked her darkness. At least he had. He definitely liked it on those late nights when she would sneak from her house to his and he would put his hands all over her and kiss her until she couldn't breathe.

"I'm sorry." She needed to think about how her actions affected him. He probably thought she was emasculating him when she beat up the dudes who fucked with him. It had probably been pretty embarrassing, like he'd been the one who cried to her so she would deal with it for him. It couldn't be further from the truth, but she could see Jimmy throwing those accusations in his face. "I should have let you handle it. I just got so angry with him."

"I know. You never mean it," he said with a sigh.

She could still save this. Guys were hard on each other. The locker room, she'd been told, was a dangerous jungle. Personally, she'd never been much of a team player. She put a hand on his. "Let's go upstairs. Talking sucks. Let's make out." She squared her shoulders and pulled on every bit of bravery she had. "I've got an even better idea. Let's do it."

His head cocked. "Do it? Make out? We do that all the time."

They did. In secret. In private. In public they were friends. Only friends. They weren't ready to tell their parents they were something more. Or their siblings. Or their other friends. She was pretty sure Kenzie thought she was simply hanging out with Cooper. If Tash thought they were close to being really intimate, she would call their parents in. Only her best friend Lou knew they were getting physical.

But she was ready for everyone to know they were more than friends. What if he wasn't?

"I think we should have sex." It was always best to be plain.

Cooper stood up so fast she nearly fell back. "Kala, we're fifteen."

She shrugged. She didn't feel like she was fifteen. Given the profession she intended to go into, she might be middle aged. Of course, her father always said she'd been born forty years old, with a taste for Scotch and violence and a bitterness he admired. "Age is just a number."

A laugh huffed from Cooper's chest. "Yeah, well, I don't think your dad would agree, and I also don't think he would hesitate to murder me."

This was not going the way she thought it would. "He won't know about the sex. I can deal with my father. He's not as bad as he seems to be. And we'll be careful. I got a couple of condoms. My parents are super open about sex. He knows how much I care about you. It won't come as some shock that we're dating."

"Dating?" Cooper said the word like he'd never heard it before.

He was obtuse tonight. "Yeah. What do you call what we've been doing for the last three months? Every Saturday night."

He seemed to think about his answer. "I don't know. Hanging out. Playing some games."

A pit opened in her gut. Maybe he'd been playing a game and she hadn't realized it. "Hanging out?"

"Kala, I care about you, too," he said, his tone low. "You know I do. You know I think you're gorgeous and funny, and I love the time we spend together, but…"

The breeze had seemed warm a moment before, but now it held a hint of a chill. That "but" was going to change everything. That "but" was going to break her fucking heart.

He hesitated, so she helped him out. It was what friends did for each other. "But I'm a lot, right? I'm a righteous bitch and everyone hates me."

He frowned. "I didn't say that."

"You don't have to," she replied, already feeling her armor slide into place. It was sad. She'd come to look forward to spending these nights with him because she didn't have to wear it. Somedays it seemed so heavy. "I have a question for you. What exactly did you think we were building up to with all the late-night make-out sessions?"

He paced, taking five steps to the edge of the pool and then back to the lounger. "I didn't think we were building up to anything. Not now. We're still really young. I know I'm supposed to do anything for sex, but I'm not ready, Kala. You're talking about an adult relationship, and it comes with a lot of responsibility neither one of us is ready for."

Ugh, she could hear his mom talking. Sometimes she thought life would be easier if Cooper's mom had been a criminal like her own. Charlotte Taggart didn't overanalyze every emotion she had. Dr. Eve McKay, well, emotional analysis was her job, and she'd passed the obnoxious behavior on to her son. "Or you don't want me."

He stopped and stared at her. "Of course I do. Kala, you know you're gorgeous."

Did she? Sure, her outer lining was physically attractive, but then she opened her mouth. Then she showed who she was on the inside, and it wasn't pretty.

Would Cooper prefer her sister? Kenzie had all Kala's outer beauty and not so much of her darkness. Kenzie wouldn't have lost her shit on a guy playing baseball. She would have checked to make sure Coop was okay and then moved on with her day.

"I just... I don't think it's a good idea for us to take this any further than we do now. We have time. All the time in the world. I like our Saturdays. We don't have to screw things up by being traditional. How about I make us some sandwiches and we play games and enjoy the rest of the night and pretend this whole talk didn't happen? But you need to chill or I'll have to ask you not to come to my practices. Okay?"

A weird numbness settled over her. It wasn't anger. She knew anger and it wasn't this.

This was her heart breaking.

He didn't love her. He couldn't. He didn't want her. She wasn't sure why he welcomed her every Saturday. Maybe he was scared of what she might do. She could be intense, and she was excellent at revenge. So fear could be the reason. Maybe he also liked making out and she was easy.

She'd been so sure of him. So certain that even when the rest of the world sucked, he was her safe place. It hadn't mattered if everyone besides her family and her best friend Lou thought she was a psychopath, as long as Coop was there.

But he wasn't there. Not really.

She thought about what he'd said before. His words hit different once she knew the truth.

She wasn't going to cry. She wouldn't give her tears to anyone if she couldn't give them to him.

"Kala?"

She stood, her heart a dull thing in her chest. "What you said before, was it about Julia Ennis or me?"

He looked a bit shocked. "What?"

"You said sometimes it doesn't work and you have to save yourself," she parroted back, the words bitter on her tongue. "Is this you saving yourself, Coop? You weren't ever going to take me to the homecoming dance, were you?"

"Why do you care?" Cooper asked, a surprised look on his face. "You don't even like dances. You call them stupid. Like you call everything fun about high school stupid. Like you call all my friends stupid."

His friends were stupid. "Your friends all hate me."

"You don't do anything to make them like you." He seemed to be warming to the argument. "You meet someone and immediately pull some crap."

"It's called being myself."

"This isn't you. This is some phase you're going through. I need you to get through it faster because I don't want to spend my entire high school experience apologizing for my girlfriend," he shot back.

"A phase? I'm in a phase? What was I before? Sweet and docile?" Where the hell was this coming from? "This is who I am, Coop. You've known me since we were in diapers. Did you think I would turn into some sweet thing who decorates your locker before the big game? Who sits around and waits for you to notice me?"

"Maybe it would be better if you did sit around and wait because what you do now is start freaking fights," he said, throwing up his hands. "I knew we couldn't have this talk. I told her…"

And she was afraid she knew who "her" was. It might be easier if she thought he'd had this talk with some other girl. Some other girl would give him advice so she would have a better shot at him. Some other girl hadn't been around all of her life. This was worse. "Did you talk to your mom about me?"

He went still, and for a moment she thought he might not answer her. Then he sat back down, his hands threaded together like he didn't quite trust himself. "We were talking about what Kyle's going through. It worries me."

Oh, this was bad. "We're not Kyle and Mae in this scenario."

"I didn't say that. I just think you're intense and sometimes we need to…"

He said a bunch more stuff, but she didn't hear it. It was a lot of word salad, and it didn't mean anything. She'd heard the important stuff. Intense. How often had she heard the word? She wasn't the Mae in his metaphor. Or was it a simile? She should have paid more attention in English, but she spent all her time thinking about a boy. Who thought she was like Julia Ennis. Which meant he thought she was a monster.

He was still talking, complaining about how often she got grounded.

"She told you to save yourself? Your mom?" At one point in time she'd called Eve McKay Auntie Eve, though they didn't share any blood. A few years before she'd dropped the honorific since she needed there to be no family ties between them. The fact that Cooper had been adopted meant nothing. He was a McKay and not her cousin.

"She said I can't control what other people do and sometimes when a person is drowning, they end up dragging the person trying to save them down, too," he admitted.

He was trying to save her? From being herself? She didn't know how to be anyone else. Sometimes she pretended to be Kenzie to fool everyone—because no matter what Coop thought, they were perfectly identical—but she wouldn't want to live like Kenzie.

He wasn't saving her life. He was saving what he valued.

The tears were there. He was choosing. His friends. His place at Johnson High School. A hole opened up inside her. A hole she hadn't realized he filled. Well, there was one thing she could give him. The last thing she would give him. Starting this moment, she would cut him out of her heart. She wouldn't hate him. Wouldn't love him. Her goal was to look at him and feel nothing. "I won't drag you down, Coop."

He took a long breath, and there was an odd relief in his expression. "Good. My mom was right. This was a hard conversation but a necessary one. I know you don't want to drag me down. I know you don't want to cause trouble."

Oh, but she did. It was there. The need to push whatever button was in front of her simply to see what it did. The impulse to sometimes burn the world down because it pissed her off. Trouble was fun. Trouble might be her true native language. "I won't cause you anything at all. Good-bye, Coop. Next time you see me, pretend you don't know me."

She turned and started walking across the backyard with far less care than she had entered. One of the motion-activated lights came on, but she simply moved through. If her shadow was the last thing he saw, it was okay with her.

How could she be doing this?

How could she walk away from him?

He was the best part of her day. He was supposed to be her dad. Not gross-like. He was supposed to be Ian to her Charlotte. She was supposed to get what her parents had, and there was no way it would be like that with anyone but Cooper. No way. She wouldn't ever feel this way again. She wouldn't ever love again. He'd been her shot.

She'd never actually had a shot.

"Hey." Cooper was suddenly behind her. "What is that supposed to mean? Pretend I don't know you?"

She stopped. It would be far smarter to keep walking. They didn't come back from this. His mom didn't like her. An ache pulsed through her. She'd always thought Eve liked her. She wondered if Alex thought she was bad for Cooper, too. Yes, it would be better to walk, but these were her last minutes with him and she couldn't lose them. No matter how brutal they became. She turned his way. He was ghostly, caught in the shadows from the pool and security lights. "It means if you ignore me and I ignore you, then you get what you want. No one will think you're friends with the nasty bitch, and you can move forward and become everything Mommy wants you to be. You might be homecoming king one day if you play your cards right and hang with the popular people."

"Don't bring my mom into this. She didn't mean it that way."

There wasn't any other way to mean it. "You have to save yourself from me, Coop. Except I'm a motherfucking hero. I'm going to do it for you. You want to let assholes like Jimmy walk all over you, who am I to complain?"

He wouldn't be hers to defend. He would be on his own.

Except he wouldn't be. He would have all his friends, and all the kids they grew up with would likely take his side because he was Cooper and she was…she was who she was.

"He's not walking all over me," Cooper argued. "I was crowding the plate. It's baseball. Are you planning on beating the crap out of the guys guarding me when I play basketball?"

"Not anymore," she admitted. She gave him a shrug like none of this truly mattered. "You've made yourself clear. It's fine. I'll move on to the next guy."

She wished she hadn't said the last part. The look of pain on Cooper's face would stay with her forever. Except it wasn't pain she saw in his brown eyes. It was so much worse. It was pity. "Kala, there's no next guy. I'm sorry. I'm not handling this well. I don't know how to tell you we're moving too fast and I'm not comfortable. I'm fifteen. I care about you. I really do, but you are so intense and I'm not ready."

He never would be. She would always be too intense. Always too much. He would find his sweet girl to take to homecoming, and then he would go through a string of them until he finally settled down with his white picket fence and two point five kids.

She would probably be dead by then, and it wouldn't matter. He'd always been a dream. Maybe he represented a part of herself craving some normalcy.

She wasn't going to get it. "You snooze, you lose, bud. Have a good high school experience. It's when you're going to peak, so enjoy it."

He went pale.

Fuck. "I didn't mean that."

"I know," he replied. "But it still hurts."

Yes, she should have kept walking. "Well, I'm sure your new friends will comfort you. Look, there's no way for us to avoid each other so how about we agree to be polite."

"I don't want to be polite, Kala. I only know if we get together now, I don't think we'll be together in the future. I don't think we make it through. It would be better to be friends now and see what happens."

Friends? She'd never really been his friend. "Sure. But in the spirit of our new friendship, I'll forego these Saturday nights. I don't think friends should do what we've been doing."

"Yeah, I'm sorry. I shouldn't have let it get this far. That's on me. Kala, I'm sorry I let you think…"

She wasn't going to stand here and listen to all the ways he'd played her. She hadn't thought he was capable of playing her. "No need. We understand each other now. You've said what you needed to say. Good-bye. Follow me and we'll have a problem."

When she walked away this time, he stayed in the shadows.

\*\*\*\*

Cooper watched Kala walk away and wished he hadn't had the talk with his mom earlier today. He should have kept it all to himself. Sucked it up like a man, but no, he had to seek validation or something. They'd been sitting in the movie theater arcade. He'd found himself alone with her while Vivi and Hunter had been playing the latest video dance game. He'd been drinking a coke, and somehow all of his worries about how close he and Kala were getting spilled out.

"Are you sure you're ready?" his mom had asked.

And he'd known he wasn't.

"You have to be careful, sweetie. She's far more fragile than she seems," his mother had said. "She loves the way her father does, and that can be amazing when paired with maturity, but right now she has all of Ian's intensity with none of the life experience that tempered him. She's going through a phase, and it's a hard one. I should know. I went through it too, and it can feel like you're drowning. The problem is sometimes when you try to save a drowning person, they take you down with them." She'd pulled in a long breath and sat back as though it had been a hard conversation for her. "I know you've cared about her for a long time, but you're both so young. Is there any way you could wait a little longer?"

He watched as Kala walked away, her slender form swallowed by darkness, and realized he might be waiting forever because his girl wasn't known for her sense of forgiveness.

His girl.

Damn. If she was his girl, shouldn't it be easier? Shouldn't it be like their parents? They were surrounded by long-term married couples who got along and never had any drama. Kala was never-ending drama.

And now she wouldn't let him walk her home. He seriously considered following her, but he valued his balls. She would take them since he'd broken her freaking heart. The look in her eyes would stay with him for the rest of his life. He hadn't been trying to hurt her. It would have been better if she'd cried, but she wouldn't cry in front of him now.

He should never have touched her. He shouldn't have moved it past friendship.

His parents were perfect. Oh, they'd had trouble in the past, but their problems had been about something traumatic that had happened to his mom. His parents knew how to talk to each other. Shouldn't those skills be in his DNA?

Except he didn't share their DNA because Alex and Eve McKay

weren't his biological parents. He didn't know what was in his DNA.

He let out a low groan and moved back to the door leading him into the kitchen. He wasn't going into that tonight. He had way bigger issues than how he fit into his family.

He pulled his cell out and pressed the number connecting him to someone who was almost as familiar as Kala.

"Hey, what's going on, Coop?" Kenzie Taggart sounded bouncy and happy, with pop music playing slightly too loud in the background.

She wasn't going to sound so happy in a moment. "I think your sister and I just broke up."

Had they been together? It wasn't like they did a bunch of stuff in public. Only in private. Just for them.

"What?" Kenzie asked, and there was the sound of someone moving and then the music was off. "You broke up with Kala? How exactly can you break up when you refuse to acknowledge her publicly? Is this more like you finally cut her loose?"

Whoa. He hadn't expected the... What did he even call the tone he heard in Kenzie's voice? "It's not like that. Look, I think we should slow down, and when I told her she freaked out on me and left."

"Slow down?" There was the muffled sound of Kenzie telling someone else to give her some space. So Tash was listening, too. All the Taggart women were going to hate him.

Anxiety made his gut tighten. He was causing trouble. It was the thing he didn't do. His parents were great. He didn't intend to ever give them a reason to regret taking him in. "Kenz, you know how intense she can be. I wasn't trying to hurt her."

There seemed to be some kind of argument going on, and then Tasha's voice came over the line. "Cooper, how long ago did she leave?"

Tasha would be fair at least. When he thought about it, he was kind of happy Kala's twin would take her side without having to hear any of the circumstances. He was pretty sure Hunter would do the same for him. "A couple of minutes. She should be there soon."

A sigh came over the line. "Or she'll go to Boba Babes and drown her sorrows. I'll call her." She was quiet for a moment. "How harsh were you with her?"

"I didn't think I was. I just..." He couldn't tell them what Kala had proposed. It was too personal. She might have told her sister, but he couldn't be sure, and he wasn't giving it away. "She wanted to go to the dance, and I told her I'm not ready to be her permanent boyfriend."

He was pretty sure he loved Kala Taggart. But he wasn't sure he could handle everything loving her would mean. He wasn't sure he could handle the intensity.

He mostly wanted to play ball and hang with his friends and yes, she was one of them, but she wanted more than he could give her.

A huff came from Tasha's end of the line. "Okay. Well, I'll bake some cookies and have a talk with her when she gets back. I think you should stay away for a while."

"I don't want to stay away from her, Tash. I..." He wasn't going to say love. He wasn't ready for that word, either. "She's been my closest friend for a long time."

"But you don't like your other friends to know," Tasha said not unkindly, though he could practically hear Kenzie cursing his name.

"She tends to be rude to most of my other friends." He wasn't the bad guy here. She was stubborn and would walk all over him if he let her.

"It's her armor. If they would give her a chance..." Tasha stopped. "None of this matters now. She'll stay away. She won't be a problem anymore."

His heart was the one breaking now. He was going to lose everyone. Lou would absolutely take Kala's side, and TJ would, too, since he wouldn't risk losing Lou. In so many ways, his best friend TJ was in the same position he was in, but he was handling it so much better. TJ wasn't going to lose his friendship with Lou because she was in love with him.

"I'm going after her." He knew in that moment he couldn't. He couldn't lose her this way. He was being a whiny ass. He did love Kala Taggart, and he wasn't sure he could be whole without her. So he would suck it up and not care what anyone else thought, and they would find a way through.

He grabbed his jacket and walked out the back, locking the door behind him. It didn't matter if she was going to throw some punches his way, he was going to make it right.

"I don't think seeing her again tonight is a great idea," Tasha replied. "Give her some time to cool off."

If he gave her time to cool off, she would ice him out. "I would rather take the punishment now than three months from now when she decides to talk to me. We've been friends forever. We're not ending like this. We'll work something out." He got to the gate and jumped it with the grace of an athlete. He didn't even put down his phone. "I'm going to make this right. Even if I have to drink way too much boba."

It was her go-to. When she was stressed, she either ice coffeed or boba'd.

"She's going to toss it in your face," Tasha warned, and he heard Kenzie's wild enthusiasm for the idea.

He would have to work on her, too. "The good news is I can always clean up. I'll text you when I'm with her."

"How do you know if she's coming home or going to one of her haunts?" Tasha asked.

"Because I'm going to check her location." He could always find her if she had her phone, and she always had her phone. He made it to the street. "Which I can't do if I'm talking to you."

"She already blocked you." Tasha sounded completely sure. "It's the first thing she would do."

He brought the screen down and realized he actually could check the app while they were talking. It was a multi-functional phone. He pulled up the app and sure enough, the only people he could select from were his brother and TJ Taggart. "Damn it."

"I told you," Tasha replied. "Give her some time. She'll come around."

But she wouldn't. It was a real panic inside him now. She would write him off entirely. "I'm still looking."

He hung up and tried her number. It rang once and then went to voice mail. She'd blocked him. She'd probably blocked him before she'd gotten out of the backyard. "Kala, I'm coming for you and we're going to talk. Pull whatever crazy shit you want to pull, but we're going to talk."

He strode into the night, confident he could fix the problem.

Two hours later, he knew the problem was way bigger than anything he'd ever encountered and that his whole world had changed.

## Chapter Two

Kala thought about going home and then turned the opposite way because going home would mean telling her sisters what happened. And then it would be real. Then she would have to admit to everyone Cooper was exactly like the others.

Fuck him. It's what her dad would say. At least she hoped he would. The last thing she wanted was her dad to sit down and give her a dad talk about how she didn't need Cooper.

Because she was pretty sure she did.

The truth was she would have to admit there wasn't one magical person out there for her. She wasn't going to have the kind of life her parents had. This was her truth, and she needed time to face it.

She considered getting an Uber out to Lou's, but her parents would get a notification she'd used the card they'd given her and Kenzie explicitly for emergencies. She hadn't figured a way around it yet. Somehow she doubted they would call needing to see her bestie a real emergency.

Of course then she would have to tell Lou. Lou would definitely look at her with nauseating sympathy.

She walked up the hill leading out of Cooper's neighborhood. A couple of blocks over and she would be in the shopping center with the boba tea shop. How late was it? She was pretty sure they were open until midnight on Saturdays.

How pathetic was it to sit and drink tea by herself on a Saturday night when everyone else was being normal?

Her feet moved out of habit, but her internal storm raged on.

Did she drag him down? Did she drag Kenzie down? Would Kenz be like head cheerleader with the entire class worshipping at her feet if she wasn't saddled down with a dark and broody and bitchy twin?

What would life look like for her siblings and parents and friends if she wasn't around? Her mom wouldn't worry. Her dad wouldn't have to explain her antics to people. Tash wouldn't be embarrassed.

Cooper was embarrassed by her. Such a fucking harsh truth to have to face. He might care about her, might be willing to be with her in the shadows, but he would never walk hand in hand with her out in the open.

The idea of being around people held little appeal, so when she realized there was a park up ahead, she changed her plans. She found a bench and sat, glancing down at her phone.

Maybe she shouldn't have blocked him. Maybe he wanted another chance.

She sniffled. She wasn't giving him another chance to make a fool of her. Nope. She was going to cut him out of her heart.

"Are you okay, honey?" a feminine voice asked.

Okay? No. She was emotionally ravaged, and now she'd nearly jumped out of her skin because she'd thought she was alone. She saw a woman walking down the trail leading to the playground equipment and the bench she currently occupied. She was probably late twenties/early thirties and was jogging. She'd pulled her earbuds out.

Kala nodded the woman's way. It was late, but it wasn't crazy late. There were a lot of people who worked out at night. It was Texas, and even the fall felt like summer during the day. "I'm good. Just chilling."

The woman stopped. "Sweetie, no one chills in a park this late at night. Not unless they're either selling drugs or buying drugs or nursing a broken heart. Guy trouble?" The woman sat down on the end of the bench leaving plenty of space between them. "I'm sorry. I'm being way too traditional. It could be girl trouble."

Kala sat back, kicking one combat-booted foot over the opposite knee. "Guys are assholes."

The woman nodded. "Definitely guy trouble then. They are assholes. It's why I so rarely work with them anymore. I'm a PI. I try to avoid male clients."

Private investigator? A cool profession. Something to distract her from the heartaches of the evening. "You're an investigator?"

She had dark hair pulled back in a ponytail. "Yeah. I usually do things like track down dudes who are cheating or dudes who skip out on child support. It's not all fun murders and stuff. Sometimes the job sucks, but the pay is so good you can't turn it down."

"Really? Like what?" Kala asked, still wanting to put off the moment when she had to make the long walk home. She was going to have to face him on Monday. She would have to walk into American History and sit in the chair next to Cooper's and pretend he didn't exist because Mrs. Jenkins had told them to pick their seats well on the first day since they wouldn't be changing. Well, everyone knew she made poor choices.

The woman sighed and glanced down at her cell phone, one handedly replying to something she read. "So many things. It's hard to be on your own. The whole spy thing feels like it's going to be super fun, but it's actually kind of lonely and the good jobs don't pay well. And when you're independent the clients range from dudes I don't like to scary motherfuckers I can't cross no matter how much I want to."

Something changed. Something about the way the woman looked at her with almost sympathy. Like she knew.

A cold chill—far colder than the early fall air—swept across Kala's skin. She stood, realizing what she should have before. Situational awareness. Her father preached it, but she'd been all in her feelings and now she was alone with someone she didn't know in a park no one could see from the roadway. What had seemed like a sanctuary moments before now felt a bit like a trap.

"I should go. Good luck with the scary people thing." She would go home and face the freaking music. Hell, Tash might feel so bad for her she made cookies or something and she could eat all her feelings, and she wouldn't think about how she'd put herself in this position.

The one with the weird chick in the dark of night. Not the one with Cooper. She'd be thinking about Cooper for a long time.

The woman stood, stepping on the paved trail and suddenly blocking Kala's way.

"Kala, I'm sorry. When I took the job, I didn't realize you were a kid," she said with a long sigh. "She's crazy, by the way, but I really do believe she's not going to hurt you if you comply."

Fuck. What the hell was going on? How did this chick know her name? Why was she looking at her like she felt bad about what she was about to go through?

What was she about to go through?

Someone had been watching her family. Someone had been looking for a weak spot and it turned out she was it. There was only one real threat she could think of right now. "How long has Julia Ennis had you following me? And by the way, I hope the payday was worth it because my parents are going to kill you, and they won't do it slow."

A pinging sound sent Kala's heart rate sky high, and then she felt a hefty dose of panic as the woman's eyes went glassy and a hole formed on her head. It took a moment for it to register. Shot. She'd been shot.

They weren't alone. This woman had led Julia Ennis straight to her, and now her parents wouldn't get the chance to avenge her. Not against this chick. She was dead.

She was dead. Fucking dead.

There were times when her perpetually dark and dramatic soul questioned whether life was worth the misery, but it was obvious now her body's answer. When she felt a hand on her shoulder, training took over and she brought her elbow up and back, hitting whoever was behind her in the gut and earning her a hearty woof.

She immediately brought her boot down where the guy's foot should be and managed to twist enough she could see her attacker.

The panic was so hard to control. She was fifteen. She was going to die and she was only fifteen, and Cooper hated her and no one would miss her. She punched out as another man dressed all in black moved from the trees, prowling toward her like death on two legs.

She didn't want to die. She didn't. She would miss Lou and her sisters and her mom and dad. She would miss her brothers and Bud.

She would miss Cooper so much.

"She's a tiny fucking girl. Someone take her down," a deep voice said.

The words did something magical. She wasn't actually tiny. She was way too tall according to a lot of insecure guys. The only thing

Cooper seemed to like about her were her already generous breasts and hips.

*Sometimes you let the crazy flow. Sometimes it's the only thing that can save you.*

Her mother's words. She might not be tiny. She might be a girl. She might be weak compared to these… How many? Five at least…assholes, but what she was—her superpower lay in her darkness, and she let it flow.

She let go of the panic. She could do this. She didn't have to go down. The guy she'd punched pulled up his balaclava, and she realized she'd drawn blood.

He cursed and held up his weapon, pointing it her way.

"Hey," one of the guys to her left shouted. "No killing the target."

So Julia wanted her alive. Likely to make Kyle come to her without too much of a fight. Or to get MaeBe to turn herself over. She wasn't going to allow it to happen. She could do this. She was a freaking Taggart, and she wasn't about to be the weak link.

Years of martial arts training came back, muscle memory proving an efficient barrier to panic. She couldn't panic if she was busy kicking ass. The guy she'd drawn blood from reached out and grabbed her wrist.

She twisted and got a good hold on his forearm. He was heavy, but she could use his weight against him. She'd flipped her dad before, and he tended to not allow her to win when they sparred. A thrill went through her when she managed to get that asshole on his back, hitting the ground hard enough the air whooshed out of his lungs.

"Dimitry, are you going to let the little bitch take you down like that?" a deep voice asked.

"Hey," another voice said. "We should move this along. The boss wants us all on the plane in less than an hour."

She wasn't getting on a damn plane.

She put her boot on "Dimitry's" chest. "I would stay down if I was you, big guy."

If she could reach into her bag, she could come up with the pepper spray she carried. Or the Taser her mom had no idea she slipped into her bag on nights like this. But it was sitting on the stupid bench.

Everything she needed was just out of reach.

"*Ya ubyu tebya, suka*," he hissed as he grabbed her ankle and sent her flying back.

She hit the dirt and groaned because he'd thrown her hard. She landed face down, her hips hitting the edge of the sidewalk hard. An ache went through her, but she could handle it. She thought about running. There was a time and a place to run, and these guys, despite their beefy bodies, probably weren't as fast as she was.

But that was the moment she realized she was surrounded.

And at least one of them was Russian since he'd told her he was going to kill her. And he'd called her a bitch. There was a lot of name calling going around tonight.

She flipped herself up and went into a defensive stance.

Five. She could handle five.

She could. She had to.

"Come on, kid," the tallest of the guys said, pulling off his balaclava, too. Military cut. Fit. His face was all planes and harsh angles. "We don't have a lot of time here. If you're a good girl, I'll let you have a snack on the plane. If you're not, I'll let Dimitry here give you a snack you weren't expecting."

Maybe darkness wasn't the right word. Maybe her superpower was her rage.

"Fuck you." She ran at the one she'd injured the first time. He was blocking her way. It was time to get the fuck out. She could make it back to Coop's house. Or not. No. She couldn't risk Vivi and Hunter. She would run for the street. She'd made the mistake of wanting to be alone. They wouldn't have been able to corner her if she'd stuck to the streets.

She punched with all her might, trying to break the guy's nose. If she did it right, she could force the cartilage up into his brain. At least in theory.

The man cursed and pulled back enough he didn't take the full force. He slapped out, catching the side of her head and sending her banging into the bench she'd been sitting on. So close to the dead body. "Dimitry, fucking take her out. You're the one with the sedative."

One of the others chuckled. "She's a hell cat. She's a pretty thing, too."

A meaty arm went around her waist, hauling her into the air.

A new kind of anger thrummed through her as she brought her head up and back, ignoring the pain in her skull. She thrashed as the big Russian held her.

And then she felt a sharp pain in her shoulder.

"Go get the car and bring it around the back. We need to take the PI with us," a deep voice said as Kala felt her body start to slow.

Sedative. They'd given her a sedative.

Now there was nothing that could stop the panic.

Things were happening around her, but she couldn't move. She slumped to the ground and felt something heavy on her chest.

She looked up and through the haze beginning in her eyes, saw the Russian, putting his boot on her chest. He spat blood on the ground next to her before kneeling down.

"I know who you are, little bitch," he said, each word snaking through her with malicious intent. "I know your cousin."

Her second cousin. Her mom's. Dusan. He was the head of the Denisovitch syndicate. If they were friends, he might…

"*Ya skazhu emu, kak zdorovo my razvlekaemsya s toboy.*"

Not friends. She could feel the world slowing down. She wished she didn't speak Russian. Didn't know what he'd said.

*I will let him know how much fun we have with you.*

She didn't think they were going to dress her up. No. She knew what the fucker was promising.

It was all starting to go dark.

Cooper. She was supposed to be with Cooper, and it was supposed to be a beautiful night. Not this. Please not this. Not when she couldn't fight. Couldn't defend herself.

But then had she ever really had a shot?

Dimitry's scarred face was the last thing she saw before the world went dark and she entered Hell.

\* \* \* \*

Cooper was pretty sure he'd never seen his father as angry as he was in this moment. He watched as Kyle Hawthorne walked toward the office. He kind of wished he could go with him.

"How long?" Alex McKay asked. He wore some kind of leather pants and the T-shirt he'd left the house in earlier.

When he couldn't find Kala, he'd panicked and called Tasha

again. It didn't matter how much trouble they were going to be in. He had to find her. He couldn't leave her alone. Despite Kenzie's protestations, Tasha had driven him to all Kala's haunts and when they found nothing, they'd come here to the club their parents spent so much time in. Sanctum.

He knew what happened here. He understood the lifestyle his parents were involved in. They were open about it. But this wasn't how he'd thought he would see the club for the first time.

"She's been gone about three hours, Uncle Alex," Tasha said.

Tash and Kenzie and all the other kids called his dad Uncle Alex. All of them except Kala. Years before she'd insisted on calling him Mr. McKay until his dad had given in and told her to call him Alex.

It had taken him a long time to figure out why she'd done it. Because they weren't cousins. They weren't related at all. Their feelings were not familial.

But she'd known long before he did.

Sometimes he felt like he was nothing more than the himbo who'd caught her eye, the dumb pretty boy who could never match her intelligence or ambition.

His father's eyes never left his. "I meant how long has she been sneaking in the house and how far did this go? You want to play adult games, son, you can answer adult questions. I need to know how far you took this so I know if Ian's about to murder you."

It took him a moment to realize what his dad was asking. "Dad, we didn't… I mean we kissed and stuff but…"

"That fucking better be all you did," a deep voice said.

It took everything Cooper had to turn and face the one freaking man in the world he wanted to face less than his dad. Hers. He'd kind of hoped his dad would handle this part. "It never went past a make-out session, Mr. Taggart. That's what we were fighting about tonight."

Ian Taggart stood at six foot five. Cooper himself was almost six two and wasn't done growing, but right now the three inches between them felt like the highest mountain. "Fighting? Do I want to know?"

Tasha moved beside him, standing with him. "Nope. You don't."

Ian's face flushed a deep red, and his jaw tightened. "She is fifteen fucking years old."

"You know she can be stubborn when she thinks she's ready for something," Tasha said.

Cooper realized what was happening. He hadn't meant to bring any of this up. He hadn't thought about anything but the fact that she was out there and she was alone. She would be horrified if her parents knew what happened. He was going to hurt his parents, but maybe it was better than hurting her this way. "It was me. I wanted to go all the way, and she said no."

Tasha's eyes actually rolled. "Dude, she stole condoms."

Alex groaned and slumped down to the chair. The infamous club Cooper had been so curious about looked a lot like a conference room. At least this room did. "Teenagers. We're not going to survive them."

Ian paced, looking like a caged lion. "All right, let me get this straight. My fifteen-year-old daughter tried to sleep with you, you turned her down and she walked out in the middle of the night alone and you let her."

"She wasn't serious," Cooper tried. "She was joking."

Ian turned like he was scenting pray. "If she was joking, she would still be at your house, and I wouldn't know a whole lot of things I don't want to know. So if she was joking, Cooper, then what was the fight about?"

He felt queasy. He fucked everything up, and the truth of the matter was she was probably going to be home at any minute. Kala could be a little on the vengeful side. She was probably hiding out.

"Cooper," his father sent him a stern stare.

This. This is what he'd always feared. He was letting his dad down. He had to be honest, had to take accountability. "She wanted me to be her boyfriend, and I don't think I want that right now. I like her. I like her a lot. She's my friend but…"

"You don't kiss your friends, Cooper." Ian bit out every word. "You don't have make-out sessions with your friends."

"Dad," Tasha began.

Ian shook his head, his fingers coming down on the conference table. He held himself there, looking like he would attack at any moment. "No. I understand Kala can be stubborn. I understand she's not everyone's cup of tea, but he led her on. What was the play, Coop? Did you think you could see her in private? Did you think you could get your hands on her and no one would have to know you thought the freak was hot?"

"It wasn't like that," Cooper replied. But he worried. Maybe it was. He did want to get his hands on her. He didn't want to deal with the ramifications of being her boyfriend. He loved her. He wasn't sure he could handle her.

He was so fucking selfish.

"Then what way was it?" Ian asked, the question a landmine.

"Hey, remember he's fifteen, too," his dad said, standing up and moving closer to him. Like he had to protect him.

"Ah, but he's not the one who's out in the middle of the night." Ian's voice was smooth, but there was no mistaking the threat beneath every silky word. "He's not the one who constantly gets told he's too much. Cooper is the athlete golden boy everyone loves, and Kala is the weirdo everyone thinks will go psycho one day. Do you have any idea how hard it is to be the kid no one understands? You don't have enough, Cooper? It's not enough to be the most popular kid in school? You have to have her, too? But on your terms."

Every word hit him like a bullet to the heart. Was that what he'd done? It wasn't what he thought he'd done.

"Ian, I think you should go find your wife." His dad sounded colder than he could remember, and he knew he was the reason his dad was fighting with his best friend. "I know the trouble with Kyle and MaeBe has you in a mood but…"

Ian pointed a finger his way. "Don't blame this on something it has nothing to do with. You wait, Alex. You wait until your daughter, the one who looks so much like Eve, gets her heart ripped out of her chest by the only boy she's ever cared about and you come back here and tell me I should be reasonable. You think I don't remember changing his fucking diaper? But I'm not capable of seeing the kid I love right now. All I can see is the little shit who told my daughter she wasn't good enough and let her walk out into the freaking night on her own."

"She wouldn't let me walk her home," he protested. And he had to watch his brother and sister. He was the oldest. He didn't have a Tasha and Kenzie to back him up. He'd had to wake his brother and freak him out by making him promise he wouldn't open the door to anyone.

He'd let his parents down that way, too.

"And don't tell him he should have called." Tasha was a well of calm. She handled the whole thing so much better than he ever could have. "No phones allowed on the floor."

"You think I don't know that?" Ian pushed off the table and started for the door. "I don't think your mom and I will be back for a while. Not now that I know I can't trust any of you."

Tasha went quiet.

"I'll go get Derek," his dad said, seeming to try to bring down the intensity in the room. Cooper recognized the name. Derek Brighton. He was a big deal with the Dallas Police Department. They were bringing in the police. "And I'll let your mom know she needs to get home because Hunter is eleven and he's not old enough to be alone. Hopefully Vivi slept through all of it."

So much guilt. So much drama.

"I'm going to call Chelsea," Ian said. "She's at home tonight so she can pull up the security cameras between your house and mine. You two need to go and sit in the lobby."

Tasha followed her dad out, but Cooper's dad put a hand on his shoulder.

"Stay for a minute."

Cooper braced for another blow. His father knew what a shit he was now. He felt like one. He felt like the worst piece of crap who ever walked the earth.

He could still see the minute she understood he wasn't going to say yes. He could see the split second when her heart had broken.

He stood there, unable to respond.

"Cooper, what you did tonight was wrong, but Ian's wrong, too." His father moved in front of him so his face was all Coop could see. "I know you didn't mean to hurt her feelings. I know she can push you. I've always been worried she would push you too hard and you would end up doing something you weren't ready for. You were right to tell her no. You have every single right to decide what you do with your body and when. And I also understand how complex your feelings are. You were wrong to go behind our backs. You weren't supposed to have visitors, and you're going to be grounded for that. The rest of it? Cooper, it comes with being a teenager, and you navigated it as well as you could."

He felt something wet on his cheek. He was crying. He hated it. His mom would tell him boys needed to cry as much as girls, but he also knew how everyone who wasn't a therapist would see him. Weak. Emotional. Still, the tears came. "I'm sorry."

He didn't have anything else to say.

His dad sighed and drew him in for a hug. "It's going to be okay. I would bet she's on her way to Lou's."

He didn't think so. Lou promised she hadn't heard anything. Lou had been the one to tell him if he didn't get the parents involved, she would. Lou had been so worried. But he wasn't going to argue with his dad. He'd fucked up enough for one night. "Sure."

His dad stopped. "Cooper, it's going to be okay. Kala is actually quite capable. She wouldn't do something stupid."

Oh, but she could. She was capable of burning down everything around them when she was angry. Was this her way of taking him down with her?

He hated he'd even had the thought. Why had he thought she was dragging him down?

Because his friends told him so. Because his athlete friends thought she was weird. Because the cheerleaders who were also flirting with him told him he could do better.

Ian was right. He was playing a role. Golden boy. He wanted to be the big man on campus, and he wasn't going to let a little thing like love get in the way.

How many times had she heard his friends make fun of her? How many times had she seen him wave it off and move on?

"Go out and stay in the lobby. Your mom will follow Tasha back to her place and take you home." His dad sounded tired.

Cooper did as he was asked, wiping his eyes and trying not to look like the snot-nosed kid he apparently still was. When he got to the lobby, Tasha was talking to her cousin. Kyle Hawthorne definitely wouldn't cry. Hell, he'd killed someone and probably hadn't cried. He'd been a badass. Kyle wasn't a Taggart by blood, but he fit in. Like Tash did.

"Remember what I said about staying inside," Kyle reminded her. He nodded Cooper's way as he moved down the hall. He was walking opposite the conference room.

Kala wasn't the only drama playing out tonight. What was happening to Kyle and MaeBe was serious and could end in someone dying.

He sat his ass down.

Tasha sat beside him. "It's going to be okay. She'll turn up and I'll have pissed off all my siblings for nothing. I'm pretty sure we're all getting grounded, and they'll blame me."

He didn't care about the grounding. He had a lot of thinking to do. He didn't like the person he saw in the mirror right now. "Are you not worried?"

"About Kala? Of course I am."

Not the question he was asking. Tash might be the only one who understood. "I mean…aren't you worried you disappointed them?"

"My parents?" She huffed. "Weirdly I will have disappointed them and they'll be proud because I covered for her. They'll ground us all, but at some point I'll hear my dad talk about how I remind him of him at this age. He would have covered for Uncle Sean. He'll say his kids are a team and he and Mom made us that way, so they can't be too pissed."

"My dad won't say anything like that. I left Hunter and Vivi alone." Guilt was a pit in his gut. He'd talked to his brother, and from what he understood his sister slept through the whole thing. They were fine, but he'd left them.

Tasha put a hand on his arm. "They're fine, and don't take my dad's words to heart. He's scared, and he kind of processes fear as anger since he understands anger better. At least that's what my mom says. Trust me, my wayward sister is going to get a full-on dose of my dad's fear as anger response." Tasha sat back with a long sigh. "She's going to be utterly impossible to live with." She turned his way, her gaze oddly both sympathetic and a bit steely. "You need to let her go. You need to break it off with her in a way that doesn't keep her dangling on a string. You and TJ are being cruel."

"TJ loves Lou." And he loved Kala.

"But he doesn't want to be with her," Tasha pointed out. "Any more than you really want to be with Kala. I don't blame you. You're obviously not a good match."

Oddly, her words bugged him. Even though he'd heard them a million times before, wondered about it himself. "I think we've always been good friends."

"She's always chasing you, and you like to be chased," Tasha replied. "It doesn't make you a bad guy, but after this if you don't let her go, you're moving into bad-guy territory."

He couldn't actually imagine his life without Kala. It somehow didn't compute in his brain. Like he needed both his golden boy athlete life and the moments he had with her.

Was he hurting her?

His mom didn't think he should be with her either. Not because she didn't love Kala. Because they were... What word had she used? Volatile. He'd had to look it up. Incendiary. Unstable. Like a bomb waiting to go off.

His mom would be upset if he didn't take her advice. What would she think of him? Would she wish she had a kid who listened? Maybe there was something in his DNA that made him this way, something buried deep inside that neither of his parents could recognize in themselves the way Tasha had talked about.

But Tasha wasn't a Taggart by blood either.

Maybe Tash was better than he was. Better at fitting in. Better at being the child her parents hoped for.

He sat for a moment, feeling heavier than he'd ever felt before. He wasn't sure how much time passed. Very little. An eternity. Tasha sat beside him, texting. Probably keeping Kenzie and Lou up to date.

He didn't have anyone to text. Not about her. His friends would say good riddance.

TJ was asleep.

He was alone.

He missed her.

Kyle walked in from the back rooms, a phone in his hand. Not his cell though. It was small. Like a burner. Why did Kyle have a burner phone?

"Proof of life," Kyle said, not bothering to look over as he walked out the door and into the night.

It was weird.

Tasha stood. "Where is he going? There's a car out there. I don't think there's supposed to be a car out there."

Something cool snaked along Cooper's spine, some instinct he'd never felt before but had been buried deep. Was it too much of a coincidence that Kala disappeared on the night everyone was freaked out about Kyle's evil ex? From what he'd gathered, this Julia Ennis person was trying anything she could to get Kyle back in her clutches.

Wouldn't taking Kala be a good reason for Kyle to walk into a trap?

They watched as Kyle got into the car and pulled away, tires screeching.

"We should tell someone," Tasha said.

Was Kala in the car, too?

MaeBe Vaughn was suddenly in the lobby, and she wasn't alone. His dad was there along with Ian and Charlotte Taggart, and all had grim expressions on their faces. Something had changed. Something big.

Tasha seemed way more capable of rational thought than he was. She pointed toward the parking lot. "He left. He went out the door and got in a car. I don't think he knew them."

MaeBe's face went pale. "Who?"

"Kyle," Tasha replied. "He didn't even say good-bye. He was talking to someone on the phone and he left. Why would he leave when Kala's missing?"

Cooper was terrified that he knew the answer to Tasha's question.

He stared out into the night as they spoke and worried he might never see her again.

## Chapter Three

Kala came awake to the nauseating sensation of turbulence. Her eyes opened and for the briefest second she thought she was on the plane that would take her to the family cabin in Colorado. They normally drove, everyone piling into her dad's big SUV. It was five hours to Amarillo where they would stay, eat steak because...her dad...and then wake up and six more hours to the cabin.

But this year she and Kenzie had a martial arts competition, and her mom had stayed with them while Dad started the vacation. They'd taken a plane to Alamosa where Dad met them, and then she'd known why they called it the Rocky Mountain Scareways.

She hated turbulence.

She wasn't on a plane to Colorado.

Why did everything ache? What had happened? The fucking Russian. He'd...had he? She couldn't remember because she'd been unconscious. Unable to protect herself. She didn't even know... She didn't know if she was a virgin anymore.

Bile rose but she forced it down. Take stock. She needed situational awareness, and she would only have a couple of minutes before they realized she was awake.

She quietly forced a deep breath down. She was by the window, though the blind was drawn. This wasn't as nice as the private plane her dad sometimes used. It was more like a small commuter jet. So there was only one person beside her. From her vantage point she could see what appeared to be a man wearing jeans and sneakers. Not fatigues.

"I could have had much more fun if you give me more time," a familiar, hate-filled voice was saying. She could barely hear him over the hum of the engines.

"She'll kill you if she ever finds out," another man said. "You need to stay away from her. You know she's a kid."

"She's not," Dimitry insisted. "She's a whore like all Denisovitch women, and they're only good for one thing."

Was the ache in her body a consequence of her time with Dimitry? How much had she lost? Tears pulsed behind her eyes, but she forced them back. It didn't fucking matter. It didn't happen. If she didn't remember it, then it didn't happen. Besides, who cared? No one did. Surely not Cooper.

She couldn't think of him right now. Couldn't think about the piece of herself she'd meant to give him, the one he'd rejected. The one someone had stolen from her.

She was going to kill that fucking Russian.

She was never going to tell anyone…anyone. Better they thought she got beaten up. She sniffled and tried to quietly move her limbs. Every movement felt slow and she ached. Everything hurt.

Kyle. She finally looked up and Kyle was in the seat beside her.

Well, of course he was.

Dimitry stood up, his big body unfurling from the aisle in front of her. He turned, and his eyes flared when he saw her. His disgusting lips turned up in a smirk. *"Ty khorosho spala? Ya znayu, chto ya–da."*

Had she slept well? He insinuated he had. Like he'd enjoyed his job and needed rest after a long night of…raping her?

She'd thought the word.

She'd been reckless and impetuous and all the things she'd been accused of being and everyone would nod and be sympathetic but deep down they'd always known she would be here. They'd always known she would get in trouble and lose pieces of herself because she wasn't smart enough to keep them.

"Dimitry, sit down and leave the girl alone. I'm not going to tell you again." One of the assholes was in charge. The big guy with brown hair and dark eyes. "We're about to land. You okay, kid? We have a medic if you feel sick."

Sick. She wanted to die. She wanted the ground to open up and swallow her whole because this was all her fault. She'd been the weak link. All she had was her strength. Would anybody even put up with her if she was weak?

"Fuck you," she replied simply. She didn't need to say anything else to these assholes.

The guy sighed and sat back down, telling Dimitry to do the same.

She sat there wondering if Kyle was dead. Probably not. His chest moved. It was good to know her cousin could sleep in the middle of his own kidnapping. Was it technically a kidnapping if he'd walked into the trap? She was the kidnappee, and he was the dude who'd been dumb enough to let it happen.

When she thought about it, it was Kyle's fault. Kyle had shitty taste in women. Mostly. MaeBe was all kinds of awesome, but she had to question his every choice since this Julia person was obviously a monster.

She felt an ache go through her as the plane hit the landing strip. She didn't even know where she was. Where were her parents? She wanted her mom. She wanted her mom to wake her up and tell her she's late and she has to go to practice, and she would start the whole day over and this time she would stay home with her sisters and brothers. She would stay in the house and never let herself think about Cooper McKay again.

Kyle's eyes came open, and there was a moment of startled recognition in them, a panic as he looked around and finally settled on her.

Yep. He'd walked into the lion's den for her. "I blame you."

He should have saved himself. Everyone would hate her now. Her aunt and uncle would be so pissed she'd put Kyle in this position. She didn't even want to think about how her parents would feel.

At least if she died, Cooper wouldn't have to look at her again.

Cooper would never touch her. She wasn't sure she would let anyone touch her. Ever again.

"Me?" Her cousin's brows had risen. "I'm not the one who snuck out of my perfectly safe house to visit my boyfriend."

The words made her stomach turn, but they were true. At least the sneaking out part. "He's not my... Well, not anymore because he's an asshole like all men. But this is about you, isn't it? At first I thought it was someone who was pissed at my dad, but then I woke up and you were here. Unless you've turned supervillain. Have you, Kyle?"

Her cousin snorted. "No."

"Then that psycho ex of yours couldn't get to Carys or Lucas or David, so she kidnapped me." It was the only possible explanation. "And you're the dummy who fell for it."

Her cousin got the aggrieved expression on his face a lot of dudes got when she pointed out simple life truths. "Yes. I'm the dummy who decided to save your ass."

"You can't save my ass if you're beside me in prison." She leaned in, her voice going low. "There are only five of them. I think we can take them."

Now he got the shocked expression she saw a lot from the people around her. "No. We're not going to *take* them. We're going to sit on our asses and wait for MaeBe to come up with a brilliant plan to save us."

"Or my parents to blow up enough shit that this person of yours shoves me back out in the world and asks them to go away." Her dad was going to be mad, but…her mom. Her mom had to be so scared. "They're going to be so pissed at me. It might be better to die."

"Don't say that. Don't joke right now."

"I'm not necessarily joking. Dad I can probably handle. He'll try to inject me with some sort of tracker, but he'll chill after a while," she explained. "My mom will never forget. Never. She's the one who saved me from the tracker the first time around. There was a lot of talk about bodily autonomy, but she will let that go now. She'll hold my ass down and put the collar around my neck. Or they'll lock me in my room. Forever. I guess they know I ditched all their GPS devices. Like I couldn't find that in my shoe. I know all their tricks. They're going to kill me."

The plane rolled to a stop and the goon squad started to stand, getting ready to move out. One of the guys she'd punched the night before stood in front of her.

"Hope your wife's got insurance on you because my mom is going to kill you," Kala said, raising her voice.

The man turned, his dark eyes on Kala. "Keep talking. I would love an excuse to spend some time with you."

Kyle hustled, getting up and putting himself between them. "You'll go through me first."

"I don't think that's going to be much of a problem." The man smiled but there wasn't any humor to it.

"Do you know who the little bitch is?" A dark voice rumbled from behind her, a familiar deep Russian accent flowing with menace.

The guy in front of Kyle shrugged. "Don't really care."

"She's a Denisovitch bitch. It took me a while to connect the two, but she's the second cousin of the head of the syndicate. Whatever this woman is paying us, do you understand what the other syndicates would do to get hold of her? We could make millions selling her."

It was good to know it wasn't merely sexual assault the asswipe was into. Trafficking was on the menu, too. She was in for some fun, fun times.

And then Kyle was pressing her into the seat, making her every muscle ache, and there was the sound of a world exploding. At least it sounded like it to Kala. Fear poured through her and her hands started to shake. Gunfire. He'd shot the Russian. He'd pulled his gun and put a bullet in him, and she didn't care the asshole was dead, except... He was the only one who could tell her what happened.

It was her second dead body in less than twenty-four hours.

She was going to die. Tears clouded her eyes.

"And now I have to share less money, so in a way he was right." The American dude seemed to be talking to Kyle, but he was in front of her so she couldn't be sure. "Do you want to say anything? I'm going to warn you, I'm not afraid of her father or whoever the hell her cousin is. I'm auditioning for a job, and I'm going to do it right."

"Should I call you John?" Kyle asked like they needed to know the dude's name.

Only one thing was important at this point. "There's only four of them now."

They could totally take them. And then she would kick Dimitry's dead body to make sure he was dead.

He could be lying. Why would he lie?

*I'm not going to be sick. I'm not going to be sick. I'm not going to fucking cry.*

A banging sound cracked through the plane, almost as loud as the damn gunshot had been, and it pretty much scared Kala just as much.

Another asshole walked through. So they were at least back to five.

"What the hell happened?" The new guy frowned as he looked over the cabin of the plane. "Why did you kill the Russian?"

The pilot had stepped into the cabin and nodded the new guy's way. So six. She blamed Kyle.

"The Russian wanted to take the little girl and sell her to one of the Russian syndicates." The guy Kyle called John huffed out his reply.

"I'm not a little girl." Kala whispered the words, but they made her sick inside. She wasn't a little girl at all, and she might have had something precious taken from her.

Something she could never talk about.

"You need to be a girl who keeps quiet." Kyle's low voice held a note of desperation. "Your bravado is going to get both of us killed. Stay behind me. We're not going to let them separate us."

Would they even have a choice? Kala turned slightly, wondering if she could tell where they were. The blind was down. Would they stop her if she opened it?

"He wasn't getting with the plan," John was saying. "I thought I'd save you the trouble and fire him. You told me to watch out for the kid. I didn't like the way he looked at her."

She felt Kyle stiffen beside her and looked up to realize they had a newbie.

Julia Ennis. Kyle's evil ex. Proof her cousin had terrible taste in women. MaeBe was a lucky accident.

She looked normal. Long blonde hair. Fit body. There was something about her face that was too sharp. As though her hard edges couldn't be contained by mere personality. This was the woman who had dragged Kyle so low.

So low. Because she "loved" him. Because she was obsessed with him. Because deep down it was simply what a woman like her did.

Some nasty questions played at Kala's brain, but she shoved them away. She didn't have to answer them now. There was plenty of time to wonder is she was even still a virgin much less ponder if she deserved all of this.

"And now you have one less person to share the pay with," Julia said with a dismissive wave. "Well, he's yours to clean up. After. For now I want you to take the young Miss Taggart to the limo. Don't take your eyes off her. She's smarter than she looks."

Kyle stood, putting himself between Kala and Julia. "I'm not letting you take her. You promised me I could stay with her."

"Well, she's not getting far, and John seems to know how to handle anyone who doesn't understand how I want my underaged prisoners treated." A long sigh came from Julia's chest. "She's going to go sit in the limo so we can talk. I'm not going to send her off somewhere. I have a room ready for you at my house, and I will allow you to share it with her. Maybe you can keep her under control. I have no idea what the Taggarts have been teaching their kids, but that one is practically feral."

She might be feral from here on out. Why the hell not? It wasn't like she fit in when she followed her own instincts. "You should remember that."

Julia glanced around Kyle's big shoulders, looking her way. "She reminds me of me at her age. Except I was better with manners. Her father should beat her more."

*Reminds me of me.* Reminds me of the woman who knew how to drag a man down.

There was more conversation, but all Kala heard for a moment was Cooper's voice.

*Sometimes when a person is drowning, they end up dragging the person trying to save them down, too.*

"Excellent. Why don't you and John take Miss Taggart out to the limo while I talk to my fiancé?"

The words jarred Kala out of the miasma of her misery. She had to be better than this. Maybe in this case, she had to be exactly what everyone thought she was. Unfeeling. Uncaring. Out for herself. Unafraid. Utterly unafraid. "Oh, my god, lady. You are delusional. He's not your fiancé. He's practically married to MaeBe."

Kyle's head shook. "No, I'm not. Mae's never going to forgive me for leaving her. We don't have a relationship anymore."

She was screwing up, but then wasn't that what she did? She tried to shake it off. "Well, if that's true, you screwed that up. MaeBe is awesome. Kyle kind of sucks. He makes everyone in the family go to his lame funeral and he didn't even respect us enough to actually be dead. At least I got an Xbox out of it."

Julia ignored her sarcasm. "It was inevitable that any relationship Kyle tried would fail. He was already in the most important relationship of his life."

Kala's only refuge was sarcasm. "Yes, with his Xbox. He loved that thing, and now it's mine."

She could practically hear Julia growl her way. There was a dark look on the woman's face that seemed to force Kyle to move.

"I need you to promise me she won't be hurt and you won't separate us for more than a few minutes." Kyle sounded so reasonable.

Julia put a hand on her cousin's chest, an entirely possessive gesture.

She put her hand on Cooper's chest when they were alone. Like she could feel his heartbeat.

What if she was fooling herself and what seemed like love was mere possession? Everyone talked about how obsessively possessive she could be. She'd heard people talk about how she wouldn't let anyone near Lou. How she horded her best friend like a dragon with gold.

Dragons weren't exactly the good guys.

"I think you want me to get her back to her parents at the first opportunity. But yes to everything you asked," Julia was saying. "She will come to no harm unless new John here doesn't want his job."

"I don't want to hurt some teenaged girl." John moved down the aisle. "Come on, kid. Try to remember I'm the one who took you down."

"Only because you had backup." Kala forced herself to move, taking in every ache. Wondering how she got them.

Wondering if they would always be there, simmering under her surface. A nightmare she could feel, sense like a shadow always at the edge of her conscious. But one she couldn't catch and kill.

"I still have backup." John held out a hand, offering her the stairs. "If we get back soon, I can make us pancakes."

"Like I would eat poison pancakes." Despite the rolling in her gut, she had a reputation to uphold.

"They're not poison." John managed to sound aggrieved.

Kala walked on, head held high. But her soul…her soul was so low. And she'd done it to herself.

\* \* \* \*

Cooper was miserable. For days it seemed he'd been locked in utter and complete hell, not knowing what was going on.

He knew it had only been a day or two, but she still wasn't home and no one wanted to talk to him. No one could talk to him since he was grounded and had barely been out of his room. And he'd lost his cell.

His parents were pissed, though they seemed more sympathetic today than they'd been the night it had happened.

That night. If he could, he would take it all back. He would do whatever she wanted. If he'd thought he wasn't ready to be Kala Taggart's boyfriend, he absolutely wasn't ready to live in a world where she wasn't.

He had to go back to school tomorrow. They'd let him stay home Monday because he'd woken up, realized she was still gone, and promptly thrown up and wouldn't eat anything. It had convinced his parents he needed at least a day. But tomorrow he would have to go, and all those friends would ask where she was. Not because they wanted to know but because they wanted to avoid her.

What was Kenzie saying when people asked? Did they call Kala in sick or had they gotten the authorities involved? He was pretty sure they wouldn't call in the police. The Taggarts were an authority in and of themselves.

Would anyone ask? Not caring seemed like the worst outcome of all. That she could be gone and no one outside her family would be concerned.

He had no idea what she was going through, and she probably thought he didn't care.

There was a knock on his door and his mom came in.

"Hey." She was dressed for the office, though he knew she hadn't gone in. She looked tired, like he felt. His dad had been at the MT building nonstop since Kala and Kyle were taken. He was working with Uncle Adam and Aunt Chelsea on logistics. Whatever that meant.

His father hadn't even bothered to tell him their weekly flight lessons were canceled. His dad had been taking him for lessons since he was fourteen. Next year he could get his license, and he'd always meant to take Kala up, to show her the world he loved so much.

He might never get the chance.

"Hey." He put down the math text he hadn't been focused on at all. Words didn't make sense to him right now. Numbers definitely didn't.

"They think they know where she's being held," his mom said, sitting at the edge of his bed.

"They do?" For the first time in days, he felt a surge of hope. "Where? Do they know if she's still alive? What are they doing?"

His mom reached out, putting a hand on his arm. "MaeBe thinks she's tracked her down because of a pizza order."

She had the worst taste in pizza. Another thing he'd made fun of her for. "Anchovies. No sauce. It's gross. How does her pizza habits… Someone was monitoring the orders for the area. Wow. That was smart."

"I believe Mae figured it out," his mom replied. "I wanted you to know. I'll keep you updated. Charlotte is in close contact with your dad."

"Does Kenz know? Someone should tell Lou." He didn't want anyone left out.

"Kenz and the others are at their Uncle Sean's for now. He'll let them know what's going on, and I imagine Tash and Lou are texting constantly." She sighed and reached into her pocket. "And I can't leave you alone in this. I can't. I know your father is still mad, but I think you've been through enough without having to deal with this alone."

She passed him his cell phone.

He took it. He wanted to call… He wanted to call her. He wanted to talk to her, but no one was going to answer that line.

"You're still grounded, but you need your friends right now more than you need a lesson," his mom was saying.

"Where is she?" He needed to know.

"A town called Winchester in Virginia. Apparently Julia Ennis has a house there. From what I understand they're going to raid the house tonight and attempt to get her back."

"I want to go. I won't screw anything up, but I think I should be there when she gets out."

His mom's jaw tightened. "Cooper, you have to understand that we don't know what she's been through. She needs her parents right now."

"She needs me. She needs to know I take it all back. Everything."

"Sweetie, you're having a trauma response. You had your

reasons for not wanting to push the relationship further."

Dumb reasons. Reasons like he was an asshole who wanted to be a golden child so his parents would never regret adopting him. Reasons like he wanted everyone to like him so his parents would never regret adopting him. "I don't care. I want to be with Kala."

"I don't think it's a good idea. Especially now. Kala can be difficult in the best of times, and these aren't the best of times. She's going to need therapy. Putting her in a volatile emotional space isn't going to help," she argued. She stood up, glancing down at her own cell. "I should call your dad and get an update. Look, with any luck at all she'll be home in a couple of days. Take this time to think about what you want to say to her."

She started for the door.

"If I'm with her, would it bother you?" Not the question he really wanted to ask. He needed to be braver. "Would I embarrass you?"

His mom's brows knitted together as though she was trying to figure something out. "Coop, why would you think that? I love Kala. I love you. I think one day you'll be good for each other, but you're so young."

"You and Dad were young, too."

"I met your father in college. Yes, we were young, but there's a huge difference between twenty and barely fifteen," she pointed out. "And honestly, it still fell apart."

"Only because of what happened to you." He didn't like to think about it. He knew his mom and dad had divorced after she had a terrible thing happen when she was working for the FBI.

"Cooper, things happen all the time. It wasn't truly the kidnapping and sexual assault I endured that broke us." She seemed to blink an awful lot. Damn. He hadn't meant to make her cry. "It was how we reacted to it. This is life. We cannot control some of the things that happen to us, but we do control how we handle them. You need to let Kala figure out what she needs because her whole world changed in the blink of an eye. You need to listen to her and support her. Do you want to talk to someone? I'm always here, but sometimes it can be easier to talk to someone who isn't your parent."

Therapy. She was offering him therapy. She thought he was weak. Maybe he was. Damn it. He knew there was nothing weak about it. She'd always told him there was strength in talking about the pain people went through. Even Uncle Ian had a therapist. So why did he go there? Why did he think he needed to be perfect?

He knew. He knew but he never said it because if he did, he knew he might not like the answer. Or he might see the hesitation in his parents' eyes.

"Cooper?"

He sniffled. He was crying again. His shit friends would make fun of him for it.

Kala would hug him and vow vengeance on whoever had made him cry.

"If I wasn't good at sports and popular at school, would you be embarrassed to be my mom? Like would you think you should have picked another kid?"

His mom's jaw dropped, and tears slid from her eyes as she moved back to him, sitting down and wrapping her arms around him. She hugged him tightly. No hesitation from Eve McKay. "I would never want another kid. Never. You are my son, Cooper. I don't care whose womb you came out of. You are mine and your dad's. I don't care if you never play baseball again. I certainly don't care if some kids don't like you. Sweetie, I'm so sorry. You seem happy."

"I am happy." He shook his head. "Well, I'm not right now. I'm just saying I'm happy you're my mom, but I worry."

She smoothed back his hair like she had when he was a child. "I love you and Hunter with every fiber of my being. The same way I love your sister. Your father and I didn't adopt you because we wanted a perfect kid. We did it because we wanted to love you. There are no expectations except we want you to try your hardest and be kind. That's all we ask." She kissed his forehead. "I love you. You made me a mom, Cooper. You made me a better person, and there is nothing you could do that would make me not love you."

He let her rock against him, a familiar rhythm from childhood he found infinitely soothing.

"Do you think about her?" his mom asked after the longest time.

He knew who she was talking about. "No. It's you I want proud of me. She doesn't know me and she never will. I'm okay with never knowing her name. This is not me yearning for my birth mom. It's me going over that night in my head and wondering if I could have done it differently. If I hurt you by loving her."

"No." She shook her head. "Absolutely not. You know what, I am interfering where I should let things play out. Not the sex part.

You are not ready for sex and neither is she, but the rest of it..." She sighed. "I'm being a therapist and not your mom. If you want to be Kala's boyfriend, I will support you. I told you. I love her, too. But you have to be prepared. She is going to need more than love for a while."

"I'll give it to her. Anything she needs," he vowed, leaning against the woman who'd changed his life utterly when she decided to adopt him. He knew the adoption had been closed and his birth mom didn't want contact at all. He was cool with it. He didn't need her. He had his mom and dad.

And he had his answer. He was being insecure, and he needed to work on it.

He would. He would do it for himself.

He would do it for Kala.

## Chapter Four

In the end it had been strangely uneventful.

"You okay, kiddo?" her dad asked for the five hundredth time.

"I would be better if Kyle stopped making me want to vomit," she replied, yawning.

Her cousin sighed and stopped making out with MaeBe. "You really are a menace."

She got that a lot.

After a long talk with Julia and some halfway decent pizza, her family had shown up and taken out all the bad guys. Not that she'd been allowed to watch. No. She'd been hustled out via secret tunnel by her mom and Tennessee Smith and coddled like a baby.

They didn't know she wasn't innocent anymore. Maybe never had been.

In the end it had been her dad, uncles, Aunt Erin, and MaeBe who'd taken out Julia Ennis.

She'd been free for hours now, but there was a weight on her she wasn't sure would ever come off again.

"Sweetie, your dad only wants you to talk to us." Her mom sat across from her, looking elegant even after what they'd been through. After they'd done what they had to do, they had her on the MT jet in mere hours. She was on her way home.

Would it feel like home?

They were an hour into their flight, and she couldn't bring herself to talk about it. Uncle Sean had tried. Aunt Erin had offered her a soda and told her it was okay if she wanted to punch something. Uncle Theo had asked if she wanted his phone and AirPods to listen to some music.

Knowing her uncle it was probably some whiny girl rock.

She didn't feel like she belonged here anymore.

"I did. I told you what happened. Cooper's an asshole, and I've learned my lesson. Boys aren't worth it. Consider me asexual from here on out. Ground me all you like. I won't be going anywhere anyway. I've seen my share of dead bodies now. I think I'll ditch the whole spy thing and become like a librarian or something." She bet Julia fucking Ennis never thought about becoming a librarian.

Her dad pointed her way, his eyes narrowing. "And that is why we worry."

She needed to deflect the parental units or she would find herself at the Ferguson Clinic for Tender Feelings. She wasn't going to have feelings anymore. "I'm fine. It was scary and I had to see Kyle in a towel and that was gross, but I'm fine. I spent my time in a cell in the basement watching the guard sneak YouTube walk-throughs of the video game he's playing. Well, played. I assume someone killed him. Should have done a walk-through of this life level, buddy."

She couldn't quite dump the sarcasm. It was a part of her.

"Kala, you need to talk," her mom said.

Was this what her mom and dad had been discussing earlier? They'd huddled together like they often did when trying to figure out what to do with her.

"About what? Do you want me to say I was scared? I was." She had to give them enough so they thought she was normal but not so much they ever figured out the truth. Because they would be…not ashamed, exactly. They would blame themselves when this was fully on her. She'd had a long talk with Julia Ennis while Kyle had been showering. She'd convinced her jailer that she was going to die of hunger, gotten him to take her to the kitchen where she'd managed to steal a knife, and then gotten caught by the wicked witch of the world.

*You are a smart girl, Kala Taggart. You could be great. You could be one of the real people of the world.*

The worst part about talking to Julia Ennis? The fact that she made some sense. Julia had pointed out that her father had trained MaeBe Vaughn but not her. He'd left her training to a martial arts asshole who'd told her she was too intense. She had to find another one. He'd liked Kenzie, though. Kenzie had been teacher's pet. Naturally she screwed that up for her sister.

*I was a lot like you as a kid.*

Kala had snorted and told her she doubted it.

*No, I was. Tell me if I'm wrong. Your sisters are far more popular than you are. Your mother's always worried. At least she calls it worry, but it feels more like she's embarrassed. They have much easier relationships with the others. Sometimes you wish you didn't exist at all. It would be easier on everyone else if you didn't.*

So much easier.

"Of course you were scared." Her mom had gone all sympathetic.

But her dad watched her like he knew she was holding back. Like he knew she'd thought about it when Julia Ennis had offered to not send her home at all.

*Once you let yourself be who you were born to be, you won't sit around and worry why you're not like your sister.*

Could her father see through her? How disappointed would he be?

It was funny. She didn't want Cooper now. Somewhere in all the hours of staring at the ceiling of her cell, she'd realized there would be no open arms for her. Oh, she was absolutely certain if she walked up to him, he would hug her and say all the right things and even take back everything he said that night. But it would be his guilt talking. It would be the Captain America part of Coop that couldn't even be really mean to a villain. She got it. She was bad for his reputation. She would only ever be a dirty secret for him to enjoy, and she wouldn't fucking be that for any man.

She didn't need him.

She didn't need anyone.

"What did she say to you?" Her father spoke in that deep voice he used when he was pissed.

Was he pissed at her? "Not much. Just some bullshit about how Kyle was her true love. She went on about that a lot. It was kind of pathetic."

"Are you telling me you were never alone with her?" her father asked, those icy eyes pinning her.

She glanced over and Kyle was already back to kissing MaeBe. MaeBe, who her father trained and treated like she was worthy. MaeBe, who Julia Ennis would never in a million years tell the things she'd said to Kala.

*When reality is flexible, we can all be heroes. We can all get what we need. When you no longer care what other people think, you're free. When other people don't matter at all, you're completely free to remake the world the way you want it. Some people would call that evil, but evil is a word used by the weak. You and I don't have to use that word. All that matters in the world we make is that we get what we want. Think about it, kid.*

Like there was something deep and dark inside her Julia had seen. Like recognizing like.

Would Cooper find some sweet girl he wanted to date and then Kala would raze the earth beneath them? Would she be the evil queen? The evil queen did not get to run away with Prince Charming.

"I wasn't the one she was interested in," Kala said quietly, hoping Kyle didn't hear her.

Kyle knew she was lying. Kyle knew exactly how interested Julia had been in her. She prayed Kyle liked her enough that he wouldn't ever tell her parents how the most evil woman he'd ever met had seen so much of herself in his cousin.

"I doubt that." Her father didn't seem to want to give up. "Julia Ennis was a woman who liked to play games. Especially mind games. You say no one hurt you."

Her calm threatened to rattle. She didn't know. She didn't fucking know. She only knew that everything hurt when she woke up and she'd wanted her mom and dad, but she couldn't now. She couldn't. Because she didn't know. "Beyond the dude I fought with? He kicked me a couple of times before he managed to shove a needle in my shoulder, but in his defense, I did break his nose."

Her mom had gone pale.

But her father merely leaned in. "Did she leave you alone with them?"

"With the guards?" She was sick of the interrogation. She wanted to put on headphones and shut out the world. Maybe if she got the music loud enough, she wouldn't hear Julia's voice in her fucking head.

"With anyone," her father clarified, every word clipped and

seemingly cold.

Why was he pushing her? Her mom had hugged her and held her hand and pulled her way too close—something she might have objected to but she had just been kidnapped. Her mom had told her she didn't have to talk if she didn't want to. Her mom had cried a lot once her dad and the rest of the family had shown up.

Charlotte Taggart had been a rock. Right up until she didn't have to be. When her dad walked out of that house and wrapped his arms around them both, her mom dissolved into a ball of emotion.

Kala cried a bit initially. Pure relief had caused it. Then the hours passed as they waited to be able to fly home and a nice numbness settled in. She'd talked to her sisters and brothers and felt absolutely nothing.

It was good, so good to feel nothing, and her father was threatening it.

"I was with Kyle. Kyle made sure I wasn't alone with her," Kala replied, feeling her jaw tense, her calm starting to shake.

"Kyle wasn't with you when you were taken," her father pointed out. "He wasn't there when the fuckers killed a woman in front of you."

"She was the one who turned me in, so who cares?" Kala asked. But she'd thought about it. Thought about the woman and wondered what made her take that job, what her hopes and dreams had been. Thought about how casually they'd taken her life. Like it was easier to kill her than it was to pay her invoice. "I would have thought they would clean up after themselves."

"We think they didn't have time," her mother explained. "We didn't connect it until Chelsea managed to find you on doorbell cams in the neighborhood. There weren't any in the park, but we tracked you there."

"So we know at the very least you were alone with them for a couple of hours before Kyle got to the airplane." Her father was relentless. "What happened during that time, Kala?"

Yep. She was starting to feel things again. Starting with anger. "General Taggart, I'm not one of your soldiers, so you don't need to debrief me."

A brow rose over icy eyes. "Excuse me."

It was said quietly, a sure sign her dad was on edge. Everyone well acquainted with her dad knew not to take him seriously when he shouted, but when he got quiet, they all took cover.

Kala didn't care. "I said I'm not one of your operatives. Or hell, maybe I can be. In that case, you'll have a report on your desk come Monday. Until then I want some space."

"Maybe we should talk this out in a session. Eve is waiting at home," her mom said.

Eve. Who already thought she wasn't good enough for her son. Eve, who was smart and could see through the whole she's-just-young thing. Eve knew about dangerous people and wanted her son to stay away from Kala Taggart.

"I'm not talking to Eve." The words came out far harsher than she'd planned to say them. "I don't need to. I'm fine."

"You are not fucking fine," her father said in that way he sometimes did. It was like the words floated out of his body. He didn't need to move his mouth. He was preternaturally still. It was intimidating. "So I ask again."

"Ian," her mom said, her shoulders squaring. "This is neither the time nor the place. We're not alone."

"No, she's not alone, but can't you see she's trying to be? Do you think I want to have this out here and now? I want five minutes when I can simply be happy I have my daughter back, but I don't know that we do. I don't know what that fucker planted in her skull. I don't know what they did to her. Charlotte, she was alone for hours with five mercenaries. Kyle wasn't there."

"Pushing her isn't going to help," her mom argued.

"If I don't, she won't talk about it." Her dad turned Mom's way, his expression tightening like he didn't dare give a moment's softness. "If this was Kenz, I would let you handle this entirely. You understand Kenz, but I know Kala. We get to her now or she loses this piece of herself. I know what she's thinking. She's thinking time will change whatever happened. Distance will make it go away, and she never has to admit to anyone what she really went through. She can shove it down and it won't be there lurking." He turned back to Kala. "It will. It will always be there waiting to poison any relationship you have. You are stubborn, my child. But so am I. I will not leave you in this alone."

Her every wall shook and those stupid tears threatened. If she ignored him, he might… He would only get more obnoxious. So she could turn it on him. "You did leave me alone. You chose not to train me. You chose to tell me I'm not strong enough. Guess what, I was. I did. I'm sorry you would need to cry on someone's shoulder, but I don't have to. I can do it alone. I don't need you."

Her mom gasped and stood, walking away with her hand over her mouth. Aunt Erin caught her, holding her hand and giving her strength.

"I didn't train you because you are fucking fifteen years old and I want you to have fun. I want you to complain about school and have the kind of life your mother and I didn't have, but trust me, that changes now. You want me to train you, I'm here. You won't have anything else to do since you're grounded for at least six months."

Three days ago she would have been thrilled. Now she wanted him to leave her alone. She was pathetic. Always begging some guy to pick her. Her father. Cooper. The asshole martial arts instructor. "I think I'll pass."

"Not your choice anymore," her father said. "Nor do you get out of this debrief. I ask again. Did they try anything? Did they succeed? I need to know what they did to you not because I want revenge. I already had that and it's meaningless. I need to know because I have to fix you. I have to take the parts they broke and put them back together because I will shatter into a thousand pieces if I don't try."

She felt the world tilt because her father was crying.

Her father. The strongest man in the world. Her father, who joked about shoving everything deep. Her father, who she tried so hard to be like because she knew she could never be her mom.

What was she doing? She was letting that woman in her head, letting her burrow into her soul and making her question the strong ground her world was built on.

"I don't know." She said the words quietly, her head down, unable to look at him when she said it.

"What?" her father asked. "Look at me when I'm talking to you."

She forced her face up. Those tears rolled down his cheeks, proof that he wasn't some larger-than-life hero. He was her dad, and she couldn't scare him away or manipulate him out of this. She couldn't keep secrets from him, not ones he worried would wreck her.

She kind of wanted them to wreck her. If she split from everyone, she didn't ever have to be here again. Didn't ever have to feel again.

Isn't that what Julia had told her? If she didn't care, she could be free.

Did she want to be free? Maybe Julia Ennis wouldn't have been such a psychotic murderous asswipe if her father had loved her. If she'd taken all that nasty energy and turned it toward protecting the people she loved.

"Kala, I can't leave this. I can't leave you. I know where you are." His voice had gone low, and she heard the emotion behind it. "Your mother might think I'm a monster, but you have to break now or you'll hold those walls up forever, and I can't leave you there. Tell me what happened."

It all rushed in. A wave that truly threatened to drown her. Or maybe she only now noticed she'd been in the water all along. Her father was offering her a way out of the river of misery she found herself in. It wasn't the same shore she'd known before, but it was something. It was a place.

She could love her friends and family and use her darkness only to protect them. She could be the dragon only a few would ever know wanted to be something else. Something softer.

"I don't know, Daddy." She could let the river take her someplace infinitely cold. Or she could let her father teach her. She could shut her heart away completely and become what everyone thought she would. Or she could guard it and only open it to those she was closest to. She could keep her parents. She could keep her sisters. She could keep Lou. "I don't know." Tears began, fat and filled with toxin, rolling down her cheeks. She let them because it suddenly felt so damn good. "I don't know what happened because they drugged me and now I don't know…I don't know…"

A deep sob heaved from her body, the feeling so overwhelming she couldn't hold herself up. It didn't matter because her father was there, wrapping himself around her. Holding her so tight that for a moment she couldn't breathe.

Then her mom was there, too, wrapping around the other side and completely encircling her, and she found herself telling them everything.

She found herself utterly broken, but now with hope that she could put herself back together.

She wasn't Julia Ennis and she never would be.

Kala held on to her parents as she tried to ride out the storm.

\* \* \* \*

"Have you seen her?" Cooper hustled to catch up with TJ. Kala had been home a full week, and he'd heard nothing more than she was fine and she would be back at school today.

It had to be really bad if she hadn't seen anyone. Were her parents so mad at her they were keeping her from her friends? She needed them right now.

He'd been in hell, not knowing what had happened. He always knew what happened to Kala. She would text him when she stubbed her freaking toe.

He'd sent her text after text, begging her to unblock him. Well, he'd sent them to Tasha since she was the only one of the Taggart sisters who was talking to him right now.

TJ stopped, looping his thumbs through the straps of his backpack. "By her, I take it you mean Kala. Yes. She was at Uncle Sean's Friday night. We had a barbecue."

So the Taggarts were circling around her. Good. He wished his family had been invited. "How is she?"

TJ seemed to think about it for a moment. "She's Kala. For a chick who got kidnapped and apparently saw a bunch of shit, she's surprisingly cool with it. And she claims her love of anchovies saved Kyle's life, so she's never giving them up no matter how stinky they are. Then she went to Chloe Lodge's party and proceeded to prove it by eating a whole large with like fifty of those fish on them. I lost a bet on that one."

Somehow in his head he'd thought she was traumatized. She was holing up because terrible things had happened, and if he could get to her, he could make it all right. He'd had this weird Romeo and Juliet thing in his head. He'd literally been making plans to sneak out and break into her house.

All he knew was he was done with everyone keeping him away from her. He should have been there when she got off the plane, but no one had even told him when she was going to land. They'd informed him she was home and she'd been looked over by a doctor. She was fine.

She couldn't be fine.

"She went to a party?" He hadn't even known there was a party.

"You're grounded, dude," TJ said by way of explanation. "I mean she is too, but apparently she's on some kind of weird training schedule, and she can earn time in the real world. I think it helped that her dad was there, too. They let us hang out in the game room while they were in... It's a room with a lot of booze, but it doesn't look like a bar. Chloe's dad is weird and intimidating. Well, one of them. The other one grilled hot dogs and didn't make fun of me when I two fisted. Uncle Ian did, though. He said I was going to get fluffy if I didn't watch it. I think he body shamed me."

Cooper ignored his best friend. "She hasn't called me. I don't suppose she earned her phone privileges back."

TJ seemed to understand there was an undercurrent to this conversation he hadn't counted on. "Uhm, I mean she's been calling Lou a lot. Lou's tutoring me and usually she's very focused, but she claims she has to answer Kala now because she's worried she'll feel abandoned if she doesn't. She had her phone on Friday. She was showing me the weapons her dad's training her on."

An armed Kala was a fearsome thing. "Why hasn't she called me? I got my phone back but she blocked me and didn't remember to fix it."

TJ's lips pursed like they always did when he was thinking something through.

When he was trying to figure out how to not hurt someone.

"Just tell me." He had to know. It was killing him.

"I think you should give her some space."

"She doesn't need space. She needs me to apologize," he said, but his eyes were on the parking lot because he was almost certain he saw Tasha parking the Subaru she drove. It must be nice to have an older sibling so they didn't have to get dropped off by their mom.

Kala offered to have Tash pick him up, too, but he'd declined. He had a weird schedule.

And if anyone saw him getting out of Tasha's car with her, they would have drawn conclusions.

He was an asshole, but he was done with all of that now. He wasn't letting anyone keep him from her. She was his best friend. He just hadn't been much of one to her. That changed. Now.

"I think she's maybe a little angry at you," TJ said with a wince. "Like she doesn't want to hear your name and stuff."

He should have known Kala would take all her hurt and put it into anger. "I can handle it."

Anything would be better than this silence.

His heart threatened to stop because she was walking up the steps with her sisters and Lou. Kenzie was bouncing as she spoke, and Kala looked at her twin with an almost indulgent smile.

That faded from her face when she saw him.

Her clique stopped, all of those feminine eyes judging him. Even Tasha seemed to have chosen her side. Which he got.

"Dude, I'm scared for you right now," TJ said quietly. "I'm going to like take a step back. Maybe you should run."

Coward. He wasn't about to run. He'd been waiting for this for over a week.

For a moment he thought she'd turn and walk away, but she murmured something to her sisters and then started walking toward him, her chin up and face in a stubborn expression. Her sisters followed, watching her warily.

Lou had her tote bag open as she approached. "Hey, TJ. Mom made blueberry today. Want one?"

TJ was a walking gut. He had that big blueberry muffin in his hands very quickly, moving in closer to Lou. "You're the best, Lou. Mom told me to eat yogurt this morning. I hate yogurt. Dad's on a job so no French toast for me."

"Hello, Cooper." Kala stopped in front of him and then looked back. "I'm fine, guys."

Tasha sighed. "All right. I have a student council meeting after school, so I need you guys to hang in the library for a while."

Kala's strawberry blonde ponytail swayed when she shook her head. "Dad's picking me up. I've got a session."

"Which I'm going to," Kenzie insisted even as they started to make their way toward the main building. "I know I didn't get kidnapped, but I'm not falling behind, and Dad can deal with it."

"Come on," TJ said around a mouthful of muffin. "Walk me to class. On the way, can you explain the whole War of 1812 thing? I have a quiz."

Lou followed him.

And Cooper was left alone with Kala.

She looked so damn pretty in the early morning light.

"Hey." A stupid thing to say, but it was all he could think of. He'd planned out this whole speech. "I'm glad you're okay."

Her lips turned up faintly. "Me, too."

"Kala, I…" he began.

She held up a hand. "No. I don't need to hear apologies. It's fine. You need to understand that I don't hold you responsible for me getting my ass kidnapped." Her eyes rolled. "I'm supposed to say a bunch of stuff about how it wasn't my fault either. Dad's making me talk to Kai. How am I supposed to take a dude with a man bun seriously? Anyway, it wasn't your fault, and we would have had that fight eventually one way or another. It's cool. What I'm trying to say is you and I are fine."

Oh, this did not feel fine. "The fight was absolutely my fault."

"Not really." She seemed way calmer than he would have expected. He wasn't sure he understood this Kala. His Kala would punch him and tell him to be better, and then they would catch up to Lou and TJ and hang out before class. "I'm the one who should apologize, Cooper. I was too aggressive, and I didn't want to see the signs that I was pushing you. I was trying to take a perceived friendship and turn it into something else. I won't do it again."

He was starting to panic. What was Kai putting in her brain? Kai Ferguson was the head of the Ferguson Clinic, a group of therapists who specialized in PTSD. He thought they would send her to a family center for a couple of checkup sessions. If they sent her to Kai… "What happened?"

A brow rose over her eyes. "I got kidnapped. I had to sit in a cell with Kyle, and he's a chatty motherfucker. Then I had to walk through a dusty tunnel with Mom and Uncle Ten, and I'm kind of half grounded, but Dad freaked enough that he lets me out if I'm serious about school and his lessons. He's training me, and Kenzie is along for the ride. She didn't even have to get kidnapped."

"Come on, Kala," he urged, "this is me. You can tell me. You have no idea how worried I've been. You have to unblock me. We need to work this out."

She shook her head again and took a step back. "No. I'm not saying I'll never talk to you again. We were friendly once. We'll be okay one day, but you have to give me space."

"What do you mean friendly? We're friends. You've been my best friend. That's what I figured out."

"That's the guilt talking, and that's why it's best we don't spend time together for a while." She held a hand up as though to tell him to stay where he was. "Not forever, of course. I'll see you at parties. Well, the family ones. You can let your friends know I won't be crashing again. I can see where that would be annoying, and I'm sorry about it."

He didn't know how to process what she was saying. "They aren't my friends. They're people I hang out with. You were right about that. Come on, Kala. Let's go and sit and talk."

If he could get close to her, get his hands on her, he could convince her. He would ease her into a kiss. She always wrapped herself around him and made him breathless. She made him feel strong and sure and true.

He was a bit lost without her.

For a half a second he thought he had her. Then the bell rang and she seemed to shake off whatever she'd been thinking. "Nope. Like I said, we can be friendly, but I need space and you'll be happier in the long run, too. Ask your mom about trauma responses. She'll explain."

"Caring about you is not a trauma response," he shot back, frustration welling. "Is this punishment?"

Her eyes narrowed, and he saw a spark of the fire that had always drawn him in. "Did you do it, Coop? Did you find a way to make me the bad guy here? I wasn't trying to get out of the role, you know. It's been pointed out to me that it's my place in the world. The good news? You're going to escape my clutches."

Now this he could work with. Sort of. "I never said I wanted out of your clutches."

"Then we were at two different meetings the other night." She took a long breath. "I promised I wouldn't do this. I'm done talking. Be nice. Don't be nice. It's not my problem. Have a good day."

He reached out for her, grabbing her elbow.

And then suddenly he couldn't breathe because he was flat on his back, staring up at the sun and trying to cup his balls. Fuck, that had hurt. She'd kicked back and then pulled his arm and somehow flipped him.

She stared down at him, her head blocking the sun. "I'm sorry. I didn't mean to do that. I'm…I'm twitchy since the incident. Are you okay?"

No. Not in any way. "Unblock me and let me in when I come to your place tonight and then I'll be okay."

Her expression shuttered, and he could see the hurt on her face. But then it was replaced with the blank look she got when she dealt with people she didn't like. People who were unkind to her. She put her wall up.

He'd never been on the other side of that wall. He didn't like it.

"Good-bye, Cooper." She turned and walked away.

He stared at the brilliant blue sky. Shouldn't it be raining or something? Shouldn't the weather know how dark he felt in that moment?

When the bell rang again, he forced himself up, brushed off his clothes, and started toward class. They had one together. He would start working on her there.

She couldn't shut him out forever.

# Part Two

## *This Night*

# Chapter Five

*Dallas, TX*
*Twelve Years Later*

"Kala, you went through something traumatic."

Kala bit back a groan and wished her father wasn't so invested in freaking therapy. "I like to call it Tuesday, Lena."

The therapist sighed and sat back. Lena Gallagher didn't normally work in Dallas. She wasn't an everyday, ordinary therapist working at the Ferguson Clinic, though for the last week she'd held sessions here.

Because apparently the Agency was worried their experimental team was twelve kinds of fucked up after their last mission.

No lies there. It had been a lot.

"All right, Kala. I have a job to do. After what happened in Montreal, the director is worried about the state of the team." Lena was in her mid-thirties, a pretty woman who dressed in a neat and efficient manner that still managed to be feminine. She reminded Kala a whole lot of Eve McKay. Lovely and intellectual, and she didn't exactly like Kala. "You've spent three days saying nothing."

"I know. It's been a good time, Doc." She was hell on shrinks. Oh, they tended to look at her like she was their Disneyland, but all of her rides were closed, thank you very much.

An elegant brow arched over dark eyes. "You know I can bench you, right? I understand that the Kara construct you use is very important to several ongoing operations, but if I decide you're not stable, I'll still pull you out of the field."

She had places she could hide a body. Always. It was probably sad that she kept a list. Uncle Jesse and Aunt Phoebe just moved and were renovating, including putting in a pool. Getting the dead body of one of your enemies buried right before the frame went in was chef's kiss. Lou's dad's place had a lot of land. Oooo, Uncle Boomer had a couple of pigs now. They loved to eat dead bodies, right? See, this was why she liked animals more than most human beings. They were helpful.

"All I'm asking is for you to talk about what happened." Lena crossed one leg over the other, showing off the red soles of her shoes. "You do that and I'll clear you. I've cleared everyone else."

"Everyone who's still here," Kala grumbled.

"Yes, I would like to talk about what happened with Captain Reed as well," Lena replied, frowning. "But we should start with how you were caught by the suspect's men."

She'd been over this a million times. Or at least once, and that should be enough. But no, the Agency needed her to go over and over it…like they were waiting for her to trip up and reveal something.

Like she was the real suspect.

Damn it. Her father had told her to take this seriously, and she was fucking up again.

"I wrote a report. Several, actually," she replied, sitting back and mimicking the shrink. Though she was wearing combat boots and ripped jeans.

Lena watched her every move and made a note in the small book she held on her lap.

Kala could guess what was in there. The rest of the team had already done their time with her.

Louisa Ward – sweet and charming. Einstein-level IQ. An asset for the Agency, with the singular exception of her poor taste in friends.

Natasha Taggart – organized and emotionally intelligent. She's the heart of the team as she manages to keep their big personalities in check.

Tristan Dean-Miles – makes things work despite his natural repulsion when it comes to making hard choices. An asset, though more behind the scenes and less in the field.

Cooper McKay – Captain America through and through.

Kala Taggart – morally ambiguous, with anti-social tendencies. Keep an eye on her.

At least that's what the last one said. She should know. She'd stolen the notes. That probably played into the whole morally ambiguous thing.

"I read the report. Now I want to hear it from you." Lena's perfectly cut bob shook. "Or we can close this report, and I can get back to DC early."

"I thought you were hanging around for a while." If she could shove the Agency shrink out early, everyone would cheer her on. It would be easier than convincing Aunt Phoebe she needed to *Poltergeist* her pool. That's what she would argue. Those X'ers knew how to use a pop culture reference to hammer a point home.

"I was. I'm here to gather information about more than the Montreal mission. I'm interviewing the team about Captain Reed and the possible reasons for his recent decision to…take a break from his responsibilities."

Zach. She carefully schooled her expression. Zach Reed had been her team's Army liaison since they'd formed. He'd been sent in to try to find the team's weakness, but he'd become a part of them. Or at least it seemed so. Now she knew he had more secrets than she could have imagined.

**Forgive me. Take care of him.**

She hadn't told anyone about the text she'd found on her personal cell the morning after the Montreal op. She had no idea why Zach would send her a message like that. She had to figure he'd screwed up and used the word *him* instead of *them*.

Which him could he be talking about?

"However, I can certainly do the work I need to do back in DC since if I decide the team needs a long time out, everything touching the Huisman operation can transfer to another team," Lena pronounced.

Uncle Sean had a freezer. He ran several restaurants, and those had plenty of places to stash a body.

Fuck. She was going to have to go along with whatever the

shrink wanted. "Fine. Do you want me to start at the beginning? It was a beautiful day in North Texas when a helicopter decided to take out my cousin's wedding. Not the helicopter itself, of course, but the assholes inside it."

A long huff came from the doctor. "What were you doing in the bar, Kala?"

Yep, this was going to be an ass kicking. And she'd already gotten such a heinous one. This op sucked. "I went to the hotel where the assets were staying." She didn't need to mention that the assets had been her cousin, Carys Taggart, and Aidan O'Donnell, one of her fiancés. Tristan was the other. They'd gotten involved in the seemingly never-ending mission to prove Dr. Emmanuel Huisman was the head of an international terrorist organization devoted to burning down the world. Carys and Aidan were doctors, and Aidan had been invited to a conference by Huisman himself. "The comms units we were using had gone out, and the big boss decided to send a couple of us there to ensure everything was all right."

The comms units had been turned off because the threesome had been having a knock-down, drag-out fight that led to some serious sex. She'd been in the audience for a bunch of the fight but had definitely been happy to leave before the sex.

Sex. Even the word was hard to deal with. It had been oddly easy to ignore sex for years, but then Cooper McKay had come back into her life, and now it was on her brain again.

"You were acting as a bodyguard?"

Kala nodded. "Yes, but you should understand I didn't leave my charge without protection. She was with Tristan the whole time."

"And you were in the bar." Lena managed to put a lot of judgment into those words.

Kala sighed. "Yes, and that is where Tasha and Zach found me. Carys joined me while Tasha and Zach went up to the hotel room to deal with the comms units. We talked for a while, and then I realized the drink I'd been watching the bartender pour was somehow drugged. I watched him open it, so he must have had the sedative already in the bottle."

"All right. I won't go into why you shouldn't be drinking on the job."

"It could have been water," Kala argued. "I wasn't drunk, and let me say if you want spies to not drink... Well, you're not going to have any spies."

Lena's lips actually quirked up. "Truth. So the bartender drugged your drink and you and Carys were taken to Toronto."

They'd been taken to hell. Absolute fucking hell.

She thought she'd gotten over what that asshole Dimitry had—or hadn't—done to her. Well, she thought she'd come to terms with it. If she'd gotten over it, maybe she wouldn't be a twenty-seven-year-old… She couldn't even think the word. It was pathetic. It was easier when she could convince herself she wasn't a sexual being. Not everyone was.

"Yes. I woke up bound to an exam table," she said, her tone bland. "Dr. Huisman was there. He intended to use Carys to get Tristan to tell him where he could find the bombmaker he's been looking for."

"And he brought you along for the ride?"

"The idiots he hired mistook me for Tasha. All they'd been told was to pick up Carys and Tasha. I was with her. They thought I was her." She kept telling herself she was lucky because if they hadn't thought she was Tash, she would likely be dead.

But she could still remember what happened next, and there had been moments during that time with Huisman that death would have been acceptable.

"Why would they want Tasha?" Lena asked.

"Because Huisman knew Zach worked with Tristan on The Jester project. Tristan had been working a long-range undercover project. He took over the identity of an arms dealer known as The Jester. Zach worked with him. The rumor on the Dark Web was that The Jester knew how to contact the bombmaker Huisman wants to work with. I don't know why the dude doesn't like give out cards or have an Etsy shop or something. He's not a great businessman. He doesn't know how important discoverability is."

"So why Tasha?"

Her humor was utterly lost on this woman. "Because somehow he knew Zach had feelings for her once. He thought he would have Tristan's girlfriend and Zach's one true love."

Luckily the fucker hadn't been completely up to date since Zach had made a serious connection with her cousin Devi Taggart before he'd decided to go AWOL.

Or he'd played her. He hadn't been able to get close to one

Taggart so he found another.

She hated the suspicions playing through her head. She'd trusted Zach. She'd gotten close to him. Zach had been the one to coax her to join him and Cooper many times. The last few Devi had joined in on, and it had felt like…like a stupid double date. Like they were all normal people having fun with their significant others and their friends and family.

It was one more lie the world told her.

Lena nodded as though pleased with the answer. Probably because everyone had given her the same one. "Did you talk to Dr. Huisman?"

"Yes. He monologued like a motherfucker. I mean it. That dude likes to listen to the sound of his own voice."

"Was this before or after he tortured you?"

She hadn't been able to move. She'd woken up on the table and been in the exact same place she'd been when she was fifteen. Wondering what had been done to her body while she'd been completely helpless. She'd sought out knowledge, trying to figure out where she ached, and she hadn't been able to move at all. "He used an experimental paralytic on me. I believe the guys in R&D got my blood work from the hospital later on. They were hoping there would be traces of the drugs he used on me."

"Drugs? You're referring to the sedative and the paralytic?"

"I'm talking about the torture drug," Kala said, keeping her tone as no-nonsense as possible. "He told me it's supposed to make it feel like my body was on fire from the inside out. The paralytic meant I couldn't fight, and he didn't need to hold me down."

"And did it?"

Kala shrugged. "I've had worse."

She'd screamed and screamed until one of the assholes gagged her, and then she'd screamed but it was a useless, futile thing. She'd burned from the inside out and prayed it would be over. At some point she'd lost consciousness.

At some point her heart had stopped.

She'd come to and the Canadian operative who'd been working with them had been pumping her chest. CPR. He'd given her CPR.

*Not today, Maggie. Not fucking today.*

Ben Parker was in love with her sister. He'd thought he was saying the words to her, and in that moment she would have done a lot to have him morph into Cooper. To have Cooper staring at her, tears in his eyes, praying she would live.

"Kala," Lena admonished.

"It's a very effective torture technique. I would have likely told them anything, except of course I couldn't stop screaming. He needs to refine it. There's a happy medium. Also, the paralytic wore off before the torture drug did, and then I couldn't control my body. I'm pretty sure I have a bunch of nerve damage. All in all, not how I wanted to spend that particular day."

Lena's expression went soft. "I'm sure it wasn't. Kala, I've read your file. You're brave and reckless and still young. You're already a hell of an operative, but this is the kind of event that can break a person."

"I'm not that breakable." She wished the woman in front of her was more like Kai Ferguson. He'd been her therapist after the first kidnapping. God, she had to number them at this point. Kai had taken her to a rage room and given her a baseball bat. And then when she'd destroyed to her heart's content, tears and screams included, he'd taken her for ice cream and they'd talked. Really talked.

She wasn't fifteen anymore. She shouldn't need to beat the crap out of a bunch of stuff to have a breakthrough.

"Everyone breaks, Kala. Everyone."

Her father had told her the same thing. "Well, I didn't have to. My team saved me, and now all I want to do is find Emmanuel Huisman and ensure he can't do it again." She knew better than to put into words what she was going to do to the doctor.

Make him hurt for days. She would find that drug and see how he liked it. Or she could go old school. There was something pure about putting real physical work behind the torture. The drug seemed like a cheat. She would slowly eviscerate him and feed him his own testicles.

Lena closed her notebook. "I'm not going to get much more out of you, am I?"

"There's not much more to get." She certainly wasn't going to tell the good doctor that when she passed out, she'd had the dream again. The one that followed her since she was fifteen.

In the dream she was always sitting and waiting. It could be on a park bench, the sun warm on her face. At the kitchen table in the house she grew up in. On the bean bag in teenage Cooper's room where they would make out and she would get so hot she didn't care about anything but him. And the door would open and she would know it was her mom.

Then Julia Ennis would walk through, the ghost she couldn't quite shake. She would start walking in as Charlotte Taggart and morph into Julia. A reminder that there were always two sides to every coin. And Kala knew which one she was.

"Tell me one true thing and I'll close the book on this part of the investigation," Lena offered. "I still need to profile Captain Reed, but I'll clear you for duty if you can be honest with me about anything. What were you thinking as you lay there?"

"I thought it hurt. I thought I wanted to die." Both truths, but not the truth. What the fuck was she so afraid of? Her father did this. Her mom still went to a survivors of domestic abuse group from time to time. She was so tired. "I wished I'd been better. Seen more. Done more. I wished I'd…I wished I'd been in love and had someone love me back."

Lena nodded. "All right. This is done, but you should know I think you should see someone regularly, and I'm not talking about just for checkups. I won't force you, but I am recommending it."

Her father could get her out of it. "Fine. I can sit in a chair and stare a couple of times a week."

"It takes more than that," Lena replied. "I'm going to ask you a question and you don't have to answer. Think about it, and if you come to a conclusion that leads you back here, well, I'm in this office for at least another few weeks."

"Shoot." She wouldn't be coming back.

"Is this how you want to live? I'm not talking about the job. You're excellent at the job. I'm talking about the walls you have up. I'm talking about the regrets you had as you lay there thinking you would die. Many people find an experience like that can jump-start a change they need in their lives."

"What kind of change?"

"For you, I believe it's the acceptance that you are worthy of what you feared you missed. It's the acceptance that you're lovable. If you don't believe it, why would anyone else?"

She didn't want to admit it, but the doc had her there. How many times had she asked the question? How often had she lied and pretended to be something she wasn't so Cooper wouldn't see she was still a scared girl who had no idea what happened to her?

Was it time to put it aside and see what she could be?

Was it time to put Cooper out of his misery? She knew she couldn't be what he needed. Cooper McKay would want a sweet wife and a picket fence, and she wouldn't ever fit into that life, but when she'd lain there praying for death, the only thing she'd wanted more had been to know what it meant to be with him.

If she did it, offered herself to him again, he could be free, too.

"Kala, are you okay? I have some tissues."

Damn it. She hated Manny Huisman. And all the stupid couples around her who made her freaking long. She didn't long. It was a dumb word.

Her father had found her mom, had forgiven her and let her love him. In his less sarcastic moments, he credited therapy for all of it.

She wouldn't ever have a real life with Cooper, but maybe they could have something, something she could hold on to when he found the life he'd been born to lead.

But she wouldn't if she didn't find a way to change even the smallest bit.

"I don't need a freaking tissue." She stood, wiping the tears. "But I'll make another appointment. I won't be happy about it."

Lena stood, her lips almost curling into a smile, but she seemed to know that might not be the best move. "I won't either."

Kala strode out, wondering if she'd just made the biggest mistake of her life. Or started down a road that might lead her home.

\* \* \* \*

Cooper sat in the conference room at McKay-Taggart, his teammates talking all around him. They discussed their plans for the weekend, how hard Big Tag was about to be on them, what they watched on TV the night before.

But Cooper's whole focus was on the door because Kala was late.

"She had an appointment with the doc the Agency sent out." Kenzie gave him a sympathetic look. "She's been avoiding the psychological debrief, but the bosses told her she has to go and say something beyond fuck you. Don't expect her to be in a good mood."

He didn't need her in a good mood. He needed her here. "Why didn't someone drive her?"

"She didn't want a lift," Lou said from her place beside her boyfriend, TJ Taggart.

"I think she said something about needing time to prepare to deal with assholes." TJ had already raided the downstairs coffee cart. He was on his second muffin. Or maybe his third. Coop had no idea where he put it. "I'm not sure if she was talking about the psychologist or us."

"Probably both," Lou acknowledged. Lou was a sweet-looking woman with brown hair and intelligent eyes behind the glasses she wore.

"Well, I don't think any of the women should be on their own." Tristan Dean-Miles sat across from Kenzie, his green eyes on Cooper. "We have no idea where Huisman is, and he's proven perfectly capable of hurting the women of the team."

Kenzie snorted. "You try telling my sister she can't get any alone time. Guys, she's still processing what happened in Canada. This is how she does it. This, and probably going all Mistress Kala on some sub's ass tonight at The Hideout. I already talked to Gabriel about finding someone for her to scene with."

"For us to scene with," Cooper corrected. "And we have an appointment tonight, so that wasn't necessary."

Kenzie put her hands up as though letting him know he was being over the top. "Sorry, Master C. I was only trying to help."

It wasn't easy being a top when the woman you were so sick in love with was a top, too. He and Kala had been raised in families who were invested in the D/s lifestyle. But both of their dads were Doms and their moms happy subs.

They had to find their own way, and he'd started by topping subs with her.

Never sex. She never had sex in the club. Sometimes he wished she would since then at least he would know if the guy was treating her right.

At least he would know who he might have to kill.

Because maybe that was what it would take. Years. More than a fucking decade and she still hadn't forgiven him for being a dumbass kid who didn't know who he was. Well, he was a man now, and he was done playing around. She'd put him on this team, insisted on him. She could have left him where he was but she hadn't, and it was time to show her what that meant.

Fuck, he could still see her in Ben Parker's arms. He'd walked out of that burning mansion with her body, and Cooper had been sure she was dead. He'd known his whole life was over because she was everything. Everything.

When he held her, felt her chest moving and realized she was alive, he'd known he was done being patient with her.

He'd given her time to heal. Time to deal.

*You've given her like a week, dude.*

He shut down the reasonable part of his inner voice. The angelic voice that told him to be patient.

*Get her in bed and everything will fall into place. That's all you need to do. Fuck her. Give it to her better than she's ever had it. Prove to her you're not the kid who broke her heart. Show her you're a man who can handle all that darkness. With your dick.*

Yeah, the devil was pretty much in charge and had been since he watched her almost die.

Kenz was giving him a big-eyed stare that let him know she thought he was being a weirdo. "I forgot you guys make appointments. The rest of us kind of go with the flow."

Sometimes he missed being on teams where he hadn't grown up with his teammates. When he'd been strictly Navy, he hadn't had to deal with people who remembered him at the age of five.

"To get back to the point, all I'm saying is Huisman is out there, and we have to be ready," Tristan reiterated.

"And Zach." Tasha walked into the conference room, carrying a laptop. Behind her, Cooper could see her fiancé, Dare, walking back to his office.

Zachary Reed. Damn, it hurt. He wasn't even sure why. He'd only recently gotten close to the captain. Zach was closer to Tristan, but the last few months he'd taken to hanging out with Cooper. He'd even given Zach flying lessons, helping him get his license. Only days before Zach had sat across from him at a diner. He'd brought along TJ's sister, Devi, since they seemed to be a couple. Or had been. Cooper had sat beside Kala, and he'd felt like they were on a double date. Like they'd done when they were in high school, sharing meals and movies with Tris and Carys and Aidan.

*I thought we were hanging out.*

Would his fifteen-year-old self follow him always?

"Zach wouldn't hurt Kala," Tris argued.

"We don't know that." TJ suddenly seemed interested in something besides his girlfriend—or a snack. TJ was mostly muscle and often slept through these meetings. "I do think Devi might need a bodyguard."

"He's not going to hurt Devi." Tris turned TJ's way. "There's something going on that we don't understand. I know Zach."

"Well, if you know him, why don't you tell us all why he skipped out on us?" a husky voice said.

Just the sound of her voice made his dick go tight. Kala walked into the conference room wearing her normal uniform of stylishly ripped jeans, an old concert tee, and combat boots, her newly pink hair in a high ponytail. She had her leather jacket over her arm and started walking toward the seat Lou had held for her.

He was going to break her of the habit. Someday she would look his way and know her place was at his side. Okay, even the little devil inside him said that kind of thinking would get him in serious trouble. *His* place was at *her* side. Yeah, he would put it like that.

There were definitely days he wished he was wired differently, wished he could give her the submission she seemed to need. Instead, what he could offer was to be the king at the side of the queen.

She stopped and then turned, coming his way. She sank down next to him, and every eye was on her. "What?"

Kenzie's lips turned up, and she shook that perfectly identical head. They'd been strawberry blonde for the last mission, but two days ago they'd shown up for work and the magenta-colored hair they'd gotten their handle from—Ms. Magenta—was back. "Nothing. Just wondering if the therapist is still alive. You look weirdly calm for having to talk about your feelings for an hour."

"Oh, she doesn't," Lou assured them. "I'm pretty sure she sits there and has a stare off with Lena. I kind of don't blame her. I'm going to be honest. I didn't like the woman. She told me I'm trying to turn TJ into my dad. I don't know what that means. She said I have abandonment issues, but I don't. My bio dad died. Do you think she means I'm trying to turn TJ into him? Because he was an asshole from everything I know, and honestly, TJ's not great at math."

Cooper snorted. Louisa Ward was considered a genius by most of the people who knew her. She was an engineer and inventor, a true innovator, but in this she wasn't very self-aware. "She's not talking about your bio dad. She's talking about how TJ is slowly morphing into Boomer."

"Am not," TJ said around a mouthful of muffin.

Kala's lips curled up in one of those pure amusement grins she rarely shared. "Last night he ate all the lasagna we had left over. Kenz made an extra-large and thought we would eat it for a week. TJ managed to down it in an hour."

"It was good," TJ said apologetically. "And it was leg day. You know I get really hungry on leg day. I'll get us takeout tonight."

Lou's head tilted the way it did when she was thinking. "Huh. That makes more sense."

"When he starts bringing home every sad-sack homeless animal he can find, we'll know his transition is complete. I don't think it's a bad thing," Kala replied, and then seemed to get serious. "Where's the big guy, and do we have a babysitter today?"

The door to the conference room opened again, and the answer was clear. Drake Radcliffe walked in followed by the aforementioned big guy, Ian Taggart, and his wife, Charlotte. Drake was in his mid-forties and had once been a deadly operative, but he'd shifted into management, and he and his wife, Taylor, were the team's liaisons with the Agency.

Kala had stiffened beside him, though her expression hadn't changed.

She was worried Drake was here to shut them down. At one point he would have cheered the very idea, but two years of watching her work had made him understand how much she needed this. She'd been born for this work. He could have been happy in any number of jobs, but there was only one for Kala Taggart. Yes, he could have been happy in several jobs, but he could only be happy with one woman. Her.

"Hey, guys. Sorry I didn't get out here earlier. I'm afraid I've been working on figuring out exactly how fucked we are when it comes to Captain Reed." Drake took a seat opposite Big Tag and Charlotte. "Taylor is still in DC. She's working the Dark Web, trying to figure out where he's gone and what connections we missed."

"Yeah, I'd like to know, too," Big Tag said before looking over to Kala. His brows rose when he seemed to realize she'd forgone her usual place beside Lou. "Did you kill the doctor? Because I don't think Phoebe is going to be cool with our normal body disposal methods. She in your trunk, daughter?"

Drake groaned. "Please tell me we didn't screw with Dr. Gallagher. She's new, and the director thinks she's the shit. She was a top profiler with the FBI and recently took the job with us."

"I didn't kill the doctor," Kala said with a long eye roll. "She's okay. I told her what she wanted to know and then set up another session with her. See, I can take one for the team."

It was his turn to stare at her, shocked. "You have a session with her?"

She turned slightly. "It's not my first time with a shrink. Besides, I get the feeling she needs to spend time with me or she won't give us the sterling review we so richly deserve." She turned back to Drake. "Is this yet another ploy to break the team up? Since the Zach plan obviously didn't work?"

Kenzie pointed her sister's way. "What she said."

"Zach didn't want to break up the team," Tris insisted. "There's something more going on here."

"I agree with Tris," Lou said quietly, her gaze seemingly focused inward, like she was seeing something she couldn't forget. "He didn't want to leave us. I saw him that day. He saved me and Aidan. He didn't have to. It would have been easy for him to walk right by, but he didn't. He told me he had to go back to hell. Said he should have known he always belonged there."

Drake's tone went low, sympathetic. "I know Zach was good to the team, but he wasn't who we thought he was."

"He's exactly who we thought he was, but apparently with a couple of extra layers," Big Tag said. "Look, I'm with Lou and Tris on this one. I'm a fairly good judge of character and nothing set me off with Zach. There's something we're missing. He's definitely not working for Huisman."

"We can't know that," Drake replied.

Cooper was kind of team Zach. "It doesn't make sense. Huisman was planning on torturing him for information. It's obvious Zach has a connection to someone Huisman is looking for."

"The bombmaker," Kala concluded. "He knows who the bombmaker is, and he has all along. If he works for anyone, it's that dude. I don't know why. Maybe he's a childhood friend and there's some weird loyalty to him."

"Have we considered Zach himself could be the bombmaker?" TJ asked.

Tasha laughed. Not a little giggle, a mad guffaw. Lou snorted along.

"Guys, don't be mean," Kenzie admonished. "Zach is not dumb."

Kala smiled broadly. "He's not, but you have to admit, the dude isn't like an engineer or anything. He's not even all that great with computers." She sobered, seeming to think of something. "Unless he's pretending. Playing dumb is always a good cover, but it's hard when you work so closely with someone. I've read Tristan's report. We know he's the one who killed The Jester and set him up to be found by Tris."

The Jester was an international arms dealer with fingers in all kinds of weaponized pies. It had been The Jester Huisman was looking for when he'd kidnapped and tortured Kala and Carys Taggart.

"My question is how did Huisman know." Tris sat back, playing with the pen in his hand, cycling it back and forth around his fingers. "About Zach. It was Zach he was serious about. I think I was nothing more than a fun diversion for him. Oh, he wanted to know if I knew anything, but it was Zach he was planning on spending real time with."

Drake opened the folder in front of him. "Let me see if I have everything straight in my head. Sorry. I know you've gone over this a hundred times. So what we know now is that Huisman is interested in the man who built several bombs used in attacks in Jakarta we've connected to the Disrupt shadow groups that we now believe are run by Dr. Emmanuel Huisman."

"And London," Tasha added. "A few years ago there was an attempted assassination on British royal family members. The bombs didn't work the way they were supposed to, but according to the experts there were signatures on the bombs that connect them to the weapons used in the Jakarta attacks. Lou could explain it better."

Lou sat up straighter. "It's actually very interesting…"

Charlotte held up a hand. "Sweetie, I know you could spend an hour explaining, but I trust you. Can we all agree if Lou believes they were made by the same person, we believe her?"

"Yes," they all said at roughly the same time. And heartily because Lou would talk for an hour, and he would understand very little because she mostly spoke science.

Lou huffed. "Fine. But you know one day I'm going to give

incredibly important information and you all are going to be sleeping or doodling and you'll miss it. To put it in simple terms, it's like art in a way. The London bombs were part of his early works. They show promise, but he hadn't figured out how to smooth over the rough edges. Move on to Jakarta and you see he's maturing. The detonators have a beautiful and terrifying simplicity. The materials he's using… Well, it's obvious he's moving into small nuclear arms. I'd love to see something he's recently worked on. I think these bombs could be used to deliver biological weapons as well. I can extrapolate where he's going from the materials he's using, but getting my hands on it, being able to reverse engineer it would tell me so much."

"We have two different definitions of the word simple, Lou," Big Tag said. "And I haven't been able to ID any other bombs. I've been talking to intelligence agencies around the world, but we haven't found anything like the signature we found on the Jakarta bombs. Of course if we did, it would likely mean Huisman had, too. The fucker seems to always be one step ahead."

"Because he's been planning things for decades," Kenzie pointed out. "He knows who we are because he's been following us since long before we joined the Agency and had our pasts erased. Stop kicking yourself, Dad. You couldn't have foreseen this."

"He couldn't have foreseen that some asshole from his past would come back to haunt us?" Kala's brows rose in a near perfect imitation of the very father she was talking about.

"Come on," Tasha argued. "How could he know?"

He did not get in the middle of Taggart sister fights. Every man who knew them knew to take a step back. He would stand behind Kala, and Dare would do the same for Tasha, and they would stay out of the line of fire.

"Well, he was Agency for years, and even after he left he fucked over like a million bad guys," Kala pointed out. "Do I need to go into all the Russian mobsters Mom screwed over?"

"Hey, I always killed them so they couldn't come back to haunt me," Charlotte explained. "And your dad tried to as well."

"The ones left remember," Kala said quietly, and Coop could sense her mood shift. She'd been joking before, but this part was serious.

Kala was like flying sometimes. He had to get a feel for the air around her, find the good streams that swept them along, and know when turbulence was going to batter them.

"Well, Big Tag didn't even kill Huisman's dad." There were times to protect himself and times to give her cover. Her mom was looking at her like she wanted to ask some questions, and he saw the tightness to Kala's shoulders. It was time to deflect. "So in addition to wanting to find a bombmaker, he used the Montreal op to begin his revenge on Ian. Who again wasn't even there when his dad died."

"Fucking Levi Green killed his father," Big Tag said in a low growl, mentioning the unalived CIA operative who'd haunted them for years. "But what we learned recently is he blames me. Huisman believes if I hadn't protected the Lost Boys, his father would be alive and all the dominoes that fell after wouldn't have and his life would be sunshine and puppies and roses. It's ridiculous but he believes it."

"I have Lena working on a profile of him," Drake replied. "And, Ian, you couldn't have known that twenty years later some kid you've never met would decide you're the devil and he needs to take you out. This isn't on you."

"It's not. I was just joking about the fact that when you take down as many assholes as my parents have, you should expect someone's going to come after you," Kala said, her tone flat. "I believe he said he would visit the sins of the father on his children. Or some bullshit like that. He's an overly dramatic motherfucker."

"Yeah, he was definitely overly dramatic when he was using my daughter as a test subject," her mother said, her tone dark. It was a good reminder that there were two Charlotte Taggarts. Or at least two versions of the same woman. One was the loving wife and mother, the mom every kid adored. One had been a Russian mob assassin, and she never forgot how to kill.

Kala had been given an experimental paralytic, and despite the fact that all the doctors said she was fine, he still wasn't sure what the long-term effects could be. Huisman had made her vulnerable and then poured fire into her veins.

He really wanted to kill Emmanuel Huisman.

"Do we have any idea where he is?" Tristan asked.

No one needed to ask who he was talking about.

"Who?" Except TJ.

Drake simply ignored him. "The last location we have for Huisman is three days ago in Algeria. He met with a group of mercenaries. We have to think he's hiring. We believe he's no longer in Africa. I've got some intelligence that has him traveling to Asia, though we're not sure where. The Canadians are going to announce an investigation into the Huisman Foundation in a couple of days."

"Are we worried that could set him off?" Charlotte asked.

"I would have to ask Lena," Drake replied. "We're considering her the subject matter expert. She's spent the last couple of months diving into his history."

"Eve thinks yes," Big Tag said, sitting back. "You have your experts and I have mine. I think we should authorize protection for the families of the Lost Boys. In particular Owen and Rebecca Shaw. They're in Sweden right now. I think we should bring them in."

"I can't authorize anything without Lena's go-ahead, but I will talk to her," Drake offered, closing his folder. "And I'd love to read anything Eve has on Huisman. As for Zach, he's disappeared off the face of the earth. I've gone over his file about three thousand times, and there's not a hint of a lie there."

"Sometimes you don't have to lie. You just have to keep your mouth shut," Big Tag replied. "We know his mother spent time in jail for cooking meth. We know she had some very sketchy contacts, but we're talking almost twenty years ago."

"Where is she?" Cooper was curious. "According to Zach, she drifted out of his life when he was a teen and never returned. He thought she was back to making designer drugs."

"She's gone, too," Drake replied. "We do know she was connected to a couple of cartels back ten years ago. The last known location we have on her is El Salvador. From there she disappears, and nothing I've found connects her back to Zach after she split. We have to consider the idea that Zach's mom is in some way connected to the arms community and knows something. I would love to talk to Zach's aunt. If I could fucking find her. Disappearing is a way of life for this family."

"Joyce lives a nomadic life," Big Tag explained. "After Zach left home, she built out a van and took to the road. I can find her. I just need some time. She's…a character."

"She also might be working with her nephew, so be careful. We have no idea why Zach killed The Jester in the first place. I think the likeliest scenario is he wanted to become The Jester," Drake replied.

"Then why not kill Tris?" Kala pointed out. "He could easily have done it."

"I wouldn't say easily." Tris looked slightly offended, but he carried on. "But Kala's right. He could have taken me out but he didn't, and not once did he try to manipulate me in a way I would say would bring him some monetary gain."

"This isn't about money." Cooper felt like he knew the guy. "This is something else."

Drake stood. "Well, you need to figure out what it is because pretty much every agent out in the field is looking for him. I can't control what they do when they find him. This is a dangerous situation. I need you guys to lay low for a while. Let Lena do her job. I'll work on the higher-ups to get more resources. I'll be in town for a couple of days if you need me."

"So we're supposed to sit on our hands?" Kala asked, irritation flavoring every word.

"Rest, Kala," Drake said. "I know you're super woman, but you went through something traumatic and you need…"

"I told you. I'm doing the therapy." Her hands fisted on the table. "I saw all the doctors. I'm doing everything the Agency asked me to do."

"We'll prep for providing protection for Dr. Shaw's family." Cooper knew what he needed to do. Give her a job. She didn't relax. The job focused her. "And we'll try to find Zach's aunt. We'll stick close to the MT building, and Lou can work in her lab."

"Great." But she sat back, and her shoulders came down from around her ears. "Logistics. Awesome."

He leaned in, his voice going low. "And we have some other projects we've neglected."

She turned his way slightly, her mouth curling in a smile that went straight to his dick. "Naughty subs. We should probably talk through the scenes we'll run this weekend."

Yep, he hoped the meeting lasted a while because he had a hard-on.

"All right, let's get to work." Big Tag stood, reaching out a hand to his wife. He always reached for her at the end of a meeting. Or a dinner. Or because they were sitting next to each other. The group started to break up, but he sat.

Mostly because of the hard-on and the utter hell he would get from everyone if they noticed. But also because he wanted to reach for her hand, not because she couldn't stand on her own. She was a force of nature. No. He wanted to reach for her hand so she would know she wasn't alone. So he would know he wasn't alone.

"You coming?" She stopped at the door.

"In a minute." He pretended to be looking up something on his phone.

And she was gone.

But this weekend, they would play, and he was determined that this time around, they wouldn't stop.

# Chapter Six

"I never realized how bad Zach's childhood was." Four days later her sister sat across from her in The Hideout's locker room. Kenzie wasn't dressed for play this evening. She'd chucked the slacks and blouse she'd worn to work in favor of leggings and a sweatshirt that hung off her left shoulder, exposing a scar she hadn't earned. It was the mirror to the one on Kala's shoulder. She'd come by it in a knife fight she'd almost lost a year ago in Beijing.

Kenzie had carefully studied the wound and then had Tris push the knife through when Lou and Tasha had balked. It had been Aidan who stitched her up, but he thought it had been an accident. That's what Kenzie had told him.

That scar bothered her. Not because Kenzie hadn't come by it honestly, but that she'd felt the need to come by it at all. Kala had argued that they could cover her shoulder. They'd been born perfect twins. Despite the fact that her parents would tell everyone there was no way they could be fooled, they had and still could be. But time and life had changed them in the slightest ways. Kenzie sometimes had way more of a tan, and Kala had to drag her ass to the tanning salon. Kala had more scars, and Kenzie kept taking those on, too.

What had felt like sisterhood at first was starting to feel like a cage.

A couple of days of intense therapy with Dr. Gallagher had her thinking.

"I don't think he told us a lot of truth." Kala turned back to the mirror where she could see her own scar because she was already in a corset and boy shorts, with five-inch heel boots that came over her knees. She was currently curling her hair. It was a 180 from how they spent most of their nights in the locker room. Kala tended to get ready simply and quickly, slicking back her hair since she wasn't there to have sex or attract a man.

She stared at the mirror. She looked a lot like her sister except Kenz didn't wear black on the dungeon floor.

Would Cooper like her in lighter colors?

"Do you truly believe he was sent in to hurt us?" Kenzie asked.

Kala rolled her hair around the large barrel iron, giving it a spritz to hold the curl better. "I know he was sent in to report back to some people who don't like Dad. I'm not sure if he was specifically there to cause trouble so they could dissolve the team, but if he was, then he kind of sucked at his job."

Because he'd saved them way more than once. Because he'd become one of them.

"I think he got in and he liked us," Kenzie said with a wistful sigh. Sometimes she thought her sister had been born in the wrong time. And place. She should be dressed in some frilly gown, staring out over the moors of England, waiting for her lover to return from war or something. "I know he admired Dad. I think he wanted to be one of us."

"Yes, that would have given him far more access." Devi Taggart settled into the chair beside Kala, putting her makeup kit down. She was in an emerald corset and shorts that made her legs look a mile long. "If he became a Taggart, he would have had access to everyone in our family. Have you thought about how convenient that could be for a man like Huisman?"

Damn. She hadn't actually seen her cousin since she'd gotten back. She'd been too busy recovering from what that asshole had done to her. Including starting PT since she'd seriously strained a couple of muscles and joints. The paralytic had worn off before the drugs that tortured her veins had, and she'd been left to spasm and jerk, her body trying desperately to expel the drug.

And her heart stopped, and stupid Ben Parker had to bring her back. Now she couldn't hate him the way she properly should since he was constantly perving on her sister and that meant her, too, since he didn't know there were two of them.

"I don't think it was like that," Kenzie said with a deep sympathy.

Devi had hooked up with Zach a couple of weeks before. It had been fast and intense. She'd even shown up with him when they'd left for the Montreal trip—something that wasn't supposed to happen. Girlfriends and boyfriends weren't supposed to know they were Agency, much less drop them off for a super-secret op with a kiss and a couple of snacks. So that had told her Zach had been serious.

Though Devi had a point. "She's right about the Taggart thing. If they'd gotten super serious, Dad would have considered him more family than teammate."

"That doesn't mean he targeted Devi," Kenzie argued.

"I've tried to tell her this. We've all tried." Daisy O'Donnell was already prepped for the night. She was stunning and oh-so feminine in her white corset and thong, long dark hair caressing her shoulders. She was with Brianna Dean-Miles. The three had grown up close, their ages ensuring they were always thrown together. They'd formed a deep and abiding friendship. Like hers with Lou.

"I saw them that night," Brianna explained. "He was into her."

"Or he's an excellent actor." Devi took a deep breath and stared at herself in the mirror before pulling out her eye palate. "I was a complete idiot around him."

Kala shrugged. She felt for her cousin, though she didn't understand the situation. She often worried she wasn't hetero or gay or anything in between. She'd only ever wanted one man. She was Cooper-sexual, and it was a problem. "He's attractive and nice. It's okay to be attracted to someone. It wasn't your fault, Devi."

She wanted to say he didn't seem like a massive asshole, but she was trying to be sensitive to Devi's obviously tender feelings. She was growing.

Daisy looked between Kala and Kenzie before leaning over to Bri, her voice a mere whisper. "This is one of those times. She said the word *nice*. I kind of thought she was Kala because of all the black, but she sounds like Kenz."

She didn't sound like Kenz just because she was being nice. She was nice. Fuck, she was not nice. Kind. She could be kind from time to time, but nice wasn't in her repertoire.

"Are they doing an op or something?" Bri asked. "The kind where one of them hides and they pretend they're one person. Because Kala always gets testy when she's the one hiding."

It was good to know all she had to do to trick people into believing she was her twin was to be a little nice. "No op. We're all sitting around trying to figure out where the fuck Huisman and Zach are. I apparently get to have a shit ton of therapy and then either go to Sweden and escort a family into hiding or hit the road looking for a nomadic auntie. All in all, not how I planned to spend the next couple of weeks. I planned to spend them wrapping Huisman in his own entrails."

"Nope, definitely Kala," Daisy announced. "Kenzie never mentions entrails."

Her twin sat back, one brow rising. "Oh, I might not mention them, but if I get the chance, I'd play in his. I'm not joking. I hate that fucker and what he did to my sister."

"We don't have to go into it." She didn't want to think about what happened in Canada because it forced her to think about what happened here in Dallas all those years ago. Or up in the air. It could have happened in the plane. It might not have happened at all. The doctor who examined her told her she didn't think so, but she also didn't have a hymen. That had been a great anatomy lesson for a fifteen-year-old. Dr. Gates had explained it didn't mean she'd been raped. It could have torn from athletic pursuits or using tampons. It didn't matter because it played out in her head over and over again. And then when she slept, sometimes Julia showed up trying to pass her crown on. "But we do have to talk about the fact that Huisman wanted Tasha because he thought hurting her would get Zach to talk."

He hadn't gotten Tasha. He'd gotten Kala and Carys, and apparently he'd shot a dude in the head over the mistake. Not that Huisman hadn't made the most of it.

Devi didn't even stop doing her eyeliner. "I've already gotten the talk, and I have my very own bodyguard following me around when I'm not with Dais and Nate. I'm excited about it since I've heard all our bodyguards end up marrying their clients."

Kenzie sat up, losing her I-want-to-murder-someone face and putting on her this-is-good-gossip one. "Who? Who did you get?"

"Landon Vail." Devi's lips curled up, but it was easy to see the smile didn't reach her eyes. "He's adorable and my type. I think he's exactly what I need to forget my troubles."

Her cousin was deflecting. And not taking the risk seriously. "Well, you can forget the whole Zach thing but try to remember the last person he had a thing for was the one Huisman wanted to torture instead of me. So you could be next if he decides he wants to see if he can bring Zach in."

"All Kala is trying to say is you need to do what Landon tells you to and stay close to home when you can," Kenzie said.

Devi sighed. "Sure. I got it. Ignore my career needs because some asshole wanted to get close to my family since he's a counteragent. Thanks, spy kids."

"Hey." Kala could only be pushed so far. "I get it. You're sad and hurt and I look like I can take some damage. Cool. I can. You want to blame me, go for it, cousin. But he's not a counteragent. Don't try to simplify this and make him the baddest of all bad guys. That man saved my life more than once, and honestly, if he shows up again, I'm going to beat on him a while and then sit his ass down and figure this out. Because something is wrong. He's not a good actor. He kind of sucks. He's also a shitty bad guy since the last thing he did was save Lou and Aidan and then text me that I should take care of our team. And I know he told Lou to tell you he was sorry. Such a bad-guy move."

Devi turned her way, eyes narrowing. "He was in love with Tasha. No one bothered to tell me. I had to overhear you guys talking about it. He loved Tasha and then she was unavailable, and so he started to look around for the next best thing."

Bri winced. "We've tried to talk to her about that, too."

"I don't think Zach was in love with Tash. He was in love with the idea of being part of a family." Kenzie put a hand on the folder she'd been reading. "He was alone most of his life, with a mother in prison and an aunt who was barely able to hold it together. He was a lonely boy who found himself when he joined the military. Tash is... She's Tash. She's gorgeous and easy to be around, and the daughter of the couple he wished had been his mom and dad."

"You are proving my point," Devi replied.

"She's fucking not." Kala knew she wasn't going to get through to her cousin. Not about Zach, but she had to make her point about safety. "What she's saying is Tasha is sweet and easy to love, and you turn into a raging bitch a lot. Don't think I'm insulting you. It's my favorite part of your personality. The point is you're not Tasha, and if Zach wanted someone sweet and with connections to my father, he could have done way better than you. You are difficult, and everyone shrugs and says it's because you're an artist, but it's because you're Erin Taggart's daughter and that shit is hardwired into your DNA. As you proved when you blamed me for all your problems."

"I didn't say your name," Devi replied.

She loved her cousin, but her cousin didn't understand her world. Oh, she thought she did on an intellectual level. They all did. They had no idea how bloody it could be. They did not understand she was a fucking wall between them and the bad shit. She finished off her last curl and put the iron down, turning to her cousin and looking her straight in the eyes. "I don't care. I don't care if you hate me. You won't be the only one. It's surprising because we're so alike, but I get it. If there's one thing I think I've figured out, it's that I can't fix other people's perceptions of me. So in essence only how I feel about a person matters. I love you so I'm going to explain a bit of the world to you."

Devi huffed. "See, this is the part I don't like. I love you, too, but you think you know better than all of us."

"No. I don't. Like I have no idea how to make clothes look beautiful like you do. I don't know how to write a book like Bri does. The list of things I'm expert at is small, but I know how to protect someone, and I definitely know when a person is being stubborn and putting themselves in danger they know nothing about. You think Huisman won't hurt you because you're a woman? You think the worst that could happen is he locks you up somewhere and you get to be the damsel in distress?"

"Kala." Her sister managed to make her name a warning.

"I think Zach doesn't give a shit about me, so I'm not in danger at all," Devi admitted. "I think this is all BS to make my mom and dad and brother feel better."

Kenzie sighed and sat back, gesturing Kala's way, permission to do her worst given.

"Even if Zach doesn't give a shit about you, there's the big old chance Huisman thinks he does," Kala explained. "If he does and he decides you're a way to get to Zach, then let me offer you some of my thoughts on him as a kidnapper. I'm a connoisseur, you see. I could write a Zagat rating system for kidnapping. Huisman is chef's kiss. I'm not joking. The man knows what he's doing. He hates women and doesn't rely merely on words to hurt us. I still feel it. I don't know which hurt more—not being able to move and being forced to watch the fucker haul Carys out or the liquid fire he poured through my veins. I like to consider myself fairly stoic when it comes to pain. I've been stabbed, shot, beaten. Stepped on Seth's freaking Legos. Don't discount those. But nothing, nothing, was ever as bad as the drug he gave me. I would have killed my own sister to make it stop. I would have done anything. I screamed. I begged. I pleaded with God to kill me. And when my heart stopped, my prayers were heard."

"Kala." Her sister could also make her name sound like the revelation of a long-held secret.

"I asked Dad not to talk about that part," she explained. "I didn't want to freak you and Mom out, but I think our cousin here needs all the bad parts or else I'm just trying to scare her. I am. The truth is terrifying. I went into cardiac arrest but only after the paralytic wore off and I tried to break my own bones to make the pain stop. My chest still hurts from where the Canadian got my heart started again and..." She winced. "I know that CPR requires mouth things, but, eww. I think that might be the worst of it. I had to wake up to my twin's dream boyfriend's mouth on me. But the point is, if you think you're safe, you're wrong. Huisman wanted Tasha. Not me. He took me because my last name is Taggart, and he blames my father for an event he wasn't even there for. Let me see, last time I checked, your last name was..."

Devi put a hand up, her expression softening. "I get your point. I'm sorry. I'm not handling this well. I really...I really liked him. I thought we were getting somewhere."

"You thought for once it was going to be you," Kala replied. She understood what it meant to pine for someone. She'd been doing it for years and years, and it was time for both of them to get this shit out of their systems and move on. "You thought for once I'm going to get the epic love story. I blame Aunt Serena. I often wonder how much better off we would be if she'd, like, written murder mysteries and we all grew up wanting to hang out in British country houses waiting to solve some rich person's untimely death. Anyway, maybe listen to Landon. About the bodyguard stuff. Not anything else. Maybe don't put the people you love through having to worry about you because you're pissed a guy turned out to be less than you thought."

"I will." Devi sniffled because she was capable of feeling. "I'm sorry, Kala. I didn't know."

It wasn't that Kala was incapable of feeling. She felt shit all the time. But she couldn't cry about it, couldn't let it out in healthy ways.

So she found unhealthy ones. Well, she was sure the shrinks would tell her dominance was a coping mechanism. "You weren't supposed to. And if anyone asks…"

Devi nodded. "I know nothing. Everything is classified."

"But if I maybe left this folder here when I went to the bar to grab a Coke," Kenzie offered, touching the file that held the secrets of Zach's life.

Her sister was way too romantic. It would get her hurt one day. Or fired. Kala grabbed the folder. "No. This is classified, and I wouldn't want Zach handing mine around even if he did think it might help me get laid. It opens Devi to things she doesn't need in her life, so I'll lock this up."

Kenzie sighed and sat back. "I just think if she knows what he went through she might be easier on him."

Kala took the folder anyway, locking it up. Her knee ached but she still kept the boots on. No one wanted a flat-footed Dominatrix. She closed the locker and when she turned, Devi was there.

"I truly am sorry. You're right and my bitch came out and you were an easy target," she admitted. "Forgive me."

There was nothing to forgive. She was a big girl. She could take it. "It's fine. Stay safe and tell me if you see anything weird. I mean anything."

"I work in fashion design. Everything is weird."

She wasn't wrong. "You know what I mean. And maybe come in for some refreshers in self-defense. We're all benched for the time being, so we can help out." There was actually one thing she felt bad about. "I'm sorry I said you were like me. I didn't mean it in a bad way. You say what needs to be said. That's all I meant."

She didn't want Devi to start thinking she was bad deep down, that she had a dark soul or that she wasn't lovable.

Devi stared at her for a moment, and there were tears in her eyes. "I can't think of anything I would rather be than like my cousin Kala. No one ever tells Big Tag he's too much."

"I assure you my mother does. A lot."

"It's all a joke when she says it. No one thinks your father needs to change anything about his big, loving, brave, over-the-top personality, but they tell you all the time. I see you, Kala. You think I don't, but I do. All of our lives, you were the protector. If you had a set of balls, no one would question it, but because you're a woman, they say you're too much. Too intense. Too bombastic. Too scary at times. You are exactly who we need you to be. Don't let anyone tell you otherwise." She reached out, putting her hand in Kala's. "I need you to know that even while I'm hurting because I thought I was in love with Zach, I see you, too. And I'm sorry I made you feel like less than you should. You should know how much we all love you and appreciate what you do for us."

She wasn't sure she believed it, but she was grateful she wouldn't have to fight with Devi. "Be careful, and let me know if he tries to contact you. You won't believe me, but I think he was into you, too, and he's a big old dumbass, so it could happen. Don't keep it to yourself. You don't have to tell the parents, but you do have to let me know."

"See." Devi squeezed her hand. "Protector."

She walked off, joining the others.

"You are, you know. You even protect me from myself because I totally would have given Devi that file." Kenzie leaned against the row of lockers.

"Because you are also a dumbass." Kala checked her lock. Not that it would matter if Kenz decided to go for it. Her sister was an excellent thief.

"Did your heart really stop?"

This was what she'd been wanting to avoid. "Yes, and you didn't feel it so we're not weirdly connected like you've always worried. It's good news because you don't die if I do."

Kenzie groaned. "You are…"

And here they were. "Too much."

Kenzie sighed, her eyes softening. "I shouldn't say that. I don't mean it. You are stubborn, though. I'm glad Ben saved you, but you should know according to Dad, Cooper completely blew our cover that day."

"How?" She'd heard nothing of this. Shouldn't someone have told her Ben Parker knew who she was? "He knows we're twins? Why the hell would Coop tell him?"

"No, he didn't tell Ben anything. He had a very large reaction to Ben carrying you out of a burning house unconscious. He thought you were dead. Ben is back to the firm belief that Kara and Cooper are a thing."

She could deal. "Next time I see Ben Parker, I'll kick Cooper in the nuts and tell him we broke up. No harm, no foul. Well, except to Coop's nut sack. I should probably warn him. He could wear a cup or something."

"You are missing the point," Kenzie replied.

"If the point is Cooper's balls, I assure you I won't miss."

"The point is Cooper went all emotional in the middle of an op."

Kala was certain her sister was embellishing. "He felt bad. Coop is a control freak. He thinks everything is his fault. He's fine now."

"He's not." Kenzie's head shook. "Watch him. He's not okay, and I think he's ready to make a move, so you need to figure out what you want. You've put him off for years. This might be your last shot with him."

So her sister thought she was going to fuck up. She had no intention. "If it's my very last shot, my 'don't collect two hundred dollars, go directly to jail if I don't take it' shot, then I should make it a good one. I might be late tonight, sis."

"Because you're going to sit down and have a long heart-to-heart discussion about years of pent-up feelings?" Kenzie asked but in a way that let Kala know it was wishful thinking.

"I thought I would ride him like the stallion he is and get him out of my system," Kala explained. "I really did do the whole almost dying thing, and when I came out of it, I realized I want to experience that man's penis."

"You are so close," Kenzie insisted. "Move about two feet up and I believe you'll find the part of Cooper you need."

"I do not need his man nipples." She wasn't giving Kenz an inch. This wasn't a love connection. It was a physical need they obviously both required to move on.

"I'm talking about his freaking heart."

Kala walked out because the one thing he didn't want from her was her heart. She was fairly certain he didn't think she had one.

## Chapter Seven

Cooper sat back and watched her work.

"You were late on Friday," she said in the deep, dark voice she used when working with subs. "Did you think I wouldn't know?"

Matt Sims was a close friend of the Lodge family and a pretty hard-core sub. Gabe preferred working with women, as it was his sexuality that tied into his Dom identity rather than his core personality. Or the dude was horny all the time and didn't want to put in the work if there wasn't a chance he might get something out of it.

So they'd inherited Matt, who was submissive to his core and also bad at being on time.

"I'm sorry, Mistress." Matt was down to a Speedo and nothing else, on his hands and knees on the floor, head down and waiting. He was in his mid-twenties and hadn't found a permanent dominant partner yet, though not for lack of trying. He'd run through most of Dallas's gay Doms. Another reason he was here with them. "I didn't hear my alarm."

They were in what Cooper liked to think of as the red room. It was a room specifically equipped for all types of punishment. Or funishment, depending on your point of view.

How many times had he dreamed of getting her in here, laying her out across his lap, and slapping that gorgeous ass until she agreed to never deny him again? So many times.

But he knew he was ready when he saw himself laid out and her giving the punishment. When he realized he would do anything for her. When he decided his love didn't have to be a selfish thing.

Convincing her was going to take time, and he was determined to be patient.

"Whose fault is that, Mattie?" Kala asked, tapping the paddle she carried against her palm.

"Mine, Mistress," Matt said, every word flavored with anticipation.

"And what happens when you're a bad boy?"

"I get punished."

Normally he enjoyed these sessions. Sometimes they were the only times he and Kala connected, but something was off with her this evening. For one thing the baddest Domme he knew looked soft, her pink hair in long curls rather than ruthlessly slicked back. He liked her any way she came, but this was a particular treat.

Like when she came to the homecoming dance their senior year of high school in a blue strapless dress, her hair in an elegant updo that had everyone thinking she was Kenz.

Even him.

When he'd walked up to her and asked if Kala had stayed home, it had taken her a moment to reply. In that instant, he'd seen the hurt. Like he should have known. Of all the people in the world, he should have known.

She'd walked out without a word and he'd…well, he'd been crowned homecoming king and everyone had cheered, and he'd known it didn't mean a damn thing.

How many times could he break her heart and still have a chance?

"It's a count of a hundred. Do you want it from me or him?"

That got his brow to rise. He sat on the spanking bench, relaxing back like it was a chaise lounge or something. He was altogether too comfortable in dungeons.

It was good to remember he wasn't the uptight, nervous, needed to be accepted kid he'd once been.

The dungeon was their place. Their palace.

Even if it needed some upgrades.

"Really? I thought this was your project for the night," he

murmured, watching the way she moved. Was her knee bothering her? She'd fucked it up on the Canada mission. Well, she'd had it injured by a man Cooper planned to kill.

"I like to give a sub a choice," she replied simply. "Me or the Master, Mattie? Know this is only the physical punishment. I've got tasks for you to complete before our next session."

"Yes, Mistress." His head turned up, staring at her with a worshipful gaze. "And if I please you, may I spend the night on the floor?"

He wouldn't be on the floor for long. He would be in a privacy room with whichever Dom caught his eye and shared his sexuality. Which was probably why Kala had offered. Sometimes he thought she would never stop testing him.

"If I punish him, he's getting rid of the Speedo. You know my punishment requires nudity from a sub," he shot back. "It's way more fun when you catch the dangly bits as they swing."

She couldn't shake his sexuality. He knew what he wanted and what he could give others. Some dude needed to get his ass whacked to feel complete? He was there for it. Someone liked to have their balls tortured? It was kind of like practice for what he was planning to do to Huisman, though he'd been far more careful with that guy than he planned to be with the doctor.

"The Mistress, please," Mattie pleaded, his head going back to a submissive position.

He tilted his head, a gesture meant to honor her. She was the one who was truly good at this.

"You make it hurt more," Mattie said with a happy sigh. "No one hurts me the way you do, Mistress."

To Cooper's mind it was code for something else. She gave Mattie what he needed and asked very little in return. She helped him without judgment. She was a goddess on the dungeon floor, benevolent in her controlled violence.

But for a moment, he saw that same hurt on her face he'd seen the night of the dance, her expression shuttering at Mattie's words.

And then everything about her was a careful blank, from the look on her face to the tone of her voice. "Then I'll have to do my best."

She pulled her arm back and a hard *thwack* bounced through the room. They'd done something to the walls that made sound reverberate. He was sure Gabe could explain it to him, but he felt the sound as though she'd struck him.

Mattie simply groaned and took it like the massive pain slut he was. Cooper watched Kala, knowing he didn't have to protect the sub. She could be mad as hell and never take it out on a submissive.

Why had she been hurt by his words? She often boasted that she was the toughest top in Dallas. Far better than any of the guys, and if they wanted, she would put it to the test. Of every aspect of her life, being a top was something she seemed most proud of. As if finding a way to serve her needs while helping others was her chief accomplishment.

What she didn't seem to understand was she did that every single day.

He watched as she took Mattie through his punishment, the sub calling out the number of strikes. Loud at first, and then with tears dripping from his eyes. Finally in a soft voice that let Cooper know he was in subspace.

She finished with one last strike of the paddle and then stepped back. "You're to go to Gabriel for aftercare. I'm in town for a few weeks, so expect that I'll show up for an inspection of your apartment, and if it's not clean in the way you have told me you expect from yourself, I'll revoke your rights to The Hideout for a week."

Mattie had rolled over on his back, a big grin on his face. "It will be clean, Mistress. And I'll be more careful about being at work on time."

Kala's lips tugged up as though she couldn't help herself. She genuinely cared about the subs they disciplined. "No, you won't."

Mattie laughed. "No, I won't. I like this too much. It's…it's the only time I relax. Thank you, Mistress. I think I'll forego the aftercare and find a hot Dom who thinks my pink ass is pretty."

Mattie got up and strode out of the room with far more confidence than he'd walked in with.

Kala frowned. "It's not pink. It's red. When I beat an ass, it's red. I get no credit."

It had been a light red. Which was pink. But he wasn't about to argue with her. He glanced down at his watch. Almost one. The Hideout had closing hours, but almost no one paid attention to them. They weren't as professional a club as Sanctum or The Club. People would still be hanging out at four a.m. most nights. Though by then they would be up in the lounge drinking beer and playing board games or in the locker rooms watching movies or sports.

Kala always left early. Even when her twin and best friend hung behind, she would head home with the excuse of her dog needing a walk before bed. At two in the morning.

"I think he was perfectly pleased. Is that our last of the night?" They'd run two scenes and had private sessions with two others. It had been a full night. He'd taken the lead on one of the scenes, but the private subs had both wanted her. He was feeling anxious. He hadn't helped her enough tonight.

She nodded and walked over to the table where her kit was laid out, carefully cleaning the paddle before storing it away. "Yes. So I guess there's not a lot more I can procrastinate over."

He didn't like the sound of that. "Why would you procrastinate?"

"Because I think we have to do something I hate doing."

Now he *was* anxious. Like moving firmly into the angst direction. "What do we need to talk about?"

There were several things Kala Taggart didn't like to do. Whites. She didn't mind any other laundry with the exception of whites and folding fitted sheets. She tended to get pissed at them and ended up needing a new sheet. She wasn't fond of cooking, but she could clean a kitchen and never complain. The only thing she really hated doing was talking.

If she thought they needed to talk, it was bad.

She took a long breath and turned, leaning against the table and looking at him across the room. "It doesn't have to be a long talk."

Such a remote goddess. "It doesn't have to be an awkward talk. Want to come sit with me?" He scooted over, offering her half of the bench. "Come here, Kala. Is your knee bugging you? Let's get you out of those heels. Sometimes the top needs aftercare, too."

She frowned his way. "How did you know? Damn it. I have to fix it. If I show everyone I'm hurting, they'll know exactly where to hit me."

She wasn't coming to him, so he stood and ate the distance between them. He got into her space. She was more willing to be open with him in this setting. When they were alone and in their element, she would let him closer. The partnership he'd begun with her had at least done one thing right. "Hey, I was watching you closely. You favored your right side. That's all. I'm sure you were in awful pain and didn't blink an eye. No one else would notice."

Her jaw firmed as she turned her head up. "I'll get better. I'm doing PT."

He reached up and wanted to run his hands through all those pink cotton candy curls, but that might be a bit much. He was being patient. He settled for clasping her shoulders. "Of course you will. You're already bouncing back. This whole benching us thing isn't about you. It's about Huisman. It's about Zach. Come on. Let's get you out of the boots. You shouldn't wear them while you're in PT. They're sexy as hell, but I'm way more worried about your ACL."

"You know heels are part of the uniform."

He had to handle her carefully. Despite what most people believed, Kala was actually pretty easy to deal with. She rarely got offended. She didn't care what most people thought. Often people mistook her deep core of honesty for arrogance. If she was wearing the wrong jacket for some party they were going to, she would shrug and ask advice and change. But this was different. This was about her ability to do her job—both as an operative and as a top. He could address one of those issues. "I think you take excellent care of your submissives, and they would likely be horrified if they thought you were in pain, Mistress. Let them have their compassion. Sometimes it's good to let them take care of you."

She was a one hundred percent service top. She didn't sleep with her subs. Oh, she would allow them to serve her at a party if they enjoyed showing off, but she wasn't the kind of Mistress who had her subs wash her car or come over to do the dishes. She was the type of Mistress who would bring a sick sub soup and order them to eat it and get well and ensure they had what they needed.

He wanted her to feel that way about him, too.

"It does hurt." She started to lean over. "I ganked it coming down the stairs. I swear if I step the slightest bit wrong…"

He stopped her, offering his leg. "Let me."

It wasn't a plea. It was a…strongly worded request. She stared at him for a moment and then slowly brought her foot up, gently placing it on his thigh. He found the zipper, easing it down, letting his fingertips brush the back of her knee and then her calf. Such warm skin, soft and silky over firm muscle.

He pulled the ridiculously sexy boot off, setting it to the side before running his hand back up to her knee. "Does massage help at all?"

"Cooper." His name came out on a groan.

"Hey, you did almost all the work tonight." He set his thumb against her calf, pressing in. One of the classes he'd taken as a member of The Hideout was in therapeutic massage. Of course he'd also taken one in erotic massage, but he had to work up to that. He had to work up to tweaking her nipples and finding that place on her glutes that relaxed her enough he could slide a finger in her asshole, getting her ready to take his cock. "I think I should contribute something."

Her eyes closed as he started to rub. "We need to look around and find some women subs looking for a professional top."

"Or I can accept the fact that everyone wants the Mistress," he whispered, finding the arch of her foot and making her moan. "I don't mind being your assistant. Besides, I give the gay guys some eye candy, and don't discount that. I'm sure it's fun to have something pretty to look at while you're getting your balls busted. By the way, did I mention you look lovely tonight? I like the hair."

"I curled it." She was also curling her toes, and that sent a thrill through him. "That feels so good. I hate massage. I don't like people touching me."

"You don't like strangers touching you," he countered. She'd always been that way. It hurt her in school where everyone thought she was some kind of freak because she had boundaries. "You're very affectionate with your friends. You just don't go around hugging every single human being you meet. You're picky, and that's fine. The physical therapist isn't recommending massage?"

She groaned and leaned back against the table, the motion causing her breasts to swell against her corset. "Yeah, but I don't have to do what he says."

"Kala," he admonished.

Her eyes came open. "I have to see a fucking shrink, Coop. I can't do it all. I need to give on something."

Compromise. He could do it. "Fine. As long as you let me know when you're tight. I can take care of it, and you don't have to deal with someone you don't know touching you."

"You don't top me, Coop," she said, and he knew the tiger was close.

Luckily, he'd dealt with her tiger many times. He squeezed her toes and her eyes fluttered. "I know. I'm only thinking of the team. We're going to get back in the field soon, and do you honestly want Kenz to take the lead in finding Huisman?"

"Fine," she agreed with a long sigh. "The things I have to go through for this team."

It was a lie she told herself. She loved her team. She would do anything for them. He needed to get her somewhere more comfortable. Somewhere he could ease that corset off her and then rub her back. He wouldn't try anything. He was being patient. "Why don't we go to a privacy room so I can work on you? You're tight, and you'll be so much more ready for whatever your dad throws at us tomorrow if you're loose."

"I think we should fuck."

He stepped back, dropping her leg. "What?"

A brow rose over her icy blue eyes. "Is it that surprising? Or repugnant?"

Holy hell. What was going through her head? "Surprising. Not the other thing. Never. Kala, you have to admit you're the one who hasn't wanted more of a relationship than we have."

"And I don't now. I'm not asking to be your girlfriend. I just think I don't have anyone I'm sleeping with now and you don't…" She stopped, staring at him for a moment. "I didn't think about whether or not you have someone. I should have asked."

"You never have to ask. You'll always know." Frustration welled where moments before he was preaching patience. This was what she brought out in him. The good, the bad. Everything Cooper McKay could possibly be, this woman unlocked. "I tell you everything. You're my best friend."

She leaned over, unzipping her other boot and stepping out. "I doubt it."

"I might not be yours, but you're mine. I hang out with TJ and Tris and the guys. I really thought Zach and I had a friendship going, but none of them compare to what I have with you. I'm not trying to replace Lou or anything, but since I walked on to this team, my focus has been you."

"Interesting." She set both boots near her kit. "We've never talked about this. I was actually surprised you said yes. We hadn't seen each other for more than a few minutes at a family get-together for years."

"For eight years, four months, and three days," he replied quietly. "From the moment you told me at graduation you didn't think we should talk anymore. You told me college would be an excellent time to move on."

"You make me sound so cold," she murmured, her eyes not meeting his.

It wasn't how he remembered it. His heart had broken, but he'd also known why she'd done it. "No, you were awkward, and you didn't know how to tell me what you were really feeling."

Now her eyes came up to catch his gaze, an almost challenging look in the blue orbs. "How was I feeling, Cooper?"

"Betrayed. Alone," he replied. "You never let go of what happened that night when I was so fucking dumb. You allowed yourself to fall into something of a friendship with me, but you held yourself apart, and then we were going to different schools. You didn't have that tether to hold on to. You decided it would be easier to dump me than to watch it all fall apart."

"There was no 'it' to fall apart, Cooper," Kala replied softly. "And don't think I sit around thinking about the fact that you turned me down that night. You were right. Everyone was right. I was too young, and we weren't good together. I was a kid, and I had this insane notion that I was in love with you."

There was the ache he felt when they talked about high school. "But you don't have that notion now."

"No. I'm not the kind of person who falls in love," she replied with a surety he prayed wasn't real. "I am the kind of person who is practical. We don't spend a lot of time in the normal world. Well, the last few weeks not withstanding we don't. It's been a long time since I had anything regular. Sex wise. You might be getting it every night for all I know."

"I haven't had sex in two years, Kala. Not since I joined the team." He couldn't say it flat out, couldn't tell her he loved her and he wasn't about to fuck around with anyone else. Not when they had an actual chance this time. They weren't kids anymore. They knew what they wanted. Well, he did. He got the feeling she was going to do a lot of hiding behind those walls she'd built.

Now that he was settling into this conversation, the shock was wearing off. He watched her. She wasn't relaxed. Anyone looking from the outside would likely miss the tight set of her eyes and how she cocked her head slightly. Sure signs she was nervous.

What if she was looking for another tether?

"I'm surprised to hear that. I assumed you were living it up on the nights you spend at The Club."

The Club was the BDSM club he'd trained at. He still went and worked a dungeon monitor shift when they needed someone and he was in town. "I tend to work on the nights I spend at The Club, though I've played a couple of times. Gabe's dad pays well. Trust me, I've thought a lot about what I can do professionally after my Agency days are done, and being Julian Lodge's private pilot wouldn't be a bad life."

"I thought you meant you considered being a professional top," she replied.

He shook his head, all the possibilities threatening to swamp him. He'd made the decision to push her after nearly losing her. What if this was her way of doing the same? Kala wouldn't ever come right out and tell him what she wanted. Not when it came to emotions she would deny having.

Why had he gotten Ian Taggart in a sexy-as-fuck woman package?

He was just lucky he supposed.

"I do this because I enjoy working with you. I have zero interest in topping subs on my own."

She considered him for a moment, and he let her brain start to make connections. "You take all the classes. You do a lot of work around topping subs."

"I enjoy it, but I don't need it the way you do, so I'm here to help out my friend. Who is you," he said with what he hoped was a bland smile. He hoped whatever expression was on his face didn't convey what he felt at the moment. Like a wolf who knew he was going to finally get to pounce. He wasn't stupid. He knew exactly what was going to come out of her mouth next. A bargain. A practical, *hey, as long as we're both here* bargain. "So neither of us has a lover right now."

Her nose wrinkled.

He was using the wrong words. He had to remember he was the romantic one in this relationship. "Fuck buddy."

"Yeah," she agreed. "I think maybe being around the rest of the team, and they're all fucking like bunnies, we might be at a disadvantage. It's not like we have a lot of time to go out there and get some."

She could walk out of this door and find ten guys willing to take her to bed right now. They would kneel at her feet or offer to top her. They would take her any way she requested and come back the next night for more, but sure, she struggled to find a couple of minutes to get off. "I feel you. It's hard. And can Lou and TJ, like, take a break every now and then?"

Her jaw dropped as she nodded. "I know. I thought once they'd done it a couple hundred times they might be chill, but no. I can't walk into most rooms in our place anymore. And I can't get any sleep because TJ convinces Lou it's normal to wake up and have sex. He's loud. I can't sleep through it."

Oh, TJ would kiss his feet if he managed to get Kala to sleep in his bed instead of sneaking into Lou's. Because she had bad dreams, and it was a comfort from childhood.

He intended to become her comfort. "Don't forget your sister."

"She and Dare do it at work," Kala said. "Dad walked into Dare's office and… Well, he did the I-can't-see thing for two days. It was kind of funny. All my siblings embarrass my father when it comes to sex. Seth sleeps with any woman with a pulse. Travis forgot to wear a condom. Tasha humps a Canadian on a regular basis, and Kenz really wants to. Though a different Canadian."

"Your dad loves Dare." Big Tag was a character. So was his daughter. "I think Parker is a different story, although the man bought a lot of goodwill with all of us. He didn't have to save you."

She put a hand up. "I can't talk about that tonight. I talk about it too much. That's what I'm saying. I need a distraction. I need sex. If you also need a distraction and need sex, then I think we should discuss having sex together."

So intellectual. So practical. He needed to be the same. He was sure his mother would tell him he should sit down and talk to her, get all their feelings and emotions laid out on the table. But oh, she'd tried to talk to him once and he'd shut her down. He was certain she told herself that rejection didn't matter now, but it did. There was still a vulnerable fifteen-year-old girl in there, and he wasn't about to disappoint her again. If she needed him to play the stud for a while, he could do it. But they didn't need a bunch of talk.

His heart threatened to clench even as his dick hardened to the point of pain.

He was finally, finally getting his hands on Kala Taggart. He had his chance. He wasn't going to blow it.

"I think that sounds like a plan. Let's start now."

\* \* \* \*

Kala was fairly certain her heart was going to explode. She was too young for a heart attack, although she sometimes thought what Huisman had done to her was very similar to *The Princess Bride*. There had been a torture machine in that movie, and it took years off the victim's life. Maybe she was actually eighty now.

He said yes. And he didn't want to wait.

And she was supposed to be this cool, sexually experienced chick. She was not supposed to be a twenty-seven-year-old maybe virgin who lied about sleeping with men because she didn't want any of them besides Cooper McKay.

He had. She knew he'd slept with women. He'd had a couple of serious girlfriends in college.

Not even Lou knew she'd never slept with anyone. She'd lied to her best friend so she didn't look like the sexless, scared-to-find-out-if-she-was-a-virgin freak she was.

Only Kenzie knew. Even her parents thought she had boyfriends in college. Her father had even praised her for not bringing the dumbasses home to meet them. Though that might have been a complaint now that she thought about it.

Cooper held a hand out. "Let's go to a privacy room. I'm not fucking you for the first time on a spanking bench."

For the first time. Oh, this was so many first times. He didn't even know how many first times were going to be had tonight.

And he wasn't going to because this wasn't about happily ever after. This was about getting him out of her system so she could properly focus on her job. She'd gone to that freaking bar the night Huisman kidnapped her because she'd been thinking about Cooper. She'd watched Tris and Carys and Aidan fighting and wished Coop cared about her enough to fight with her.

She had to get him out of her head, and not sleeping with him hadn't done the trick. So here she was. But no one else had to know about it. "The bench is fine."

He stared down at her. Without her boots, he had a good five inches on her. And a hundred pounds of muscle. Pretty muscle. She'd never seen him naked before. Tops didn't tend to get naked during scenes.

Shit, was she a top so she didn't have to be vulnerable?

She wanted to punch her therapist.

"The bench is uncomfortable. It's supposed to be. It's a punishment bench. And it's too low for what I want to do. I know they clean in here, but I'm not laying on the floor."

"Why would you do that?"

"So I can eat your pussy," he said like that was a normal thing to say. He tugged on her hand. "I'll tell one of the subs to deliver your bag and boots to the locker room. They'll be thrilled."

She tugged back. "But if we march through the dungeon, everyone will know."

He stopped, those gorgeous eyes of his narrowing. "And that's a problem why?"

He wasn't thinking. "Cooper, I told you I wasn't angling to be your girlfriend. We don't need all these people in our business."

"Are you ashamed to be seen with me?"

It was time for her eyes to narrow. With irritation. "No. I don't want people talking about me."

"You don't care if people talk about you. You roll your eyes and walk away. So this is about me. I don't care if they know. I'm going to ask how this is supposed to work because the team is usually in pretty close confines. Hence your father's regular bouts with hysterical blindness. Are we going to go to seedy motels? I'm not against that. It can be sexy, but again, I thought we were all about expediency. We're not going to be doing it in whatever safe house we find ourselves in? What's the point then?"

She hated that he sounded so practical and that he was using her own argument against her. Did she care? Did she care if everyone knew she finally got into Cooper's silky boxers? Didn't they all already think she pined for him? When they broke up, it could really be over. Or she could tell whoever asked they could bite her ass and it wasn't any of their business. Because it wasn't.

She looked down at the hand on hers. Would she be able to come back here after it was over? Able to watch him with some sweet sub who would give him everything he needed?

Was she doing this to break with him or to break with everything in her life and start over? Was the idea of splitting off and working for someone who hadn't been there when she was born playing around in her head?

If she left, she could be free. Free to be whoever she truly was. Lou didn't need her anymore. Her sister was going to end up with that Canadian operative. She would have to watch them all settle in and become something she could never be.

"Okay."

The hand around hers softened, and she realized he'd been holding on pretty tight. Had he thought she would run? He seriously underestimated how shitty her knee was.

"Okay? Okay, we can go to a privacy room or okay, we're not doing this?" Cooper asked, his gaze intense on her.

"Privacy room," she whispered. "And anyone who has a problem with it can kick dirt." She thought of another positive. "Hey, they'll probably start betting on us, and since we're not really together except for the sex stuff, we can control it. We can make some money off this."

Rent wasn't cheap, and it was good to multitask.

He huffed and then did something completely unexpected. Kala thought she was pretty good at tactical maneuvers, including figuring out what her opponent's next move was in any fight. She knew Cooper's style, and he was laid back and patient.

This man was anything but patient. He leaned over and shoved his big, stupid strong arms under her knees and lifted her against his chest.

She hadn't been picked up since she was a kid and her dad carried her around. Well, not when she was conscious anyway. "What are you doing?"

"Saving myself time. You're right. I'm incredibly horny, and now I have a fuck buddy. Also, there are a bunch of stairs between us and the privacy rooms. I'm thinking of your knee."

Good. She could go with his reasoning. It also felt nice.

He managed to get the door open, and immediately the industrial thump of music was all around her. And sex. She could hear the sounds of sex and pleasure, and was she about to find out what that really meant?

She needed this. She would be a better operative for doing this, and no one ever had to know how afraid she'd been all these years.

She heard someone gasp as Cooper strode by the main stage and then felt every damn eye on her. He stopped when he found Mattie at the edge of the crowd, looking up at a big guy with wide eyes. Flirting. He was a lot more flirty after a good thwacking. If he got some tonight, she'd done her job.

Mattie turned and stopped, staring at them.

"When you get a chance, deliver the Mistress's kit and boots to the locker room. Her sister is in there, and she'll store them for her," Cooper commanded. "They're in the red room."

Mattie nodded. "Yes, I know which room and yes, I will." He put a hand over his heart. "Are Mommy and Daddy actually going to do it this time?"

"Hey," Kala began. She'd known this would happen. The subs liked to gossip. Despite the fact that it was discouraged. Sort of. In theory. In practice, the club ran on it. "I can still spank you."

She shouldn't have let Cooper pick her up. It made her look weak. It made her feel so good.

It was expedient since she had an injury and there were many stairs that could exacerbate the injury.

Cooper started walking toward those dangerous stairs. She glanced up at him, allowing her arm to float around his broad shoulders. He wore his leathers, no shirt beneath the black vest on his chest so she could feel warm skin. His jaw was tight and with the barest hint of stubble.

"Kala." Lou ran across the dungeon floor, TJ following after her. "What happened? Should I get one of the doctors?"

Oh, bestie. She'd kind of hoped they would get by her. Lou might be a sub, but she could be super stubborn if she thought someone could hurt a friend. "I'm fine."

Cooper kept walking.

Lou followed. "What is going on? Did your knee give out? Was it the spanking bench in the red room, because I told Gabe I thought we should get another."

"Lou, baby, I don't think this is about a bad knee." TJ put a hand on his girlfriend's elbow. "We should give them some space."

"Space for what?" Lou asked as though she couldn't wrap her head around why Coop would be carrying her upstairs and toward the privacy rooms.

Cooper didn't say a word.

TJ whispered something to Lou and then her eyes went wide and she watched them. Her best friend sent her a look of pure surprise. And maybe a little hurt.

She told Lou everything. Almost everything. Since the incident in Canada, she'd held a lot back. Or maybe it started when Lou and TJ got together and Kala realized how she could fuck things up for her friend and her cousin.

Cooper blew right past the bar where everyone was not paying any attention at all. Nope. They were all staring. Every single one of them. Daisy's jaw had dropped, and she pulled her cell out of her boobs and started texting. So her sister would know in seconds.

It didn't matter. This was what she wanted. What she needed. When they broke off whatever they were starting, everyone would think she was the heartless bitch who walked away from perfect Cooper.

"Three is open," a deep voice called out. She glanced behind Cooper and his brother, Hunter, was standing at the entry desk to the privacy rooms, dressed in his leathers and a big old grin. He gave her a thumbs-up as Cooper simply walked on.

He got them inside the privacy room labeled three and closed the door behind them and stopped. For the first time since he picked her up, he looked at her, staring right into her eyes. A long moment passed.

"You can put me down," she said quietly, the intimacy hitting her like a kick in the gut. She was in a room with Cooper and they were supposed to have sex. He was probably thinking she was incredibly experienced. Since that was kind of the vibe she put out.

"I'm worried if I put you down, you're going to run away," he admitted. "And I don't want you to run away. I think we need this. Both of us."

Yes, they needed to indulge so they could both move on. "I don't care what they say, Coop. This is a private thing between the two of us. Which is why we should have stayed downstairs. No one would think anything of us holing up in a room together on the dungeon floor."

"We should negotiate." He set her on her feet, not taking those big hands off her until he seemed certain she was stable.

She was anything but. Her heart rate had tripled, and she could feel her stupid nipples hardening because there was every possibility that he was about to see them, and they wanted to put on a freaking show. "There's nothing to negotiate. We have sex when we're horny and that's that."

"We have sex when it's convenient and we're around each other, and we're free to have sex with anyone else who catches our eye?" Cooper managed to make the question sound like an accusation.

Did he think she was trying to trap him? "I thought you said you weren't sleeping with anyone else. If you want someone else, you should go for it."

"I wasn't talking about me." His jaw was a stubborn line as he got into her space. "I won't take another woman while I'm in your bed. I'll be utterly devoted to you and your pleasure. I'm talking about you, Mistress Kala."

She barely bit back a laugh. She'd obviously done an excellent job at building her reputation as a sexual powerhouse. It was good to know Cooper had an ego. Sometimes she thought he was far too perfect. He didn't want anyone to think she was cheating on him. Which she wouldn't be because they weren't together, and he should have thought about that before he paraded them through the dungeon. "I'm not your girlfriend and I'm not your submissive. However, I can agree to not sleep with anyone while we're sleeping together."

It made sense. There would be way less drama and no need to worry about things like sexually transmitted infections. From him, obviously, not her since she hadn't and never had wanted to sleep with anyone except him.

Would sleeping with Cooper awaken a sexual animal inside her? It was an outcome she hadn't considered but could actually work in her favor. She'd always worried about her lack of sexual response to anyone but him. What if getting a taste of him opened her up to sex in all its various flavors? She might be normal. This might help her be normal in one thing.

Cooper stood there, staring at her, and she couldn't quite name the emotion in his eyes. Or she was afraid to because she sometimes didn't get the same cues her sister and friends picked up on. Was he changing his mind?

"I'm here, and now I don't know quite what to do," he said, his words cutting through the silence. "I feel like I've…like we've danced around this forever, and now I'm a little scared I won't live up to what you expect."

Good news for him. She expected nothing except awkwardness and probably disappointment. And yet she was still going to have this time. "Why don't you kiss me? Forget I'm Mistress K. Treat me like you would any woman you want to sleep with."

"Never." His hands were on her cheeks, brushing back and sinking into her hair. "You are not any woman. You are *the* woman. You're Kala, and I can't ever forget that."

She would have said something back, something like… She didn't know what she would have said. Hopefully something sarcastic to break the emotional cocoon she found herself in, but it could have been something stupid and sappy because she felt it. He saved her by lowering his lips to hers and kissing her for the first time in over a freaking decade.

They'd only had three months of this. Three months where he'd put his hands on her and she felt like the woman she wanted to become. When Cooper kissed her she felt safe and normal. She felt like the Kala she was, and that it was okay to be her.

She knew now that was an illusion, but she sank into that kiss. For a moment, she allowed herself to be fifteen again, the world laid out in front of her, with all the roads still open and waiting for her to choose. She let her hands find his lean waist, brushing past the leather of his vest to soft, warm skin.

She followed his lead, the same way she had when they were kids. He was dominant but it didn't bother her. This man would never harm her physically. She trusted him with her life, so when his tongue dragged across her bottom lip, she opened her mouth. His tongue found hers, and her whole body came alive. So often her body was nothing more than a tool, a weapon she used against the enemies. She trained it, fed it properly, maintained it, but now she realized she'd been missing something essential. Every inch of her skin hummed with need and he'd barely touched her.

He kissed her for what felt like forever, and the world fell away. The thoughts that were always in her brain, picking at her and nagging like incessant insects, were silent now, and she was nothing more than a body meant to touch and caress and kiss.

"I'm never going to be able to last, baby," he whispered against her lips. "It's been too long and I want you too much. So I need to get you across the finish line first. Turn around."

Normally the bossiness would bug her, but she wasn't the expert here and he was. So she turned and let him loosen her corset and drag it off her. When his hands slid up to cup her breasts, she practically melted against him. She let her head fall back on his shoulder as he played with her nipples.

"Have I told you how fucking hot you are?" He growled the words against her ear. "I can't watch you work without wanting you. Hell, I can't be in the same room without wanting to fuck you, baby."

He hadn't talked like this when they were kids, and the words felt jarring, a reminder that he thought she was used to this, that he believed she was the sexual being she presented herself as. It was easy to turn and kiss him again. When he kissed her she could pretend the years that had passed between them weren't an ocean she had to find a way to navigate.

His fingers slipped under the waist of her shorts, easing them down.

She was comfortable with her body. It was certainly not the first time she'd been naked in front of a guy. She'd brought plenty of dumbass counteragents or dudes she needed something from up to her room and gotten them comfy and distracted. Boobs were great distractions. But this was usually the moment she knocked the guy out. Or killed him when he decided it was a great time to attack.

She was naked in front of Cooper. He'd touched her before, put his hand between her legs and rubbed, but this was different. This felt more serious. Or less serious because it meant less, because they both knew this wasn't forever.

She had to shut the voices out or she would lose it. She moved into his arms and went on her toes, pressing her lips to his again.

She let him take the lead and found herself on her back in moments, Cooper's big body covering hers as he pressed her into the mattress. She'd worried his weight might bug her, but she liked it. He felt warm and reassuring. He kissed her, his tongue delving deep, and then pressed kisses down her neck and chest until he caught a nipple in his mouth, the sharp tug sparking something deep inside her pussy.

Desire. She'd thought she understood the word, thought she remembered how it felt to be young and to think she was in love, but this…this was a drug she could get addicted to. This was a wave she could ride and for a while be outside herself, be someone else. There was no future for them, but for a brief moment, he could be hers.

He sucked her nipple until her hands fisted in the comforter and she groaned, her toes curling. Then he worked his way down her body, kissing along her belly until he was right above her pussy.

She wouldn't be able to take it. What if she didn't like it? What if he didn't like how she tasted? She was so weird, and what if this part of her was weird, too? Regular sex seemed safer. He would like regular sex and then she would know. "Cooper, just do it. I don't need the rest."

His head came up, eyes flashing like he was going to argue with her. There was the top who would need a sub. This was why it couldn't work but they'd agreed to this, and she was seeing it through. She was going to know. Going to know once and for all of time that she wasn't a virgin.

"The rest is the fun part," he grumbled. "I told you, I won't be able to last. I'm lucky I haven't gone off yet."

She didn't want to fight and she didn't want to lay there worried he wasn't enjoying it. The actual sex part was something every guy liked.

She should have talked about sex with her sisters more. She tended to leave the room when Tasha and Kenz started up, and Lou blissfully didn't seem to need to tell her everything about her sex life with TJ. She'd learned at a young age to tune her parents out. She'd gotten the meaningful stuff. Wear a condom. Sex is important. Yadda, yadda.

He was so gorgeous, and the idea of disappointing him damn near killed her. What was she doing? She was thinking again, her brain caught in a never-ending wheel moving her toward panic.

"It'll be fine," she insisted, tugging on his arm. What should she say? "I need you. Please, Coop."

She needed to know. It was perverse. She'd waited all this time, and suddenly she had to know. She couldn't wait another second, and she was well aware if Cooper drew out the foreplay she would freeze up. A vision flashed through her brain. A vision of herself laid out for a monster. Had he laid her out on a bed? Or just did whatever he'd done in the car they'd transported her in? Had he waited until they were on the plane?

"Please." She hated to beg but she couldn't stop the words. She was at an inflection point. She did this with Cooper and gave herself a chance at finding something normal or she might be done trying at all.

"Damn it," Cooper cursed and lifted his hips. "I'm not even going to get my damn pants off. We can forgo the condom?"

"You know I'm on birth control," she replied, her nerves flaring. They were doing this. It was happening. She was ready. Was she ready? "We're both regularly tested. It's fine."

Cooper managed to shove his leathers down and then he was spreading her legs, lowering himself on top of her.

Suddenly his weight did bother her, but he was kissing her again and she let it go. It would be fine. This was Cooper, and she did want him. He made her feel more than anyone ever had. He could show her this world. It would be okay.

He thrust inside her, and she winced at the fullness. It wasn't pain. Not exactly. She was all kinds of wet down there, but it also wasn't pleasure. It wasn't comfortable.

Cooper went still. "You feel so fucking good, baby. Better than I could have imagined." He stared down at her, and the lust in his eyes seemed to clear. Concern replaced the desire she saw there. "Are you okay? Fuck. Baby, did I hurt you?"

She felt her jaw clench. "I'm fine."

He reached up and brushed something off her cheek. "You're not."

Crying? She was fucking crying? She didn't cry. The last time she'd cried it was because she was pinned down by a paralytic. Huisman didn't need to tie her down to make her feel like a bug pinned to a board, studied for the amusement of others.

In a moment she was back and she felt the fire in her veins, knew she was going to die, and for the barest moment she'd been okay with it because it would free everyone she cared about. It would free him.

"Baby, stop," he said, and then he gritted his teeth and gasped.

She went still, felt him move inside her, his warmth filling her.

Cooper pushed himself off, rolling away. "I'm sorry. Kala, what the hell happened? You were somewhere else for a minute." He scrambled to his knees, looking down on her like she might be dying.

She was. On the inside. Of embarrassment. What had she done? She needed to play this cool. Long breath. Nothing was wrong. She forced herself to roll over, getting off the bed and going for one of the robes the dungeon monitors stocked the privacy rooms with. "It's all good. Can't be sexually compatible with everyone, I guess."

She belted the robe and turned, and Cooper was still on his knees though he'd tucked his cock away. She hadn't even gotten a good look at it. His mouth was open as he stared at her like she'd said something unbelievable.

She simply shrugged and tried not to think about how sore she was. He was big. She should have known he would be big. But it didn't look like she'd bled or anything. She hadn't felt some tearing sensation.

So she would make of that what she would.

She was not going to cry. He didn't seem to want to say anything. This was going to be one of The Hideout's shortest hook-ups, it appeared. "Now we know. It's good to know."

"We know nothing," he replied, his eyes narrowing. "And I'm worried I know less than nothing. Kala, get back on this bed. We're going to talk."

There was a knock on the door, something that was never supposed to happen. Privacy rooms were private, and unless there was an emergency, no one was supposed to interrupt.

Thank god something had blown up or someone had died and she would feel bad about it later because right now, that knock was her salvation.

"Go away," Cooper said in his absolute dommiest voice.

She had to admit. It was still hot, but now she knew she was only sexual in an intellectual fashion.

Hadn't she known that all along? Hadn't she known the loving relationship her parents shared wasn't something she would ever have?

It was good to know.

She moved to the door.

"Kala, do not answer," he ordered, getting off the bed.

Did he even know her? Well, she'd proven he didn't, but he should know she didn't follow orders. She opened the door, and her sister stood there. Kenzie was in street clothes, and that told Kala everything she needed to know.

It was time to leave this dream behind and move back to reality.

"Huisman?" she asked.

Her sister nodded, her expression tight.

"Get dressed, Coop. Time to get to work." She walked out and didn't look back.

# Chapter Eight

Cooper sat back in the conference room they kept in The Hideout. It was meant for things like board meetings, but too often it turned a great night into a work conference. Like tonight.

Not that it had been great. What the fuck had happened? One minute he was absolutely sure she'd been right there with him, moving with him, kissing him as though they'd never been apart, and the next she was pushing him off her and he was proving he needed help for premature ejaculation.

"Dr. Rebecca Walsh-Shaw's car exploded roughly an hour ago. It was her personal vehicle and was sitting in her driveway," Big Tag said.

Kenzie gasped, sitting up, with tears already forming in her eyes. "Rebecca?"

Her mom sat forward. "She's fine. She started it from inside her house so it would have time to warm up. Lucky for all of us, Huisman's bomb didn't take into account the fact that she always starts it before she actually leaves the house."

"Where are they now?" Kala asked, her tone entirely professional. She hadn't even looked his way since she'd walked out of the privacy room.

And he was angry about it. It sat in his gut. He wasn't sure if he was angry at her or himself. He'd told himself to be patient, that she was working through something. She had been the one Huisman tortured, and his trauma from thinking she was dead didn't begin to touch what she'd been through. But then if he'd tried to talk to her, had tried to get her to understand they could be more than an itch to scratch, she would have walked anyway.

She put him in an impossible position time and time again.

When would he stop paying for the idiot his fifteen-year-old self had been?

"Packing as fast as they can. Damon sent a couple of his men to escort them to London. Hannah was already in England. She's at Oxford, but Arran is going to have to be pulled out of school," Big Tag replied. "The Swedish police are watching them for now. Once they're at The Garden, they'll have twenty-four-seven security. But I have to worry about Jax and Tucker. Robert's already got his family at The Garden. They've been living in London in a townhouse, but it's better to close ranks at this point."

He studied Kala as they began to talk about logistics. Which was supposed to be his area of expertise, but his brain wasn't working on anything but her right now. Tristan was saying something about flying to Colorado to escort Jax Lee and his family back to Texas. Someone talked about Wyoming. He was pretty sure that was where Tucker lived. All of the men from the team so long ago would have to go into hiding.

Kala was perfectly flawless. She'd changed into street clothes, and gone were the pretty pink curls, replaced with a ponytail that accented her high cheekbones and the lips he'd kissed.

He'd kissed her and it had been everything. It had been like coming fucking home, and then it had all gone wrong.

How had it gone wrong? In the beginning she'd responded to him. There hadn't been any hesitation in her kiss. She hadn't fought him when he'd picked her up—and he'd done it for exactly the reason she thought he had. So everyone would know. He knew she would want to keep it on the down low, but he had no intention of being her dirty secret. He could be her booty call but not a secret.

Not like he'd made her when they were young.

He shoved aside the gut-gnawing guilt he felt.

She'd had a reaction. Likely to his weight being on her. Had she felt pinned down? Had it been too much dominance for the

Dominatrix?

"I've called the Swedes, and they're going to work with us," Big Tag said, running a hand over his barely-there hair. He'd seen pictures of Big Tag when he'd had blond hair that brushed his shoulders, but as long as Coop could remember he'd had a high and tight. He'd likely gotten pulled out of a privacy room, too, since he was almost certain Big Tag and Charlotte had come from Sanctum.

"They're sending us CCTV footage from around the neighborhood," Drake said since the gang was all here. It was a whole lot of Agency in his happy place. "I'm surprised Huisman didn't find a way to turn off the cams."

The woman at the end of the table cleared her throat, and all eyes turned to her. "Have we considered the fact that this might not be Huisman?"

The profiler/therapist the Agency had sent was here as well. She sat beside Drake, who was as casual as he'd ever seen the man in sweats and a T-shirt, with rumpled hair. Like he'd rolled out of bed to get here, which he probably had. Unlike Ian and Charlotte, he hadn't been at Sanctum since his wife wasn't with him.

Lena Gallagher, however, looked like she was ready for work. If the late hour bothered her, it didn't show. She wore a perfectly tailored business suit, her chin-length bob smooth and straight, and her makeup done.

Big Tag's brow rose. "Who the hell else would it be? Dr. Walsh is a renowned neuroscientist. She's a researcher at this point and working on curing Alzheimer's. Do you think the disease is sending out bombs to kill her?"

Big Tag was spicy when he was tired. Kala's gaze slid his way, her eyes flaring slightly as if to say *here we go*. He let his lips curl. She was endlessly amused by her father, and they loved to watch when he got started up. Cooper loved sharing it with her.

And then she shut down as though she remembered what had happened.

Was that all she was remembering?

"Well, Mr. Taggart, it feels petty for Dr. Huisman," Lena began, ignoring the sarcasm from Big Tag. "I've made a study of the man, and he tends to be a big-picture sort of guy. Don't get me wrong. I'm certainly not saying the doctor isn't capable of murder. He obviously is, but I believe he would do it in a more spectacular fashion."

"He likes bombs," Kenzie pointed out. "He's blown up shit across the globe. Sounds like Huisman to me."

Kenzie was glaring at the psychologist, which was odd because Kenz was almost always friendly. But then she kind of glared at him right now, too. He would bet Kala hadn't said a word about what had happened.

If he hadn't made a big deal, hadn't let his ego get in the way, she wouldn't have had to. She might have been able to quietly disentangle herself.

Thank the fucking universe for his ego because he wanted to be entangled.

"Huisman isn't the only one who is heavily connected to bombs," Lena pointed out, also ignoring Kenzie's pointed jabs. "What I mean by the big picture is everything Huisman has done to this point has benefitted his plans for the Disrupt organization. The shadow one, of course."

"Uhm, pretty sure Kala would disagree," Lou said. She'd been watching him, too, obviously trying to figure out what had happened.

"I don't know about that," Kala replied. "In this I might agree with the doc."

"How so?" Charlotte's head tilted slightly, taking in her daughter. "I think what was done to you was pointedly about the grudge he has against your father."

"But that wasn't his plan." Kala turned in her seat, facing her mother. "Taking me was a mistake. He even told me he hadn't planned to move so quickly, but he wouldn't waste the chance. He wanted information from Tristan, and more importantly, Zach."

"Exactly," Lena said, nodding Kala's way with an approving smile. "Huisman's plans were about discovering the identity of the bombmaker, which brings us to Zach."

"Yes, he obviously knows more about the bombmaker than we understood." Big Tag sighed as though tired of the whole thing. "But if you are trying to convince me Zach planted that bomb, you're barking up the wrong tree. Zach barely knows Dr. Walsh. He met her briefly once. He has no reason to hurt her."

"Unless he's in league with Huisman, and he lied about wanting information from Zach." Lena sat back. "We've already established that Huisman's true goal is chaos. What better chaos than to be working with a member of your team? Especially if there's a possibility of Zach returning in some way to the fold. He would be able to give you a lot of misinformation. It's obvious you don't believe Zach is capable of this kind of crime, but we have already established he's murdered one man in cold blood."

"The Jester," Charlotte said. "Who is an arms dealer who fed multiple wars and criminal organizations. I get what you're saying, but you don't know Zach. There's something bigger here we don't understand."

"All right." Lena studied Charlotte for a moment. "You care for Zach and I understand, but I would like for the group to at least consider what I'm saying. I wasn't placed in this position for my good looks. I know what I'm talking about, and in this case I believe I can think more clearly about the situation." She held up a hand as if to ward off the inevitable arguments. "If I'm wrong, all you've done is be more careful. I suspect you'll hear from Zach at some point, and he'll come with explanations and apologies. He'll play on the sympathy he knows he'll get from you. Be careful, Mrs. Taggart. Your operatives need to be careful as well." She stood and collected her designer bag, settling it on her shoulder. "Now, I'm going to get back to my hotel and get some sleep since it's easy to see I'm causing problems here."

Drake looked up at her. "Lena, you don't have to go."

She shook her head. "They're emotional, and I'm making it worse. I'll be back at the Ferguson Clinic tomorrow. Mr. Taggart offered me an office in his building, but the clinic is quite nice, and I won't be a focal point there. Please keep me up to date on anything I need to know. Kala, I'll see you soon."

Cooper winced at the thought but Kala merely nodded, and Lena exited stage left. He wondered what she thought about being dragged into a meeting at a lifestyle club. Drake was in the lifestyle, and he and his wife attended a club in DC, but somehow he couldn't see the perfectly controlled therapist being interested in D/s. He could be wrong.

Drake looked Ian and Charlotte's way, his eyes narrowing. "You know who she is and what she's here to do."

Charlotte tucked a strand of strawberry blonde hair behind her ear. "I know she's trying to sway my team to believe Zach is the bad guy here."

"She's not wrong," Ian said tightly. "I'm not saying Zach is evil, just that we should be careful and keep an open mind. We don't know what forces are pushing on him right now, what kind of trouble he's in. We don't know who or what he's protecting."

"Well, I would think it's the bombmaker," Tristan said with a frown. "At least it seemed that's what Huisman believed. But I can't see Zach trying to kill Dr. Walsh. He wouldn't have any reason to."

"Unless he was working with Huisman," TJ replied. "I know. I don't believe it either, but Huisman plays games. What if this is all part of his game?"

"I need to see the bomb," Lou said resolutely. "Can I get on a plane? I suspect the Swedish police aren't going to turn it over any time soon, and getting my hands on it would help enormously. I've studied the bombmaker's work. I can tell you if it's his."

Drake nodded and sighed as though happy to have something active to do. "Yes. I'll inform the Swedish police you're coming. You and TJ can fly out tomorrow."

"Tris can go with them," Big Tag said.

Kala's hand came up. "I think I should be the one to go."

Ian's eyes lit with what Cooper always thought of as his karma's-about-to-bite-your-ass expression. "Nope. You'll be hiding because your sister is going to Toronto to update the Canadians."

Kenzie jumped in her seat, hands clapping. "Really?"

Ian groaned. "Well, now I'm thinking I should send someone else. Tasha could go with Dare."

"I'll be good. You know I will," Kenzie promised. "And I'll get way more out of Ben Parker than anyone else will. He's the subject matter expert on Huisman. I'd like to know what he thinks of the attack on Dr. Walsh."

She managed to sound halfway professional.

"I think it should be me," Kala argued. "Kenz is way too interested in Parker's abs."

Kenzie's jaw dropped. "Seriously?"

Big Tag shook his head. "We are not fighting about this. Kala, you aren't going. You have an appointment with Dr. Gallagher and physical therapy you shouldn't miss. You are not clear to be out in the field yet, and honestly, the last fucking place I would send you to is Toronto. So stand down. I can't send you to Sweden because there's only one Ms. Magenta out in the world at a time, and it's not you."

A faint flush stained her cheeks, but she let out a deep breath and stared straight ahead. "Understood."

"All right, then let's get out of here." Big Tag stood. "Drake, why don't you come by our place tomorrow for breakfast and we'll discuss this situation. I know exactly what Dr. Gallagher is here to do, which is probably why my wife wants to murder her."

Drake groaned and stood. "All right. Let's get some sleep."

The rest of the team made for the door, Kala pushing her chair back and starting to exit. Kenzie followed her, obviously wanting a word. Cooper meant to have one, too. He stood, ready to corner Kala and get to the bottom of whatever had happened in the privacy room.

"Not you." Big Tag blocked his way.

There weren't many men who were as tall as Cooper, but Big Tag looked him straight in the eyes. "I need to talk to Kala."

Big Tag glanced around, making sure they were alone and the door was shut. "You need to tell me what the fuck happened tonight."

Well, there was a reason the man worked for the Agency. "I should point out that it's none of your business, but I'm curious as to which of our so-called friends saw you walking in and immediately informed you Kala and I are taking our relationship to another level. Again, not anyone's business but ours."

One side of Tag's mouth curved up. "Impressive. I almost want to honor that because it truly should be your business. If all I'd heard was that you finally got your hands on my daughter after all these years and she seems happy, I wouldn't be having what is likely going to be a very awkward conversation. But she does not look happy, Cooper."

"It didn't go the way we thought it would." He wanted to walk away, but no one knew Kala like her father did. Not even her twin. Lou might have all the information, but she couldn't know what it felt like to be Kala. The closest he had was Big Tag. "I wanted to go slow. She wanted fast and then... I think she was reliving something. She went somewhere else for a moment. And I'm a guy so..."

Big Tag slumped back in his chair, a weary sigh coming from his chest. "So your dick didn't care that she was having a post-traumatic episode and the inevitable happened. Tell me you wore a condom."

Sometimes it was best to be upfront with the man. He sank back into his seat, too. "Nope. I know my last tests came back healthy, and quite frankly, if she wants to baby trap me, I'll walk right into it. I'll happily provide logistics for her ops with one of those baby carriers strapped to my chest."

"Damn it. I want to hate you," Ian admitted.

"Because of that night." They hadn't talked about it in years. Years where he was completely uncertain how this man, who was such an important part of his life, felt about him. Maybe it was time they all talked about it, stopped pretending it wasn't a wall between them.

Icy blue eyes pinned Cooper. "You made her feel small."

"I know." There was nothing to do but take whatever Ian was going to give him. He'd been wrong, and they were still paying for it. "And I continued to do it because I was too scared to talk to her about what happened. Not just when she was kidnapped, but what my words to her that night did to her. Now she doesn't want to."

"Oh, I assure you somewhere deep down she wants to, but you might not like what she has to say," Ian countered.

Her father didn't understand how far he would go for her. "I would take it. You need to know if I didn't think I'm the best man for her, I would walk away in a heartbeat."

"I'm worried you're the only man for her, and if she can't have you, she'll be alone forever." Ian's expression softened slightly.

Cooper touched his chest, placing his hand over his heart. "I'm right here. I've been very clear about wanting to try. I haven't looked at another woman since I joined this team. I've supported her work both with the Agency and in the lifestyle. Then she comes to me tonight and wants what she calls 'stress relief,' and I was willing to be that, too, because I know it's bullshit. She needs another name for it. She can't love me because I hurt her and it's scary, so I let her hide a little while longer."

"See, this is why I can't hate you," Ian admitted. "You really do know her."

Tonight made him question what he thought he knew. "Not everything. I don't know what was going through her head tonight. But then she didn't want to talk to me about what happened in Toronto. I had to read the reports to know the basics, and I'm sure she hid the worst of it."

"Her heart stopped."

Those words felt like a land mine he'd stepped on. Cooper felt sick. He'd known it was bad. Sometimes he thought he was still stuck in that moment when Ben Parker carried her out of a burning house.

"That wasn't in the report."

"It wasn't in the one the team got, but I assure you, it was in the one the Agency has," Ian explained. "Why do you think I'm benching her when she wants so fucking badly to get back into the field and prove to herself nothing changed? She didn't even want to see a cardiologist to make sure her heart's okay. I had to force her. She's pissed at me, and when she's mad at me, it's one less person she's willing to talk to. I tried to get her to see Kai when we got back, but she insisted she was fine. I don't know whether to be relieved or worried that she's agreed to see Dr. Gallagher."

Cooper knew that particular truth. "She thinks if she convinces the doctor she's solid, she'll back off. We all know she's here to evaluate us. Probably to finish the job Zach didn't manage to do." If they shut down the team, it wasn't like Kala would come home and start a job at MT. They would move her to another team, another handler, and he would be right back in the Navy flying helos.

Or he would cash out and start his life back here. Either way, he wouldn't be with her.

"I only want her to talk to someone," Big Tag admitted.

"I wish she would talk to me. She does about some things." She talked to him about how afraid she was to lose Lou when she and TJ got together. How it felt like everyone was going to leave her behind as they started their lives. She'd been halfway through a bottle of Cab that night, and they'd sat on the roof of The Hideout, looking out over the Dallas skyline. She'd let him hold her hand, and for once he felt like he was giving her something. "Should I walk away? Would she be more open to a relationship with the men she sees if I wasn't in the picture?"

"The men she sees?" Big Tag's expression went blank. "Have you met these men?"

"No. She's very private about her sex life."

Ian nodded. "Yes, she is. And isn't that odd since no one else is. Her sisters can't fucking stop talking about their sex lives. Lou and TJ just do it wherever they happen to be standing. I do not know how she works when he's on top of her all the time. Kala is surrounded by people who are perfectly comfortable talking about sex, and do you know how many boyfriends she's brought home?"

He was sure it was at least one or two. "She had a couple in college, from what I understand."

"Did she?" Ian asked. "Or did she tell us that? I don't know because I never met the fuckers, and when I followed them around for a couple of days, I realized they were just men in her classes. She had no interaction with them outside of class, so unless they were fucking in the closet…"

A chill went through him. "Ian, tell me she's not a virgin. She can't possibly be a virgin."

One big shoulder shrugged. "Well, probably not now unless you didn't actually make it inside her."

He felt his whole world shift because all this time he'd thought she was trying to find happiness the way everyone did. He'd thought she was dating and hadn't found the right one, thought she was enjoying sex the way she should when she was young. He'd heard stories she would tell about seducing targets. "Why? Why would she lie about it?"

"Because it's easier than admitting why she's afraid of sex. Look, Cooper, I know why she's been skittish. It's a combination of something that happened to her when she was young and you. I'm not going to tell you about the event. That has to come from her. But I will talk about you. She is now and has always been sick in love with you. Kenzie fell in and out of love a million times. It's why I'm not worried about the Canadian. She'll move on eventually. But Kala is a different story. She's me, and if I hadn't found my Charlie, I would have been alone. Don't get me wrong, I had girlfriends and I had subs, but I wouldn't have opened myself up to anyone but Charlie. I had one shot, and for a long time I thought it was over. When I thought Charlie was dead, I shut myself off. Only thing that saved my relationship with my brother was his wife. Hell, there were times I didn't want a relationship with anyone. It would be easier to go lone wolf and let the job be my life. I worry she's in that stage right now, and whatever the hell happened tonight is going to push her to do it."

"I love your daughter," Cooper said quietly, emotion welling through him. "I've always loved her. I was a child and I wanted to fit in. I thought if I did everything right, made everyone like me, showed everyone I was good at sports and popular, then I would be worthy of them."

Ian looked at him with something akin to sympathy. He didn't pretend to not understand. "Your parents loved you from the moment they saw you. It never mattered Eve didn't carry you. They didn't give a crap you don't share DNA. I assure you I love my Tasha every bit as much as my biological children, but I do understand that it can feel like you don't belong. Have you thought about finding your biological mother?"

He shook his head. "I don't need to meet her. I have a mother, and I don't need anyone else. I got over it, but how I felt when I was fifteen hurt the girl I loved then. She scared me back then."

"Because everything that makes her a strong, resourceful woman made her a difficult child. That's the sharp edge of parenting they don't tell you about. It's hard when you can see so clearly what a teacher calls stubbornness will one day be determination," Ian admitted. "You have to figure out how to balance fitting in with not losing what makes your child special. It was easy as breathing for Kenzie. Tash had to learn. My boys are knuckleheads, and oddly that made everyone love them, but Kala was different."

"And I made it worse because I wanted her but I didn't want anyone to know I wanted her. Like she was something I should hide." The old guilt settled on him, and now it held a new edge since there was something he didn't know. And something he did. He'd wrecked her first time. "I should leave."

Ian's face fell. "And I'm back to hating you."

"She didn't trust me enough to tell me she was a virgin," Cooper argued. "I don't know how to deal with that. I joined the team because I wanted another chance with her, but I worry I'm hurting her. Seeing her… She almost died. I wanted to fucking lie down and die with her."

Ian slapped the table, the sound reverberating through the conference room. "Then live for her. Don't give up. If you genuinely believe you're the best man for her, you don't give up. Not until she tells you she can't love you and asks you to leave. Has she done that?"

"No. But I can't do what I want to do."

"And what's that?" Ian asked.

This was the crux of his problem when it came to sex with the woman he loved. "Top her. I know she identifies as a Domme, but she needs a top, Ian."

"I would say she's actually more of a switch," Ian said, proving he didn't have a problem talking about sex. "But there's a wall she can't break down on her own. So you might have to be sneaky. You already are. You think I don't see you manipulate her?"

"It's not manipulation." Cooper didn't like the word. "It's about figuring out how to get her what she needs when she doesn't think she needs it. Things like affection and taking care of her. So if I stop by a bakery on my way to work, I pick up a chocolate croissant because she'll tell herself she doesn't need the carbs. But if I paid for it, she doesn't want to waste the money."

Ian shrugged. "All right. I'll give you that, but it's still a way to top her. A sneaky top. Now you have to figure out what will make her comfortable in bed. And you need to do it fast, son. If you give her a couple of days, she'll talk herself out of it. But if it was right there and presented in a way she understands, then maybe…"

Oh, he had his thinking cap on. Big Tag could come up with a plan. "What are you planning?"

A smile hit the big guy's face.

An evil smile. Cooper sighed because this was absolutely going to be embarrassing.

\* \* \* \*

Kala stepped out of the conference room, ready to pretty much run and hide. A cowardly thing to do, but here she was. She'd tried to dip her toe into the ocean, and now she felt like she was drowning.

And she definitely hadn't known how to swim.

"Hey." Her sisters moved in, Kenzie taking the lead, but Tash close behind. "I think we should talk."

The last thing she wanted to do was talk. She was so done talking. Talking was what got her in trouble in the first place. Or maybe she should have talked more to Cooper and then she would have realized it wouldn't work.

It hadn't worked. It was an actual ache in her gut, and she finally understood how much she'd been counting on having a few weeks with him. A month or two. A year, tops. She could have sunk into it, guarding herself, of course. She could have put off making decisions.

"I don't think Zach has a reason to bomb Dr. Walsh, if that's what you're asking." She knew it wasn't, but she wasn't doing this here. "We'll know more when Lou gets a look at the bomb. Way to get yourself a free trip to Stockholm, bestie."

Lou was coming out of the conference room, TJ behind her. She looked at Kenzie and Tasha, obviously taking in the scene. "You guys, you know better than to corner her. She'll talk about it when she's ready to talk about it. You'll do way better offering her late-night waffles. Somewhere in the middle of her third she might drop a moment of truth."

Her bestie knew her way better than anyone else. Even her twin. She and Kenzie loved each other but didn't always understand the other's motivations and actions. Like Ben Parker. Ick. She did not get the attraction. He was cold and ruthless. He was an obvious playboy, an agent who used his looks and magnetism to get what he wanted. She would always have to question his intentions. Cooper was earnest. A woman tended to know where she stood with him.

Shit. She was like Parker. It was an opposites-attract thing. Coop was the Kenzie in this situation.

Damn. She was always the bad guy.

"I'm afraid I'm not hungry tonight." Kala started down the hallway. She wanted to get home and get to bed and be alone. The only problem was she'd come with Lou and TJ. She needed to be less dependent. She was their constant third wheel, and it had to grate. The last thing she wanted to do was fuck up her best friend's relationship.

Why hadn't Cooper come out of the conference room? She glanced back and her mom was exiting, talking to Tristan. The door closed and Kala stopped, waiting for it to open again.

Shit and balls. There were only two people left in that room. Cooper was in there and so was her dad, and the chance that they were talking about the op was zilch.

"Who told Dad?"

Everyone seemed to take a step back as though she could take them out with a mere glare.

Her mother stepped in. "It wasn't your sisters. They won't give me anything. It was him."

She pointed Tristan's way, and he paled. "I didn't. I said something offhand because it's…I…okay, I might have mentioned in a casual way some of the events of the evening. It's not like he wouldn't find out. But like I said…"

She punched him. Right in the nose. Let Aidan set the fucker. He was somewhere in the building. Tristan had two people he could count on, and both of them had MDs. He didn't need to go around tattling on her like a fucking toddler.

Tristan groaned, putting a hand over his nose. "Damn it, Kala. You can't expect to sleep with Cooper after five thousand years and not have anyone talk about it."

"I told you," a feminine voice said, and then Aidan and Carys were moving toward their Dom. Carys was in street clothes and had an ice pack in her hand. Like she'd expected the violence.

Aidan chuckled and looked Tris over. "Just had to gossip, didn't you? You had to tell Big Tag, let him know you knew something he didn't, and now here we are."

"It slipped out," Tris complained.

Why were they still in the conference room? Her mom was standing in front of it like she was guarding it or something. Kala was pretty sure she should get in there and stop whatever the hell was happening.

Her mom put a hand up. "Unless you want to sit down and talk about what happened tonight, you should go to the locker room."

She put her hands on her hips and stared her mom down. She wasn't a child anymore. She hadn't been for a very long time. "You don't think I have a stake in whatever the hell Dad's doing in there?"

"I think your father loves you and wants the best for you." Her mother was unmoving. Charlotte Taggart was a force of nature, representing strength and love and devotion. She was everything that was good in Kala's world.

She turned and walked away because she couldn't punch her mother the way she had Tris.

She was antsy and emotional. Could she find someone who wanted to spar at this time of night?

She strode down the hall, conscious of how everyone in her way suddenly decided they needed to be somewhere else.

The evil Domme was pissed, and everyone was scrambling for cover. There were days when she would find it amusing. Today was not the day.

Up ahead she saw Kenzie and Tasha still arguing with Lou about how to handle her.

She didn't want to be handled.

Maybe the decision whether or not to stay with the team would be easier than she thought it would. She should go to the locker room and get ready for the ride back, but she just couldn't. She couldn't. She couldn't get into TJ's truck and pretend like nothing happened.

She couldn't stay here and watch as Cooper walked out of the conference room, shaking hands with her father, likely commiserating over how hard she was to deal with.

So she turned and walked out of the club. She could walk. Or call a ride. It didn't matter.

"Hey, you okay?" Lena Gallagher stood outside the entrance, her cell phone in hand. "I thought y'all would be going a little longer. I was waiting to see if I could catch a ride with Drake. We're at the same hotel."

"I'm fine," she lied. "It's getting late, and the parents get crabby when they miss bedtime."

She looked behind Kala as though trying to catch sight of someone. "Any idea if Drake came out?"

She shook her head. "I lost track of him. Sorry. I'm going to head home."

"I know you hate me, but give a sister a ride?" Lena asked, sounding less shrinkish than usual.

"I was going to walk," she admitted. "I didn't bring my car."

"Do you live close? This seems like a kind of deserted part of town and it's late," Lena said, glancing down the street as though looking for danger. "I know you're a badass operative, but still… Also, is this club what I think it is?"

Kala stared at the darkness and remembered another night when things with Cooper McKay went hideously wrong and she'd walked away alone. Huisman was out there. Was she really this dumb? Was her pride worth living through that nightmare again?

Or was that precisely the point?

Did she make the same mistake again and again because deep down she knew she deserved whatever happened to her?

That was the moment TJ stuck his head out the door. He hadn't changed from his leathers, merely thrown a T-shirt over them. He pointed her way. "Kala Taggart, I swear to god if you try to walk home, I will fucking find you and drag you back, and I will tell everyone I found you crying like a girl who lost her favorite teddy bear. I have secrets, sister. I will tell every one of them if you leave this club without me or Cooper."

Fucking TJ. She sighed. She'd just come to the revelation herself, so she couldn't exactly argue. She could, but it would be counterproductive, and going home with TJ and Lou would be better than anyone else. "I'll be here when you're ready."

He sighed as though he'd expected more of a fight. "Were you serious about not being hungry? Because there's a Waffle House on the way. I mean, if you want."

He was a walking never-full gut. But she did like waffles, and Lou wouldn't push her. Lou would talk about everything else that happened in the club and what she was going to do in Sweden. Listening to Lou would be soothing. If they stayed out long enough, Kenzie might fall asleep, and then she could avoid her twin's questions. "I could eat."

TJ's expression suddenly turned sunny. "Cool. Give me ten and we'll pick you up here."

He walked away but not before she saw Lou standing behind him. Sneaky bestie.

God, she would miss Lou if she left. The thought of not having her around nearly brought tears to her eyes, but she had to think about it.

"He's your cousin?" Lena asked.

Kala sank down to the bench Gabe had built. The Hideout was a work in progress. It wasn't much to look at right now, certainly not from the outside, but every week the board worked on it, and slowly it was becoming something they could all be proud of.

What would it look like ten years from now? Would it rival Sanctum or The Club? Would she ever see it again if she walked away from her team?

"Yeah. He's my uncle Theo's oldest," she replied. "I have a ridiculously large family."

"Yes," Lena agreed. "Four brothers on your dad's side, and your mother has a sister."

"It's way bigger since my parents collect people. My parents have had the same close group of friends since long before I was born. They're family, too. It can be a lot sometimes," she admitted. And wonderful, but it also was hard because she didn't fit with them. "How about you? You have any siblings out there?"

Lena sighed, and her eyes found the darkness again. "No. I'm afraid I'm on my own. My father was involved in the intelligence business at one point, and he was killed in the line of duty. Not that I spent much time with him. My parents weren't married. He didn't want a kid at the time, but I like to think if he'd lived, he would have been a better dad."

"I'm sorry." Maybe she shouldn't get to know this woman. It was easier to hate her when she was nothing more than an Agency spy sent to break up her team. Which she was thinking about doing herself. "Was it hard to work in intelligence? Or was it easier? Everyone thinks I'm here trying to be my father, but it wasn't him. It's something I needed to do."

"This work fills something inside me," Lena explained. "It's gotten me to where I need to be to do what I want to do. If that makes sense. I have goals and dreams and plans like everyone else. Being here gets me closer to achieving the goals."

Did she have goals beyond the next job? Anything that didn't involve work? Cooper had been…not a goal exactly, but definitely a dream.

Lena got quiet, and the silence sat between them, not a comfortable one. It was awkward, and Kala remembered that wasn't the only question Lena had asked. "It's a BDSM club. Did you not get the background research on my family? I suspect it's one of the reasons the Agency watches us so closely. Can't trust those perverts."

Lena sat down beside her. "Of course I have read all the relevant background, and your parents' lifestyle was covered. I wouldn't say it's perverted. Simply more open than most lifestyles. And since you're in an honest lifestyle, do you mind if I ask a couple of questions?"

"Is this a session?" If she could fit in one of the required sessions, the night might not be a total loss.

Lena snorted like she knew exactly what she was thinking. "Not a session. This is just me asking some questions so I can work better. The whole team is involved, correct? I can understand you all better if I'm informed."

Lena made it sound so reasonable, but Kala's suspicious nature still made her careful. "Sure."

"So I do understand that there are a couple of different ways to play… That's the word, right?"

"Yes," Kala allowed. How long would TJ be? Lou had already changed. She wouldn't take any time at all. She would grab her bag, but TJ probably wanted to look pretty or some shit.

"So there are different ways to play. Pain can be oddly relieving for some people. For some people who don't like traditional therapy, the careful administration of pain can release pent-up emotions. Are you a submissive, Kala?"

Kala sighed. Naturally, she was a woman so she should submit to someone. "Nope."

"So you prefer to be the one inflicting pain?"

Kala lifted a brow, staring plainly at the therapist. "What happened to the careful administration of pain to relieve inner turmoil? Your disdain is showing, Dr. Gallagher."

"Sorry. I'm not disdainful at all," Lena countered. "I was simply surprised. I've heard the lifestyle can often provide a place for the other side of a person to come out. You deal with violence in your daily life all the time. You're in control. You have to be. I'm surprised you prefer to dominate. I guess some of us are simply wired one way and don't have another side. See, I'm learning."

Learning she was a violent freak? "Yeah."

Lena sighed and sat back. "And I've put my foot in my mouth again. I'm truly not judging you. I find you fascinating. If I looked merely at your records, I would say you're the perfect lone wolf operative. I would say you would be able to work the blackest ops, but then there's the issue of your team."

"What about them?"

"They ground you," Lena replied. "Working with your family gives you something a lot of other operatives don't have. It can be good in that they can act as a check and balance to your—and every other operative's—darker impulses. And bad in that you're forced to think about them before the mission. What I'm trying to figure out is where's the line. Where does family loyalty come into play before the job? If I was talking about your twin, I would say that line is very thick, and she would struggle to ever cross it. I believe Kenzie would throw the job out to spare her friends' feelings, much less their lives. You're different."

"Of course I am." It was nothing she hadn't heard before, but she was raw tonight and Lena's words were touching all her nerves.

"Stop being so defensive, Kala. I think you take the job more seriously than anyone on the team. I genuinely believe you are one of the brightest operatives we have working today," Lena explained. "One of my jobs at the Agency is to identify truly gifted people. I think you qualify, and before you say because I'm some kind of brutal monster, I'm talking about more than your skills at taking down the bad guys. I'm talking about how you can see patterns and recognize danger before anyone else knows it's there."

Comforting words. Words she should listen to. Lena might be helpful if she decided the team would be better off without her. She might be someone Kala could bounce ideas off of. She certainly couldn't talk about this with her mom or dad or sisters. Lou would get worried, and that was the only time her bestie would go behind her back. "The team exists because of me."

"Why would you say that?"

"It was my idea," Kala admitted. "I knew from a very young age this was the kind of work I wanted to do. Kenzie went along with it. It helped after she got into these young adult novels about spy school. I got her into those, too. I wanted her with me. I knew our parents didn't want this life for us, but I had to do it."

Sometimes she felt so guilty about dragging Kenzie in. She should be happily dating and living the life of…whatever she wanted to do. Kenzie would likely be married with a kid or two by now if she hadn't followed Kala.

"And you've done an enormous amount of good," Lena countered. "Our parents don't always know what's right for us. They're simply humans who take into account their own damage and trauma. I'm sure your father's prior employment with the Agency played into his desire to keep you away from intelligence work."

"He still came out of retirement when I wouldn't be swayed. It wasn't like I wanted to work for my father. I kind of rebelled against the idea," she admitted.

"And now?"

"I kind of like being close to them, but it can also be a heinous pain in my ass. Like tonight." Tristan should have kept his mouth shut. Then his nose would still be in the same place.

Her gaze was on the street in front of them, watching in the distance as cars lazily drove by. Even at this time of night, there were still people out and about in Dallas. Roughly two miles away it would be different since the rambling house she and her sisters lived in was in a nice, solidly suburban-feeling neighborhood, but here the city still held sway.

"What happened tonight?" Lena asked.

And she realized she should have kept her mouth shut. No one would have told Lena shit. It was one thing to tattle to her father, another to the Agency. They would definitely like to know if two of the operatives on a team were suddenly fucking. Which they weren't.

Luckily, she had plenty of recent events to fall back on. "The Zach thing. My parents liked him. Not that I didn't. Zach was cool, but I hold myself apart better."

"Precisely why I think you're an excellent operative," Lena allowed. "I believe you'll give my theories some thought. I assume the rest of the team feels like Kenzie and your mother."

In this she could be honest because they all would. "Tris is close to him. He firmly believes there's shit we don't know about. My mom, Kenz, and Tasha are definitely team Zach, and Lou is, too. TJ will be more cautious. He would hear Zach out, but he would also make sure the team was safe while he did it."

"And Cooper?"

Kala shrugged. "I don't know. You would have to ask him."

"Do you have something going on with that young man?" Lena asked. "There was a certain tension between the two of you tonight."

"Nope. We grew up together and now we work together, and that's all she wrote." And all she would ever write because it turned out she wasn't a sexual creature at all. Another way she didn't fit in. She spent half her time at a sex club, and the one time she tried had been a spectacular failure. Though it wasn't like Coop had been some sex god. Disappointing was definitely a word she would use. She'd heard rumors that he was great in bed. So it probably was a her problem.

"You should be careful with him," Lena advised. "I like Cooper. He's a lovely young man, but I don't think he's going to ever become a true operative. I think he'll play around with it for a couple of years and then go back to his first love."

"Flying." She'd always known that truth, too. "He'll either go back to the military or go civilian. He'll want a family and roots." Would she get an invite to his wedding one day? Hear about the birth of his first kid? She wanted that for him, but damn it hurt. "Yeah, I suspect he will. I'm sure we can find someone else for logistics."

The door opened and Drake strode out, stopping when he saw Kala sitting there with Lena. His eyes widened. "You two okay?"

Lena waved him off, standing. "Just having a chat. You heading back to the hotel?"

He nodded. "Yes. I've got a conference call with the Swedes in a couple of hours. You need a ride?"

Lena straightened her skirt and settled her purse on her shoulder. "Yes, thank you. And Kala, I hope you think about what I've said tonight. I do think you can do great things, but you have to believe it, too. We can talk more at our next session."

She gave Lena a jaunty thumbs-up before she walked away with Drake.

She wished the parking area didn't wrap around. Had her parents snuck out the back door? Had Cooper?

She groaned. How had she fucked things up so badly?

"Are you sure you want me to help? I mean, I could send someone who's not like related and stuff. I think Gabe's still here. He's used to weird projects," a familiar voice said as the door came open. "Also, why? I would like to know why? Do I want to know why? Maybe I don't." Her brother Seth stopped, his skin flushing slightly. "Oh, hey, sis. Uh, you doing good?"

What the hell? "I don't know. Am I, Seth? Who are you talking to?"

Seth hung up really fast. "Dad. He wants me to come out to Sanctum tomorrow. I think he's pulling a prank on Uncle Adam. You know those two. It never ends."

She stared at him, trying to tell if he was lying. Seth wasn't a great liar, but he did know how to add in some truth to throw things off. "Is this about me?"

Seth held a hand up. "No. Dude, I do not fuck with you. Like whatever happened tonight between you and Cooper is your business." He seemed to think of something, and his jaw went tight. "Unless he did something he shouldn't have. Do I need to deal with him?"

Her singer-songwriter brother wanted to fight with Coop? "I think I can handle it."

"You shouldn't have to," Seth replied. "If he fucks with my sister, I can take care of it. I know I'm not some badass operative, but I'm still a damn Taggart. I know how to get some revenge, and not merely through song. If I decide Coop needs some justice, I'll administer it."

So weird how nice it was to hear those words. She took it for granted that no one would protect her because she was the protector. Kala sighed and walked to her brother, wrapping her arms around him. "I think that's sweet, Seth, but I can handle Cooper. He didn't do anything wrong. We just weren't meant to be."

Seth only hesitated for a second, likely out of shock that she was being so affectionate. Then his arms came around her. "Are you sure? You've loved him for a long time, and I know he's been waiting to make a move. You don't see how he looks at you."

She sniffled and pulled back, looking him over. Her snot-nosed, obnoxious brother was a handsome young man. He was talented, and someday he was going to be a star. She loved him so much, loved them all. "Sometimes it's not enough. And you're one to talk. Should we discuss your situationship with Chloe Lodge?"

Her brother immediately backed away, holding up his hands. "Nope. She and I do not get along. She's uptight and picky."

"And you think she's hot," Kala teased because this was a place where she felt comfortable.

"She is but...she's not for me," he admitted, and there was a hint of sorrow in his words.

"And Cooper's not for me." She reached out and squeezed her brother's hand before releasing a long sigh. "Well, let me know if you need help on the prank front. I still need to get Uncle Adam back for fucking with my security system."

Seth winced. "Yeah, you should do that. No one should fuck with your security system. Just so you know, that's my stance on this, and if it ever happens again, I won't be a part of it. Never."

Okay, that was weird, but there was the sound of a car stopping and then a honk.

She turned and Lou waved at her from the passenger side of the truck. She was about to tell Lou to give her a minute so she could interrogate her brother further, but then her sisters were walking out the front door. Tasha held hands with Dare, and Kenzie's eyes lit when she saw Kala.

"Gotta go. Don't want to keep Lou and TJ waiting." She bounded down the stairs.

"Coward," her twin called out. "You know I'll still be there in the morning."

But she might not. Kala settled herself into TJ's truck and put off the problem of her sisters for another day. Tonight she would drown her sorrows in waffles and bacon and put off the moment when she had to be alone again.

## Chapter Nine

"Seriously, guys, no one has to stay with me." Cooper tried not to think about his very precarious position.

Not so precarious, actually, since he was securely tied in here. Big Tag hadn't forgotten how to tie a dude down. He had forgotten how to give a man some dignity. At least they'd let him get under the sheet before they'd gone to work.

"I think he'll be fine." Seth Taggart had shown up, pulling his truck in behind Cooper's SUV. Kenzie was somewhere in the house but had declared she didn't have any part in this and all of her twin's revenge was going to be on the men of the family. And she'd promptly run off, dialing someone on her cell phone.

Probably Tasha.

Big Tag made a tsking sound. "Seth, I thought I taught you better. You never leave a sub tied up and unattended. Anything could happen. A robber could come in and see our friend Cooper laid out like a feast."

"A robber is not making a feast out of me." He should have known Big Tag would be obnoxious, but when he'd laid this plan out, it had halfway made sense.

And he was so desperate, halfway worked for him. If he let her sleep on this, it would be done. She would talk herself out of ever trying again.

He might never know what happened to her. He wasn't sure he could live without trying everything he could.

So that was why he was naked, his wrists tied to Kala's mattress, and nothing but a thin sheet covering him. He'd argued they wouldn't be able to properly tie him up without the right equipment since he didn't want to be tied to the headboard. It wouldn't give him the freedom he needed for what he was going to do.

Not a problem. Big Tag simply stopped by Sanctum and suddenly they had all the under-the-mattress restraints they needed.

Seth looked like a younger version of his father. "I'm with Coop. No robber is taking anything from him. Also, I'd kind of like to not be here when she shows up. She's going to figure out you took down her security cams so she couldn't see us walking in, and that is a revenge I don't want."

Big Tag shrugged. "If Coop here does his job properly, she won't care."

"Also, should I really be doing this? Trying to get my sister laid?" Seth asked.

"Holy shit," a feminine voice said. "I thought you were sneaking him in so he could talk to her. Whoa. Daddy, I think we should do this to Ben. Think of all the intel I could get."

Kenzie was dressed for bed in PJs, with slippers on her feet and her hair piled high on her head. She did not look anything like the deadly operative he knew her to be.

Her father's eyes rolled. "Absolutely not. And I thought you wanted plausible deniability."

She shrugged. "Curiosity got the better of me. So what'd you do to my sister, Cooper?"

Now he saw the folly of his own actions. He was trapped with Taggarts. "I tried to start a relationship with her. Like I have been for years now."

"Don't," Big Tag said, putting a hand on his daughter's arm. "I've already put him through the ringer. Do you think I would be doing this if I wasn't certain he's telling me the truth and he wants to make things right?"

An evil smile lit Kenzie's face. "You would if you were going to murder him. Or let Kala murder him. I think it could be rough on her. You should let me do it."

Damn. He always thought Kenzie was kind of Team Cooper. Not Team Murder Cooper. "I love your sister."

Kenzie's nose wrinkled, and she huffed. "Fine, but you should know it's about fifty-fifty whether she makes a meal of you or makes you into a meal for Bud Two." She turned to her dad. "And if she sees Seth's truck here, she'll know something's up and she'll run the other way."

Big Tag sighed. "I didn't think about it. I had him give me a ride here so your mom could go home and help with Colton. Travis has a big test in the morning or I would have had him over here, too. He hates being left out of family projects, but that's what you get when you don't wear a condom."

"Speaking of." Seth seemed intent on not ending Cooper's torture. "Where do you keep them, sis? We should leave a few. Maybe we could decorate the bed. You know, like some people use flower petals except we use condoms."

"You are not decorating the bed," Cooper began.

"Eww, not romantic," Kenzie argued. "I could go in the back and pick some daisies. Hey, Bri, have those daisies you planted come in yet?"

Was anyone asleep? He hadn't seen Brianna Dean-Miles, the newest resident of the house. She'd moved in mere weeks before, and she seemed to be getting into the flow of giving no one any privacy at all. It was how this household ran.

"Oh, hey, Coop." A wide smile spread across Bri's face. "You are looking good, buddy. Is this one of those nights Tasha warned me about?"

Kenzie snorted. "Tasha warned you about the guys invading because we made cookies and have better Internet. She was not talking about naked pilots tied to beds. Though I do see where we've missed a fun activity. I think we should decorate Cooper. After all, he's a gift."

"Not so sure about that," Big Tag snarked. "He's very shy for a Dom. Didn't get a good look at his dick, so I have to withhold saying he's a gift."

This was his life now. "For fuck's sake. Maybe I didn't want my future father-in-law seeing my junk swinging."

Seth's head shook. "I don't think it can shake like this." He stared at the sheet. "It's not making much of a tent, though. Are we sure about this? Has anyone seen him in all his glory?"

Cooper groaned. "Just because you walk around half naked all the time doesn't mean I do, man. I haven't taken a single submissive in two years because I love her. So, no, I didn't walk around showing off my junk. I only wanted one person looking at it."

"How do you think I got my Charlie?" Big Tag asked as though this was a completely normal Taggart family conversation.

Which Cooper supposed it was.

"No." Kenzie's head shook, and she put her hands on her dad's arm. "You are done, Dad. Time to go. She can only eat so many waffles."

"Yeah, but TJ's with her. It could still be hours before they run out," her father replied, though he was grinning as she pushed him toward the door.

"Nope," Kenzie insisted. "He said the magic words, and now you're done."

"Magic words?" Seth asked, not moving from his place.

Brianna took that one. "He said he loves Kala and now we're on his side, and this is serious. I mean it's not so serious we're not going to decorate him, but it is serious enough that we're going to kick you out so you don't ruin this for Kala."

"I thought we didn't leave subs tied up," Seth complained, though his ass had been arguing the opposite way mere moments before.

"He's not a sub," Big Tag admitted. "I can totally leave a Dom tied up. Ask your dad, Bri. Hey, Bud, you know what to do."

Cooper turned his head in time to see the twins' big mutt lumber through the door. He was a massive thing who would likely make any intruder think twice. For two seconds, until Bud started to lick the dude to death. The big dog walked right up to him, and for a moment Coop was worried he was about to get licked, too.

Nope. It was worse. Bud took the edge of the sheet between his teeth and ran off with it.

"You actually trained the dog to do that? What is wrong with you?" Cooper asked, knowing the answer.

"Hey, Cooper, I was wrong. You are a gift, buddy," Big Tag yelled as he turned and walked down the hall.

Kenzie said something he couldn't hear.

Unfortunately, Big Tag was loud. "It was a compliment. I didn't think it would be that big. His dad's is tiny."

Brianna had walked after Tag and Kenz, and Coop found himself alone with Seth.

"It's not so big I can't take it off," Seth said in a slow drawl. "You should think about that."

He did not need a lecture. "Come on, man. Put a sheet over me. This is awkward."

Seth shrugged. "I don't see why. How is this different from the locker room at The Hideout or that time at The Club when Julian made all the Doms run a mile naked in high heels to show us what it feels like to be a sub? Remember I got the five-inchers, and I'm pretty sure it's because he thinks I'm after his daughter."

"Yeah, well, I'm starting to wonder if I didn't fall into your dad's trap," Cooper admitted.

"Nah." Seth crossed his arms over his chest. "Dad only pranks people he cares about. See, that's where people get confused about him. If my dad is yelling, everything's fine. If he's pulling dumbass pranks, you're cool. It's when he gets quiet and agrees with everything you say that you know you've lost him. He truly believes this is what's best for Kala. If he didn't, well, there's a certain freezer at Top where we put those problems. It's best they're kept on ice."

"Your dad isn't going to kill me," Cooper argued.

"No, but I might," Seth countered. "You see, Dad believes you're the only guy for Kala. Like Mom was the only woman for him. Personally, I think we can do better than an asshole who told her she wasn't good enough for him in high school."

"I never said that, and how the fuck do you know about what happened?" He hadn't thought Kala would tell him. "From what I can tell she didn't talk to anyone but Lou."

"I know I have a certain reputation as a dumbass artist who wouldn't understand intelligence work if it hit me over the head with my own guitar." Seth moved around the bed, getting closer to the door. "It isn't easy being the artist in a family full of badasses. But there are rewards to be had if one is smart. You see, I cultivate that shit because then no one suspects me of anything. No one would think that I would perhaps read my sister's journal because I happen to know she won't tell anyone when she's hurting. I have always known Tash and Kenz will be okay. They're resilient. They bounce back from everything, but not Kala. I knew it when I was fucking five, man. So I do what I need to do to protect her in a way she finds acceptable."

Coop wasn't sure about that. "I don't think she would find it acceptable to read her damn journal."

Seth leaned against the door jamb. "But then how would I have known to tell her I had a bad dream and couldn't sleep alone and I didn't want to disturb Mom and Dad? For three weeks. Kala sometimes needs a place to put all that anxiety and fear. Some people take all the bad shit and spew it on the world like a snake spitting venom. My sister puts it into caring for the people around her. She's got it in her head she's some kind of monster who doesn't feel things the same way everyone else does."

So Seth did know what was going on with his sister. "That's not true."

"I mean it is a little. The part about her not feeling things the same way. We don't talk about it but come on, man. She's on the spectrum. We all know it. I have been around so many artists whose brains work differently, and they get the shit kicked out of them for not being normal."

"Neurodivergent." He knew the term, and now he wanted to kick himself for not seeing it.

"Yep. There are so many people out there who don't fit the norms, but there's nothing wrong with them. Their brains just work differently. Mom and Dad had been planning to have her tested in high school." He shrugged. "I'm also excellent at eavesdropping. When I get caught, I give the 'rents a cute dumb boy look and they assume the earbuds in my ears are working. They are, by the way, just not how they think they are. You see, a long time ago Lou figured out how to make it so they amplify sound from the outside." He waved his hand. "You don't need to know the specifics. Anyway, they were trying to figure out how to talk to her about it. They wanted to test her in case she needed accommodations, but they were worried it would make her feel even more different. Before they had a chance to, want to guess what happened?"

"That night." He felt a bit sick.

"That night." Seth's eyes narrowed. "I don't know a lot about what happened that night. I know my sister blames herself. She wrote about what happened between the two of you, but not what happened while she was a guest of Julia Ennis. The last entry in her journal was a poem. Did you know she used to write poetry?"

She'd never told him. "No."

"I doubt anyone does. Maybe not even Lou. I know because I'm a sneaky bastard who won't let her be alone even when she thinks she should be. The poetry was her outlet. She wrote one last poem about a week after she got home, and then she never touched that journal again. She thinks she threw it away, but I have it. One day I'm going to ask her if I can put them to music because her poetry is an insight into a truly beautiful and unique soul, and it should be heard if she allows it." Seth stared down at him. "My parents put her in therapy and didn't talk about getting her tested again. I'm pretty sure the therapist told them she's on the spectrum but functions so highly she wouldn't need anything but emotional accommodations, and here we are. By the way, no one gives anyone emotional accommodations. We think everyone's brains must obviously work the same way and anyone different has problems. My sister is perfect the way she is."

"She's not," Cooper argued. "She *is* perfect but her life isn't, and it can't be without me. I know I sound like an arrogant prick when I say that, but no one in the world is going to love your sister the way I will. No one. I might not have a technical word to describe how she thinks, but I studied it and I learned how to talk to her, how to give her what she needs in a way she can accept. I was stupid in high school, but I've changed. All I want is her. Do you think I want to be an Agency operative? Dude, I barely hold my shit together when she's out in the field. I'm there because she's there, and that means it's the only place for me to be."

"All right," Seth said with a long sigh. "Then I should tell you what she's said about what happened to her."

Cooper shook his head. "Abso-fucking-lutely not. That is her story, and you're not telling it. If I find out you've told anyone, we're going to have a problem."

Seth's lips quirked up. "And that is the right answer. The truth is I don't know. I know it still affects her. She still wakes up scared sometimes, but she sleeps with Lou now which is good because it would seriously cramp my style."

She was going to sleep with him from now on. He would take care of her, and eventually she would tell him her secrets. "Don't worry about it. I'll take care of her. I'll figure out a way, but you are going to give that journal back to her when she's ready."

"Journal?" Kenzie walked back in. "Who has a journal?"

Seth's entire expression changed. Gone was the intensity, and in its place the aw-shucks smile he was known for. "I've been using a notebook I stole from Kala to write some lyrics."

"Dude, she's been looking for that," Kenzie complained. "We'll deal with that another day. You need to leave. Kala's tracker says she's three blocks away. Lou must have convinced TJ he'll get a stomachache if he eats too much."

Seth smiled his sister's way. "Then I should get the old man home and tuck him in. It's way past his bedtime. Cooper, you got a nice set of balls on you. They're very well formed."

Cooper's eyes rolled. "And you say you're not like your father."

Big shoulders shrugged. "I never said that at all. 'Night."

One problem walked out the door and another strode in. Brianna Dean-Miles had a bottle of champagne in one hand and a bunch of daisies in the other. "This is all I could find. We need to up our decorating game."

Cooper closed his eyes. It was going to be such a long fucking night.

* * * *

"'Night," Kala said as TJ took Lou's hand.

Lou turned slightly before they got to the door to her and TJ's room. It used to just be Lou's, but now there was no way to deny TJ lived with them. His boy stuff was all over the place, though she would give it to her cousin. The Army had trained him to be neat. "You sure you want to sneak in tonight? You could come in now. It's pretty late."

Kala snorted. "No. We're good, Lou. Besides, he's going to want to do stuff to you."

TJ's head shook. "Nah. We did that earlier, and I ate too many waffles. I got a pooch going. But I think you should sneak in. We have an excellent routine where I can pretend my cousin isn't sleeping with us most nights."

"I agree with TJ." What would she do when she wasn't living here? Would she move to DC and deal with it? She could do it. If she lived alone, she would learn to not need anyone. Maybe that was the problem. She was codependent. Or just dependent, since it wasn't like

Lou snuck into her bed. "Why fix it if it isn't broken? Thanks for the waffle. I had fun watching the waitress taking bets on when TJ would explode."

TJ chuckled. "I'll take a run tomorrow and it will all be gone." He grinned. "And then I'll need another breakfast."

"You know the word *breakfast* means to break your fast, buddy. I don't think you ever fast," Kala quipped.

"That sounds terrible," TJ said as he drew Lou into their room.

They would probably still do it. Sex seemed to work for them. Lou wouldn't lie to her. If it was terrible, Lou would tell her. Kenzie had in the past. She'd talked about one boyfriend who was terrible in bed.

So it was just her.

She stared at her door for a moment. It was her room, and it wouldn't ever be theirs. She was solitary, and that was okay. It was okay. She would be okay and they would be okay, and one day years from now they would think of her fondly.

It was going to be okay, and she wasn't going to end up in Lou's bed tonight. She was going to suck it up and deal with her problems on her own. If she had trouble, she would put it where it should go—deep down in her gut or in the therapist's office. Lou shouldn't have to be her emotional support friend forever.

Lou and TJ would get married and then have kids and they would move on. They would have a life.

She had to be ready for that. Tash and Dare were getting married soon. Kenzie would either catch her...*ick*...Ben or wake up and realize he was a douchebag and find someone else. Tris had his subs. Even Zach apparently had a whole other plan no one knew about. There was comfort in evil plans.

She was all she had, and tonight had proven it.

The door to her sister's room opened, and Kenzie stared out, Bud Two at her side. The big mutt almost always slept on Kenzie's bed when they were home.

"Go in your room," her twin said, eyes narrowed. "And I swear if you try to run, I will catch you."

What the hell? "I'm getting that a lot tonight. I'll go to bed. No need to chase me down."

Kenzie stood there, not saying a word. Weirdo.

Kala was happy she wasn't cornering her, trying to get her to talk about what happened tonight. No way. No how. There weren't enough waffles in the world to get her to talk about what happened tonight. She opened the door and turned, closing it quickly in case Kenzie changed her mind.

"Don't scream."

Kala turned and did not scream. She wouldn't fucking scream. But she did feel her jaw drop.

Cooper McKay was laid out on her bed. Naked. And there were daisies. On his dick.

Oh, damn. "Tell me my father didn't put flowers on your penis."

She stood there for a moment because of all the ways she'd thought the night would end, this hadn't even been a thought. Like she'd contemplated what she would do if aliens attacked but only because she'd gotten the dude from Bliss's weekly newsletter warning of impending mating seasons for some alien life-forms. It was weird, and she kind of dug it.

But this… Nope. This was a total surprise.

Cooper's arms were splayed out, the restraints coming from under the mattress—a setup that absolutely did not belong to her. His head turned. "No, the daisies are from your sister and Bri. They're kind of dicks. Like leave a man some dignity. Nope. Your father is the one who tied me down. There was a sheet involved at one time. Did you know your dad trained your dog to pull the sheets off naked dudes?"

Her father was such a menace. "I think he just taught him how to retrieve stuff." He was naked on her bed. Naked. She forced herself to stare at his face. "What are you doing here, Cooper?"

His gaze went grim. "I'm here for you, baby. What happened… We didn't go about this the right way."

"Is there another way to go? We fucked. It didn't go well. We're not compatible."

"Yeah, it might work like that if everyone was the same and needed the same things sexually."

Of course. It was her fault, but then she knew it.

"Don't," he said, his voice going deep. "You listen to me and not the negative voices in your head. There is nothing wrong with a couple not being able to go from zero to penetration in a heartbeat. You tell me something. If one of your subs talked to you about this, would you tell them to give up? If they said they truly cared about their partner and wanted it to work, what would you tell them?"

"To talk to each other. To try new things." She would likely read up on sexuality and try to help them through the problem.

"Why can't you give yourself the same grace, baby? You deserve it, too. Unless you want to tell me you don't care about me and you don't want to try."

This...this was her out. This could be payback for everything he'd done to her over the years. For every time he'd made her feel small and unworthy. Even though she knew it wasn't what he'd meant to do, the feeling had been real all the same. All she had to do was tell him she didn't give a shit.

He stared at her with such earnestness.

What did she want? Petty revenge or a couple of months with him? Did she owe herself grace?

Why was her father such a weirdo?

"What do you think we should do? Is this an invitation for a session? Are you submitting to me, Cooper?" She wasn't sure she wanted that.

"If that's what you need," he offered. "I'll give you anything you need. If you want to whip my ass, it's yours. I don't think you understand how far I'll go for you. I'm not the scared kid I was when we were fifteen."

"I doubt you were afraid. You were embarrassed."

"I was afraid," he corrected. "I was afraid I wouldn't live up to what my parents expected from me. I didn't understand what they expected from me. I thought I had to be the best at everything, and that included socially. I thought if I was the golden boy, they wouldn't care that I don't look like them."

He'd thought that? Damn. She made fun about her emotionless state, but she could actually feel emotion well. It was kind of gross and not something she could ignore. "Because you were adopted? You thought they would only love you if you were perfect?"

It was kind of hard to keep her eyes on his face. He was such a beautiful man. She'd seen him in leathers and without his shirt on. She'd seen him in shorts, playing sports, with his whole body glistening with sweat, but there was something about him laid out that made her insides shake. Her pink parts.

Hadn't she learned she wasn't sexual? Except she could feel an ache begin low in her pelvis.

Her sexual organs were eternally optimistic, it seemed.

"I did, but I grew up and realized they love me. For who I am. They don't need me to carry on their DNA. They wanted a kid to love, and I was lucky enough to be that kid," Cooper said. "I was insecure. I was young. I know I hurt you and I never meant to, but I did. I need you to understand this right now. I don't want anyone but you. I want you because you are everything I need in a woman. Even the frustrating parts. I think this whole let's-have-sex thing might be a way to get me out of your system before you move on, and I'm willing to take the risk. But you should know what you're risking, too."

Every word threatened to shred all her plans. "What am I risking, Coop?"

"Me winning. You can try to fuck me out of your system, but the whole time I'll be plotting and planning to find a way that I'm so burrowed in, you won't ever be able to leave me behind. I'm going to make you love me, Kala Taggart. I'm going to be the one thing you can't ever compromise on."

She was fairly certain she'd never heard any threat as terrifying as the one Cooper had just issued.

*I will let him know how much fun we have with you.*

Nope. That was it. Yep. Twelve years later and that fucker was still in her head. Definitely scarier than Cooper thinking he might be able to love her.

If she walked away from Cooper now, the Russian asshole might always live there. No matter how afraid she was of truly loving Cooper, she was more afraid of not ever feeling anything but afraid.

So she took a long breath and gave in. "What do I need, Cooper? I'm sure my father, the sex therapist, was embarrassingly thorough."

Cooper seemed to relax. "You need to explore to your heart's content. You need to be in charge in any way you like. I'm not saying I won't ever want to be in control. I can assure you I will, but not until you're comfortable."

Did he know? She didn't even fucking know. It wasn't like she'd bled or anything, but then she was pretty sure even if she'd been a virgin, she wouldn't have had a hymen anymore. She'd killed a dude with her thighs once, and he'd been a twisty, turny motherfucker.

Not knowing. It was a curse in its own way.

"Why do you think I wouldn't be comfortable?" Kala asked,

laying a trap.

Ah, there was the tension. "I don't know. Probably because you're a top. I only know what we did earlier didn't work. We went too fast. We need more time. I've wanted you since we were fifteen. I want to take my time, to sink into this thing I've longed for almost half my life."

He definitely wasn't the same boy. The man knew exactly how to talk to her. The man was infinitely more dangerous.

Well, her sister had told her if she tried to run, she would hunt her down, and Kenzie could be mean when she wanted to. Kala's brain ran through all the scenarios of her leaving this room and taking to the road to live a vagabond life, and almost all of them ended with the cops being called and her and her sister becoming viral video stars for all the wrong reasons. She couldn't run. Decision made. "So I can do whatever I want."

"As long as the first thing you do is get this fucking flower off my dick," Cooper pleaded. "I'm worried it's like covered in poison ivy or something. It tickles."

She couldn't help the laugh that boomed through the room. It was funny. It was wild. It was...kind of perfect when she thought about it. Sometimes she thought things had to be normal to be perfect, but what if her life was different? What if she got to decide what was perfect and everyone else could fuck off? Why was that so hard?

She moved to the bed, staring down at everything he was offering her. So much more than merely a beautiful body. He was offering her something she'd never had. She could touch him and rub her body against his, and it wouldn't freak her out because she was in control.

He was hers. Like a sub but with sex. And she was an indulgent Mistress—she wasn't. She was pretty hard-core, but tonight she was playing a different game.

A thought struck her as she stared down at the pretty white flower covering Cooper's penis. Sort of. She could see the head kind of peeking out. But she was stuck on what had to have happened. "Did my sister see your penis?"

Cooper flushed. "I mean, it's not like I planned it. There was supposed to be a sheet. I agreed to a sheet, and your dad took it because he said he wasn't sure my penis was like a gift or something, and your sister then decided to decorate me. And for full disclosure, Bri saw it, too. But if I have sex at the club, everyone's going to see it."

"I should have seen it first. I'm totally going to see Ben Parker's dick first. You're going to help me make that happen." They were being honest tonight. She usually didn't like to ask questions she didn't know the answer to, but she was going all in. "Why haven't you had sex at The Hideout?"

"You know why. The same reason you haven't," he replied. "Because neither one of us wants to hurt the other, and we weren't ready."

"I was ready at fifteen," she murmured, reaching out to put a hand on his muscular thigh. She loved his legs. They were strong and masculine, and she used to love the way they felt when they brushed against hers.

"You weren't, baby," he said quietly.

She also loved that he was honest. She wasn't a fool. He worked around her half the time, offering up something she could accept without giving up her pride. She was starting to wonder if her pride was overrated. "No, I wasn't. But I might be now."

She watched as that little flower no longer covered so much of Cooper. His cock stirred to life and lengthened in front of her eyes, the daisy falling away.

Damn, that was hot. She had to swallow her drool. Now that the formalities were out of the way, she could indulge. She could look to her heart's content.

He was every bit as beautiful as she dreamed he would be, with long, strong limbs and a well-defined chest. She'd seen him without his shirt a thousand times, but this felt different. She put a hand on his chest, feeling the hard muscle covered by warm skin. He had a light dusting of hair that felt good under her palm. And his nipples were hard. Cooper loved to torture a sub's nipples during their sessions. It didn't matter if they were guy nipples or chick nipples, Cooper twisted them all the same.

She reached down and ran the tip of her index finger around his left nipple, watching it pucker even further.

His lips curled up. "You're going to kill me, aren't you, baby?"

It wasn't something she would ever admit, but she loved it when he called her baby. Like they were together. Like they would never be apart again. She let her finger circle him one more time and then brought the heat. She pinched down and twisted and watched his toes curl, his cock bob, and the breath hitch from his chest.

This she knew how to do. She was the mistress of pain as pleasure. It was why all the subby boys and girls came to her. How many times had she brought a sub to orgasm? Service had become her sexuality. She'd taken no physical satisfaction from those encounters, merely the knowledge that she had a purpose in a world she felt apart from. D/s gave her a place where her violent tendencies could do good. Where she wasn't the person Julia Ennis had told her she was destined to be.

Nope. Not thinking about that bitch or anything about that time tonight. Cooper was giving her a gift, and she was going to take it. She moved to his other perfectly formed nipple and gave it the same attention. Cooper gritted his teeth, and his hands gripped the ropes that bound him.

Did he like it? He could be pretending for her. "Is this okay?"

"Baby, you know it is. You know how to watch for signs. My cock won't lie to you. My body won't. I'm your sub tonight."

Strangely, she didn't like those words. "You're not my sub. You're just...mine for tonight."

"For as long as we want," he said quietly. "I want the deal we made before back in place. I want to be the man you come to when you need, Kala."

"When I need sex?"

"When you need anything."

It wasn't like she didn't have people in her life who would do anything for her. Her family was wonderful. Her parents would literally go to the ends of the earth for her, but hearing the words out of Cooper's mouth filled some place inside her she hadn't known was empty. Why did it have to be this man? Only one. Only him.

She stared down at him as she started to unbutton her blouse, easing it off her shoulders. This was happening, and somehow she trusted it this time. She didn't have to worry about pleasing him, about rushing through the part that scared her so she could feel his arms around her. They would get to the part where she was wrapped up in him, but now she got to explore.

She hesitated when she got to the button of her jeans.

"What is it? Don't stop, Kala."

She frowned down at him. "Well, if I'd known I was going to get naked, I wouldn't have eaten all those waffles. TJ is a bad influence."

His laughter boomed through the room.

Somehow him laughing made all her insecurities fly away, replaced with an eagerness she'd never felt before. She wanted this, wanted this time, wanted him in a way that was bigger than sex, and somehow that made it okay.

He watched her as she undressed, his eyes seeming to eat her up. He'd seen her in various states of undress, but now she wondered how much he'd hidden from her because there was no way to deny the hunger in his eyes. She couldn't pretend this was about convenience. Oh, she likely would tomorrow, but for tonight she wasn't lying to herself.

Tonight, this was everything.

Being naked with him felt right. So did having him tied down for her pleasure, so score one for her father. Eww. She'd thought about her dad.

"Do not think about your dad or your brother or Kenzie," Cooper ordered in his dommiest tone.

The man did know her. "My brother was here, too?"

Cooper's eyes were on her breasts. "I want to fucking suck on your nipples, baby. I want them in my mouth and hands and god, at some point I want to hold them together and slide my dick in between them."

All interesting thoughts. She never realized how easily distracted he was by sex. She could have fun with that, but he hadn't answered her question. A feeling of power coursed through her. How could it not when he was looking at her like he wanted to eat her alive? "Focus, Coop. My dad brought Travis here?"

His eyes stayed on her as she prowled around the bed. "Seth. And your parents should have spanked him more."

She trailed her fingertips down his body, lightly scraping across his chest down to his abs. "He would have liked it."

"Your brother loves you," Cooper said, and his breath hitched as she touched his cock. "He cares about you more than he shows. Also, he's a sneaky bastard, and he's listening in way more than you think he is."

Seth? She loved Seth, had always felt a connection to her brother, but he didn't pay attention to much beyond his music and sex with lots of women. "I don't want to talk about Seth. Tell me more about the nipple thing. I like it when you talk."

Dirty. She liked it when he talked dirty. She could get hot listening to him tell a sub what he planned to do to them, and she didn't get off on stuff like humiliation play. But when it came out of his filthy, gorgeous mouth, she suddenly reconsidered.

"Do you know why I had them tie me down like this?"

She climbed on the bed, finally letting her hand find the part of him she'd been fascinated with since she learned what sex was. She tossed away the flower. Her sister was a weirdo. He didn't need decorating. He was a work of art all on his own. "I would think the headboard would be easier. You wouldn't need an under-the-mattress restraint system."

She licked her lips as she touched him for the first time. His cock practically pulsed in her hands, and Cooper groaned, a deep, sexy sound. She wasn't going to think about where that restraint system had come from. It was hers now.

"If they tied me to the headboard, you wouldn't be able to sit on my face, baby," Cooper said. "And I really, really want you to sit on my face."

For a second the words didn't compute, and then a vision of her riding his tongue washed through her, lighting a fire inside. She thought she'd wanted before?

"I want you to ride my face and then my cock. I'm your fucking stallion tonight, baby. Don't think about it. Don't let in any intrusive thoughts. All you need to know is I dream about eating your pussy. I think about it when we're sitting in a conference room and when we're on an op. It's distracting. You have to do it or I'm going to get myself killed in the field because all I can think about is how good you're going to taste on my tongue and how tight you'll be around my cock. When I'm in a knife fight, sometimes I think about the way those perfect tits of yours will bounce when we fuck."

He was saying all the right things, pushing every button that would allow her to see past those nasty thoughts encumbering her every happy moment. "So I'm doing it for my country, when you think about it."

"You're doing it for me. You're saving me, and quite frankly, everyone who rides in a plane with me because I think about fucking you there, too. Remember when we dropped two thousand feet over the Atlantic a couple of months back? I said it was because I thought Big Tag needed a jolt of adrenaline every now and then. Nope. My dick was so hard, it bumped the damn yoke, Kala. Guess who I was thinking about?"

He'd been thinking about her? Well, there was nothing else to do. "I am a dutiful operative. So I just move in and put my pussy right on your face? Will you be able to breathe?"

"I will," he promised and looked like a man who was so very close to getting what he wanted. "It'll be weird at first, and then I promise you won't think about anything but how good it feels. Try it. Try me."

How could she possibly deny him when he asked so politely? It was awkward but she moved up his body, stretching out so their skin touched. So her breasts grazed over his belly and chest. So she felt his erection against her skin. She breathed him in, shutting everything else out. What had been weird in the club suddenly seemed okay here in the safety of her room. He was giving her permission to do all the weird shit she'd ever wanted to do to him. Like smelling him and rubbing her cheek against his chest so she could feel his chest hair tickle. Like running kisses over his collarbone and nestling her face against the warm curve of his neck.

"It feels so good, baby. So good to be close to you," he whispered.

So good. So right. Like something fell into place, and she was whole for a moment.

She paused at his face. She'd memorized every line and plane, and yet this felt new and fresh. She lowered her mouth to his, the kiss oddly sweet. Or maybe just sweet. Maybe she needed to stop with the fucking adjectives that put her on the outside and simply accept this was her world and it wasn't so bad.

Right now it felt like heaven.

She kissed him for the longest time and he let her, their tongues playing. She sucked his bottom lip into her mouth before running her tongue across it.

Cooper groaned and squirmed, his cock rubbing between her legs like it was trying to burrow inside. Hours before she would have taken this as a cue to get the train moving, but not now. Now she wanted to go slow, to make this last. To give him everything he wanted, and he wanted her on his face. So she was going to do it.

She kissed him one last time on the mouth before brushing light busses over his nose and cheeks and forehead. "Tell me if you're uncomfortable."

She brought her body up, kneeling above his mouth, her lower legs pinning his arms down. She balanced against the headboard. He was perfectly placed, and it wasn't as awkward as she thought it would be.

"You're so fucking gorgeous," he muttered, bringing his head up, and she suddenly felt his nose right in her pussy. "You smell so good, baby. Give me a taste."

She was in a haze of lust as she lowered her pelvis down and felt the first long lick of his tongue. Heat flashed through her, a revelation. What the hell? This wasn't the little pleasures she'd given herself with her fingers and a vibrator. This was something else entirely.

She couldn't think. All of those voices that nagged at her fled entirely as Cooper speared her with his tongue. He ate at her pussy, drawing one side of her labia into his mouth and then the other, sucking and licking and worrying her clit with his tongue. She thought she would survive it, but she found herself moving with him, seeking more. The shy part of her was utterly muted, and she found a fierce pleasure she'd never felt before.

"More," Cooper groaned against her tender flesh. "Give me more. I swear if my hands weren't tied, they would be digging into your sweet ass, pulling you down on me."

She had zero idea how the man was breathing, but in that moment, she didn't care. He was telling her what he wanted, and she gave it to him. She seated herself on that talented tongue of his and rode him. Moving in an instinctive rhythm, she rolled her hips and found the perfect spot. His tongue went deep and something…probably his nose…rubbed against her clit. It didn't matter. All that mattered was the magnificent flood of pleasure invading her veins.

She felt alive. So fucking alive.

"Baby," Cooper was saying against her skin. "Baby, please. I'm dying. Please fuck me. I'll beg all you like. I'll make you breakfast in the morning and rub your feet before we go into the office, just please put that gorgeous pussy close to my dick and I swear I'll do all the work."

Oh, she liked it when that man begged. A languid pleasure still pulsed through her, but she worked up the will to move down his body. Now she understood what she'd done wrong the first time.

She'd been wet but not entirely ready. Sex wasn't merely about her pussy. Her mind was ready. Her soul was ready.

She felt like a new person, like some part of her had just been unleashed, and she liked this aspect of herself. She straddled his hips, taking that glorious cock in hand and placing it right where it needed to be.

Cooper's face was a mask of desire. "Do it, Kala. Ride me."

She lowered herself onto his cock. Cooper's moan filled the room as his hips bucked up.

"Understand this, when my hands are free, they're going to be all over you," he vowed.

It didn't scare her the way it would have five minutes before. She wanted his hands on her. They didn't need the ropes. This wasn't anything but love and pleasure, and she wasn't even going to pretend she hadn't thought the word love. This was love.

She followed his lead, moving her hips in time with his, loving the way he filled her. He stretched her pussy in the most delicious way. There was a sharp edge to it, but she even liked the ache it caused. She rode him, not expecting anything but to watch him find his pleasure. So when she found the perfect spot, she was shocked, but her body took over. She ground down, rubbing that spot deep inside her. Cooper's jaw clenched, and she felt the moment he came. It sent her over the edge again, the pleasure even more forceful than the last time.

She collapsed on him, not minding the way they were still connected. Sex was messy and sticky and kind of amazing. She lay her head on his chest, listening to the beat of his heart. It was thundering, but hers was already slowing into a peaceful rhythm.

So often she thought she should have simply thrown herself into the deep end, gotten it over with, moved on from him.

In this moment, she was so grateful she hadn't. No matter what happened, she would have this night to remember.

"Can I say it, Kala?" Cooper asked quietly.

She wasn't ready. She couldn't believe it. Not right now. "Not yet."

"Just so you know I'm thinking it."

*I love you.* The words played in her head as she lay there, surrounded by wonder.

Deep in the night, she woke, the dream flashing through her system. It had started with Cooper on top of her and then morphed to the Russian, and she'd looked back and saw a line of hims waiting for their turn.

She shot up and forced herself to breathe.

It was okay. It shouldn't be surprising she'd had the dream tonight. She wasn't going to let it ruin what had been a great night. She glanced over, and it looked like she hadn't woken him.

She eased out of bed. Kala wasn't sure why, but she didn't have the dream when she slept with Lou. She had in the beginning, but her bestie would pat her back and talk to her until she got back to sleep, and after a while she simply slept when she was in Lou's bed.

She picked up Cooper's shirt and drew it over her head. It came to mid-thigh, so it would work. She would nap in Lou's room. Then she would sneak back here, and Cooper wouldn't even have to know.

Moving quickly and quietly, she slipped into Lou's room. TJ had recently replaced Lou's bed with an oversized king they'd had to have custom sheets made for. Lou barely moved when she eased into the bed. Lou's room always smelled like lavender, the scent immediately dispelling the dream.

"Scoot," a voice whispered.

She managed to not freak out. Cooper had followed her. "What are you doing?"

Lou's eyes opened, and a grin hit her face. "Oh, this is going to be fun. I think he's getting into bed with us. You dream again?"

Kala nodded. "Yeah. I was going to take a nap and go back."

"I sleep where you sleep," Cooper said, and in the moonlight, she could see he was in his boxers and nothing else. He slid in and wrapped his arm around her waist. "And keep it down. I don't want to wake up TJ."

"Oh, you can't." Lou turned her head slightly. "You're not going to wake up, are you, babe?"

TJ sniffled and turned over. "I'll take two and a side of fries."

Lou snorted. "See. No waking him up. Now pretend you're sleeping, Cooper. I need to talk to bestie."

Cooper yawned against her neck, the warmth of his breath hitting her skin like a blanket. "I'm already there. But, Kala, I sleep where you sleep. Always. 'Night."

He cuddled her like a teddy bear.

Lou's hand came out, touching her cheek. "Was he good to you?"

There were moments when Kala felt like the world was dark, when those voices she had made it feel like she was in a constant storm. But then there were moments like this when she felt all the love that surrounded her. When she knew how blessed she was to have these people in her life. When she felt worthy of them.

"Yes," she said quietly to the woman who had been her best friend for half her life. It was a sort of love affair, friendship. In the beginning it was exciting and new, and if it survived all the changes people went through, it became something soft and precious. It rounded out and became a foundation to build parts of a life on.

Could she do the same with Cooper?

"I'm so glad," Lou whispered. "So happy. But now you're going to be a complete perv, right?"

Probably. She kind of already wanted to do it again. "Maybe I should have woken him up and fucked him again."

"She learns," he said and kissed the nape of her neck.

"Not here," Lou shot back like she would actually do it.

She wouldn't. "Maybe in the morning."

The world was soft and warm, and she fell into a perfect sleep.

## Chapter Ten

Cooper strode into his dad's office the next morning with a sense of satisfaction he'd never felt before.

He had her now. Oh, he was sure there was a piece of his baby trying to rationalize the emotions of the night before, but she'd let him take care of her this morning. He'd worried she would pull away and try to pretend around her roommates, but when they'd had breakfast, she'd sat on his lap and eaten her toast as TJ had complained about all the extra people in his bed.

Like he'd noticed. How the hell did Lou get any rest when the dude talked about tacos in his sleep?

"You look happy." His dad stared at him from behind his desk, considering him. "I'm a little scared to know what put that look on your face. I thought you would be on your way to Stockholm. Ian told me he was sending Lou and TJ off on some classified mission. Should we warn the Swedes about him? As a country, they're not known for their abundance of food. He could clean them out."

Normally he probably would be flying the jet, but not today. He and Kala had dropped Lou and TJ off at the private airfield before coming into the office. Even if Tag had ordered him, he would have refused the assignment. He was sticking close to home for now, and home was one Kala Taggart. Kenzie had taken a commercial flight to

Toronto and complained the entire morning. "Drake decided to go with them. He got his license a couple of years back. They're in good hands."

His dad stood and moved around his desk. "All right, then what's put that smile on your face."

He was surprised Big Tag hadn't spilled the beans. It wasn't like everyone at the club last night didn't know. "You talked to Ian and he didn't tell you where I spent last night?"

A brow rose over his father's eyes. "He said he knew something I didn't know in that asshole way of his but then he got a call, and I still don't know what he knows. He had to leave Sanctum early last night. Does it have something to do with why Lou and TJ are taking on Scandinavia? I heard Kenz is on the road, too."

The door to his father's office burst open.

"Alex, it happened." His mom walked in, her eyes wide. Coop was standing to the side so she didn't see him. "I just got off the phone with Hunter, and he said Cooper walked through the club last night with Kala in his arms. They went to a privacy room. Together. Without some sub to filter for them. He finally threw her over his shoulder and carried her away like I said he would eventually. Now I'm worried she might not take it well. He needs to be patient with her. You have to talk to him. I actually think he might need to be a bit subby in the bedroom a couple of times. How do we have this talk? Should we have this talk? He's almost thirty. It's going to be weird, but I'm worried he might scare her."

Oh, what did his mother know that he didn't? "Why would I scare her? Also, I did not throw her over my shoulder. I was a gentleman and picked her up. Her knee was bothering her."

His mom started and stared at him for a moment.

His dad snorted and moved to the couch. "Do you know what I never thought about when I became a dad? This discussion. This one right here."

His mom's cheeks were stained a bright pink. It was kind of nice to know something could shake Eve McKay's cool. He'd seen his mom be unshakable through many a family drama, but this was freaking her out.

Damn. Was it because she still didn't think they could work? He needed to make a few things plain. "We don't have to have any talks because I'm a man and I make the decisions about my love life. I need you to understand. I love her. She won't let me say it yet, but I love her and I'm going to make this work. This isn't some phase."

His mom's expression changed from embarrassed to confused. "Why would you say that?"

Did she remember nothing? "When we were kids, you said she was a phase I was going through. She's not."

His mother's head cocked slightly as though she was trying to remember. "Are you talking about what I said the day she went missing? After she punched the pitcher who brushed you back and you were complaining about her?"

It was his turn to be embarrassed. He didn't like to think about the dumbass kid he'd been. "I wasn't complaining, exactly."

His mom huffed. "You were absolutely complaining, and I didn't say *she* was a phase. I said she was going through a phase. Do you think I don't remember this conversation?"

"She does." His dad sat on the couch, watching them warily. "You have no idea the guilt she went through when she realized it was a fight that sent Kala walking. Your mother thought the conversation you two had at the arcade might have something to do with it."

He didn't want his mom to blame herself. "It did and it didn't. But, Mom, I remember distinctly you telling me that sometimes when a person is drowning, they take down the person trying to save them."

His mom let out a frustrated groan and sank to the couch beside his father. "I was talking about Kala. It's hard to be different. Ian and Charlotte and I talked a lot about how the things that would make Kala an incredible woman one day made it hard for her to fit in. She looks exactly like her sister but her brain functions very differently."

"Yes, I got this lecture from Seth last night," he replied. "And I had to listen since I was tied to a bed at the time. You're right about the subby business, but I think she'll get over it pretty quickly. What do you know about what happened that night, Mom?"

His mother took a long breath and seemed to think for a minute, and then tears welled in her eyes. "I'm so sorry, baby. I can't. I know I'm not technically Charlotte or Ian's therapist, but I can't tell you because it would be a betrayal. I'm going to ask you to be patient with her. When she's ready, she'll tell you."

He looked to his father, who shook his head.

"Ian's been my best friend for far longer than you've been born, son. I would do anything for you, but telling you this wouldn't merely betray the most important friendship of my life, it would hurt whatever you've got going on with her. If you love her, let her come to you."

He knew this. Knew they were right. The night before he'd told Seth he didn't want to know. But now, in the light of day, he couldn't help but worry. She might never tell him.

"How can I fix the problem if I don't know what it is?" Frustration welled. They were so close.

"Fix?" His mother stared at him for a moment. "What about her are you trying to fix, Coop?"

"I didn't mean it like that."

His mom's head shook. "But that's the word you used. Words are important. Words can show us how we feel when we're not willing to admit it. I'm very worried that you think Kala is broken and you can fix her. She is not broken."

"Of course she isn't. I didn't mean it that way." It could be hard to be the child of a psychologist. They were always looking for something deeper. "I meant we have an issue and we can't address it until I know what it is. I can't know if I'm doing what's right for her if she won't talk to me."

"And if she's never comfortable talking the way you're used to?" his mother asked. "I'm not saying I think she won't, but you have to be prepared for the fact that some things are hardwired into a person. Kala is a deeply loving human being, but I don't think she sees herself in this fashion."

He was confused. "But why? Look, I know something happened that night, but she's surrounded by a family that supports her. I know her parents got her into therapy after."

"Therapy only works if you understand why you need it," his mom explained. "I think it did work to make her more functional and it helped her find coping mechanisms, but there's something more. Sometimes we're born with these shadows. Like you when you were a teen. Baby, did your father or I do anything to make you think we loved you or your brother less than Vivian?"

She knew? How did she know? He'd tried so hard not to talk about it. "Never."

Vivi was the miracle child. His mother had been told it was highly unlikely she could ever conceive, so they'd adopted Cooper first and then Hunter. Right after Hunter's adoption was finalized, she'd found out about Vivi. Not once had these wonderful parents treated him differently than the girl who had their father's eyes, and everything else made her their mom's mini me.

"And yet there were times when you worried you didn't belong in our family, that you weren't enough for us," she said with flawless accuracy. "I know you never confronted us about it, but it was there. We had to give you space and time and hope you worked it out because it wasn't about us. It was about the voices in your head. Kala inherited all of Ian's darkness. All the things that made him a brilliant operative made it hard for him to experience true joy. We like to think everyone starts out the same and time and trauma change us, but it simply isn't true. Kala sees the world differently, and that also means she sees herself differently."

"Big Tag is utterly confident."

"About some things," his father agreed. "Ian was always confident when it came to his jobs, but he wasn't confident when it came to believing he deserved all the good things in life. It took Charlotte and a whole lot of therapy to make him see that he self-sabotaged and that what he viewed as anger was actually fear. You've only ever known Ian after Charlotte."

"You can be her Charlotte, but you have to be patient, and you can't view her as something you have to fix." His mom's jaw firmed, and he watched her make the decision to say what she said next. "I talked to you that day because I was worried for her, too. I love Kala. We're not supposed to have favorites, but of all the kids who grew up with mine, she's it for me. Even when she thinks I'm uptight and too intellectual. I worried that you wanted a life she's never going to be able to live. She's not ever going to be your sweetly submissive wife who says all the right things and supports your career."

What was she thinking? "I never..."

His father's head shook. "You wanted to be the fucking homecoming king, buddy. Do you think I don't remember the whole family helping you campaign? You wanted to be the most popular kid at school. Don't try to deny it. You might have told yourself it was because you needed to be the best for us, but it was about you. It was about the voice in your head that said if you didn't have a crown on, you weren't special enough."

"Your father isn't saying this because he thinks less of you," his mother began.

Cooper had been around long enough to know what his mother was going to say next. "If I don't acknowledge the problem, I can't avoid repeating the behavior that got us in trouble in the first place."

"I'm worried you still think she's going to change and give you some kind of white picket fence life," his mother said quietly. "Do you want to be with the Agency for the rest of your career?"

Not really, but it didn't matter. "I want to be with her."

"But in the back of your mind, what does your life look like twenty-five years from now?" His father asked the question that threatened to turn his stomach. "Don't tell me you haven't thought about it because I know you have."

He had. He saw himself with Kala and a couple of kids, and he would work as a pilot and she would…

Damn it. He told himself over and over that he would be whatever she needed him to be, but did he mean it?

His mom stood and wrapped him in a hug. "You need to be patient. With her. With yourself. It's okay to sink into this relationship, but you have to be realistic. You have to be ready to compromise."

He knew in that moment there would be no compromise. He knew it deep in his gut, a feeling he'd avoided since he was a kid and he'd felt her pull. It had always been her. In some ways, he had tried to figure out how he could have it all, have her and the white picket fence he'd thought he wanted as a kid.

Fuck it. All he wanted now was her. None of the rest of it mattered. They would have kids or not. They would stay in this life or move on to new careers when they got older. The only thing he wasn't willing to compromise on was spending his life with her.

But he knew it would worry his parents if he didn't at least pretend to think about what they'd said. "I will spend some time thinking about it."

There was a brief knock and then Kala was in the doorway, her eyes on him. Her expression was blank, and he wondered exactly how much she'd heard. His girl was a brilliant spy. It wasn't like it shocked him she might have listened in.

"We need you in the conference room, Cooper," she said quietly. "I'm afraid we have the footage from the police, and it's not exactly great."

"Kala," his mom began.

Kala gave her a half smile that proved she didn't act around her family. There wasn't an ounce of humor or happiness in her expression. "Sorry, Eve. We have to go. Lena's here, and Cooper needs to keep me from punching her in the face. She's extremely pleased with herself."

She turned and walked out. His mother frowned. "She heard something. Damn it, she's going to take it all wrong."

And he would have to deal with it. Lucky for him, sex was now firmly on the table, and after the night before he kind of thought it might work on her. He only knew one thing.

She wasn't getting away from him this time.

\* \* \* \*

Kala sank down into her chair, grateful someone had dimmed the conference room lights.

It was awesome to know Eve McKay still thought she was a time bomb waiting to hurt her baby boy.

Well, it wasn't like she was planning on marrying him. It had been right there on the tip of her tongue to explain to Alex and Eve that all of her intentions toward Cooper were perfectly sexual, and they didn't have to worry. When he found his perky former cheerleader ready to have his babies and make him all the sandwiches he could eat, she would fade away into the shadows and never be seen again.

Could she do it? The idea of walking away from her team made her heart ache, but could she hang around and watch them all get married and be happy and she would stay…Kala?

She would be a terrible mother. She wasn't affectionate. She wasn't sweet and kind and loving.

"Are you okay?" Lena asked from her place at the end of the conference table. She'd been sitting in the shadows for more than twenty minutes. She'd been the one to bring them the footage they were about to review.

Kala cocked a brow and turned her way. "I'm fine."

Lena stared at her for a moment. "Is it about the footage? I told you what's on there." Lena had been waiting in her office when she'd come in this morning.

"And I know that sometimes cam footage doesn't tell a person the whole story." She knew what Lena thought, but Lena came in with preconceived notions. Or maybe she herself was the one with a hard belief when she should keep an open mind.

"Do you not trust me?" Lena asked with a sigh as though she couldn't believe such a thing. "Drake himself sent that footage. He would be here if he wasn't accompanying Louisa."

Kala noted she didn't mention TJ. Lou would be the important one to someone like Lena. TJ was just another soldier, and he could be replaced. There were certainly days when she thought about replacing her cousin, but she didn't like the idea of someone else thinking he wasn't important. "Of course I don't trust you. I don't trust anyone."

Lena chuckled. "Now that might be the first real lie you've told me."

"The first? You've kept count?"

Lena waved a hand. "Of course not, but I do find your honesty refreshing. Although sometimes we like to lie to ourselves. You trust your team. Maybe too much."

She did trust her team. She knew her team. It's what happened when you grew up together. "I do trust my team, but you should know I don't truly trust anyone else."

Another lie. She trusted her cousins. And most of the people at The Hideout. She wouldn't like tell them classified secrets or shit. Especially Brianna, since she seemed to be rolling down the same road as her romance-writing mom, but she certainly trusted her. Oooo, she wouldn't trust her brother with any of her friends because his dick was dumb and wanted to know every woman in a biblical sense.

But she would trust Seth with her life.

Yeah, when she thought about it, maybe she wasn't as isolated and gloomy/broody as she thought she was. She blamed her parents. They had too many friends. If they'd been the proper spy parents she'd deserved, she would have been an only child—created by accident—who they carried with them around the world, never making friends, only enemies to be taken out at a later date. But no. They had to settle down and have a billion kids and dogs and make her love them all.

It was gross.

"I don't think that's abnormal for a woman of your talents," Lena said, the shadows throwing across her face. "You have a healthy skepticism. I certainly worry more about the other members of the team. I think Kenzie could be easily manipulated with the right tools. You should know I told Drake I don't think Kenzie should be the one to deal with Benjamin Parker. I think you should handle the relationship. I was overruled."

She bet she'd been. Even if her dad agreed with Lena, he wouldn't hurt Kenz that way. "Kenzie isn't as naïve as you think she is. My twin just likes to look on the positive side of things."

"I still think it would be better for you to manage the relationship."

"If she did, Ben would be dead now," Cooper said from the doorway. He was a big, muscular shadow standing there, and she felt a rush of arousal go through her system.

She was a big old perv now. Even after what she'd heard, all she could think about was getting into that boy's manties. She had so little time with him. Shouldn't she take advantage before she did the right thing and gave him up to some whining sheep who would give him what he needed? Who would have a ton of kids and go to PTA meetings and not embarrass him because she was weirdly socially awkward.

Until she needed to give him up, shouldn't she have him as many times as he was willing?

Would he be willing after what his mom said? Or was he reconsidering.

*I sleep where you sleep, your arms a blanket around me.*
*The dark is softer when you are near.*
*I am unafraid and dreams are sweet, all my shadows silenced in the song of your breathing.*
*Where your life entwines with mine, I am safe.*

Kala took a long breath, trying to banish the sudden well of emotion that threatened to swamp her. It had been so long. So long since words invaded her head like a damn Taylor Swift song she couldn't stop playing. She resisted the urge to grab a notepad and write it down. It wasn't like poetry would ever pay the bills, but her heart clenched at the thought of writing again. It wasn't for anyone except her.

"Her sister has emotional connections to the man," Lena was

saying. "It's not a good idea to let her direct communications with him."

"I assure you Kala does, too. But she has the emotions you think she should have about a foreign operative," Cooper said as he sank down next to her. "What you don't understand is the amount of restraint she's shown in not murdering him."

He was being over the top. She didn't truly want the man dead. Maybe maimed. What was a little maiming between friends?

The door opened again, and her parents walked in. Tristan had gone with Kenzie. Tasha had the day off because she and Dare were visiting wedding venues.

They were very light today, the team spread out over the globe. It kind of made her nervous they weren't together.

See, this was why it would be easier on her own. She wouldn't worry.

Except then she wouldn't know where Lou was, or Kenz or Tash. She wouldn't have eyes on her brothers.

"Well, I believe Kala can easily control her emotions in a way Kenzie cannot." Lena sat back, crossing one leg over the other.

Her dad snorted. "Sure."

Jerk. She didn't have emotions. Maybe one. She got pissed off a lot. That was an emotion. Shit. Now she had horniness. She blamed Cooper for that one. Was horniness a proper emotion? Because if it was then she'd moved from having a feeling to having feelings. With an *s*.

Her mom slapped at her dad's chest, a familiar gesture. "Stop."

Her father sat down, his expression going grim. "All right. Let's get this done. Lena, you have the footage. I'll send it to the rest of the team tomorrow. I want them focused on their jobs today, and I'm pretty sure this will be distracting."

Cooper leaned over. "What is he talking about?"

So her dad had seen the footage. It wasn't surprising. Her parents were the heart of the team, and they would get all the intel first. Though it was good to know she'd been the second of the team to learn what had happened. "It's the footage from Rebecca Walsh-Shaw's security cameras."

She sat back, her stomach threatening to turn. She wasn't going to think about what Eve had said. It wasn't new information, so there wasn't anything to process.

Cooper's hand slid over hers as the grainy footage came up. The Land Rover sat in the drive in front of a nice house in what looked to be a suburban neighborhood. The time stamp read five forty-five a.m., but it was still full dark. A big figure moved into the frame briefly before disappearing.

"He knows there's a camera there," Cooper murmured.

Kala stared down at where their hands were entwined. "You don't have to hold my hand. I'm fine."

She saw the moment her father's head swerved around like a predator scenting prey.

She should have kept her mouth closed but that hand in hers...did something to her. Something that would hurt later. It was neither pissed off-ness nor horniness.

It was...longing.

Cooper didn't seem to care that everyone was looking their way. "You take my dick, you get my hand, too. I do need someone to hold my hand through this because everyone is on edge, and I don't know what's happening. I need my emotional support grump."

Her dad snorted, and his head shook as he sat back.

Her mom smiled approvingly Cooper's way.

It wasn't fair her mom liked him and his mom thought she was a walking disaster.

"Is he under the car?" Cooper asked, moving on smoothly. Like she would just accept that he would hold her hand in public.

It felt nice. And he needed it. She was nothing if not his longtime friend. She spanked asses when subs told her they needed it. She'd done far more intimate things for the subs under her care. So it was fine to give Cooper what he needed.

"He is," Lena replied, and Kala could feel her judgment from across the room. "He's good. The only time the camera catches him is that brief moment before he goes under the car. We believe he attached the bomb to her vehicle at this moment. The rest of the footage is normal until the vehicle explodes almost an hour later."

"Okay," her dad said, his eyes now firmly on the screen in front of them. "I want to see the enhanced footage again."

"Enhanced?" Cooper whispered the question.

"Just watch," she replied with a sigh.

Lena clicked a few keys on her keyboard, and the video changed to a series of still shots, mostly from the beginning of the cam footage. She zoomed in on the figure who wore all black, the hood of his jacket pulled over his face, obscuring his features. She didn't zoom in on the face, however. She went for his left hand, zooming in far enough that it was clear he was Caucasian with large hands and a scar that went from between his thumb and forefinger, trailing up to the arm of his jacket and disappearing.

Cooper's hand tightened around hers.

"And there it is." Her father sat back.

Cooper let go of her hand. "It's not Zach. Someone fucked with the footage."

She'd thought about that, too. "I checked it out. I even took it down to my Aunt Chelsea and had her review it. She says it hasn't been tampered with."

"You did what?" Lena asked, genuine surprise in her tone.

Did Lena even know who she was? "Trust but verify, and I don't know anyone who is better at verification than my Aunt Chelsea. I think you'll find she's still got clearance. Though if you want to fire me, I could use the nap."

She didn't know what the hell she would do if she got fired. Given all the shit she pulled, she probably should have a plan B. She might go the private detective route, but her friends Harlow and Ruby already had that going. She could do the professional Dominatrix thing.

"What did Chelsea say?" Cooper asked. "Because whoever fucked with the footage wants us to believe that's Zach. You know he had his hand cut and had to do PT for six months after one of the first missions we ran together. He took a knife to the hand in Hong Kong."

Yep. She knew it well. She'd known he wouldn't think straight about this. "She said there was zero proof it was altered. It's Zach."

"It can't be Zach," Cooper said stubbornly.

"Of course it can be." Her father was a realist. He moved his hand to the control panel and flicked a switch, bringing the lights back up. He looked a bit weary. "We knew he was hiding something. I didn't think it was this big."

"He wouldn't kill someone," Cooper argued.

"Sweetie, you've seen him kill people," her mother said with sympathy. "But I do tend to agree with you that I'm not sure we should immediately jump to conclusions. Which is why we're sending the two of you on an assignment."

She'd expected something like this. "You want us to find his aunt and figure out if she knows anything. Shouldn't I just go after Zach on my own?"

"You're not going anywhere without me," Cooper said, his tone deepening. She turned his way, and he shrugged. "No one goes alone, and I'm the only one left. Unless you want to hang with your dad."

It wouldn't be bad if her dad would let her work in peace, but he would want to talk. For a dude who claimed to shove his feelings real deep, the man loved to talk about other people's feelings. She wanted to avoid all the feelings talks. It would come, but she could put it off. Maybe even long enough that they would have broken this unwritten contract of theirs and she could chalk it up to random, meaningless sex.

Damn it. Her father would never buy it.

"He's not wrong," her dad replied. "And neither is your mom. I want you to find Joyce Reed. I've sent her dossier to you along with a map of the national park I'm fairly certain she's living in right now."

"National park?" Cooper asked.

"I might have mentioned she's nomadic," her father pointed out. "I've had some people I know tracking her movements, and she's definitely not doing seasonal work right now. She'll often work the holiday season to collect the money she needs to move around. About four times a year she'll work for a couple of weeks. She recently did a three-week stint in a town close to the Rocky Mountain National Park, and my investigators believe she's camping there for the time being. They've found her van parked at the store she was working at, and the owner admitted to letting her stay there."

"Then we should simply watch the van," Lena said with a shake of her head. "We don't need high-level assets out in the wilderness. We can send someone else."

"I want Kala and Cooper to handle this," her father said, turning Cooper's way. "Read the dossier. She requires a somewhat soft touch. Joyce has seen some shit."

"Soft touch?" Coop asked, his lips quirking up, and then he brought her hand to his lips, kissing her knuckles. "I will attempt to make up for my partner's blunter approach."

Her father's eyes went right to their entwined hands, brow rising, but the bastard had a grin on his face. "Oh, Joyce will love Kala. It's men she can be nervous around, and by nervous, I mean she can shoot first and ask questions after she's buried your body."

It was Kala's time to chuckle. And not think about how good it felt to sit here with him, to have his affection in a place where someone else could see it. "Somehow I think Coop will be okay. He knows how to handle an angsty chick."

"They're my favorite kind," Cooper replied.

"I'm pretty sure from here on out they better be your only kind," her dad said with a smile that was only half predatory. Seventy-five percent.

"Ian," her mother said, his name a clear warning.

Yeah, maybe she should rethink the in-public thing. Her father shouldn't threaten Cooper when this relationship was completely casual and had an open end date that would probably happen sooner rather than later.

"Don't push her, Ian," Cooper said quietly, and he turned her way when she started to pull her hand back. "It's hold my hand or sit on my lap."

A weird thrill went through her. She was almost never challenged. Her siblings would poke her, but they wouldn't ever throw down some arbitrary choice she didn't have to make. Dom wanted to play, did he? She pulled her hand away and stared at her temporary lover. "I don't have to do either."

Cooper glanced between her and her father, and she was suddenly well aware that Coop was now trapped between two stubborn Taggarts. If it bugged him, he didn't show it. He simply shrugged. "Then let's negotiate."

Her dad huffed, an annoyed sound. "And it's time for me to leave."

Her mom winked her way. "I think that's a good idea."

"And I don't." Lena slapped her hands on the table. "Look, I get it. You're family. But I'm here as a representative of the Central Intelligence Agency, and you are running this like some family bakery or something. The emotional connections between your operatives alone makes me want to question your leadership choices."

"Question away, Doc," her father said with a shrug. "You want to fire me, cool. I would love some more golf time."

"You're acting like you can fire us," her mother challenged.

Lena took a long breath. The doc was definitely overstimulated. "All I can do is suggest. And right now I suggest that Kala remains here in Dallas. She's doing some important work both mentally and physically."

"I have the exercises I'm supposed to do for my knee. I'll do them." She knew what she'd promised and she wasn't going to back out, but the truth was she could use some time away from everything. Everything except him.

Negotiate.

She understood negotiations. Negotiations put things in plain words and let her know what was expected. She didn't pick up on nuances sometimes, not when it came to the interpersonal. A contract. She loved a contract. Maybe they could talk about one between them.

Though she wasn't his sub. And he wasn't hers.

"Kala, I scarcely think the Agency wants to lose its most valuable young agent in the damn forest," Lena complained. "I don't like the idea of you being completely dependent on McKay in a world that is utterly foreign to you. I'm trying to look out for you since it's very plain your father is pushing this new…relationship."

Cooper sat up straighter, seeming to decide this was a serious conversation. "First off, she wouldn't be dependent on me. You said Rocky Mountain National, right? She spent most of her summers in the Colorado mountains. Trust me, I'll be nothing more than the dude who carries a bunch of stuff and cleans up after us. She knows the woods. Her dad's an asshole who dumped her in the middle of the woods and forced her and her sisters to find their way back."

She didn't blame him. She'd requested the test when she was fourteen, and she was pretty sure her dad had been following them, waiting in case they needed help.

"Can't go raising soft kids," her dad replied. "They either came back or got eaten by a bear."

Her mom rolled her eyes. "Yeah, because you didn't have most of the town of Bliss watching for them. Those wildlife cameras just popped up overnight."

She wasn't sure who Lena thought she was. "It'll be good to spend some time in nature. I'll be fine, and I'll take a sat phone with me. Well, Cooper will. Those things can be heavy."

She kind of hoped it took a couple of days to find the woman. It would be nice to be alone with him in a place she loved. Alex and Eve would come out there from time to time, but never for the weeks and sometimes months her parents did. Once they got good Internet, her parents had spent most of the summers in Colorado.

"I don't think it's a good idea. I actually was going to propose that you and I go to Langley for a couple of weeks. I think you can help me with the profile of Zach Reed. Your father seems to think his aunt is going to… I don't know, open up his baby book and you'll know what he's doing. It makes no logical sense."

Her father's eyes narrowed, and she could tell Lena hadn't spent a ton of time around her dad. His voice went soft, a sure sign he was about to do some bad shit. "We don't understand the same logic, Doctor. You are not her boss. I am."

"Yes, I have a problem with that, too," Lena added. "Kala doesn't need a firm hand. She's smart and capable, and sometimes you treat her like a child."

Her mother's hand disappeared, going under the table and likely squeezing her dad's thigh. Her mom's hand was a leash, hauling back the biggest, baddest guard dog in the world.

"Baby, move back a little. I know you just bought that shirt, and blood is hard to get out," Cooper whispered.

He knew nothing about laundry. Blood was actually quite easy to clean up.

Her father's eyes remained on Lena, but his words were for Kala. "Which assignment would you like, Agent Taggart?"

That was easy. "Uh, you're asking me if I want to spend a week in the woods talking to a nomadic crone or in DC talking to assholes? I very much like a crone, thank you. I also think Lena is discounting the intelligence we can gather from talking to Zach's aunt."

"Really? You think you can get something from her or are you simply attempting to take a couple of days off with your new boyfriend?" Lena asked.

Her mom sat up at those words.

Kala didn't care. She waved her mom off. "I'm going to work and fuck his brains out. I can multitask. It's all cool. I got this."

Lena sighed and stood. "Well, I can see I'm not needed here."

Her father watched the doctor as she strode away. "You two pack up. Cooper, you can take the small jet." He stood. "Don't forget the first part of your multitasking is to keep your eyes and ears open."

And her legs. Those were going to be wide open. She gave her dad a salute. "Will do, general."

Her father shook his head and stared at her for a moment. "You know what you're doing?"

She shrugged. Her father, she almost always understood. If it had been someone else, she would have wondered if he meant what she was doing with the op or with Cooper. Her dad? Oh, he was always asking about the most embarrassing thing. It was easy to be around her dad because he was so predictable. "Probably not. I mean, physically yeah. I think I got it down. I don't know. I do have some questions."

Her dad was out the door very quickly.

And she was alone with Cooper.

"So a couple of days in the woods," he said, his lips curling in the sexiest grin. "Whatever shall we do?"

She could think of a few things.

## Chapter Eleven

Cooper checked out the van, but it looked like Zach's aunt lived lean. There weren't a bunch of mementoes stocked there. There wasn't much of anything beyond some blankets and pillows and a couple of books and dry goods. It looked like she'd taken a lot with her when she'd walked into the woods.

"And you're sure Joyce isn't in trouble?" the man who owned the store asked. He'd been introduced as Buddy. Buddy owned this general store and was friendly with their target.

He shouldn't think of her as a target. She was Zach's aunt, and maybe she could explain why one of his best friends had lost his damn mind.

More importantly, she might be able to tell them how to get Zach back in the fold.

"I'm sure. I promise you, she's not in trouble." The man who'd picked them up at the airport was acting as something of a go-between with the suspicious small-town citizens. Henry Flanders knew pretty much everyone in Southern Colorado. He and his wife were very important to the communities. They weren't in Bliss, but Henry still had pull. "Do you want to talk to the sheriff? I assure you he wouldn't be cooperating if he didn't trust these people."

"They look like Feds," Buddy said with a frown.

Kala snorted. "Do not. I mean, I know he does. He's Navy, by the way. I'm way cooler. I'm with the CIA."

What? "Uh, hello, undercover?"

Kala waved him off. "I'm not lying to the people here." She turned to the man. "Look, I spent a lot of time in these woods, a lot of time in Henry's town. I understand you deserve your privacy, but I have to weigh that against Joyce's nephew's safety. I need to find Zach, and she's my best bet. Now *he* might be in trouble since his ass apparently tried to explode a friend of ours."

"He did?" the man asked, eyes wide.

He had zero idea what she was doing. Was she planning on handing over the mission briefing to the dude who ran a small general store?

"He didn't do a great job," Kala admitted. "Which is why I wonder about the whys. See, I don't like to admit this but he's actually competent. He doesn't make mistakes. He wouldn't simply guess and hope he hits his target."

They'd spent the last night prepping for the op and then falling into bed together. And on the kitchen table. And on the couch. Brianna had protested that she used the couch, too, and Kala had given her permission to go to town on it. Bri had not been amused.

Having her sit next to him in the copilot's seat had been… Well, it was his two favorite things together. Chocolate and peanut butter. Flying and Kala.

Now he wondered what she'd been thinking about the whole time. What had she worked out in that magnificent brain of hers? She wouldn't talk about what his mother had said, waving him off with promises of not getting her butt hurt. She'd been more willing to talk about a contract. He now had the right to hold her hand when she didn't need it to stab someone with—she'd insisted on the wording—and the right to sleep next to her when they were in the same place at the same time. Because it was easier than making two beds.

His girl was so fucking romantic.

"You thinking he could be in trouble?" The store owner was coming around. It was clear Kala's openness was winning him over.

Kala nodded. "I do. I think he's in serious trouble, and he's my friend. I understand if you want to contact her and tell her we're coming, but she could help us help him."

"Oh, I can't contact Joyce. When she goes off the grid, she's really off the grid," the man said. "But if I hear anything, I'll let Henry here know and he can contact you."

Henry had their sat number. "We'll be monitoring the situation from Bliss. If anyone needs help, we'll be able to come in via chopper if we need to."

"We aren't going to need a chopper." Kala stepped away from the van and picked up her kit. They'd carefully packed the night before, Kala checking his twice. Not because she didn't trust him, but because it was kind of her love language. Making sure he had the things he would need so she didn't worry. Because she would worry. Now he wondered how worried she was about Zach. About the whole team.

Despite all the sex of the last few days, there was something brewing inside his baby. Some storm she wouldn't talk about until it turned into a hurricane. He intended to calm that storm before it blew them both away. "We'll be fine."

He picked up his pack and looked out over the trail. It began behind the store and would take them into the Rockies. Henry had given them a map with the known trails, but both he and Kala knew they would be going off the beaten path. Henry and some of the citizens of Bliss had marked up possible places where she could be camping. And there was a place they shouldn't go into because of alien mating practices. He hadn't completely understood what that old dude had been saying, but Kala had listened to him carefully and promised she would allow no aliens to breach Cooper's... Well, he was pretty sure she'd been talking about his asshole when they'd discussed probing.

It was a weird place. He'd only been to this part of the world a couple of times, when his parents had visited the Taggarts during the summers they spent here. The family owned a cabin in Bliss, and Kala had gone with her dad even after her sisters had stopped.

He'd missed her those summers.

And sometimes he'd been relieved because he didn't have to be "him" when she was around. His youthful self had enjoyed playing the popular kid who didn't ask the hard questions, who didn't have to feel the way she always made him feel. Kala challenged him. She poked and prodded and forced him to be better. When he was younger it sometimes rankled. Now he understood how good she was for him. How she made him a better man. Like his parents had done for each other.

Now all he had to do was convince the most stubborn woman in the world that he was good for her, too.

"We're hiking the main trail to Big Meadows, and we'll camp there tonight," Kala explained. "I've talked to the park rangers and they've agreed to help, but no one's seen her since three days ago when she was camped out near Alberta Falls. We can get there in the morning and that's where we'll start. Thanks for the ride, Henry, and please tell your daughter I said hello."

Henry snorted. "Really? We're pretending I only have the one?"

Kala settled her big pack on her shoulders. "You have a lovely daughter named Poppy, who is the best, and you somehow ended up with Lucifer."

Henry's sigh spoke of long suffering as he turned to Cooper. "Lucy. Her name is Lucy. Lucy Brooke Flanders. She's… Well, she's actually a lot like Kala, so they don't necessarily get along. I'll send her your well wishes."

"For her hair to fall out," Kala quipped.

"Well, that's progress. The last time she hoped for Lucy to get stabbed. And offered to be the one to do it." Henry slapped his shoulder in a manly fashion. "I'm going to have to go with Kala's dad on this one. Wear a condom, man. Kids will kill you."

"Lucifer certainly will," Kala grumbled. Cooper wanted that story out of her, but it would have to wait because he planned on spending this time they had together talking about the future. And the past.

They began down the trail.

*Day One*

Hours and hours later, Cooper settled in by the fire Kala had made with a practiced hand. He'd passed all sorts of survival courses, gone camping with his family, and learned how to survive, but Kala thrived out here. She seemed beautifully settled as she stared into the warm glow of the fire. He studied her profile, loving the strong line of her jaw.

"What are you thinking about?" he asked.

They'd had a shockingly good meal of rehydrated beef stew, and he'd learned Kala made it herself. She owned a dehydrator and apparently tested out new recipes from time to time. It was a hell of a lot better than the prepackaged MREs he bought. He'd eaten the food she'd cooked and felt…taken care of. So often the people around her didn't realize she was taking care of them in little ways. They only saw the warrior.

She settled back against the log they'd dragged over to form a sitting area. "I was thinking about trying this meatball recipe, but I'm not sure how well it'll dry out. I was also wondering if it might not be fun to try a couple of recipes and have a dehydrated dinner party, but then Lucas would get all chef douche on me and stuff."

"We could have a sub dinner," Cooper offered. "You know they would love to see you in a more relaxed setting."

Her nose wrinkled. "I want to hate that idea."

But she didn't, and it gave him an excellent way to bring some domesticity to their new paradigm. "We can have it at my place since it appears I'm living alone again. Nate was supposed to take over Aidan's room. I thought Zach might move in for a while."

"It must be nice to be alone," she said.

"I hate it. I never wanted to live by myself, though I am considering talking to Tris's parents about buying the place." When they'd all gotten out of college, Tristan's parents had bought the four-bedroom ranch house he and Tris and Aidan had lived in for years while they'd built their careers. It had been a way station for him and Tris as they'd been in the military and then the Agency, but he was giving up his commission. He only wanted to work with his team, and honestly, only until she wanted out.

His plan was to follow her. If that meant he became a commercial pilot because they could use the money, he was up for it. If he only ever flew for the Agency…or hopefully for McKay-Taggart someday, he was okay with that, too.

"Really? You don't think it's too big? Or are you planning to get some more roommates?"

The thought made him shudder. The only one he would have considered was Zach. He loved his friends, but he was over the whole woman-a-night thing, party-all-the-time phase of his life. Not that he'd actually had the woman-a-night thing. He'd been more of a serial monogamist, and even then there hadn't been many girlfriends. But he'd liked a party. Now he wanted to sit down at night with her and watch TV and pet the dog and have her fall asleep on his lap. "No. I just think it's time, and I have some money to invest. A house is almost always a good investment. Besides, maybe someday someone will want to move in with me."

"That's what I'm saying," she replied with a nod. "You can charge rent if you own the house. I do think there are a couple of guys looking for a new place. James doesn't want to stay with his parents anymore now that he's done with grad school. I'm pretty sure I heard one of the line chefs at Top is looking for a new place. His apartment got flooded, and it'll take weeks to get it back in shape."

She could be very literal at times. "Baby, I wasn't talking about one of the guys. Don't get me wrong. I was planning on letting Zach stay with me but only because I thought he was settling down with Devi. I don't want a roommate who brings home women every night."

"Well, he was probably going to bring home Devi," she pointed out.

"No, he was probably going to drop his stuff off and then spend every moment he could at Devi's." At least that had been the plan when they'd talked about it. It was hard to believe Zach hadn't meant every word, but then there was a lot he didn't know about the guy. "I was talking about you. I was hoping maybe you would move in."

"Why would I... Is this because I make the bed and you don't like to make the bed?" Kala asked, her eyes narrowing.

*It's because I fucking love you and want to spend every moment with you and want us to build something beautiful together.* It's what he wanted to say, but he had to be patient. "Yes. I hate making the bed."

She sobered and sighed. "No, you don't. I know it seems ridiculous..."

"It's not." She had boundaries she thought she had to defend, but she was allowing him to gradually remove some bricks. Soon he would have a whole door, and he would be on the other side of all her walls. "We move as fast or slow as you want."

She chuckled. "Sure, babe. This is all on my time."

She wasn't wrong, and it felt like an opening since she wasn't shutting him down. "How honest can I be?"

"And not scare me off?" She seemed to think about the question for a moment. "Hit me. I can handle it."

He wasn't sure, but this was a good opening. "If you would have talked to me, I would have been your boyfriend after that night. I knew I had screwed up so royally and it made me ache inside, but I would have done anything to have changed that night."

She was silent for a moment, her head turned up to the stars. "If it helps, I think you were right."

"About the sex, yes, I was." He was only going to agree with her so far. "But not the rest. I know I sometimes made you feel like I was hiding you, but when you started school again, you were the one who ignored me. I can't help but think it's because you blamed me for what happened to you. I'll take it. I'll take that blame because I never should have allowed you to leave."

"Like you could have stopped me," Kala argued.

"I could have tried." He remembered back to the night and the awful time when he'd had no idea where she was. "I was sick. So sick. After your parents went to find you, I sat there praying I would see you again. And when I did, you looked through me. I know it's not fair. I know I'm the one who screwed up, but I hated the fact that you couldn't look at me because you were the only one who really saw me."

"I think everyone saw you, Coop. You were like the king of high school."

"They saw the me I wanted them to see. They didn't see me. They saw the scared kid who thought he had to be perfect or his parents might regret adopting him."

"You know that wasn't true."

She'd told him a million times. Naturally she was the only one he'd told, and when she'd stopped talking to him, he'd stopped talking about it. Years and wisdom had solved the problem, but he'd missed her. "It felt like it at the time. And it wasn't anything my parents did. It was me. I wondered if there was something I should know, some, I don't know, weird DNA trick waiting to make me someone else. Like badness or laziness can be inherited. I know nothing about my birth mother. I'm okay with that now, but at the time I questioned everything. Including why she gave me away."

"She probably wanted what was best for you and she couldn't give it. Or she didn't want a kid," Kala said with her usual logic. She frowned. "But it was probably like the first one. Like she loved you and stuff but didn't have any money."

He grinned her way. She wasn't trying to be mean. She often said what she was thinking around him. Kala would be utterly closed lipped around anyone she didn't know, but she let all her thoughts flow with him. Even if she didn't admit it, she felt safe with him. "Baby, what else went through your head? Please? I want to hear it."

She frowned and looked adorable with all that pink hair piled high on her head. "Fine. I was thinking she also might have been on the run from a drug cartel and she had to give birth in a bathroom and she knew a kid would weigh her down while she plotted her bloody revenge and one day when she's killed everyone she needs to, she'll come back and be like 'hey, I'm your mom.'"

He reached out and brushed a hand across her hair. "You should have been a novelist."

"Too many words. But I do like a good story." She moved closer to him, dragging her blanket along. "You don't still think that way, do you?"

"No. Not at all." He stroked her hair again and she sighed and laid down, her head on his lap, eyes facing toward the fire. "I know my parents love me. I know they want what's best for me."

She snorted. "They definitely want that."

"And what's best for me is you," he said quietly.

Her hand came out to cover his knee in what felt like a deeply possessive gesture. "Your mother would disagree, and you're a bastard because I didn't want to talk about this."

He wanted her possessive. She was a Taggart lion, and they didn't share the things they loved. He wanted to be something she didn't share.

"We don't have to, but I don't think you understand what she means, baby." He kept up the slow stroking of her hair since he could feel her relaxing. "Even if we don't talk about it, I need you to hear me on this. I love my mother. She would never ask me to choose. Never. But if on some separate plane of existence there lives an Eve McKay who would, I would choose you. Always."

Her jaw went tight. "You just told me how much you care about their opinion."

"Yes, I do, and you don't understand her opinion. You always hear the words, but you often don't get the intent behind them, especially when deep emotion is involved."

She sat up suddenly, turning to him. "Because I don't have emotions."

He groaned but forged ahead because this was a conversation they needed to have. "Because you feel so fucking deeply you sometimes struggle to understand what other people feel. Especially if they aren't perfectly clear in their wording."

"You make me sound like a weirdo," she complained but with a huff that told him she wasn't mad about it.

"I make you sound like someone who thinks differently, someone who sees the world in a way I can't comprehend but I'm always in awe of. I am fairly certain my mother worries I won't be good enough for you."

She snorted.

"I broke your heart once and you didn't let me back in for twelve years, Kala. Twelve years where I felt untethered," he explained. "Twelve years where I felt like I didn't know who I was. Where I questioned if I ruined both our lives with a couple of foolish words and teenaged insecurities. I worried I wrecked us because I wasn't as mature as you were. I have definitely spent the last twelve years worried that I don't even know what I did to you because you won't talk about it."

She sighed and moved back to sit against the log. At least she was still close, their hips touching. "There's not a lot to talk about."

"You were gone for days."

She was quiet for a moment and then her head tilted slightly. "I wasn't tortured, if that's what you're worried about. I just had to listen to that Julia chick go on and on about Kyle. That was gross."

So she wasn't going to talk. Damn it. He wasn't sure they could move forward until he truly understood what had happened the other night. "Okay. Was it something else? Something that happened in college, maybe? Or on an op?"

He worried about her on ops. Worried about the men she targeted deciding to take advantage of her. She was the strongest woman he knew, but there was only so much strength could save her from.

"This is one of those times when I wish I was Kenz and I could give you a cute girl smile and pretend to not understand you. I can do it, you know," she said quietly. "I can be Kenzie when we're in the field. I can lie and be charming. But I can't with you."

He let his arm drift over the back of the log so it was almost around her shoulders. "I'm glad. I want to be your safe place."

"I think you're my weak spot."

He turned slightly. "I'm not. I'm exactly what I said. I'm your safe place and you're mine. I feel so bad I made you think I wasn't for a long time. I know in that head of yours what's happening between us is some kind of meaningless sex thing, but it's not that way for me."

Her eyes closed, and she seemed to come to some decision. "It's not meaningless."

"Again, I'm glad to hear it."

She opened them, those clear blue eyes boring into his soul. "But I also don't think it's forever. I'm not going to make that mistake again."

"Not a mistake. I was wrong." He could see the way her hands fisted and knew she was getting emotional. He wanted her that way—if the right emotion was involved. He was pretty sure she was feeling anxious and for her it came out as anger, and he didn't want that between them. "Forget I said anything, baby. Come here. The solar's got plenty of charge, and I know you're listening to an audiobook. Let's eat some cookies and listen."

Her brow cocked. "You want to listen to fairies fucking?"

"Sure, why not." He didn't care as long as she relaxed. "You had to listen to my music the whole flight. Come here. We won't talk about anything but books and the op if you like."

He held open the blanket he'd placed over his lap.

She didn't move.

Had he lost her?

"I don't know." She said the words solemnly and pulled her knees into her chest, wrapping her arms around them.

"You don't know if you want cookies? Your mom made them. They're delicious."

She swallowed and seemed to find some courage. "I don't know if they raped me or not. The asshole who put a needle in my neck promised me he would pass me around to all the guys while I was sleeping, and I don't know what he did. I know I was sore, but I didn't know how it would feel so I can't be sure if it was because of a sexual assault or because I nearly took them all down. They were shitty fighters, by the way. I saw a doctor, but it was days later, and she couldn't be certain. I've thought a lot about it lately, and I don't think so. I think I would remember being sore the way I was a couple of days ago. But maybe your dick is bigger."

His heart threatened to seize, and the world blurred as he stared at her. "Kyle said…"

"Yeah, I know what my cousin said. He wasn't there the whole time. And now that I… Well, I think maybe he was right and there wasn't enough time nor inclination for a group of mercenaries to gangbang an unconscious fifteen-year-old. The one who led them shot the Russian dude who threatened me. He wanted to sell me to a syndicate. Obviously not the one my mom used to belong to. He said people would pay money to be able to brag they hurt Dusan Denisovitch's cousin. I don't know if he did it because he didn't want to have to protect me from his own men or because he didn't want to share the money. You're right. I struggle with emotional reasoning sometimes. Especially when I was younger. He said he didn't have to share the money, and I believed him."

Well, he'd wondered and now he knew. "You were a virgin."

"Maybe. Maybe not," she replied. "I won't ever truly know because all the people who could have told me are dead, and I'm also okay with that. I just…sometimes I wish I knew. I wish it wasn't always there under the surface, this thing I can't quite see. I don't know if what's dancing around underneath me is a shadow meaning nothing or a shark that's going to eat me from the inside out. I know I lied."

"About having sex?" She'd alluded to previous boyfriends, but she'd never gone into details. Certainly not with him. "Not really, now that I think about it. You allowed people to think you had."

"I wanted to be normal."

"You are so much more than normal." He reached out and cupped her cheek. "If there is one thing it seems I learned since high school that you didn't, it's that normal isn't something we should aspire to. You're you, and I that-word-you-can't-hear-me-say-yet you for it. I was a stupid kid who didn't understand the magnificent woman in front of me. I do now. You think I'm going to revert back to form, like I'm going to wake up and want some sweet thing who doesn't growl at me, who doesn't fight the whole world."

"Who could be a good wife and mom." Her words were so hollow it hit him in the gut.

"Are you fucking kidding? Baby, I'm going to have to ask what drugs you're on now. You don't think your mother was a good mom?"

"She was the best."

"And she was weird as hell. She talked openly about her days as an assassin and regularly got caught having sex with your dad. She spent every Saturday night at a lifestyle club, and I'm pretty sure she helped bury a bunch of bodies because one of my core childhood memories is of our parents having a big fight about the hole they'd just dug and your mom complaining about the Agency needing to pay for dry cleaning. I won't even go into your dad." Maybe he was asking the wrong questions. "Did you want something more normal? Did you want a white picket fence and perfect childhood?"

"It was perfect."

There she was. "Yes, it was. And whatever life we can have together will be perfectly ours. I don't want anything else. Anything less than the weird, magical world we can create together."

She was silent for a long moment before turning her eyes his way, tears shining there. She never, ever cried. "I don't know what I want, Coop. I don't know that I want a family I might let down. I love my parents. I love my sisters and brothers, but sometimes I think about how much easier it would be if I didn't."

It made him ache because he knew he'd been the first real crack in her life. Sure, she'd gotten bullied for being weird and she'd known from a very young age that she didn't fit like the rest of her family, but she'd persevered. She'd been strong even as a teen. It had been his betrayal that sent her here. Made her question. "It won't be because no matter what your inner voices are telling you, you won't be able to turn it off. That love you feel isn't some switch you can flip. If it was, you wouldn't be sitting here with me right now. You are a warrior goddess but what you don't understand is what makes you truly strong is the delicate place inside that holds all your love. Even when it hurt, there was a part of you defending that place in your soul. If you could turn it off, you wouldn't be the one everyone goes to when they need something."

"That's not true. Everyone goes to Kenz unless they need someone fucked up."

She thought she was nothing more than an enforcer? "They go to Kenzie when they want a shoulder to cry on and someone who will agree with them. When they need real help and advice, they come to you. They come because you'll tell them the truth and won't judge them."

"Oh, I judge plenty," she began.

She was not going to turn this into a rundown of all the dumb shit her cousins did. "All I'm saying is when they need a stereotypical mom they run to Kenz. When they need a dad…"

She groaned. "I know. I know they call me She-ian."

"Yeah, like they call your Aunt Erin, who you think is the coolest woman on the planet. Also not a typical stand by your man, have dinner on the table and spurt out twelve kids trad wife. This is where you think my mom is saying one thing when it's another. She's using a bunch of therapy speak. She was worried we were getting in too deep as kids, and she's worried I'll hurt you now because I pretended to be something I'm not."

"Something you're not?"

"Yes. Baby, I'm good at one thing on this planet, and it's not flying. Though I'm excellent at that. My parents are super smart. They're problem solvers. They can save the world. I can fly anything with wings, but that's not the job I'm truly excellent at. I'm good at doing that word we're not saying yet when it comes to you. I might have been shitty at it in the past, but…"

She moved suddenly into his space, and her lips were on his. "Shut up, Coop. I can't. I can't fix things tonight, but I can promise you I'll think about it. I can promise you that I won't make decisions without talking to you."

Shit. She was serious. Kala was the ultimate independent woman. If she was offering to discuss the future, then he had a real shot.

He wrapped his arms around her and sank into the now.

\* \* \* \*

Kala felt his tongue slide against hers and wondered how the hell she'd ever lived without this. How had she gotten through life without his hands on her, without the comfort of knowing he was hers?

How would she ever go back to not having it?

She kissed him, moving her body so she straddled him and got his cock against the juncture of her thighs. She didn't make a move yet, simply wanted the feel of him. The warmth of him.

Every word he'd said slid into her soul, finding all the cracks in her walls. But instead of breaking her down, she somehow felt stronger. Like instead of splitting her walls, he'd simply found a way to the other side and then him being there strengthened her.

She'd meant what she'd told him. This wouldn't be fixed in a night. It wouldn't be decided by sex and talking. Time was what she needed.

She knew one thing. She was going to tell Lena that. Time. She needed time to decide if she would take the woman up on her offer because so many things Cooper said made sense.

Her mother wasn't normal. Her father was so far from it he defied the very word.

And yet they were happy. They loved their family, loved her so much they'd supported her when they didn't agree with her decisions.

Was that all that was required? Love.

What if she was being a coward by not asking the real questions—the ones she was afraid to ask. The ones that might mean she needed some help, and help seemed like weakness.

But she would never say that to a friend. Ever. Why did she deserve less?

*Stop.* She was going to spiral if she kept down this path. "Cooper, I need something."

"Anything," he replied.

She knew exactly what could take her mind off all the questions roiling around in her brain. There was something they hadn't done yet, and she wanted to know what it felt like. He'd spent an enormous amount of time pleasuring her with his mouth and tongue, and she wanted the same. She tossed the blanket aside and slid down his body, putting herself between his knees. He'd changed into sweatpants after they'd gotten the tent set up. Just one. They hadn't even brought two, and she hadn't pretended when she'd laid out their sleeping bags. One on bottom and another as a blanket, zipping them together to form a double bed.

For as long as they were together, she would be with him. And she would think about everything he'd said, about whether she could put aside the scared little girl and be the woman he needed.

She stared at him as she allowed her fingers to find the waistband of his sweats, dragging them down so his cock bounced free.

"Fuck," he hissed between clenched teeth. "You're going to make me beg, aren't you?"

She'd been thinking a lot about where they could go with this. "I don't know if I'll ever want you to spank me, Coop."

"I don't need to."

"But I do kind of like the violet wand." She'd been introduced to it in her training classes at The Club. Every top was expected to experience what their subs went through, and she'd found the violet wand rather stimulating. What would it be like if she truly trusted the person on the other side?

His lips kicked up in the most devilish grin. "Oh, I can handle that, baby. And while I don't think I ever want to lay over your knee, either, we can talk about other forms of play. You'll find I'm quite open for the right woman. For a very specific woman. Touch me."

So bossy. But it didn't feel wrong with him. She wrapped her hand around that gorgeous dick of his and gave him a firm squeeze, loving the groan that went through her man.

Her man. For now.

Forever.

She would fuck up anyone who hurt him. Even if she had to leave, even if it couldn't work, she would watch over him.

Which was exactly what the fucker meant when he'd said she couldn't shut it off. She would never get the quiet she thought she wanted. Her heart wasn't something she could cut out and throw away. Her love for him would always be there, the delicate part she protected because it made her who she was.

Was she lying to herself? Trying to take some easy way out because heartache was too much for her fragile fucking soul to handle?

"Baby, ask the important questions later. Focus on the task at hand. Please," he said with a low growl.

The man did know her. When she thought about it, he knew her better than anyone. She lowered her body down until she was right where she needed to be. Her skin felt electric. She didn't have to decide. She could have this night and many more. They could explore. They could have fun.

She could give herself the time she needed to trust again. Not in him but in herself.

She licked the head of his cock. "I'm not sweet."

His hand came out, running along her hair like she was something precious. "You can be."

Delusional man. "I'm difficult."

His eyes closed as she sucked his head inside her mouth. "I like difficult. I like a challenge. I don't want a sheep, Kala."

She gently dragged her teeth over the delicate skin, making him hiss. "I'm possessive."

"So I have seen, baby," he replied.

"I might be a little on the vengeful side." She used her free hand to cup his balls. She liked the way they felt. The way he smelled. Masculine and clean and extremely aroused. For her.

"As Jimmy Roads probably still understands," he said between clenched teeth.

"Am I doing this right?" She wasn't sure. She'd seen some porn and listened to her sisters talk about the act since they had never once been taught shame, and that had been a mistake her parents made. But she hadn't done it herself. "Also, it might have been more than Jimmy."

"Fuck," he cursed as she licked him again. "You're doing it perfectly, and I'm going to die soon if you don't take me inside. Your mouth is going to feel so good, baby. Not as good as that sweet pussy of yours but almost. Put that tongue on me. Use your teeth, you gorgeous predator. I'll love all of it."

She settled in and let all those voices flow out of her head because he was more important. He needed her. Wanted her. So it was easier to shut off the negative flow that seemed to always fill her brain and concentrate on what mattered.

Her body never faltered. Her body always wanted him. Her body didn't ask why, simply knew its mate and craved him.

It was enough for now.

She lowered her mouth down, sucking him deep and tasting his salty essence on her tongue. She rolled his balls in her hand and fucked him with her mouth until his fingers tightened on her hair.

"I'm going to come, baby," he warned. "I'd rather you were riding me when I do it."

She gave him one last lick and sat up.

She wanted something else tonight. Now that she'd said it out loud, gone through all the logical twists of the situation she'd been in that night, she wanted more.

By the light of the fire, she pulled her T-shirt over her head, exposing her breasts. She stood and eased out of her pajama bottoms, taking her undies with her and kicking off her shoes.

He shoved his pants down further and got ready for her to

straddle him.

Instead, she held out a hand.

"Kala?"

"Come with me. I made a bed for us," she offered.

He scrambled to his feet, shucking his clothes before taking her hand and letting her lead him to the tent. They would put out the fire later, but for now it gave the tent a gauzy, fantastical lighting.

Like they were in a faery forest and he was the man of her dreams, the one who didn't want the princess. The dumb one who fell for the assassin.

Her reading was one of the only girly things about her. Or maybe it was time to throw out all those gender norms because they meant nothing. Her reading was part of her, like her writing had been. It was part of who she was, pieces that made a whole.

He was the biggest piece. The one that had been missing for so long.

"Let me lie down, baby," he offered. It was a tight space, and she was sure he was trying to make things easy on her.

She went first and laid her body on the bed she'd created, her head on the pillow, looking up at the most gorgeous man in the world as he stared down at her. Vulnerable. She was so vulnerable, and it was okay this time.

"Are you sure?" he asked, his voice low and soothing, offering her everything. He wouldn't mind if she wanted something different. Wouldn't argue or fuss. He would give her what she needed.

But what she wanted was to be able to do everything with him. To have their intimacy wash away her doubts and fears so she was at peace with her past because either way, she was okay.

She held a hand out, and he fell to his knees.

He lowered himself on her, his mouth meeting hers. She wrapped her arms and legs around him, holding him close. All of her possessive tendencies flared when she was with him. She wanted him beside her so she could watch over him, make sure he was okay.

She gasped when his cock rubbed over her clit, pressing the piercing there down. So wet. She could feel her arousal coating his dick, making them ready for what came next.

"I'll never get used to this," he whispered before he thrust up inside her.

She held on as he began to move, allowing her body to follow the rhythm he set. There was no panic this time, no shadows worrying at the edge of her consciousness. This time there was only her and him. Kala and Cooper.

He kissed her over and over as his cock worked inside her, finding the place that made her moan, that sent her over the edge, her whole body tightening with pure pleasure. She held on so tight, not wanting the moment to end, but still, a deep sense of satisfaction flooded her veins as he stiffened above her. The heat of him filling her up was a drug she was fairly sure she was addicted to now.

But nothing was better than the way he felt when he dropped down on top of her, completely spent. His face found the crook of her neck and he held her.

"Baby, I…"

"I feel the same, Coop." She couldn't hold the words back. Didn't even want to. She'd always known she loved him.

"But you're not ready to hear it," he whispered. "You're not ready to say it fully."

"Not yet. But someday. Soon. I promise." She held on to him and wished they never had to leave these woods.

Cooper chuckled. "I think if we ever have a wedding day, we should invite Jimmy. Like don't we owe it to the dude to feed him chicken or beef? Give him a couple of drinks? He was probably the worst thing you did to a dude when you were younger."

"Uhm…." Maybe she was ready to leave.

## Chapter Twelve

*D*<sub>*ay Two*</sub>

Kala groaned as they started up the hill. "She gave you an F."

Cooper snorted behind her. He'd been the one up early this morning, waking her with coffee and protein bars and kisses. And she hadn't even karate chopped his throat or anything. She'd known it was him.

She hadn't dreamed the night before.

"I think I probably deserved it. Also, she let me make up that paper."

Why had she ever broached this subject? All of her sins were, as Shakespeare put it, remembered. "Mrs. Teacle was cheating on her taxes. You didn't even cheat. You just didn't understand *The Scarlet Letter*."

"I watched the *Wishbone* version. They left things out."

"And Mrs. Teacle left out forty thousand dollars' worth of winnings from Vegas." It was a case closed in her head.

"You're a menace."

*Day Three*

Cooper knew he should be irritated that Joyce Reed was nowhere to be found. They walked from known campsite to known campsite, stopping at Ranger stations to ask around. Other than that, it was the two of them, and they didn't seem to be getting anywhere.

Definitely should be irritated, and yet he couldn't work up the will. All he could find was this weird sense of contentment when she didn't hesitate to allow him to give her a hand up a slippery rock surface. "So Jimmy. Mrs. Teacle, who gave me a valid F and wasn't expecting a group of teen hacker vigilantes."

Her nose wrinkled, and she looked adorable. "It wasn't a group, per se. It was me and Lou."

Lou had helped her get revenge on anyone who Kala vaguely believed hurt him, and the last two years of high school, Cooper had been her accomplice in some shady shit she pulled on people who hurt Lou. The first time she'd asked him had felt like sunshine coming back in his life. Now he could see it had been a test to see if he could leave a little of his Captain America, right-is-right and wrong-is-wrong mentality behind. His baby was on the morally gray side even back then. "You don't need more than you and Lou. I'm only trying to get a full accounting of all the villains my personal Batman took out."

"Black Widow, please," she corrected as she moved along the tree line. Above them a gloriously blue sky shone down.

She was happy here. Relaxed and in her element in a way he hadn't known she could be. She was a mystery, and he loved uncovering new facets of her.

"Black Widow," he agreed. "So we have Jimmy, who got a smack down. Mrs. Teacle got a couple of weeks in prison."

"Minimum security," Kala pointed out. "And she had to sell that Porsche that made her look like a douchebag. You're welcome."

He wasn't done. They'd been spending a lot of time going over her list. When they weren't fucking. They'd done a lot of fucking. She seemed to be making up for lost time.

He was her only lover. He intended to keep it that way.

"Susie Clifton, who broke up with me right before prom, had some very nasty texts about her that her friends on the cheerleading team released to the school website." He was still surprised at that one. He shouldn't be. She'd loved him back then. She just hadn't trusted him. "My traveling team coach, my boss at the ice cream shop."

She turned, her thumbs under the straps of her backpack.

"There's probably more. You're lucky I didn't keep up with you in college. And you know what? You've never once risked prison time to get revenge on someone who hurt me. Where's the love, McKay?"

Oh, she'd started using that word. Maybe not exactly the way he wanted her to, but it was creeping into her vocabulary in non-ironic ways. He moved in, standing over her. When she wasn't in fuck-me heels, he had a good half foot on her. He let his hand caress her cheek. "Point them my way and I'll take 'em all out. I promise."

Her lips curled up slightly. "What are you going to do? Give them a good talking to?"

Oh, she thought he was soft. Luckily, he knew how to speak Taggart. "I promise you if I get my hands on Manny Huisman, I won't talk to him. I don't know. Maybe I will. We can have a conversation about internal organs while I feed him his. He's a doctor, right?"

There was a hitch to her breath that got his cock hard. "A bad doctor. A doctor who should definitely be experimented on. Tell me more."

He whispered in her ear and knew they were camping right here tonight.

*Day Four*

"What do you mean he wasn't there?" Kala held the sat phone to her ear and thanked the universe her dad was better equipped than the Agency. He'd sent this brand-new state of the art baby with them, and her sister was coming in perfectly clear even though they were miles and miles away from the nearest cell tower. It didn't matter because this sucker was pinging around space.

Her twin sniffled. "They said he was on another mission. But I know he was in Toronto before I got there."

"How would you know?" She was a menace? Had Cooper met her twin?

"I make friends. I might have made friends with a couple of Canadian analysts we've worked with. You know, the ones you haven't met."

That was fair. She could be hell on an analyst. It was best to let her twin deal with the admin stuff. Or Coop. He was good with that. If they ever managed MT, she would be the big-picture chick and Coop would deal with the day-to-day stuff.

Was she actually seeing a future where she was married to Cooper and they took over McKay-Taggart? It wouldn't happen. It was far more likely Tash would take over. Tash could do it all.

Although it wasn't like her dad was some easy to get along with dude, and he'd managed. Of course, he tended to be more open to therapy than she was. It might be time to think about why it worked for the old man.

For now, her sister was really better at parts of this game they played. "So you got some Canadian analyst to betray her country and tell you where their very valuable assets are?"

Kenzie huffed over the line. "It's not like that. We were talking. I took her out to lunch and I mentioned how sad I was to have missed Ben." The sniffling started again. "She said he took off right after the meeting where they informed everyone the Agency was coming in. She wasn't sure he knew it would be me, though. Do you think he was trying to avoid Dad? He hasn't been particularly nice to Ben."

Because Ben was an asshole, but that was Kenzie's type and she was trying to be more magnanimous. Her sister couldn't help her terrible taste in men. "I think he'll be more polite from now on since Ben did the whole save-me thing. I'm surprised. Carys told me you made up in the hospital."

"Babe, what are you doing?" Cooper strode into their camp, two big fish dangling from his line. "You know that's for emergencies only. Is that Kenz?"

Yum. Trout. They were eating well tonight. And she knew what the sat phone was for. "It is an emergency. Kenzie got to Canada and Ben fled before they were supposed to meet."

Coop's eyes went wide. "Damn. Continue, but can't you put her on speaker?"

Yes, she was totally in love with this man. She put her sister on speaker. "Tell us everything."

"Is that Coop? Are you still doing him?" her sister asked. "Tell me, is he as good at oral as I've heard?"

"And I'm out." Cooper walked away.

"Who the hell did you hear that from?" Kala asked. "But for the record, yeah."

*Day Five*

Finally they were using the sat phone for what it was meant to be used for. Intelligence. Cooper sat with Kala between his legs, lying back against his chest as her father's voice could be heard coming from the sat link.

This was why he'd refused to bring a laptop along. Oh, he'd said it was because of the weight and delicacy of the thing, but he hadn't wanted visuals. If they'd had this meeting coming in on a screen, he wouldn't have been able to get Kala to relax against him.

Just a couple of days and she was already so much more affectionate.

"Lou, what did you find out?" Big Tag asked over the line.

"I spent three days in the lab with the Swedish police, and there's zero question in my mind the bomb placed on Dr. Walsh's car was made by the same person who created both the Jakarta bombs and the London bombs from a couple of years ago," Lou explained.

"But they aren't the same as the ones Huisman used to blow up his own house?" Kala asked.

He ran his hands over her arms and wrapped one around her, just below her breasts. He didn't want to think about that day. He dreamed about it far too often. Lately he'd been the one with nightmares and Kala the one to soothe him.

She would smooth back his hair and kiss his forehead even when she was half asleep.

"No," Lou replied. "Those were much more rudimentary. And I probably shouldn't use that word because they weren't. I only mean by comparison. It's obvious Huisman has some arms dealer connections. The bombs he used in Toronto are what one would expect. This one is something else. A leap ahead."

"So we believe Zach is working with the mysterious bombmaker," Tristan asked. "I don't want to believe it, but it would explain why he did what he did with The Jester."

"You think he killed The Jester because he was going to out the bombmaker?" Cooper asked. He didn't want to believe it either, but the evidence was stacking up against his friend.

"What other reason can you think of?" TJ asked. "He knew Tris had found The Jester and was going to bring him in for questioning.

Zach got there first. He hired the assassin to take the fall for him, but I would bet anything he did the deed himself."

"Yeah, I don't buy the whole the assassin got scared off and came back thing. It was a sloppy story in the first place," Kala said. "But I also don't think we're being very creative. There could be several reasons he did it. He could be protecting someone."

She was such an enigma. He would bet she would be the first to go all paranoid about a team member who'd obviously betrayed them. But when she cared about a person, she had a lot of rope to give.

He hoped Zach didn't use it to hang them all.

"Well, that's why you're in the middle of the wilderness." Charlotte Taggart's voice came over the line. "Any word on his aunt yet?"

"We're talking to some rangers this afternoon," Cooper replied. "If we don't find her in a day or two, I'm afraid we're going to have to get transport to another part of the park."

Rocky Mountain National Park was four hundred and fifteen square miles of wilderness. They'd searched from where Joyce had left her van, but now he had to consider she'd gotten some kind of transportation to another part of the park.

"If you don't find her soon, I'm pulling you," Big Tag said. "The Canadians think they have a potential line on where Huisman's hiding. They know he's left Canada. They have a private jet flying out a few hours after he blew up his house, and it seems to have flown directly for Russia."

Nice. "Non-extradition treaty. Of course that's where he went. Does he still have millions of dollars?"

"Of course he does, babe," Kala said, and he could practically see the expression on her face. It was her dumbass-said-what face. "He would have prepped for all of this. He's an asshole but a prepared one. I assure you the fucker has cash everywhere."

She wasn't wrong.

"What is he planning on doing in Russia?" TJ asked.

"Probably make it his base," Kenzie replied. "We know he's interested in shaking up Southeast Asia. There are some soft targets that would disrupt western supply chains if they were hit. And we always have the threat of losing Taiwan and the supply of semiconductors. The Canadians are specifically worried about that."

"But not worried enough to send Ben Parker," Tristan quipped.

Tris was an asshole. "I'm sure he was on an important op."

Kala snorted. "Sure he was. It was super important that he avoid my sister. He's still butt hurt because he thinks Coop has the hots for her."

"For Ms. Magenta," Kenzie corrected.

"Well, he can't tell the difference, and Coop lost his shit," Big Tag complained.

Her hand came up, covering his, and her head tilted so he could see her shake her head.

"I thought she was dead. Damn straight I lost my shit," Cooper said as she winked at him and resettled. He was going to murder Huisman.

And he wished he could murder Julia Ennis and all the bastards who'd worked for her. Maybe in the next life.

"Well, I'm her dad and I didn't lose my shit," Big Tag shot back.

Charlotte snorted. It was funny that he knew exactly who'd made that sound.

"Well, it's for the best," Kenzie said, and he could practically see her chin come up in that "I'm going to martyr myself for the sake of the team" way. "It's done and we don't have to worry about him anymore. So now that we all have our assignments, let's talk about the important thing. There are bets at The Hideout that Cooper's going to come back from this assignment as Kala's sub."

"I'll take that bet," TJ said.

And they were done.

*Day Six*

Cooper was almost sure they hit paydirt when they saw the small cloud of smoke coming over the ridge. "Maybe the hiker was right."

They'd met with a hiker early this morning. She was walking the Continental Divide trail and had been more than happy to join them for a coffee when she'd come across their camp. She'd told them about the older lady she'd met the day before about four hours walk to the west in one of the remotest parts of the trail. She'd called herself Joyce and had given the young woman some granola and filtered water and a place to rest for a couple of hours.

And she'd mentioned the woman's handsome son, who'd shown

up at the end of their visit. Though she hadn't been introduced, she'd gotten a glimpse of the man before Joyce had hustled her off.

Tall. Dark hair. When they'd questioned her she'd said she couldn't be completely sure it was Joyce's son, but she'd given her impression of his age—roughly thirty.

Zach. Zach was here.

Or someone Joyce met in the mountains. One of the things her dossier included was her penchant to make new friends wherever she went.

It also mentioned she might be developing early stage dementia.

"You think she was talking about Zach?" Kala asked.

She'd lost her relaxed humor the minute they'd realized the mission was truly starting. He was dealing with the operative part of his baby, and she could be intimidating. This wasn't the woman who'd spent a shit ton of money on a sat call comforting her sister because her Canadian crush hadn't met with her. Big Tag would try to send that bill to the Agency. Good luck with that. No, this was the woman who'd once left the very same agent her sister was in love with on a plane filled with people who wanted to kill him while she'd used the last parachute.

The trouble was he was attracted to both the kind, loving sister and the deadly operative. "I think we need to be ready in case it is. Our main objective is to bring Zach in."

A brow rose over her blue eyes. "It is?" She frowned. "You called my father."

Worse. "I couldn't get hold of him. I talked to Drake. Baby, you know we're supposed to report in. This could go wrong, and the guys in Bliss need to be ready for an evac if we need it."

"I would rather have had the option, Coop," Kala argued. "This isn't a military op. I don't need instructions."

"We do need guidance."

"I don't. I need to have some flexibility in the field." She sounded irritated.

He stood by his action, but he maybe should have kept it to himself. The truth of the matter was Kala would do what she thought was right, and damn orders. But they needed backup if bad shit went down. He moved into her space, putting his hands on her hips. "I wanted us to have backup. Forgive me."

She sighed. "That's not fair, McKay. You know I can't say no to puppy eyes."

He curled his lips up. "Excellent. Then let's take a break right here."

She went on her toes. "Horny bastard. And no. She could move. We're going in. But later."

He was worried there might not be a later and they would lose this easy companionship they'd found here in the woods. "Fine, but I think on our next vacation I want you to take me to the cabin."

She turned and started down the trail that led into the valley where the smoke was coming from. "You hate the cabin."

He followed her, keeping his voice low. He'd noticed she'd moved her SIG into her shoulder holster. "I don't hate it. I didn't like it when we were teens because you ignored me the couple of times we came to visit. You would be off hanging with other kids, and I wasn't allowed. I actually think a couple of those dudes talked about dating you. Like together. Like Aidan and Tristan together."

She snorted, an oddly sexy sound, but then he found everything about the woman hot. "You're talking about Charlie and Zander Hollister-Wright. They were not truly interested in me. They were interested in making my friend Paige jealous. Gosh, I haven't been back in forever. I didn't even ask about them. The last time I saw her, she was going into college, and they had decided to keep the relationship friendly. Her dad was so cool. He talked about his balls a lot. Fun guy. Well, one of them. You know when it comes to identical twins there's always a fun one."

He was pretty sure that was open to interpretation. In his mind, she was the fun one and Kenz was a little much with all the drama. If Kala had been in love with Ben Parker, she would have simply kidnapped the man and given him the choice to love her or die.

Actually, that would be a fun scenario. "Hey, baby. How open are you to fantasy play?"

She turned, her eyes lighting up. "How open are you to pointed ears and wings?"

Touché. "Definitely something to talk about."

"Who the hell are you?" a feminine voice asked. And then he heard the sound of a rifle cocking.

He held his hands up, turning. A woman with steel gray hair cut in an almost military style stood a few feet down, right inside the tree line. "Just hiking, ma'am."

Joyce Reed wore cargo pants, the legs stuffed inside sturdy boots. She had on a threadbare sweater and glasses held together by tape, but there was a steady look in her eyes that let Cooper know she saw him just fine. The rifle was held with a firm, practiced hand. "You hiking, too, young lady? I'd like to see your hands."

Kala wasn't holding hers up. She simply watched the woman with a wry smile. "I think you see them fine, Joyce. And no, I'm not hiking for fun, though I will admit I've had a good time. Name's Taggart. Kala Taggart. My dad sent me."

Could she not follow a damn plan? They were supposed to be honeymooners. Drake had sent them their cover. It was very thorough, including all the documents they would need, but did Kala use it? Nope. She told the target her name like it wouldn't send her running.

The rifle stayed on her. "You Big Tag's kid?"

"Yep," Kala replied.

"Prove it," Joyce challenged.

He wanted to turn to Kala and ask her how she planned to do that since they were literally traveling undercover. He hadn't brought along his real passport or driver's license. Only Henry Flanders knew who they were, and he was hours away.

"My father's favorite piece of advice is to wear a condom," Kala deadpanned.

The rifle came down, and Joyce grinned. "Damn, Big Tag forgot his own advice and has a kiddo. I mean, I heard he did but here you are. You are way too pretty to be that big bastard's kid. Who'd your momma cheat with?"

Kala moved down the small hill they were on, holding a hand out. "According to my dad, the UPS guy. It's nice to meet you. I work with Zach, too."

Joyce shook her hand. "With my nephew? He's in the Army. He's a captain."

Shit. His aunt didn't know about Zach's Agency work? "Yes, we're both in the military."

Kala's head turned slightly and she frowned his way, but when she turned back to Joyce she said, "I'm in Army intelligence. He's a grunt. He's carrying my stuff around, if you know what I mean."

Oh, if she could be snarky, so could he. "I'm also ensuring my charge stays loose, if you know what I mean."

Kala laughed, the sound booming through the woods. "Good one, babe. Joyce, this is my…boyfriend, Cooper McKay. He really is Navy."

"And I would bet you go by Mrs. Black." Joyce proved she was astute.

"I prefer Ms. Magenta," Kala corrected. "But you can call me Kala because this isn't some Agency operation. This is about Zach."

"What has my boy gotten into now?" Joyce asked with a sigh. "Or the better question…what has my sister dragged her son into? Come on. I've got some whiskey back at camp. Zach's not here right now. He comes and goes, but you can at least tell me what's going on."

Kala began to follow her.

"Baby, you know we're not supposed to… You're going to tell her." It was inevitable. He hoped they had cells for couples wherever the Agency was going to hold them.

Kala smiled and followed.

* * * *

Kala sank down on the bench Joyce had placed in front of the firepit someone had dug. Given how perfectly precise and deep that sucker was, she was betting it hadn't been Joyce. She noticed the way Joyce held her rifle. She was firm and had a steady hand, but she hadn't held the rifle above the middle of her chest even though she'd been below them. The older woman also avoided shifting her left shoulder when she'd set down her pack and welcomed them into camp. She had an old shoulder injury according to her records—yes, she'd read them—and it looked like it definitely still bothered her. She wouldn't be able to lift the shovel enough to dig a pit as deep as the one in front of them.

Zach was here somewhere, and she had to pray he didn't run.

He saved Lou and Aidan when he didn't have to. He talked to Lou. Maybe he would talk to her.

But first she was going to work Joyce for every bit of intel she could, and she would use the woman's obvious love for her dad. "This is nice. I haven't spent a lot of time in this park, but I did go hiking and camping in the national forest land around Bliss."

Joyce sat down on an old camp chair across the pit from Kala and

Coop. Cooper had immediately taken the seat beside Kala, his big presence reminding her she wasn't alone in this op. Nope. She had a keeper, and he might not like the way she played this game.

"Oh, I love that town. I sometimes work in Creede. Just temp jobs where they need me. And sometimes the lodge on Elk Creek Pass has seasonal work." Joyce sat back. "I love it here, but it'll be too cold soon. I'll have to move on to Arizona and California. The desert is beautiful, too."

"I bet it is. How long have you been on the road?" Kala asked.

Cooper turned his head her way and gave her a grin and a wink that said *you're doing great, babe*.

She was pretending to be her sister. Everyone loved Kenzie. Everyone talked to Kenzie. Kenzie cared about people.

Although it wasn't like she hated the woman in front of her. Not at all. Joyce seemed kind. Kala cared about Zach, and this woman had been his rock. Was she pretending to be Kenz or was she simply uncomfortable with the part of herself that actually wanted to know Joyce's story? If she knew Joyce's story, she would probably like her for herself and liking people…it was hard.

Cooper had said she felt deeply. Cooper knew her. Was he right and she was being a coward because caring about people meant opening herself up to hurt? Because the truth of the matter was, she did want to know Joyce's story, the one beyond what was in her file. She wanted to know why she roamed the way she did when once she'd had a place to live and roots.

She also wanted to know why she kept staring at Cooper like he was some golden god of a man deigning to visit her home. Joyce wasn't even trying to take her eyes off him.

The older woman seemed to realize she was staring and shook it off, moving her attention back to Kala. "Oh, I started van life years ago. I never liked to stay in one place too long. It was what I loved about the Army. Never stayed at a base more than a year or two and then we moved out."

"You had a stellar record," Cooper pointed out. "I'm surprised you left."

Her eyes were back on him, concentrating in a way that made Kala uncomfortable. Like she was looking for something in his eyes.

Or Cooper was a work of art and she could still see and appreciate him.

She needed to tamp down her jealousy. Tolerance was more of a Kenzie trait. She could do it. She didn't have to plant a flag and defend her territory from an elderly woman who in all other ways seemed super sweet.

"I didn't want to. I had to. My sister got into some trouble," she said quietly. "Shannon was ten years younger than me. Our momma called her an accident, and not a happy one. I'm afraid I was more of a mother to her than our own. By the time she came along, Mom was bitter and angry all the time. She would tell Shannon that she only had her to spite her biological father."

Sometimes she was reminded how lucky she had it. Her parents were all kinds of awesome.

And weird. Not normal. Not normal did not mean bad.

She'd picked up another inner voice lately, but it was kind of at war with the others. With the ones that told her not normal wasn't bad, but she was. Her sessions with Lena had concentrated on how useful she was to the Agency since she didn't have much of a moral compass. Lena had even made some reference to her father Dextering her—putting her talents to good use since it would be so easy for someone like her to go bad.

It wasn't anything she hadn't heard before, but lately it bugged her.

She'd had all the love she could have gotten, so why was she still the way she was?

"What kind of trouble?" Cooper asked.

Joyce's gaze moved back to Kala. "He likes to pretend, doesn't he?"

See, now she liked the woman again. "It goes with being as hot as he is. He thinks he's a good liar. Obviously, I've read a dossier on you. So has he. We wouldn't be here without all the intel we could find."

She nodded. "Good, then maybe you can explain what's going on with Zach. He won't say a damn thing beyond he's on leave, but I don't believe him. Something's gone wrong. I have to wonder if his damn father ain't back in the picture. Or if it's… Well, the fact that he's here tells me a lot."

Oh, she was interested in all of those words. She wasn't sure what Zach being here told Joyce since she'd asked Kala why he was here, but she'd become confused a couple of times already. Kala zeroed in on what seemed the most important thing. "Zach's dad is in the picture? From what my father discovered, it was a boyfriend who got Shannon in trouble. She was a chemistry student, right?"

"She was the smartest person I ever met," Joyce said with a sigh. "Sometimes I think her life would have been easier if she hadn't been brilliant. It's hard to know so much more than the people around you and to still be stuck in a dismal existence. Our mom put food on the table but not much else. I would work after school so we could buy clothes. Momma spent all the extra money trying to find some new man who would take care of her for more than a night. When you grow up like that you often react one of two ways. It put me off any kind of relationship, and my sister only wanted someone to love her. Wanted to prove she was better than Mom gave her credit for. That girl got a full-ride scholarship to Stanford University. Do you know how hard she worked for that? I still...I don't know why she gave it all up for a man. She could have been something."

There was a lot of nuance left out of her dad's report. "So Shannon gets out of Iowa, goes to California and meets Zach's dad."

Her eyes slid away, sorrow on her face. "Raymond White. He was older than Shannon. At the time she was a senior, and she worked in a lab. I don't pretend to know what she was working on, but I know Ray targeted her because she worked in that lab. He was a low-level drug dealer at the time. He convinced her to use the lab to make some designer drugs that bumped him up a level in his organization. She proved to be excellent at creating drugs. If she was a bartender, she would have been called... What's the name for it now? It's real fancy."

"Mixologist," Cooper provided.

"Did she stay with Ray?" Kala prompted. "I know he was arrested a couple of times."

Joyce nodded. "I was already in the Army then. I didn't know what was happening. She would write letters to me. About her classes and how she was up for a big internship, and then one day they stopped. It was a long time before I could get leave, and when I finally found her, she was pregnant with Zach and fully in Ray's world. I tried to get her to go back to school, but she loved him. She had a nice house and said he treated her real good, and they had a baby on the way. I didn't know better. I had no idea how they were making their money."

"She was still cooking drugs?" Cooper asked. "Did she take them?"

"No. Never. She never did her own drugs," Joyce said like that was some kind of virtue.

Kala didn't get that. Shannon had actively harmed the world for money and love.

"She certainly didn't when she was pregnant. I was in Germany at the time. I thought she was like our mom. She found a man and didn't need her family anymore. I was hurt, but at least I thought she was happy. She sent pictures when Zachary was born, and everything seemed fine. Then it all went to hell. That's when I got out."

"She was arrested." Kala knew this part of the story.

Joyce nodded. "The cartel they worked for decided Ray was cheating them, and he went on the run. Shannon was left holding the bag. I came and got Zach, and that was when I found out she was pregnant again. And she was facing seven to fifteen years in prison."

"Zach told me he wasn't sure why you didn't give him up for adoption. He knew about his sibling," Kala said.

"About his brother," Joyce corrected. "Shannon had a boy. As for Zach, Ray knew about Zach. The cartel knew about Zach. We decided it was better that I watch over him, but we had a shot at hiding him."

And that was the moment she looked at Cooper and Kala's world shifted.

*Or if it's... Well, the fact that he's here tells me a lot.*

Joyce hadn't been talking about Zach. She'd been talking about Cooper. She'd been staring at Cooper like she knew him.

Which she did.

"Joyce, I'm going to need you to tell me where your sister stashed her second son."

## Chapter Thirteen

Cooper wasn't sure what was going on, but it was clear Kala had picked up on something important. It was there in the way she'd sat up, in the gleam in her eyes. Sometimes he simply liked to watch her work. But there was a weird feeling in his gut, some instinct that put him on edge.

"Zach told me his brother was given up for adoption. His mom was in prison and wouldn't be getting out for a long time, so she gave him up. I suspect the dad was completely out of the picture by then," he said, trying to move the conversation along.

He thought about making some excuse to leave. He wanted to check around, to see if he could figure out if Zach was coming back or if Joyce was getting confused. She'd said Zach had shown up but that he came and went. This wasn't the kind of place where one simply showed up out of nowhere and left just as quickly.

And it wasn't like they didn't know where he'd been last week.

The thought of arresting Zach made him kind of sick to his stomach, but he had to do it. He had to bring him in, and then they would figure everything out. Now that he knew more about Zach's mom's story, he understood how he could have had ties that dragged him down.

Could his father have resurfaced and brought him into something dangerous?

"Ray came in and out of Shannon's life. I still don't think he knows about…" Joyce nodded his way like she couldn't stand to talk about the other boy. She probably felt guilty for not taking him in when she'd taken in Zach, but she'd had her reasons.

"But he knows Zach?" Cooper hadn't thought a lot about Zach's father. Zach didn't say much about him. Were they in touch?

Joyce nodded. "He lived with them for about six months before things got real bad, and he left them hanging out to dry. The cartel got upset with him. He was skimming the profits."

"Joyce, I need to know about the adoption," Kala said, leaning in.

"I'm sure it was closed if she was in prison and worried about someone finding out." Cooper knew a bit about adoption since both he and Hunter were adopted. Kala should know something, too, though he was pretty sure Tasha's adoption hadn't been entirely legal.

Kala's eyes stayed on Joyce. "You helped her."

"She's my sister," Joyce said. "Of course I helped her. I'll always help her."

"Do you know where she is?" Cooper asked. Maybe they were going about this the wrong way. Maybe bringing in Shannon Reed would tempt Zach to come in and explain what was happening. "The last time I talked to Zach he said she disappeared when he was fourteen. He said she'd fallen back in with a bad crowd. Was it with his dad?"

"She stopped cooking drugs, if that's what you're asking about," Joyce replied with a frown. "No. While she was in prison she made other connections. I thought the cartel was bad."

He was interested in those connections. They might tell him something about why Zach was doing what he was doing. "If she wasn't cooking drugs, what was she into? Zach made it sound like she was still involved with something criminal."

Kala frowned his way. "I'm fairly certain she started making bombs, Coop. I would bet anything she's our bombmaker and Zach is trying to protect her. Now let me ask my questions."

Damn, it stung when she talked like that.

She softened. "Babe, I'm sorry. I think…I think it's important."

He thought the fact that they might know the name of the bombmaker everyone was looking for was kind of important. But hell, he was just the dude who carried the backpacks. "Sure. Proceed."

Kala looked like she wanted to argue with him but turned back to Joyce. "You helped her pick. You picked the adoptive parents. How did you do it? Did my father help you? Does he know?"

Something cold snaked up Cooper's spine. What the hell was going on? He felt dumb. She knew something he didn't. "Why would your father know about Zach's brother?"

But Kala could be hyper focused at times. She ignored him. "I need to know, Joyce."

Tears shone in Joyce's eyes. "He didn't. Lord, I didn't tell him. I talked to him right before I went out to visit Shannon in prison. I called him because I knew I was going to have to get legal custody of Zach, and Big Tag always helped out his old Army buddies. He gave me some good advice."

Shit. Did Big Tag have something to do with this? Kala was going to be pissed if her father knew something and hadn't told her.

"You didn't tell him about your sister's pregnancy, but he told you something, didn't he?" There was a breathless air of expectation in Kala's voice.

A tear slipped from Joyce's eyes, caressing her cheek. "He told me all about his best friend. He said Alex was looking for a kid to adopt."

The world seemed to slow, time slipping into some weird place where he was there and not there.

Alex was looking for a kid to adopt.

He was the kid Alex McKay adopted.

In a closed adoption. His parents didn't know who the birth mother was, had been told to never expect contact with her. The records had been buried.

"I put you in the safest place I could, Jonathon," Joyce said. "That was what she named you. She knew it wouldn't stick, but it's what she calls you when she dreams about you. Jonathon Michael Reed. You were safe. I made sure you were safe."

"Babe, are you okay?" Kala asked. "Do you need to...like do you want a hug?"

He was Zach's brother. His full-blooded brother.

No. Fucking no. Hunter was his brother. Vivi was his sister. Alex and Eve McKay were his parents.

"Jonathon, don't be mad at her. She was trying to save you. She knew they would use her babies against her." Joyce stood up, her arms coming out. "I missed you so much. Zach missed you."

Zach played some fucking hard-core games. "My name is Cooper."

"Joyce, I think he needs a minute." For once Kala sounded like the cool voice of reason.

It wasn't fair to think it, but he wasn't feeling very fair in the moment. How could she have brought it out like this? She'd known where this was going. She'd used that big brain of hers to pick up on clues he'd missed, and she hadn't thought maybe they should have a private conversation? "Did my father know? Fuck. Why did I even ask that question? Of course he didn't. My dad is always left out of the spy shit, but I can't believe for a second that your dad didn't realize it. Which means he probably knew my biological brother wormed his way onto my team. Maybe I should ask if you knew."

Kala's face flushed and then became a perfectly polite blank. "If I knew I wouldn't have asked the questions. I would have brought it in front of the team, and we would have figured out how to handle it. Joyce said my dad didn't know."

Cooper stood. Tag could play some deep games, too. And maybe Kala wasn't the only one who'd never forgiven him for being a dumbass kid. "Sure, he didn't. Your father is the absolute most paranoid asshole in the history of time, with deep connections to people who can find any record they want to, but he let his best friend adopt a kid without knowing anything about it."

"He wouldn't have wanted to jeopardize the adoption, and why would he have any reason to think there was something weird about it?" Kala asked.

"He wouldn't have found anything." Joyce looked miserable standing there staring at him. "I have connections, too. So did Shannon. If he'd looked, he would have found what we wanted him to find. One of the women she connected with in prison was involved in a group of radicals."

The hits fucking kept coming. "Disrupt? That group?"

Kala frowned. "If she was involved in Disrupt, wouldn't Huisman know how to find her?"

Awesome. Something he'd put together before her. "Not if she did what she seems to do and left the group and went on the run."

"That wasn't the name, though I do think at one point she did some work for them. You have to understand how scared she was when she was in jail. The cartel could get to her in there. She needed protection," Joyce tried to explain.

He didn't want to hear it. He still didn't buy that Big Tag hadn't known. Nothing this woman told him would change how he felt, and it was time to do the fucking job they'd come to do. "I'm calling Flanders. He can meet us in the meadow about half a mile back. Joyce Reed, I'm taking you into custody."

Her eyes went wide.

Kala stood. "Hey, we need to talk about this."

"Now you want to talk? You didn't think about talking before you blew up my entire childhood?" He loved her but damn it could be hard sometimes.

"I wasn't certain." Kala's tone was so even, he knew she was forcing herself to stay calm. "I thought she might be talking about you, but I wasn't a hundred percent. I didn't think it was a good idea to stop the conversation. You know some people freeze up."

"So it was all for the op."

She nodded like it was good he understood. "Of course."

He was afraid he understood all too well. "I kind of thought you cared more about me than an op."

"I do. Didn't you want to know? Coop, Zach is your brother, and he's doing all of this to protect your mom."

"Eve McKay is my mother," he insisted. "I doubt he's protecting her. And Zach is not my fucking brother. He's a liar who betrayed his whole team. That team. That's my family."

"And he was part of it. Babe, I know you're upset, but think about how he treated you."

He didn't want to think about anything at this point but getting home to his parents. He wasn't being reasonable, and there were warning clangs going off in his head that he should slow down. Cool off. "That was my family, but if you Taggarts kept this from my dad…"

"You Taggarts?" Kala asked.

"I mean your dad."

She shook her head. "No, you didn't. Which Taggarts are you talking about? My mom? I'm pretty sure if Dad knew she did. He likes to play the spy, but he's actually a surprisingly gossipy old dude. My sisters? I don't think so. You're talking about me. You're sitting there wondering what? If I knew about this the whole time and suddenly decided to spring it on you here and now? Do you think I set the whole thing up?"

Of course he didn't. "Did you?"

She huffed. "Why, Coop? Why would I do this? You're not acting rationally. I know it's a lot to take in, but I need you to be Cooper McKay right now. You know I wouldn't do this to you. I'm as surprised as you are."

He couldn't tell. "I would bet your blood pressure didn't even rise."

"Ah, we're at the cold-blooded snake phase of the argument. Well, I'm sorry. I was trying to do my job the only way I know how, and it did not include a bunch of drama."

He got into her space, something nasty twisting inside him. "Oh, because you never cause drama."

She stared straight at him. "I don't. I handle this job with precision. Do you think I lost my shit when I found out my sister got shot? I didn't. I did my job."

She was bringing this up? "You're mad at me because I was upset I thought you died?"

"You blew a whole lot of cover," she shot back. "Why do you think Ben Parker wasn't there when Kenz got to Canada? We lost a valuable asset because you couldn't keep it together."

"Because I thought you were fucking dead." He shook his head, anger flaring. He loved this woman and she was bitching at him because he was upset she got hurt? "I suppose if it had been me, you would have shrugged and moved on, Ms. Magenta to the core. Do I mean anything at all to you? Is this your way to get back at me?"

Her shoulders fell. "Of course not, and yes, you do. But Coop, what we do is important, and we can't allow personal feelings in. Not until we're alone." Her head shook. "This is stupid."

"Of course it's stupid. It's my feelings so it's stupid."

"Damn it. I didn't mean that."

He shook his head. "No, you didn't. It's all feelings, isn't it? You don't have any so all emotions are useless."

A blank expression spread across her face, and he could see her shutting down. "I think you should go and call Henry. I'll handle the rest of the interview. You're obviously too close to this. If I'd known you were Zach's brother, I would never have brought you with me."

He felt his fists clench. "Oh, do you think you can bench me, baby?"

"I think I just did, and don't call me that again," she said quietly. "If this is what you think of me, our relationship is over."

He should have known how she would handle this. "One fight? One fight is all it took? The great Kala Taggart can't handle a single argument?"

"I'm not doing this with you right now." She turned to Joyce, who stood watching them, hands shaking. "Joyce, I'm not bringing you in, but I would like to talk further with you. Is it all right if I hang out with you? Maybe bring in my dad? Your sister is in real trouble, and so is Zach. It's serious, and I want to help."

So fucking kind. So reasonable for someone who'd lied. Never for him. No. She wouldn't ever play a role for him. He loved her and this was how she treated him?

*Like you're her safe space. Like she doesn't have to pretend with you.*

He wasn't listening to that fucking voice right now.

His whole life was a lie, and so was she. How did he fucking know that he wasn't bait? That she and her father hadn't used him like they'd once used Dare. They'd nearly wrecked Dare's life. He knew what they were capable of.

*And you were with them. You were there. And you know she's right about what happened with Parker. You set the whole team back with him. This is the spy game, not some fun afternoon in the fucking park.*

Was she serious? Was she picking the job over him?

Or was he being a butt hurt idiot, and she was trying to keep things together?

"I'm not going anywhere, Kala." He was right about a few things, and they would need to sit down and discuss this whole situation when he'd calmed down. Deep inside he trusted Big Tag. He loved Kala. It was too much to process right this second. The best plan of action was to pull everyone in. If Zach was worried about his aunt, he could come to Dallas to find her. "Not without Joyce Reed. You're not my boss in the field no matter what you seem to think. I'm calling it. We head back."

That brow cocked, a sure sign she was getting stubborn. Getting more stubborn. She'd been born that way, and he wasn't handling this situation properly, but then she'd done absolutely nothing to handle him properly either. Why did it always have to be him?

Joyce started to move.

That wasn't happening. "Move again, Joyce, and I'll have you in cuffs in a heartbeat. You can either come in willingly or I'll drag you."

"Or I can take you out right here and now, brother," a deep voice said. "Hands up, Coop. Right fucking now. Don't think I won't take out a knee or something."

Zach stepped out from behind a massive cedar wearing fatigues and holding a Glock on him.

"Don't you fucking call me brother," Cooper replied, anger surging at the sight of him. But he put his hands up. "Kala, get behind me."

All Zach would have to do was get hold of Kala and Cooper would be forced to do whatever he wanted.

"Boys, there's no reason to fight. Jon…Cooper, Zach loves you," Joyce said.

Kala still hadn't moved.

"Coop, I'm not joking," Zach said, his eyes moving from Cooper to Kala and back again. "Do not make a move. I won't kill you, but I can't let you take her."

A long sigh came from Kala. "But girls are too emotional to make big decisions. Sure."

"I said get behind me," Cooper reiterated between clenched teeth.

"Who the fuck do you think I am, McKay?" Kala asked. "I was right. You want some sweet thing you can protect. I don't need protection. If I wanted to take Zach out, I would have done it. I think it would be way more productive if we all sat down and had a chat. Joyce, you got any booze? I could use a drink."

Oh, she was fully in her Ms. Magenta, badass persona, and he didn't think he would be getting her back anytime soon. It was time to retreat. Lucky for him, he had the sat phone and could call for reinforcements. He would walk away since she didn't need him and call back to base. Drake, not Big Tag, who would absolutely side with his daughter no matter how she wanted to fuck up an op. Kala was Big Tag's precious girl who could do no wrong.

He kept his hands up, moving back toward his pack. It held the blankets they'd wrapped themselves in, the meals she'd made for them. "Fine. You guys have a blast. I can see I am not needed here."

He would walk away, throw it all in Drake's lap, and quit. He would go back to the Navy and not come home again. Not for a long fucking time.

Zach sighed. "Don't reach for that pack, man. Please, Coop. Don't make me do this."

"He's not going to listen," Kala said with the saddest sigh. "He thinks I betrayed him."

"How would you know?" Zach asked.

"He's not thinking logically," she replied.

"Fuck you both." They were acting like this was a nothing situation. Like it happened every day and he should chill.

"Auntie." Zach said her name like it was an order she should know how to obey.

"I'm so sorry, Jon," Joyce said right before picking up her rifle and firing.

A dart hit his thigh. Damn. He'd thought it was a real rifle, but then he'd also thought what he'd had with Kala was real this time, and he was wrong about that.

Still, he looked her way as the drugs started to course through his system. She ran toward him, getting her arms under him, though his weight immediately dragged her down.

She was the last thing he saw as the world went dark.

\* \* \* \*

Well, that had gone about as poorly as it could.

Kala eased Cooper's unconscious body into what seemed like a comfortable position, gently maneuvering his head onto a pillow she fashioned from her jacket.

Her heart ached. It felt like it had broken utterly, but she kept her expression calm. There would be time later to cry. Alone. She wouldn't call Lou or her sisters. She wouldn't contact her mom.

She would deal with this alone because that was how she was going to be for the rest of her life.

"Are you okay?" Zach asked like he hadn't betrayed his team and walked out and oh, never mentioned he had ties that they couldn't imagine. Also, he was a dumbass because he offered her a hand up. "He didn't mean any of that, you know. He was overwhelmed."

She calmly took the proffered hand and allowed Zach to haul her up. Then the minute she was on her feet, she used her other hand to punch him right in his nose. Hard.

He groaned and winced. "Damn. I should have seen that coming."

"Zach?" Joyce asked, pointing the tranquilizer gun toward Kala.

That was not happening. "I will fucking end you if you tranq me."

He waved a hand his aunt's way. "Don't. She's the reasonable one. And honestly, I deserved that punch and more." He stared down at Cooper. "I know you won't believe me, but I never meant for him to find out. Certainly not that way. I guess somewhere in the back of my head it would come out one day and he would be happy about it. That's never going to happen."

She wasn't so sure. "Cooper can be very forgiving. I think once he calms down and you explain the situation to him, he'll want to talk. He'll certainly be curious."

"Yeah, but I think he'll be talking to you," Zach returned. "He didn't mean a word of that, Kala. He loves you. I've always known that."

But he didn't. He was pretending she was something she wasn't. Or maybe there was a softer part of herself that he brought out, but she couldn't shove the rest of her soul away and become some chick who hid behind him during a fight.

The sad part was she couldn't even argue with Cooper. He knew her. He was right about most of it. She was ruthless. She did put the op first. If he'd been carried out of that house in Toronto and she'd thought he was dead, she would have broken inside, but no one would have seen it. Not until her whole team was safe. She owed it to the op and her team to keep her personal feelings hidden away. And for Cooper that meant she didn't have any.

He was so lovely, and she'd been right all these years. They couldn't work. He was holding on to someone who never existed.

He thought she was capable of betraying him. It was the most ridiculous accusation, and if he thought about it for two minutes, it wouldn't have come out of his mouth. But it had. When he didn't think, didn't plan his words, he told her what he truly thought of her.

Her whole soul felt heavy. The tears were right there, waiting to come out in a torrent.

And then she could be done with them. This would be the last time she would cry for Cooper McKay. He made the decision for her, and there was a piece of her grateful to him for doing it.

She took a long breath and looked up to Zach, who was still holding his nose. "Did I break it?"

His head shook. "Nah. You pulled your punch. Or you were too impatient and didn't wait until you were solidly on the ground. Want to go again?"

No one ever said Zach wasn't fair. She actually believed the man would stand there and take the punch. And not because she was a girl and it wouldn't hurt. This was precisely why she thought Cooper was being too emotional. If he hadn't been, he would have seen how calm Zach was. "I'll pass. You going to give me hell? I meant what I said. If you use one of those darts on me, there won't be a place on earth you can hide."

He holstered his Glock, slipping it under his arm. "Auntie, stand down. She's not going to freak out on us."

Joyce was crying as she looked down at Cooper. "He looks like my granddad. I saw it the minute he walked into camp. Does your momma know he's here? Zach, something's happening. Something you're not telling me."

Zach sent Kala a "see what you've done" look. "Pretty sure Mom knows nothing, but then I've barely talked to her. Finding her is one of my problems. How much has Kala figured out?"

"Enough to know she's the bombmaker." Apparently he hadn't been listening the whole time. "Did she make the bomb you put on Rebecca's car or did you learn how to do it, too?"

Zach's head fell back on a groan. "I should have known this would get heinously fucked up. The truth of the matter is I panicked when I screwed up with Tris. If I'd been thinking and not worried about losing my friends, I could have saved it. You want a beer? There's also whiskey, but it's not what your dad drinks."

She stared down at Cooper. "What was the dosage?"

She wanted to know if it was meant for a man or a bear. If it was a bear dose, she needed to get him to medical care.

Zach moved to the cooler, pulling out two longnecks. "Kala, I wouldn't hurt my brother. It's precisely why my aunt is carrying a tranquilizer gun with man-dosed darts and not something with real bullets. She's an excellent shot, but she can be paranoid at times."

"It's not paranoia, son," Joyce argued. "The damn Agency

walked into my camp in the middle of nowhere looking for you. So it's not paranoia. But he is right that I can shoot first and then really wish I'd asked some questions. Though I don't think I would have seen that face and shot."

So Cooper would be okay, and that was all that mattered. Now she had a job to do. She took the beer and pulled the cap off. She should throw it back in his face since the last drink she'd taken from an actual bartender had been drugged. She stared at it for a moment.

"It's not the same as Canada," he said quietly, tipping his own beer back and taking a long drink. "That asshole got you because you like super-bougie vodka. You watched him open the bottle. Watched him make the drink. If you weren't so fancy, the bottle wouldn't have had a cork that makes it easy to drug."

"I also tested the fucker." He was right, and honestly, if he wanted to drug her, the rifle was still loaded. Deep down she trusted this man. "How was I supposed to know Huisman spends his time developing new ways to rape women? Asshole."

Zach tipped his bottle her way before taking a seat. "With you, sister. Now tell me what's going on with Devi."

She sat across from him and rolled her eyes. "Sure. Let's gossip about my cousin. No, Zach. You either talk or I call Henry Flanders right now and maybe you get away. Don't think I'm not serious. I just wrecked the only good relationship I've ever had. I would rather you tell me what I need to know than fight you."

Zach sighed. "It's two against one. I know you're good, but I might have been holding back on you."

Yeah, she got that. "I think I can convince your aunt to help me out since you didn't talk to her about what's going on. Joyce, your nephew has been working with the Agency for years. Now I believe he worked his way on my team because he knew about Cooper, but he's also used that position to protect his mother, who is an illegal arms dealer."

"Is this true?" Joyce asked.

"She's not a dealer," Zach returned. "She doesn't want to be in this world, but once you're in it's hard to get out. She didn't realize what Disrupt would try to do with her bombs."

A laugh huffed from Kala's chest. "She didn't realize they would use bombs to blow shit up? Really? Do they have another use? Like an anxiety-inducing footstool?"

"You know as well as I do that sometimes war is necessary," Zach replied evenly, his eyes on her. "She's not what you think."

"Shannon is a good girl deep down." Joyce sniffled but kept that rifle close. "She thinks she's helping people."

Joyce was delusional, but she wasn't about to argue with the woman. From what she could tell, Shannon and Zach were the only family Joyce had in all the world. Well, apart from her sleeping Prince Charming. Who'd lost all his charm.

He'd said all the right things, and she'd fallen for it. Because deep down she was just a pathetic girl who wanted some man to love her. Wanted a particular man to love her.

But she didn't have to be. Lena could help her become something else. Lena could help hone her into the weapon she'd always dreamed of being in her darker moments. A weapon for good, but who didn't have to feel this awful cloud over her head all the time.

How could he think she wanted to hurt him?

*Because everyone sees you as the villain. It might not be fair, but with your talents, they always might.*

It hadn't been the happiest thing she'd heard in therapy, but at least Lena didn't hold back. Kai was always soft and gentle with her. He never would have put the hard truth out there. Kai asked questions. Lena gave truth.

"My mother has done some things she's certainly not proud of. She did them to survive. Auntie, you start packing up." Zach sighed and sat back, scrubbing a hand over his slightly shaggy head. He'd let his dark hair grow out and was now sporting a beard.

How had she not seen the similarities in their faces? Cooper and Zach had the same basic coloring, but almost identical jawlines and lips. "With the kind of information I'm sure she has, she could have come to the Agency at any time. Or the FBI."

"She's had enough of prison," Zach said. "And I can't convince her she can make a deal. I can't justify everything she's done. I can only tell you she didn't want to be involved with Huisman. She's been working with a couple of groups in Africa and Southeast Asia."

Joyce started to move, throwing her possessions into a ragged old backpack.

Kala concentrated on the discussion at hand. "Let me guess. Rebel groups."

"Yeah. She became friends with a woman in prison who was

active with a group trying to free her home country from an authoritarian leader. It became her cause. When she got out of prison, she went underground, and I didn't hear from her for years," Zach explained.

"So you didn't go into the Army in order to gain a position you could help her from?" She was still trying to grasp where this story intersected with finding Cooper. It was obvious now how Zach had been trying to get close to his biological brother. Zach had encouraged Coop to spend time with him, hanging out and going to the movies when they weren't on a mission. When he'd gotten close to Devi, they'd gone out a couple of times. Cooper had begged her to go with him so he wasn't the third wheel.

She'd gone because it was fun to pretend for a moment that she was with him for real and they were a couple out with friends and family.

Devi was going to be devastated.

"I've been honest about why I went into the military. I got a full-ride scholarship to a local college, but the job market when I came out wasn't great. I went into the military because it was the only way to get out of the trailer park I grew up in, no offense, Auntie."

"None taken. I got out, too," Joyce replied as she took apart her water filtration system. "I always wanted better for you and Jonny. For you and Cooper."

"Did you know what your mother was involved in when you went into the military?" Kala took a sip of the beer. It was cold and cheap, and she would probably be drinking on her own soon, so she should get used to cheap. "I want to know when you decided to infiltrate your biological brother's life, and how did you know since the secrecy around it has now been well established?"

She didn't believe her father would know and not tell his best friend. She didn't believe Alex McKay would know and not tell his son.

She wished Cooper had the same faith in her and her family.

"I knew because I found pictures hidden in my aunt's closet." Zach stared into the distance, like he was lost in memory. "I was twelve and looking for blankets, but I pulled it out and the box fell on my head and spilled everywhere."

"I should have watched him more, but I had to work so he was alone a lot," Joyce admitted.

"You did the best you possibly could," Zach assured her before focusing on Kala. "I asked about why there were pictures of my mom with a baby who wasn't me. I had seen all the pictures of my birth, so I knew it wasn't me. There was also a medical bracelet with the name Jonathon Reed. I confronted her when she got home from working twelve hours, and she broke down and told me everything. Including the plot to ensure my brother was adopted by Alex and Eve McKay."

"I also told him it was to protect…Cooper. To protect him," Joyce said with a firm tone. "We never meant to bother him again. He wasn't supposed to know we existed."

"And I screwed that up. I honestly didn't mean to ever seek him out. I hadn't heard from my mother in years at the time." His eyes got that far-off look again. "And then I heard some news. My unit had been working with some Agency operatives, and I was in a debrief at Langley and I overheard a conversation about a new team that was forming. They were looking for a military liaison. This particular group I'd worked with before, and they asked my opinion. They were worried about giving this Big Tag guy too much power. Well, I knew that name. I was curious. I offered to check it out, and then I found out who was on the team."

He'd likely seen the name McKay, done some research, and figured this was the way to meet his brother. "You should have come forward."

"Why? I never meant to tell him. Ever. I meant to be his friend, his brother in everything but name," Zach explained. "I thought the danger was probably past, but I didn't want to wreck him. He loves his parents. He didn't seem to need to know more, so I let it be. But that doesn't mean I didn't grow to love him. He's got a huge family. I do not. Yes, I wanted to be close to my brother. I still do."

She wasn't getting into this with him. Let the shrinks do their jobs. It was enough to know her father had no idea. He would have looked into Zach, but with no reason to question the connections, why would he have found them? Her father wasn't a god, no matter what that T-shirt he wore said. "When did your mother get in touch with you?"

His eyes closed briefly, and when he opened them again, there was a certain amount of resignation there. "During the investigation into The Jester. I was working with Tristan on another team, so she had no idea about Cooper. She'd been dealing with The Jester, and when she refused to make bombs for the Disrupt group, he threatened to out her. At first she was afraid of going to jail again."

She knew how this ended. "And then she was afraid of Huisman."

"Yes. I managed to take out The Jester, but Huisman is smart and he has connections no one in our world has," Zach admitted. "I thought she would be safe with Tristan pretending to be The Jester. I thought I could manipulate the situation, but at some point, Huisman figured out her name and he started to look for Shannon Reed. He figured out I'm her son, and here we are."

Kala glanced over, and Joyce was making quick work of the camp.

"Huisman didn't care about Tris and Carys, did he? He didn't give a shit about me." Bitterness tinged Kala's words. "We were all incidental to the one he was trying to get. You. Huisman always wanted you. Hell, he even got the wrong sister. He wanted Tash because he knew you would do anything for Tasha."

"I would do anything for you," Zach rasped out. "He had me the minute he took a member of my team. Kala, I would never betray my team that way."

"No, but you'll lie to us," she shot back. "You'll keep pertinent information. If we knew, we would have been on guard."

"And I think about that every single day and twice as much at night. I know I broke trust, but she's my mother."

She was going to have to make a decision and soon. The truth was she could probably take Joyce and force Zach to come with her. But she wasn't sure that was the way to go. They needed to lower the temp, not raise it. "You made your choice. I respect it. Are you going to respect mine?"

A chuckle came from his throat. "I'm glad it was you. Yeah, I'm going to respect it, but I need more time. You can force me to come with you, but everything falls apart the second I'm in custody. Let me figure out where she is. I'm the only one who can get her out of hiding. Once she's safe, I'll come in. I promise, Kala. I just want her to be safe."

"We can ensure that." Well, the team could since she would likely be on her own by then.

His head shook. "Somehow I think your father will ensure I'm in prison. Which I'll be willing to do after I finish what I have to."

"This isn't merely about finding your mother, is it?" He was definitely hiding something.

His head shook. "It's best that I leave you out of it."

"Or you can bring me in and I can help you."

His lips curled up slightly as he took another sip. "I know you would. But it's too dangerous, and quite frankly, my brother would be pissed if I dragged you into it."

She wasn't going to let him bring Cooper into this. "Your brother made himself plain."

"No, my brother had a hissy fit that he will be deeply apologetic for later on, and you know it," Zach pointed out.

She knew his brother better than he did. "*In vino veritas* and all that. In this case the rage was the wine."

"There's no truth in rage and you know it." Zach's gaze softened. "Kala, this isn't about him. He was put in a terrible position and freaked out. It wasn't the best reaction, but it could happen to any of us. This is about you. He said the wrong thing and now you're retreating. Don't."

She could turn this around on him. "Says the guy who ran away and broke my cousin's heart."

He flushed. "I didn't mean to do that."

"Did you get close to Devi so you could stay close to Cooper?" Their time was almost up, and her decision was pretty much made. But there was still intel to be had. "Since Tasha friend zoned you, and you're definitely not Kenzie's type since she only likes douchebags."

Zach leaned in, his eyes steady on her. "Abso-fucking-lutely not. Kala, I'm crazy about Devi. I meant everything I said to her. I meant to come back after the op and move in with Coop and start a damn life. I was ready to throw in the towel when it came to my mother. I figured saving her from The Jester could be my last act as her son, and walking away from all of it could be my first act as Devi's man. That's what I wanted."

"You had a funny way of showing it." Although now that she thought about it… "The bomb on Walsh's car was a warning."

"Of course it was. I had to get you guys to take this seriously. I know you are, but you'll get more backing if they think Dr. Walsh is in real danger. Which she is," Zach insisted. "They all are now that he's out in the open."

"He's not exactly out in the open, is he? Do you know where he is?" The most important question she would ask all day.

Would it be easier to find him without the encumbrance of a team? She could focus entirely on hunting Huisman down and then her family would be safe. It might ease her conscious about leaving them, though she knew it was for the best.

His expression went dark. "If I knew where he was, I'd be there. And then he wouldn't be in this world any longer. I think if I present his head to Big Tag, I might have a better chance of coming out of this with my own still on my shoulders."

"That chance gets better if you come in with me now," Kala offered.

He seemed to think about it for a moment. "I can't because the minute I come in, it's not just up to your parents. If it was, I might never have left. If you think I wouldn't love to shove this problem on your dad, you're so wrong. I hate this. I got too used to having a team. I fucking miss all of it. But you have to let me do what I need to do. I can find my mother and get the intel we need to take down Huisman, but I can't do it if I'm still working for the Agency. I didn't plan for things to turn out this way, but here we are, and I have to find the silver lining."

"Of being on the run? You have to know we're not the only ones looking for you." The whole Agency wanted Zach brought in. "They sent a shrink out to talk to all of us so she can profile you. They're serious about catching you. So is the military."

"Yeah, that career's down the drain." He finished off the beer. "It's all gone, Kala. My career, the family I wanted, Devi… Let me do one good thing. Let me figure this out. I can't do that from a prison cell. I'm close. I'm meeting with an old friend of my mom's in a couple of days, and I think he might have some actual intel for me. I swear I'll find a way to share it with you, but I have to be out in the field. I have to look like a rogue CIA agent."

"You are. A rogue CIA agent, that is." There was no way around that particular truth. "You built the bomb?"

He nodded. "From some of my mother's notes. The Jester had a bunch of her research, and that was one of the things he was planning on selling. Obviously I'm the one who took his laptop. I'll send you what I have if you let me go, and I'll stay in contact with you. Only you."

"Or you could play me and never see me again because I was

dumb enough to let you go."

"I wouldn't do that to you. I wouldn't do it to him." He glanced over to Cooper. "If you believe nothing else about me, know that I love my brother."

She did believe him, and that was why she had to do what Cooper would never forgive her for. Let Zach go. She stood. "I'm calling my contact and getting out of here. You've got maybe twenty minutes after I make that call."

Zach went still. "You're letting me go?"

"Are you going to call me when you have what you need?"

"Yes." He stood and walked to her, bringing his hands up and then stopping. "Can I touch you?"

She'd never noticed it before. Zach was a touchy-feely guy, but he was always cautious with her. She appreciated it. There were times when it was too much to be touched without knowing it was going to happen. Not with Coop. She was used to him, but everyone else. Even her family sometimes. "Yeah."

He put his hands on her shoulders. "Kala, thank you. I know this might cost you. I won't let you down."

"How do you know? To ask if I want to be touched? I try to look normal." Maybe she wasn't as good at it as she thought she was. She'd gotten used to burying the flinch she sometimes got when she was younger. "It's not anything against you."

Zach's eyes shone with tears as he gently pulled her in for a hug. "I know. It's how you're wired. I know because Coop told me. I know because he spends so fucking much of his time trying to make the world easier for you. I love you. I never used to say those fucking words until I got on this damn team. Didn't even think I knew how to love. I blame your parents. And his. Please don't give up on him."

She was not fucking going to cry. "I think it's best if I do. I don't belong. Not really."

"You do, sister. You don't understand it right now, but you are the center of the freaking universe for so many people. I know sometimes it seems dark, but I'm here for you. Whether or not you give my brother a real shot."

"No you won't. You're going to be running around the world chasing down a bombmaker," she said, trying not to sniffle.

He chuckled. "Always so literal. I meant it in a metaphorical fashion. Also, I promise I'll get a phone and call you. I'll find a way to keep you updated."

"If it helps, I think running around the globe trying to chase down a dangerous person sounds like fun." She kind of wished she could go with him.

But she had to ease out of her situation. If she didn't, her parents would be hurt.

And confused. A confused Ian and Charlotte Taggart could prove difficult to deal with. She had to make the transition work.

Or her dad would be pissed she'd had Zach and let him go and maybe she wouldn't have to worry about it.

He squeezed her gently and then stepped back. "I assure you none of this is fun. I need you to tell Devi if she doesn't start taking her security seriously, I'll be forced to do something about it."

"I already talked to her." How would he know? "Do you have eyes on her?"

"I love her. Of course I do, and she's behaving in a reckless fashion. I have to hope Huisman doesn't know about her, but it might not matter since her last name is Taggart," Zach said gravely. "He wants to hurt all of you. You have to be careful."

"She's got a bodyguard," Kala explained, stepping back. Damn but she'd missed Zach. She hadn't realized how much because she'd been so involved with Cooper. She'd been lost in how good it felt to be close to him and hadn't considered all the other people around her.

"She's pissed and reckless, and I don't think whoever you put on her can handle her," Zach admitted. "Just tell her to take the threat seriously or she'll have to deal with me."

Kala kind of wanted to watch that throw down.

"I'm ready," Joyce said. She stood near Cooper's sleeping body, looking down on him. "I don't want to leave him like this."

"We have to," Zach said with a frown as he hefted his pack. "Hopefully someday he'll forgive us."

Zach and Joyce walked into the thick woods and Kala pulled out the sat phone, making the call she needed to make.

Then she sat down and held Cooper's hand.

For the last time.

## Chapter Fourteen

Cooper came awake slowly, coming to his senses and trying to find his way through the fog.

Why was he in a fog?

He reached out. Kala should be close. She rarely got out of bed unless he was awake. She waited for him to draw her close and make love to her before they rolled out of bed and started the day.

It was kind of his best life.

Fuck, he had a brother. Another brother.

He forced his eyes open. His body felt weighed down. Drugged. He'd been drugged. Zach had shown up and Kala had gotten the truth out of Joyce and he'd been… Fuck, he'd been a dick about it. But damn it, she could have handled it differently.

"Well, good morning sleeping beauty," a familiar voice said.

His father. "Where am I?"

"You're at Big Tag's cabin. I flew out as soon as Kala called. She thought you would probably wake up before I could get here, but the flight time from Dallas is only two hours. Cooper, I didn't know."

He took a long breath, trying to focus. He glanced around and saw he was in a bedroom, laid out on a big bed. The blinds were mostly closed, but he could see a thin stream of light coming through them. "How long was I out?"

That seemingly nice old lady had tranqed him. His aunt. Biological aunt.

Zach was his brother, and he'd yelled at Kala. He'd said some mean things to her, and she sometimes took things far too literally.

"It's been eight hours," his father replied. "Your brother flew me out here. He's going to fly the other jet back. We need to talk. I know this is a shock, but what did you do to Kala?"

So many things. He forced himself up, swinging his legs over so he was upright. And that felt terrible. He caught sight of a picture on the dresser to his left. Big Tag and Charlotte were in the middle, their arms around their kids. Kala stood to the side, her face solemn while all the others were grinning like mad. "Where is she?"

He should talk to her. He'd been too harsh. Way too harsh.

His father looked tired. He was wearing slacks and a button-down, proving he'd likely come straight from the office, gotten into the private jet, and flew all the way to Colorado. No one ever said Alex McKay didn't show up for his kids. "She's out in the kitchen, I think. She's been on the phone with her father or on her laptop. I don't know what happened. That's why I asked. All I know is I haven't seen her look that hollow in a long time. Hunter offered to fly her back. You know when I was a kid growing up I never thought having two corporate jets would be so necessary to my existence."

He tried to stand but fell back on his ass on the mattress.

"Go slow. You took a whole lot of sedative," his father advised.

"Yeah, from fucking Zach." It had been on his orders. He was so angry at Zach he could barely breathe.

"Kala had the doc around these parts come out and check your vitals. He said you were fine," his father explained. "I know she was worried about you, but she won't come back here. She said she was planning on heading home with Hunter. Naturally Hunter needed to go into town for a couple of things before he turned the plane around. I'm glad you're up because I don't think I can keep her here much longer. She might try to walk home."

She wanted to leave him? Damn, had she even blinked when he went down? Or had she been so far in badass operative mode that the fact he was knocked out didn't even faze her? He'd sat by her hospital bed for hours and hours holding her hand, but she was working?

A bitterness welled, an unfamiliar feeling. He wasn't this person, but he couldn't help it right now. He was sick physically and his head was still spinning and she wasn't with him, wasn't worried about him. "Well, if she wants to leave, that's her prerogative. Where's Zach? Is he being held at the sheriff's department? Or does Big Tag have a lockup here?"

He wouldn't put it past the man. Was his dad feeling betrayed? He had a very hard time believing Ian Taggart didn't know something.

His father shifted, staring at him for a moment as though trying to figure out how to handle him. "I thought the two of you were doing okay."

"We were." He sighed. "And we will be. I'll calm down and apologize. I said some harsh things, but I was in a bad place. A place she kind of put me in."

"I assure you she didn't put any of us in this situation. That apparently was the Reed sisters," his father replied. "Kala wasn't even born when we adopted you. Why would you blame her?"

He understood the logic and yet he still had this feeling. "She figured it out way before I did and instead of letting me in on the secret, she kept going. I was a complete idiot. I sat there while she played detective. I mean, I've always known her job came first, but damn it hurt."

His father's eyes were steady on him. "I don't think she meant to hurt you. I do think she sometimes gets lost in her own thoughts. You know this. You know her. What did you say?"

Cooper shook his head. "Nothing that wasn't a normal, natural reaction to finding out I've been lied to all my life."

His father sighed. "That feels dramatic."

"Really? You're not mad?" Cooper asked.

"I'm surprised. I have some questions, but if you're asking if I'm angry that I adopted you and got to be your father, the answer is no. I can't be angry about something I love," his father said. "From what I understand, the Reed sisters were in a desperate situation and Joyce thought you would be best protected if you were part of a family she knew and loved."

"She manipulated the system and put you and your wife in a bad situation," Cooper countered, unwilling to give up on his anger. It felt good. It felt right to be angry.

His father's brows cocked up. "My wife? You're not calling her your mom anymore? It didn't take much to shake you."

He was screwing this up. "I didn't mean it that way. I'm only pointing out what happened."

His father leaned forward, his eyes a steely green. "I'll tell you what happened. I got the son I always wanted, and if they'd asked me directly if I would take you in, I would have. You know Ian and Charlotte pulled some shady shit to save Tasha. Should she be angry with them that they didn't go through the most proper of channels?"

His father wasn't listening to him. "Of course not. Tasha was in real danger."

"Tasha was in an orphanage," his father pointed out. "Your biological mother thought a cartel would take you in order to force her to do their bidding."

"If she was so worried about it, why didn't she make a move to protect Zach?"

"They already knew about Zach." His father sounded deeply annoyed. "They didn't know about you. I would bet she was worried about your biological father as well. From what I can tell, she spent time in jail for him. He could have threatened to hurt Zach to get her to do it. Look, we can argue all night about what they did, but all I know is the result. I got my son and I'm happy with it. Like I said, if they'd asked, the result would have been the same. I'm sorry if you feel like you missed out on something. I suppose deep down you've always felt that way, and I understand. The unknown can be intriguing, but I'm going to ask you to not talk this way around your brother. I assure you he's already wondering if his place with you is about to be taken by Zach."

"The only place I want Zach Reed is in jail, and that's the only good thing to come out of this day," he announced. He was feeling stronger now and got to his feet. "Dad, I'm not saying this the right way. I don't want to have anything to do with Zach or Shannon Reed. I know Kala is upset that I didn't react the way she wanted me to, but for fuck's sake, can't I have a bad reaction every now and then? I can't walk on eggshells around her for the rest of our lives. I accommodate her on everything. Every single thing. It can be exhausting. I need her to be okay with this one thing that hurt the hell out of me."

"I didn't mean to hurt you," a quiet voice said.

Well, of course, she walked in when he was being an asshole. "Kala."

She stood in the doorway, her hair up in a ponytail and dressed to fly. She'd changed into leggings and a long shirt, but she hadn't put on makeup or jewelry. She looked younger than normal, and his father was right. There was a hollowness to her eyes. "Are you feeling okay?"

"I feel like shit," he replied.

"The effects of the sedative should wear off completely soon. The doctor said getting some food into your system might help. I made some soup. It's in the kitchen. Sorry it was all my dad had here." She didn't walk into the room, merely stood at the door as if she didn't think she belonged here.

"I don't want food. Kala, we should talk."

"I don't think that would be productive," she said, her tone firming. "I think you said everything you needed to say, and I do not have a comeback. I heard you loud and clear, and we should both try to be polite from now on."

Polite? There was nothing polite about her or their relationship. "Dad, could you give us the room?"

His father stood, but Kala held out a hand. "There's no need," she said. "I was just checking on you. Hunter should be here soon, and we're going to head to Dallas. You two can stay here for the night so Cooper's ready to fly tomorrow morning. I'm sure my dad will have a meeting on the schedule for tomorrow afternoon since everyone will be back in Dallas."

"You're not going anywhere. You're going to sit down and talk this out with me."

"I think I'll go see what's taking Hunter so long," his father replied, his discomfort plain.

He eased his way around Kala and moved down the hallway.

"Cooper, don't be difficult about this. I'm trying not to be," she said with a sigh.

"You? Not be difficult?"

Her eyes narrowed. "I said I was trying. I didn't say I was capable. I don't want to have this fight. I don't see the point in it. You don't trust me. I get it. If there's no trust, we have nothing."

And she wasn't trying to be difficult? "How can you say that?"

"You literally accused me of knowing the circumstances of your adoption and not telling you."

She was forgetting certain parts of this morning's conversation.

"How long did it take to figure it out, and why didn't you bother to tell me?"

Her shoulders shrugged, a weary motion. "It wasn't long, Coop. It was a whole fifteen-minute conversation, and I couldn't be sure until she said it out loud. I'm sorry I didn't stop down for a session with you. I was trying to figure out what was going on with Zach. It's the whole damn reason we were in those woods in the first place."

"Yeah, the mission." He wasn't able to keep the bitterness out of his tone. "The mission always comes first."

"It does. It has to. And you always knew that about me. Did you think you could change me?"

"I don't want to change you." He didn't. He just… He wasn't even sure what he wanted at this point except to have her fucking hold him. Which was stupid.

"You do," she said with the saddest look on her face. She moved now, approaching him. She moved into his space, and her hands came up, cupping his cheeks. "I know this thing has been between us for a very long time, but this is the reality, and it didn't take long to break us. I know it's my fault. I don't behave the way I should."

Damn, but she could break his heart. "I don't want you to change, Kala, but can I have an emotion, too?"

Her lips curled up slightly, and she was looking at him like she was studying for a test to be held later. Or memorizing him. "You have all the emotions, babe. You are a fully functional human. And for some reason, I'm not, and I don't think that's going to change. We're always going to end up back here, you and I. If you can't trust me when all logic says I didn't betray you, how will you handle it when the logic goes against me?"

He sighed, his hands going to her hips. At least she was touching him. "I didn't honestly think you had anything to do with the adoption. Obviously."

"But you thought I might have known something and didn't tell you. You definitely thought my dad knew," she pointed out. "If he knows something, I usually do. Mostly because I'm very nosy."

He needed to calm down. "I don't blame you."

"But you did, and deep down there's still a little bit of you wondering if I didn't do it on purpose. It's a good way to throw off Joyce. I couldn't have known Zach would show up. Or maybe I did, and this was how I threw off Zach."

She didn't understand. "I don't think you're working with Zach."

"Can I hug you?" she asked.

"You can always hug me." Even when he was so angry he couldn't breathe, he wanted her arms around him.

She wrapped him up, laying her head on his shoulder. "You're going to be all right. This doesn't change anything for you. Your parents love you."

"I know." He was calming down now that she was close. He could smell her, feel the warmth of her body against his, and somehow it was easier to breathe. "I'm sorry I said those things."

"I'm sorry, too," she whispered. When she pulled back there were tears in her eyes. She stepped away, wiping at them. "And I'm sorry about...all of it, I guess. I don't mean to be exhausting. But I don't know another way to be. I'm always going to be difficult, and you're always going to deserve more."

"What?" He wasn't sure how they'd gone from her comforting him to... "Kala, I apologized. I didn't mean it." He hated how red her eyes were. She was the strongest woman he knew, and he'd brought her to this. He reached out, taking her hand in his. "I'm exhausting, too. Baby, you can't take every fight and turn it into a breakup."

"We've had plenty of fights, Coop. This is something else. This is me recognizing that it won't ever work. Deep down you don't trust me, and I understand. I'll always be a spy, and you'll always wonder if I won't give you up for the mission. Hell, I don't know. Maybe I would. I can be ruthless. I'm a Taggart, after all."

Fuck. She'd taken everything he said literally.

*And how did you mean for her to take it, asshole? You know how her brain works and you still talked to her like that. Don't tell yourself you're the only one putting work in. She's spent days and days taking care of you, opening herself up to you physically and emotionally when it scares the shit out of her.*

"I love you, baby." He held her hand. "I had a bad reaction to some freaky news, and I put it on you. It doesn't mean anything. You said it yourself. It doesn't change anything."

"It doesn't change anything for you," she replied. "I was talking about your life. This is a blip on your road, and you get to choose how to process it. You can be grateful you had a mother who wanted to protect you. You can ignore it entirely because you're happy with your life. Or you can turn it into something it's not."

"What is it not?" Cooper asked.

"An offense to you," Kala replied with quiet certainty. "Everything these people did was with you in mind. You should accept it even if you don't agree with how they went about it. There was no malice here. Not from your biological mother. Not from Zach or Joyce. Not from my dad, who did not know what had happened. And not from me, who just can't be the woman you need me to be. If I can understand that and not be angry with you, can you do the same for me?"

"I'm not angry." He wasn't angry with her. He wasn't sure how he felt about the rest of it.

"You were."

"I'm not now."

She stared at him for a minute, and then her head shook. "But you will be."

"Kala, I'm not mad." He was getting frustrated though, and he needed to tamp it down. "I was, but now I can see you handled it the best way you knew how, so let's forget the rest of it. I think I've earned some grace from you."

"By putting up with me? Is that what you're doing? Earning something by tolerating how hard I am to live with? Do you know how that makes me feel?"

She was misunderstanding him. "I didn't mean it that way."

She shook her head. "It doesn't matter because when I tell you what I did, I assure you there won't be a lot of grace."

He dropped her hand. A cold suspicion snaked up his spine. She wouldn't. She wouldn't do this to him. She would know how important it was for Zach to be secure and ready for questioning. "Where is Zach?"

"Probably on his way out of the country," she admitted with a deep resignation in her tone. "He's looking for Huisman, but also for his mother. I've already typed up the reports. It's everything I can remember from the conversation we had, including the fact that he's promised to contact me again when he can and he's worried about Devi."

She let the fucker go? Maybe he was being hasty. "Did he hurt you?"

Her head shook. "No. He didn't hurt me or threaten me in any way. If you're looking for some way to make this not my call, you won't find it. I could have easily gotten Joyce and forced Zach to come with me. I probably could have taken them both, but I chose not to."

"You chose."

"Yes," she replied simply. "That's what the job is. Choices. I think we have a better chance of getting to Huisman if Zach is out there. He's got connections we don't, and I believe him when he says he'll come in when he can."

"Why the hell would you believe him?" The question came out on a harsh rasp.

"Because he loves you," she said with a sigh that felt like resignation. "Because he wants to get to know his brother. Because I think he truly cares about Devi."

He huffed at the irony. "Now you believe in love. When it's convenient for you."

"I never said I didn't believe, Coop," she argued. "Trust me, I do, and I do not in any way think it's convenient. I simply don't think there's any for me."

How quickly she forgot. "I loved you."

She was silent for a moment, staring at him with solemn eyes, and he realized his mistake.

He couldn't seem to stop making them today. "I love you, but you have to understand why I'm upset. You knew I would want Zach brought in. You let that fucker take me down and then what? You sat down and had a sandwich with him over my drugged body?"

"It was a beer," she corrected.

Well, of course it was. His girlfriend. Sipping beer over his unconscious body.

"I made sure you had a pillow," she offered and sighed when the silence lengthened between them. "What did you want me to do? Should I have killed Zach? Taken out Joyce? I made sure you were okay and then I calmly did what I had to do. I didn't fall to my knees and scream. I am what I am, and it's never going to be what you need. I've known it for a long time, babe. I love you, too, but I don't think my love is ever going to be enough for you. I don't think I can love enough for anyone. It's not your fault. It's all me. I don't have anyone to blame. I was born this way. Kenz got all the gentleness. Sometimes I wish you fell in love with her and she loved you because at least then I would know you were happy."

She kissed his cheek and turned and walked out of the room.

He felt his fists clench at the irony. Now she told him? Now? When she'd utterly betrayed him? Now she used the words he'd longed to hear.

He felt like she'd kicked him in the gut. There was a part of him that wanted to chase after her, to force her to fight with him.

He was too dramatic? He loved her. Of course he was going to lose his shit when he thought she was dead. The fact that she wouldn't meant… What did it mean? Did she have to love him the exact way he loved her? Would her quiet mourning mean less than his histrionic one?

What the fuck was he doing? He needed to chill this thing out. His father was right, and he was behaving in an overly emotional fashion.

Wasn't this exactly what his mother had warned him about? That he would try to mold her into something she wasn't. That he'd decided he loved her a very long time before, and he'd been chasing her ever since without truly knowing who she was and accepting her.

Accepting Kala meant embracing all of her, including the parts that sometimes felt remote. She wasn't. She often seemed standoffish when she was thinking, but she didn't want to be alone. Well, she did, but she rarely didn't want him around. He was the one who could soothe her. What did he get in return?

He got a part of her absolutely no one else got. He got her softness.

His heart clenched. She was more fragile than anyone thought. She hid it, and she would never complain, never treat him like shit even when he'd done the same to her.

A laugh huffed from his chest. Nope. His girl would keep it all inside. She would show her love in different ways, including protecting him like he was something precious. Even when they weren't together.

She was exactly the woman who would see her boyfriend get his dumb ass tranqed because he couldn't keep his shit together in a potentially dangerous situation, put a pillow under his head, probably kiss him on the forehead and then sit down and get the damn job done.

If it had been him being carried out by someone, she would have died inside but not given up the op. She would have sat by his bedside and held his hand—unless she needed to stab someone.

She was never going to be some swoony, romantic heroine who needed him to save her from the bad guy.

But she did need him to save her from the black hole that sometimes threatened to swallow her whole. She needed him to pull her back to the real world and remind her how much her love was worth.

He sat there for a moment and realized that while he'd thought he'd made a decision before, this was really it. She'd done something he never would have done—allowed Zach to go free. She'd handled things in a way that hurt his feelings. She hadn't chosen to scrap a mission to save his pride.

What the fuck was his pride worth?

It certainly wasn't worth the woman he wanted to spend the rest of his life with. He stood, glancing at the clock and realizing how much time had gone by while he'd sat here.

Nothing was more important than Kala. Nothing. If she didn't want to work with him anymore, he would take it. He would support her. It would be her choice.

Although he would try to sway her because he loved working with her. He wanted to work with her at the Agency until she was ready to embark on something else.

If she wanted him to hear Zach out, well, he was already rethinking that, too.

What the hell would he have done had he been the one in Zach's position? While he certainly wouldn't have ended up leaving his team, he might have found a way to put himself on it so he could get to know his brother.

He should have done his job, sat beside her and worked it out. He might have been able to talk her into bringing him in, but no, he'd gotten his butt hurt because she hadn't wailed and cried and made an already dramatic situation worse.

He was going to have to buy so many chocolate croissants and give a million foot rubs and probably agree to another dog because he was pretty sure Kenzie would try to keep Bud 2 and Kala had never not had a dog in her life.

But the most important thing he could do was put his arms around her and ask her for forgiveness.

He walked out into the hallway and into the big living room

where his father was sitting in Big Tag's lounge chair, a serious expression on his face. He looked up. "Are you feeling okay?"

"No. I feel like an asshole." He glanced into the kitchen. "Where's Kala? I need to grovel."

His father's expression grew even more grim. "She left half an hour ago. She told Hunter if he wouldn't take her, she would find her own way back. He did it because… Well, I don't think he's ever seen her cry."

He'd brought his gorgeous girl so low. He pulled out his cell.

**I'm going to be back not long after you, baby. We need to talk. I love you. Love you. I'm so sorry for the way I behaved. Please meet with me. Tell Hunter he better keep you safe. You are everything to me.**

He sent the text and looked to his father.

"We need to get back to Dallas. I have to get my girl."

\* \* \* \*

Kala stared at her parents across the conference table. "I'm fine."

If only they were the only ones who'd shown up. Unfortunately, Lou was here, too. At least TJ was off somewhere probably trying to find a street food vendor.

Her father's brow cocked. "Sure. That's why you didn't go to your own home last night and instead spent the night in a sex club."

Well, she'd known damn well what would happen if she went back to her place. First her sister and Bri would be all over her asking what happened with Cooper, and then at some point in time Cooper would show up, and she couldn't handle it.

He would show up because he was stubborn and didn't like to fail at anything. She was good at failing, so she accepted the reality of their relationship better than he did.

If she stayed with him, it was only a matter of time before he resented her. It was better to break it off now when there were still some good feelings between the two of them. They still had a shot at seeing each other every now and then and wishing each other well.

Like well was what she wanted for him. She wanted spectacular, fabulous, amazing. He deserved a beautiful life and everything he could possibly want. Even if it wasn't with her.

"Cooper already came by this morning, and he looked like shit,"

Lou announced. Her bestie had come in with a bag for her, a fresh change of clothes, and some makeup. "He said he was an asshole."

"He wasn't. He was fine." Kala was calm and cool. She hadn't slept much but she'd used the punching bag they kept in one of the rooms. She'd tried to cry but it wouldn't come. Thank the universe she had a key to this place because otherwise it would have been a motel room. She'd known she needed time alone. Not that Hunter had been very talkative. He'd just flown the plane and told her if she wanted to talk, he was there. He'd told her whatever Cooper had done, he would be horrified to know how it affected her because he loved her.

But he didn't.

"That is not what he told me." Her father naturally had found her. Stupid trackers. She knew what happened. Her dad called Lou and her bestie pinpointed her location. Lou had done something to them—there had been a whole lot of technical stuff. The end result being she had a brand-new tracker. Not that it stopped Huisman last time, but maybe the next asshole who drugged her and tortured her wouldn't have the same level of tech.

"You know I am always on your side," Lou began cautiously.

This would hurt most of all, and it was precisely why she should have thought this whole thing through. Lou and Cooper had been friends for years. It wasn't fair to ask her to choose. She wasn't going to ask her to choose.

Lou was the only one who had always been hers. Always. Except now she was TJ's and she was happy.

"It's okay." She was going to stay calm through this. Get through it. Tomorrow would be easier. After they settled the situation with Zach, she could move into her new role and start to find the distance she needed. She could sink into a long-term op and not come out for months, maybe years. "I'm not going to make things difficult."

Her mother's brow cocked. "You're not going to make things difficult? This time? You choose this time to go down easy, baby girl?"

She should have known her mother would have problems with her stance. But there would be no explanation that would serve her mom or any of her and Cooper's friends. He was the sunny guy everyone loved and she was… She was Kala. They were always going to come down on his side. So she wasn't wasting her time and energy. "Yes."

A frustrated huff was her mother's only response.

Good. They were getting the picture. "So can we get off the topic of my love life and get down to business since I'm due to leave for DC in a couple of hours?"

More like eight, but who was counting. She'd made the arrangements to travel back to Langley with Lena. The big bosses wanted an update on the situation with Zach. Her father had agreed with the way she'd handled things, though he'd wished she'd tried harder to get him to come home.

Her father stared at her like he could see straight through her and knew everything she was thinking and planning on doing for the rest of her life. He didn't, of course, but this was one of Ian Taggart's patented dad stares. It worked like a charm on her siblings every single time.

Not on her. She simply stared right back.

"Should we go and make some coffee or something?" Lou asked. "This looks like it's going to last for a while."

Her mother's head shook as she sat back. "They can do this for hours."

"There's zero reason for you to go to DC right now," he said, obviously giving up.

"On this we will have to agree to disagree," she replied.

"Who convinced you to go to DC because I know it's not Drake," her father shot back. "I talked to him this morning, and he's happy with a conference call."

"Kala, you can't leave Cooper hanging like this," her mother argued.

What had he been saying to her parents? "I didn't. I said what I needed to say in Colorado. It's not like I up and refused to talk to him, but at some point the argument is done and things are over. I'm going to DC for work. I need some time to think about my career."

"He told me what he said to you," her father explained. "I know it was shitty, but you have to understand that he was in a bad place. He also told me that in the middle of that shitstorm he questioned whether or not I knew and let it happen."

She should have known that Captain America would own up to his mistakes like the stalwart hero he was. "If it helps, he thought I was in on it, too."

Her father sighed. "He had a bad reaction to some shocking news and he's trying to own it. You do neither of you any favors by hiding like a coward when I know damn straight you aren't one. You chose to let him in."

"I think what your dad is trying to say…" Lou began because she was always the peacekeeper.

"My father doesn't need a translator, Lou. He's trying to tell me I made my bed and I better fucking let Coop lie in it, too." She knew exactly what her dad was saying.

"He's trying to say you can't fold the first time there's pressure on you," her mother argued.

"First time?" Kala felt her eyes go wide. "I assure you this is not the first time."

"Don't you think I understand that?" Her father stood and started to pace, a sure sign he was getting emotional. "I know how much that one night cost you. I do not intend to allow you to waste another fifteen years of your life because you can't handle the fact that he said some stupid words. I know they hurt you. I've said shit to your mother that hurt her."

"Same." Her mother nodded in agreement.

They were always in tune. Always.

And yet she knew they fought.

Her father stopped in front of her, kneeling down. "Kala, I know it's hard for you to process a fight like this. I know because that's how it was for me in the beginning. It feels like there's no way out, but there is."

"I've made my decision, and though I know you all think I'm some kind of selfish shit, I'm actually doing this for him."

Lou sent her mom a look. An *I told you* look.

"I know that, too. I know what's going through your head," her father insisted. "You think you're too dark for him. You think you're sparing him because one day he's going to wake up and realize he needs some sweet princess who won't ever give him a moment's trouble. You think he can't possibly know what he truly wants because he keeps saying he wants you. That can't be right because you don't deserve it. You don't deserve it because you're not good enough."

"Ian," her mom began.

"I can say it because I felt it, too. I've had all those dark voices in my head. I am so sorry you inherited them. I wouldn't wish that part of me on anyone, much less my daughter. You have to be stronger than the voices," he urged.

But her voices were so silky and smooth. Her voices didn't feel all that dark. Her voices sometimes told her how nice it would be without that light in her eyes all the time. She was born in shadows, and it was only her connections to these people that forced her into a mold she didn't fit. How much easier would it be if she could simply be herself?

"I want to know what Lena's been saying to you in therapy," her father announced.

Oh, they were not going there. "Therapy is private. I believe at one point in time you told me therapy is sacred, and I never had to talk about what was said there."

"Yeah, when you were a kid and I was worried about you never talking about what happened in Virginia. Now you're an adult and I feel like I'm in some kind of battle where I don't even know the rules of war," her father said, running a hand over his head. He stood and started pacing again. "I don't like that woman, and I'm working to get her off this case. Drake is going to find someone else."

"I can't put my finger on it, but she gives me bad vibes. There's a smugness about the woman," her mother added, "like she knows something and she's going to use it against us."

Well, it was obvious Lena wasn't all Team Taggart. "She's been helping me see some things more clearly."

Now her mother leaned forward, a tense expression on her face. "What things, exactly?"

"Kala, when I had my sessions with her, she spent most of the time focusing on my friendship with you," Lou said. "It was weird. Everything was focused on you. She was supposed to be learning about Zach and how he functioned in the team, but it was you she wanted to talk about."

"Lena thinks I'm being wasted on this team." She winced when she realized how that sounded. She hadn't meant to be arrogant. She was simply stating the facts, but she'd learned that people often associated facts with internal feelings. Damn. She couldn't seem to stop screwing up.

Her father put his palms flat on the table, staring down at her. "If you think for one second you'll be allowed to go solo, you do not know me at all. I'm going to ask you what you would do if Lou up and told you she was leaving the team and going into the field on her own?"

Kala snorted. "She would never do that."

"But if she did?" The question came out between her father's clenched jaw.

"I would stop it, but it's not the same. Lou isn't a field operative. It would be too risky."

Lou held up a hand. "For the record, not something I would do."

Dad ignored her. "So if Lou decided to do something you felt was dangerous, you would stop her."

"Of course." It wouldn't matter that it should be Lou's decision. She wouldn't be able to watch it happen. Any more than she would be able to watch Coop do it since he wasn't a field operative. He was too emotional, too tied into his own morality to make the hard calls.

Not that she would be able to help them if she walked away. They wouldn't be in her life all the time. They would be reports, whispers, stories she heard when—if—she called home.

The thought made her ache. Would that ache go away if she was far from them? Or would it become a part of her, some pain inside that never went away?

"She's your best friend," her father said with a grave tone. "You love her, but no one put her in your arms when she was born. You didn't watch her grow up. She's not a piece of your soul, walking this earth. What do you think I'll do to stop you from hurting yourself?"

"I'm not hurting myself. I'm doing my job, and I think in order to do it to the best of my ability, I might need to work alone. Hell, I get benched half the time as it is." Did he think she wasn't an adult? Hadn't thought this through?

Lou had gone pale. "You can't leave the team. I'm here because of you. I'm here to work with you. I'm here because I don't want to lose you, and that's what will happen if you go off on your own."

The words hit her squarely in the chest. Wasn't that exactly what she'd been thinking? Now that TJ had Lou, she didn't need her anymore and it was okay to let go.

But what about Kenz? Kenz had Tash. What about Devi? She was reckless, and Bri and Daisy wouldn't be able to hold her damn feet over the fire to get her to see reason. What about her brothers?

What about her tiny nephew?

*Don't you think they're all better off without your darkness? Without you in their lives, maybe there won't be danger since you're the most dangerous thing of all.*

God, that voice still sounded like Julia Ennis.

"You will hurt yourself if you walk away from this team." Her father straightened up and had his "decision made" face on. "If you isolate yourself, it'll be easier to give in to all of your dark impulses. I should fucking know because that's what I did. Only nearly losing Liam O'Donnell to that fucker Eli Nelson brought me to my senses."

Her mom cleared her throat.

"Well, and your mom died. I try not to think about that part. Honestly, meeting your mother, being with her before she pulled all that bullshit fake death thing was what made me reconsider. After my mentor John Bishop died, I went deep. I pulled away from friends and family. I was starting down a very dark path where I stopped seeing people as humans with hopes and dreams and lives and started seeing them as chess pieces to move around."

"Isn't he Henry Flanders now?" Lou asked.

Her father pointed Lou's way as though she'd made his point. "Yeah, you get too deep in this 'career' and there's a whole lot of faked deaths. It's a real theme. My point is it took loving your mother to make me reconsider, and then even when she was gone, I was too changed to go back. If you leave this team behind, you won't return. Cooper is your shot. Baby girl, please take it. Whatever he did, however he hurt you, it's fixable."

But she wasn't. For all her father thought he knew her, the situation wasn't the same.

Was it?

She stared at him, not knowing what to say.

Her father shook his head. "You're not going to DC. I'm still your boss, so unless you want to quit, you'll stand down. Stay here. Go home. It doesn't matter as long as you're in Dallas. We have a meeting in the morning now that everyone's home. I expect you there at eight a.m."

She knew an order when she heard it. He would move heaven and earth and probably cut her off at the knees. She needed a new plan. "Sir, yes, sir."

Her father turned and walked out.

Her mother stood up. "And I expect you at the house for dinner on Sunday night for Travis's birthday. If you're not there, I'll send someone to find you. I know you think your father is the hard case, but only because you've never put me in a corner. You try to walk away from this family and you'll find out how hard I can fight, my love."

Her mother knew how to make an exit.

Kala watched her, not truly understanding why her heart felt so twisted. There was anger at them not respecting her decisions and treating her like a child.

There was this odd warmth that came with the knowledge that her parents wouldn't ever let her go, wouldn't ever stop fighting for her. Even when they had to fight her.

It was a lot. So much damn emotion, and she didn't handle a regular amount of emotion well. She looked at the last person in the room. "Do you have something to say before you walk out?"

Lou's head shook. "I'm not leaving. I brought a bag with me. I took the second privacy room. Where you go, I go. So if you're leaving the team, I'm coming with you."

Fuck it all.

Too much. It was too much. She stood because she needed some air. She walked through the conference room doors.

"Just remember I can track you, and if you think you can cut that tracker out, you're wrong," Lou yelled after her. "Why do you think I put it in your ass cheek? Your arms aren't long enough to get there."

She'd told her it worked best in subcutaneous fat and her butt was the only place she had some. Liar. Her best friend was a liar who was trying to keep track of her.

Because she loved her. Because she worried about losing her.

Too much.

She let the door slam shut and strode to the front of the club in time to see her parents leaving in the massive Navigator her father drove.

They had no right to tell her what to do.

Couldn't they see this was for the best?

Had her father thought about doing the same thing?

She drew in a deep breath and wished she was back in the woods with Cooper and they'd never found Joyce, never revealed the secret of his birth. She wanted to be with him in that space where nothing mattered but the two of them. Where she'd felt safe to be exactly who she was. Where who she was had been a woman in love with a man.

"I knew I'd find you here," a familiar voice said.

She turned, trying to tamp down her shock. Because the man standing in front of her shouldn't be looking for her at all. The man in front of her had no idea who she really was.

Ben Parker stepped from behind the big oak tree.

She was fucked.

## Chapter Fifteen

"What are you doing here?" She had a million questions, but it seemed like the most important one.

Ben Parker was handsome—if one liked the type. Which she did not. He had golden hair he kept in a stylish cut and light blue eyes that could go from warm to icy in a heartbeat. At six foot six, he towered over her.

Whoa. She'd never realized the man actually looked a lot like her dad.

Ewww. What was her twin thinking?

He stared at her for a moment, taking her in like she was some gorgeous piece of art. She wasn't. She probably looked like shit, but Ben Parker didn't seem to mind. He just didn't realize he had the wrong sister since he didn't understand there was a sister at all. "I know it was cowardly of me to leave Toronto when you were coming up to see me."

"I was coming to give your team a briefing." He was annoying. She didn't need this right now. She already had way too much rolling through her. It would be great if she could start a fight with this man. Maybe get him to throw a punch and get a lot of this awful emotion out of her system in a wholly violent fashion.

But that would likely end in her team cutting ties with Parker and his team. They needed the Canadians. They had more experience with Huisman.

This was what she'd tried to tell Cooper. There were times when one sucked it up and did their job. No matter how badly it hurt.

"Did you? You were the only one who could do it?" Ben asked.

She could fix this whole situation right now with a few carefully chosen words. She could tell him her boss had forced her to come since she seemed to be the only one who could properly play Ben Parker. That's all she'd been doing. Playing him for intel, and wasn't he a moron for falling for it?

Except that wasn't what her sister had been doing. Her sister was at least half in love with this man, and that meant something. Kala disagreed with her. Kenzie could do better. Parker was nothing but a hot dude in a nice suit.

And yet he'd saved her even when he'd thought she was doing exactly what she'd thought in her head—playing him.

Her sister was in the middle of an epic love story, and she could cut it off right here and now.

She forced her expression to soften. "No. Of course not."

He moved in, standing over her. He was close, but he didn't touch her.

If this was Cooper, it would be a move that threatened to melt her panties off, but she mostly thought Ben looked like a big old goofball. "I thought so. I'm sorry. I'm afraid it's hard to think strategically when it comes to you."

*Be Kenzie. Be Kenzie.* Do not tell him what you want to which is to ask him if he thinks strategically at all? Does he know the meaning of the word? Because she wasn't sure they spoke the same language.

But she was Kenzie, and she was sure her twin would be all gooey at this point.

Did Kenzie think Coop was a big old golden retriever? Did she barf in her mouth a little when Kala curled up on his lap? But would also do anything to see her twin happy?

Like Kala was about to do.

If she was so fucking filled with darkness, why was it easy to make this decision?

"You wouldn't meet me in Toronto. Why?"

He stared down at her like he was memorizing the moment. This man wasn't playing. He was in deep. "You know why."

Oh, this made her slightly ill, but it was the only thing she could think to do. Tell the truth. Or at least a version of it. "Because of how Cooper reacted. But that wasn't me. I can't control how he reacts or feels, Ben."

Cooper would always be the guy who had big reactions because he felt things deeply and didn't have a switch inside that told him it was wrong to show the world. He never hid his feelings because he wasn't ashamed of them.

Was that why she did it? Or was she afraid they wouldn't be accepted? Those voices always told her to keep it all inside.

"He loves you," Ben said.

"But I don't love him." Such a lie. And it came out of her lips so easily. This. This was why Cooper should run. She could lie, and she didn't even feel bad about it because it wasn't for her. It was for Kenzie.

She was certain if Cooper was in the same position, he wouldn't be able to lie at all. His Captain America stalwartness would force the truth from his mouth.

There was an intensity in Ben's eyes that likely would have Kenzie swooning. Kala thought he looked like a starving dude who'd found the last Snickers bar on earth. "I don't know what to do about you, Maggie."

He called them Maggie, a nickname for the Agency code name they used, Ms. Magenta. It was good to hear that name because it reminded her beyond a shadow of a doubt that this was work and she shouldn't punch him in the face and tell him to back off. Because she wanted to. Intimacy was hard for her. It was why Kenz so often handled the jobs that required flirting.

"I don't care about Cooper. He's a friend, but he's never going to be anything more," Kala said, forcing herself to move closer even when every single instinct in her body screamed to get away. Only Cooper got this close. Only Cooper got to kiss her and love her and hold her against him. To touch her when she wasn't expecting it because it was always okay for him to touch her.

Only Cooper.

How would she move through life without knowing he was waiting for her? He would find someone, but it would probably be some airhead who wouldn't know how to take care of him because he obviously had terrible taste in women.

Ben Parker's lips hovered above hers. "And what am I?"

She had to find a way to tag out. She was willing to, maybe if she had to and couldn't figure a way out of it, let him kiss her. Not like a full-on kiss. More like a peck. She could handle a peck. She was not going to barf. Barfing would totally give up the game. "I don't know. I think we should figure it out. I have some things I need to do, but I could meet you later."

"Sex club things?" he asked, his jealousy obvious.

"It's a lifestyle club," she returned. "I haven't had sex with anyone, Ben. Not since I met you."

God, she hoped her sister hadn't lied to her about the op when she and Ben had found themselves pretty much alone. It was in Croatia, and they'd spent a night in a castle hunting down an informant at a party given by a billionaire.

Ben's hand came out and caressed her cheek. "That was your choice, baby. It would have gone very differently if I'd been in charge." He leaned over and brushed his lips against hers.

Thank the universe he didn't try to use his tongue. Ick. Ick. Ewww. Ben lips. Lips of Ben. She was going to need all the mouthwash. Vodka was a disinfectant, right? Her sister so owed her.

*And how will you hold this shit over her head for the rest of time and long after we are dead if you walk away from your family, moron?*

She stepped back, praying she hadn't actually gone green. "Meet me in two hours. I know this restaurant where they'll give us a private room and we can talk. It's called Top."

Her uncle's place. Uncle Sean would ensure privacy for the two of them. He would also ensure security.

"All right," he said and reached for her hand. Then dropped it as he glanced to the left and his eyes widened. "Well, shit. Your timing is perfect as always, McKay."

Kala felt her heart squeeze as she caught sight of what she'd missed while she was pretending to be lost in her sister's crush's eyes. Cooper stood about twenty feet away, having obviously come in from the back parking lot. He stared at her like he hated her. It was right there in his eyes, the betrayal.

She fought back nausea. Real nausea this time. She'd been ready to walk away from him for his own sake, but this…he hated her. It was there in his eyes.

He would never speak to her again. Never.

"She's all yours, Parker," Cooper said with a shake of his head. "Maybe she can string you along for years like she did me. Good fucking luck."

He strode off, his boots ringing against the concrete.

If they'd made that sound in the first place, she wouldn't be in this position, but no.

God, she felt so hollow.

This was what she wanted, and now she couldn't stand the thought.

She had to go after him. The impulse to chase the man down was right there. She could chase him down and beg his forgiveness.

But she couldn't, and there would be no forgiveness for her.

"Well, that's going to make things awkward," she said and sighed before turning to Ben. "I'm sorry you had to see that. We are friends. I've never led him to believe anything else. I promise."

Kenzie never had. And she was Kenzie right now.

Because if she had to be herself, she would likely lie down and wish she could fade.

He reached out and stroked her hair. "All right. We can talk more about it at the restaurant. I'll be there in two hours. Maggie, don't stand me up. I know I should be all modern man about it, but I'm afraid I'll hunt you down."

"I'll be there." Her sister would drop whatever she was doing and haul ass to see this man.

Her sister might have a future.

Hers was over.

She turned and walked back in the club. Where she wouldn't be a member for long because she would leave this place to Cooper. And her friends. And everything.

She turned the corner and he stood there in his jeans and T-shirt, his eyes on her. He'd obviously gone around to the back entrance. "Cooper, I..."

"That was such a nice thing to do for your sister, baby," he said, his jaw going tight. "I am so fucking proud of you. I told Lou to go get your toothbrush. And some mouthwash. And a bottle of vodka. It's a disinfectant, you know."

The world slowed down and something untwisted inside her. Something that had been knotted and gnarled unfurled, and she knew she would never question this man again. She strode up to him, putting her hands on his cheeks and kissing him for all she was worth. "I love you."

A long sigh went through him. "I love you, too, baby. I love you so much. I'm so sorry about what happened in Colorado."

"Then kiss me and get all the Ben cooties off my lips and then I think we need to try something new." The tears were right there, but she couldn't let them out. It was time to see if Cooper could help her with that, too. It was time to trust him in the ultimate way.

Cooper practically inhaled her. His mouth claimed hers in a way he never had before. There was no tentativeness in his kiss this time. No holding back in case he moved too fast. There was nothing but pure desire in his kiss.

"So we don't need the mouthwash, apparently."

Kala broke off the kiss and turned to her best friend. "I just gave him cooties, too. If I have them, he has to have them."

There was a hint of tears in Lou's eyes. "Then my work here is done, and I can go meet TJ for lunch. Though he's probably already had it. It's okay. He likes Second Lunch, too. Why do I want to marry a hobbit?"

Her bestie turned and started walking away.

There was one thing Lou could do for her. "Hey, I need you to tell Kenz she needs to meet Parker at Top in two hours."

Lou didn't even bother to turn around. "Coop already did it."

Cooper's lips curled up as he stared down at her. "I was on the phone to her the minute I rounded the corner. Also, I told her she has to do your laundry for the rest of the month and has to make at least three batches of those cookies you love."

The ones with butterscotch chips. She craved them.

Damn it, she loved them all.

"I was going to walk away."

His expression softened. "I wouldn't let you. Never again."

"I don't think I'm good for you."

"I get to decide that, Kala. I know you have control issues and I'm willing to accommodate you, but not on this. I decide who I love and it's you. It's always been you." He kissed her again.

She melted against him. It felt so good to lean on him in every way. It would be a hard conversation with Lena, but she was doing the right thing.

And maybe she should find another therapist.

Nothing mattered except being with him right now. "Then I'm going to need you to do something for me."

His hand moved over her hair. "Anything."

"Tie me up, and let's get some tears out of me, baby."

\* \* \* \*

Cooper stared down at her, the sight so fucking beautiful to his eyes. Kala was naked and bound. And she wasn't spitting bile his way. She was calm and collected.

"Are you sure?" He didn't want to push her in any way she wasn't fully on board for. "I've told you in the past. I don't need this. We can play and top subs together and then fuck like wild cats. I don't need for you to submit to me."

"I think I need to submit to myself, Coop. I know it sounds weird, but I can't cry. I need to. I want to. I want to find that place where I can forgive, but I don't think I can until I let this poison out of my system. This works for my mom and my sisters. I'm never going to be your sub, walking around on the dungeon floor and calling you Master, but I might need this. And I'll only ever accept it from you."

She was going to get him all kinds of emotional. This. This was what he'd always wanted. This was why every bit of pain he'd felt was worth it. His mother was wrong. He didn't want her to change. He didn't want her to leave her world and come to his. He just wanted to be on the inside with her. "Excellent. Then while we're working through your issues, we'll deal with a couple of mine, too. I have you all tied up, gorgeous. Nowhere to run. So guess what? We're going to talk."

Her jaw dropped. "That is evil."

Oh, but he was the top right now. He reached over and rolled one tight nipple between his thumb and forefinger. He'd selected the apparatus in the center of the main room. It was a nice setup, with drop down adjustable chains for the sub's wrists and more on the floor where he'd bound her ankles. Gabe had taken a very literal definition of dungeon when designing this particular part of the club. It was dark and medieval looking. They'd tortured many a submissive right here, but he never thought he'd see her like this. She was stretched out and utterly helpless. He had access to every inch of her body, from that glorious mouth of hers to her breasts and ass, and that pussy he loved to play with. He reached down and toyed with the piercing on her clit. "Want to tell me the story of how my virgin bride ended up with a hood piercing?"

Her lips curled up in the hottest smile. "Coop, if that is how you ask me to marry you, I'm saying yes."

No grand gestures for his girl. Making a big deal out of it would cause her anxiety and stress. She was all about the little things, the daily shows of love and affection. "We're going to the courthouse Monday. No muss, no fuss. Party it up this weekend because you're going to be a married woman next week. Now, story."

He touched that ball that sat on her clit and watched her breath hitch.

"This is supposed to be about me crying it out," she complained.

As he was acting as her Dom for the next hour, he had no choice what to do next. He brought his hand down on her ass. Hard. One and then two and three. She shuddered. "And we'll get to that. It's going to take more than pain to push you. The good news? You've come to the right place. We're going to work through some things, you and I. Story. Now."

"Fine." There was some of the fire he'd expected. "I got it so I could feel something. I don't know why I'm not normal, but I didn't have a lot of sexual feelings."

He slapped her ass again. "We're not using that word anymore. There is no normal. There is you and me and how we are. You are a perfectly made Kala Taggart."

Her gaze seemed to darken. "I am so far from perfect."

He sighed because damn, but she looked perfect to him. He let his fingers trace the graceful line of her spine. "We all have things we want to work on. But I need to make one thing very, very clear to you. You are the best partner I could possibly have. I do not want some sweet thing who'll have my babies and make my lunch and never complain. I want you. I want to love you and fight with you and grow old with you. If you decide you want them, I want to raise a couple of the weirdest kids in the world and make them call your dad Grumpa."

Her eyes were suddenly shining. He'd known it would take words to get to her. Words she couldn't shut out or ignore. "I'm scared I won't be a good mom."

Another swat and then another until he counted out ten. "You're already an excellent parent."

"What does that mean?"

"You take care of your subs. You take care of your cousins. You take care of your siblings and ask very, very little in return. The trouble is you think the only way you could possibly be a parent is to be the ideal vision of what society thinks of as a mom. You're not the most openly affectionate person. You don't wear your heart on your sleeve. You probably will tell our kid to walk it off if he or she falls down. It's okay. I'll be there."

Her jaw dropped. "Oh, shit. I'm the dad."

He moved in, framing her face with his hands. "We're going to be the parents we're going to be, and it will work, baby. We're going to throw out every expectation except one."

A tear fell on her cheek. "What's that?"

This was the most important rule of all. "That we will never leave the other behind."

"Never."

He stepped in close to her and turned her around so she was in front of him. He'd taken off his shirt and shoes and socks but still wore jeans. They wouldn't be on for too long. He pressed his chest against her back, wrapping an arm around her waist. "I know sometimes you try to drift away, but I'll always bring you home to me. I promise you. I won't ever leave you alone. You are not merely more than enough for me. You are my whole fucking world."

Her head fell back. "I think we can skip the tears. Let's get to the sex."

Oh, she wasn't getting off that easily. No way. He stepped back and reached in his kit. Luckily, he left it here in his locker at the club since this was where they played. He pulled out a thing he'd thought he would never use. Nipple clamps. Beautiful ones he'd purchased with her in mind. He would never use them on anyone else. They were for her.

He brought them around and showed them to her. Pretty alligator clamps with jewels that matched the one on her clit. "First, I get to dress you."

Her eyes narrowed. "I'm paying you back. You're going to love what I put on your dick."

He probably would. He knew he was a pervert, and he was perfectly happy to try anything she wanted. "I'm willing to play a lot of games with you, baby."

He leaned over and got his mouth on her nipple, licking and sucking until it was perfectly hard. Then he slipped the clamp on, watching it bite into her gorgeous flesh. He caught her gasp, such a fucking sexy sound coming from her. He treated her other breast to the same. How had he gone so damn long in life without having this every day? Without being able to touch her and stroke her and lick her to his heart's content. He stepped back and stared at her for a moment. Even in bondage his girl looked fierce.

"We're going to see how you like this later, Cooper," she said with fire in her eyes.

"You have a safe word, Kala. It's okay to use it. I want to get you where you need to go, but I don't want to break you."

"Then play with me. Be my badass boyfriend right now. If it's too much, you'll know."

"You'll tell me," he corrected, cupping her cheek.

"I'll tell you," she whispered and then went right back to her ferociousness. "But I'll also wake you up one day with clamps on your nipples."

She probably would. He could handle it. "Tell me why you would think I could misinterpret that scene with Parker. Don't lie to me. I saw your face when you walked in. You thought I meant what I said."

"Well, you said I strung you along, and I probably did."

His head shook. "No, you did not. You never played me. I broke your heart and it took a while, but you were my friend again before we hit our senior year. You were the faithful one. You would have stood by me no matter what. I was a weak boy. But I need you to understand I'm a man now, and I could have found you fucking Parker and I would have asked why. Because I believe in you. I know your heart."

"I didn't think I had one."

"Oh, you do, and it's so big, and I mean to protect it for the rest of my life," he vowed. "So tell me why you thought I wouldn't know. You have to say it. We can't fix a problem if we don't acknowledge it exists. Say it."

A stubborn expression settled on her face. "Because we had a fight."

Not the answer he was looking for, and in this room, that meant punishment. He wouldn't always be her Dom. But there would be times when she needed it, and if he needed it, she would do the same for him. There would be no one else he would ever allow to top him. They could be fluid in their roles with each other. He moved around her gorgeous body and picked up a wooden paddle. "Is that your answer?"

"It's what I said, Coop. We had a fight. You thought I betrayed you."

He brought his hand back and smacked that stunning ass. One and two and three and four, until she gasped and wriggled. There was a perfectly placed mirror across the dungeon, and he could see the way her tits bounced, making the jeweled clamps jiggle. He paddled her until he counted to ten in his head and then backed off, staring at the glorious pink her backside was becoming. "I told you I acted like an idiot. You're the one who left. You're right. Your father would have told mine if he'd known. I'm not used to Ian Taggart without almost god-like powers. I was kicked in the gut, and I acted like an idiot. Also, you're right about me as an operative. I'm only going to work as support from now on unless you need me and then I'll follow your lead in the field."

Her head came up. "I didn't mean you should quit."

"I'm not quitting," he promised. "I told you. I'm your backup. I'll hang with Lou and Tash and let you and Kenz and Tris handle the forward-facing jobs. Now tell me what was underneath it all. You know. I need to know what sent you running that night. I unearthed it and let it loose on you."

"I don't know what you're talking about."

So stubborn. Another ten had her eyes misting over. His baby was a hard bottom when she wanted to be. It was probably because she'd survived spy training, which included a shocking amount of torture. This felt like a regular Saturday for the woman who'd survived what Huisman had put her through. "All right. Let's try this another way. Tell me why you stopped writing poetry."

Now her head turned, eyes flaring. "What?"

"Eyes front," he bit out and gave her another five.

She did as he asked, but proved she could stare a hole through a mirror. "How do you know I used to write? I never showed you."

She still hadn't answered. Another five had her going up on her toes. "It doesn't matter how I know. I want to know why you stopped."

"Because it was stupid. I wasn't good at it."

Oh, they might have more sessions like this if she kept talking that way. He got in close, letting his hand slide along her hip until he could touch her pussy. He leaned in close, looking at the picture they made in the mirror. "I know someone who disagrees."

"I'm going to kill my brother," she vowed, but her breath hitched and her pelvis tilted slightly so the tip of his middle finger slid over her clitoris.

Right where he wanted to be. He let her feel his erection nestled against her ass. He toyed with her clit, feeling how wet she already was. She might not be a sub, but being naked and bound and spanked was doing something for her.

"Why did you stop? You didn't write for anyone but yourself, and then you didn't write at all after I fucked up. It wasn't the kidnapping that made you stop writing. It was me."

She pulled at the chains and leaned back against him, trying to force his finger to rub again. "I was a dumb kid, and I grew up."

So he pinched her clit between his thumb and forefinger and gave the piercing a careful twist.

She gasped and grumbled as he stepped back.

Pain alone wasn't going to fix this. She could take pain. She needed something else. He stepped in front of her, bringing his hand up. Tenderness might work where pain didn't. "Please. I think we break if we don't acknowledge this, and I do not want us to ever break. This is the most important relationship of my life. Tell me."

Yep. There they were. Tears filled her eyes. "I don't want to."

"Because you can't trust me. Because I hurt you."

She closed her eyes, tears dripping from them.

"Because I wasn't faithful the way you were. It was me." He knew deep down that was only part of the answer, but he needed to lean into it. She could handle pain. He could go and get a cattle prod and she would likely roll her eyes and tell him she'd had better. What she couldn't handle was guilt. He was taking it all on himself, and while he knew he was part of the problem, her secret tender heart wouldn't let him carry the whole load. "I did this to us."

She sniffled, another sign she was ready to break. "It wasn't you."

There she was. "I hurt you so badly you stopped writing."

"It wasn't just you," she admitted. "I was hurt, but I would have gone home and hated you and written a million shitty teen angst poems about how you broke my heart. That was what you broke. She broke *me*."

"She? Are you talking about Julia Ennis?"

"She told me I was like her. She said I reminded her so much of who she was at my age, and I could be someone. She had a very narrow definition of what *someone* means. Not many people counted as important. She told me other people were sheep."

Something she said a lot. "Honey, you don't mean it the way she did."

"Don't I? I've been working through this in therapy, and I think maybe I'm everything Julia said I was. Why did I walk away? Because I thought walking away was the best thing I could do for you."

How could she believe that? "Do you know why I never stopped trying to be in your life?"

"We were thrown together. Our parents are close. We should have been like brother and sister."

He shook his head. "I could never be your brother. Never. Kala, it's always been you. Even when I was a moron, I knew it was you. I was desperate to stay close to you in high school."

"Not desperate enough to ever ask me to a dance," she whispered.

His fault. "I'm so sorry, baby. I wasn't as strong as you were. It took me years to figure out what you did. What other people think of us doesn't matter if we're okay with who we are. And now I'm worried some of those voices in your head aren't your own. Julia Ennis was mentally unstable."

Her eyes came up, a grave truth in them.

He shook his head. "You are not unstable. I worry that you struggle with some depression, the kind that needs to be treated, but you are not unstable. Baby, how can you think that? You are the reasonable one in the field. You can shut off your emotions and do the job that needs to be done. That's the definition of stable. You are not now, nor have you ever been like that woman."

"She obsessed over my cousin. I obsess over you," she said, her voice threatening to break. "You're the only man I've ever wanted. The only person I've ever wanted."

The words were a balm to his soul, and he needed to find a way to give them back to her. "And I am so honored because you're my person, too. What do you think Julia Ennis would have done if she'd been in your position that night? She wouldn't have walked away. She wouldn't have stayed away and still helped me from behind the scenes. Even when you were pissed at me, you wouldn't let anyone else hurt me."

"I think she would say she did the same for Kyle."

He had to make her believe. "It's not the same. Not in any way. You barely talked to me in college. She would have done anything to get Kyle back. Anything. She would never once have thought to walk away because she was a narcissist. Can we agree on that one thing first? You are not a narcissist."

"Lena thinks I might be, but she also thinks it's a good trait for an operative since I'm obsessed with my job," Kala explained.

Oh, he was going to have to deal with Lena. He would start with going to Big Tag and demanding they bring someone else in. "It's a terrible trait, and you know that deep inside. You do your job for the betterment of your country and everyone around you. You do not do this job for you. If you were doing this job for you, it would have been easier to call your cousin and apply for a job as assassin. Because you like to stab people who deserve it. So we're tossing all of that out. I don't think Lena is the right therapist for you. So now we're at the truth. Say it out loud. You walked away because something inside tells you that you're not worthy of the love you've been given."

Her eyes caught his, her jaw tightening and then releasing as though she'd made her decision. "I'm not worthy of the love I've been given. I don't belong here. I don't fit."

It was out in the open, and now they could work on it. "Baby, you think you don't fit because you're the damn sun. You don't fit into orbit because you're the person we all orbit around. I know you think it's Kenzie, but you are the hand that guides us, not Kenz. You are the strong voice of reason even when that voice is very sarcastic. It's you, Kala. It's always you."

He stepped in close and kissed her, sure now that everything would be all right.

"I need you to hold me," she said, her breath hitching.

He knew how hard it was for her to ask for affection, for anything really. He had her out of the bondage in a heartbeat and turned her around, pulling her back against his chest. He had to be careful with the clamps that still decorated her gorgeous body. He wrapped her up while she cried. Told her he loved her over and over. Promised it would all be all right.

Her head fell back, arms coming up to cup the back of his neck. "I love you, too. Even though you're an asshole and my nipples have gone numb."

He felt a smile spread across his face. "Well, my love, we'll have to do something about that."

## Chapter Sixteen

It felt so good to cry, but now that she'd done it, there was another feeling she wanted to experience again. Love. The physical kind. He'd done everything she'd needed him to do. She believed him. She wouldn't question him again, and she'd said the hard truth.

She could work on it. She could do anything if this man was with her.

*You're the damn sun.*

The words had done something to her, opened some place inside her that had always been closed and locked away. If she was the sun, it was time to do some glowing.

After he got the damn clamps off her.

Cooper stood in front of her, the sweetest smile on his face. And his gloriously masculine body on display. He reached over and toyed with one of the jewels hanging off her nipples.

Kala yelped. Nope. Not as numb as she'd thought.

Cooper chuckled and dropped to his knees. "Do I get to tell our subs this story?"

Their subs. She'd always thought he would eventually leave and she would have to deal with them on her own, but it was kind of like they had a bunch of puppies they'd adopted and now she got to keep them. "I will murder you."

She had a rep to keep up, after all.

He winked and leaned in, his eyes turning up to look at her. "Understood, baby."

Then his hand came up and she gritted her teeth as he released the clamp and the blood surged back in. Pain bit through her but his mouth was on her, his tongue soothing the pain. Though she had to admit, the pain did something for her, too. It went straight to her pussy.

She might have some switch in her. The sight of Cooper on his knees in front of her got her motor going. She let her hands come up, stroking through his silky hair. He was so fucking gorgeous. Another snap of pain as he released the second clamp and then tongued and soothed her poor, irritated nipple.

How had she ever lived without this connection? She'd never viewed sex the way her sisters and friends did. She'd always known it would be sacred for her, and only with him. "Say it again."

His head tilted up and he smiled at her. "I love you."

Three words that should send her screaming, but they were from him so it was okay. "I love you."

"You better because the things I'm about to do to you absolutely require love." He stood and before she could protest, he picked her up, cradling her to his chest.

Yeah, she thought that was hot, too. "You can't pick me up whenever you want to."

"Watch me," he replied with a grin.

Damn, but it was good to see him looking happy. All the more because she was the reason for it. She put the smile on his face. "Are you serious about getting married?"

He reached his destination—a padded table that was the exact right height to fuck on. Her whole body tightened with anticipation as he set her down, lying her back on the table. "Yes. We can go on Monday. I think we have to wait three days, but that's enough time to plan a party for after. Spread your legs."

There was only the tiniest part of her that chafed at the order. The larger part of her knew what he was about to do and heartily agreed. She spread her legs and allowed him to lean over and get his mouth close to her pussy.

His big hands pressed her legs wider, and she damn near came from the first lick of that talented tongue. How did he do this to her over and over and it always felt new and exciting? And safe. She was so safe with this man.

He dove in, fucking her with his strong tongue while he held her legs open for his feast.

Desire poured through her veins. This was the only place where her brain turned off and her body could hold sway. The only place where she didn't need to think about anything but his next touch, the next kiss. She could breathe in this place, let go and be a version of herself she never thought she could be.

The orgasm hit her hard and fast, a wave rolling over her skin. And still he didn't stop. He kept it up until she came a second time, this one stronger, threatening to become her whole world.

Then he stood, his eyes dark on her and his lips glistening. He stared at her while his hands worked the fly of his jeans, and he pushed them off and over his hips. He tossed them aside and moved into place between her legs. His big hand stroked his cock. "Come here."

She brought her torso up, and his free hand wrapped around the nape of her neck, dragging her in for a long kiss. She could taste herself on him, his tongue diving deep as his cock started to invade. He stretched her as he thrust in, his tongue sliding along hers. Connection. This was the connection she'd longed for. With him. She'd spent so much of her life worried she was cursed and weird because she never had these feelings for anyone but him. Now it would be the joy of her life.

His hands moved, cupping her hips and holding her in place while he started to fuck her with power and precision. He tilted his pelvis and managed to hit her clit with every thrust. And whatever place inside that only he could light up. Her hands found his back, sinking in.

He held her close, only pulling away as far as it took to make it feel good. Her legs wrapped around him, nails sinking into his back. She couldn't stand to be even an inch away from him. She kissed his neck, needing every bit of her skin touching his.

Her whole body tightened as she was blasted with pleasure. Cooper stiffened and she felt him come, sparking even greater sensation. He held her tight even as they both came down.

When she laid back, he moved with her.

"Forgive me," he whispered against her breast. "I was dumb and mad and took it out on the one person I never should."

On the safest person. He'd done it because she was safe. People weren't perfect. Sometimes when overwhelmed, the way they asked for help looked like a fight. She could get that. "Forgiven. And babe, forgive me for being a big old scaredy cat and running away the first fight we have."

His head tilted up, a satisfied grin on his face. "Forgiven."

He pushed himself up and immediately slid his arms under her, hauling her against his chest. It seemed to be his go-to move.

She liked it.

"Let's take this to the privacy rooms. We don't have long before one of the subs will be here to set up for tomorrow. I'm pretty sure it's Devi's week, so she'll be hauling a bodyguard with her, and I'd like to avoid Landon seeing you all sexed up and hot as hell," Cooper said as he started for the stairs.

She was all for it but heard the beep that let her know the alarm was being reset. "I think she came early."

"What the…"

Nope. It was totally her dad, and he was carrying a bag from her favorite bakery. It was sweet. Her dad had come back to try to persuade her with chocolate croissants.

Or he'd drugged them and this was his kidnapping play. A sucky thing to do, but she wouldn't put it past him if he thought she was leaving.

He turned, but she could see he'd put a hand to his mouth. To stem the vomit. Well, he'd walked into a sex club.

"Hey, Dad, you should leave the croissants. We're planning on having a lot of sex," Kala announced. "Unless you drugged them. Then you should give them to Seth. Didn't Lou tell you Cooper showed up?"

"She left that part out," her dad said. "She told me about Ben making an appearance, and I thought it might be a good time to try to talk to you again. Lou thought that was a great idea. Boomer should have spanked her more. I take it you two are okay, and why the hell would I drug you?"

"We're good," Cooper replied, and there was a light in his eyes as he looked down at her. He was having fun. "And she thinks you were going to lock her up until she came to her senses. It's cool. I figured out another way. I don't know why you and Dad always tell me my dick is stupid. It was very smart this time."

Her father dropped the bag. "I need a drink. And I wouldn't drug you. I would trick you into the cage. Take care of her and…"

"We don't need a condom," Cooper called out. "We're going to have the kids call you Grumpa."

Her dad sighed and strode out the door again. Like she would get tricked. Maybe if there were chocolate croissants. Or pizza.

Cooper laughed and started for the stairs again.

"Hey," she said.

He turned and lowered her close enough to grab the bag of treats her father had so thoughtfully brought her.

They would need some energy. They could get pizza later.

She snuggled close as he carried her to the privacy rooms.

\* \* \* \*

Kala slipped out of the room where Cooper lay sleeping. Her phone had been ringing for hours, and though she didn't want to have this talk, she was a rip the bandage off kind of girl. She pressed the screen to answer this latest call. "Hey, Lena."

A long sigh came over the line. "Finally. I thought I was going to have to haul you out of that club."

Stupid trackers. She was going to tell Lou to change the damn frequency on hers. "Seriously, you turned on my tracker because I didn't answer my phone?"

"It's been hours and hours, and I was getting worried about you. So am I picking you up from the club or are you meeting me at the airport?" Lena asked, her voice crisp and professional over the line. "I'm calling security for the plane because your father is an asshole."

She wasn't sure what her dad had done, but she did know her parents wouldn't ever let her leave. Neither would Coop. They would track her down, and no one would care that she was on a super-secret mission. They would charge in and toss her over a shoulder and put her in a locked room.

It was easier to stay.

Nope. She was changing her thinking. She wasn't going to make things less than they were. Especially her feelings. She was staying because this was her place. Because they loved and needed her, and she loved and needed them.

Yes, she was kind of a grump, but there was nothing wrong with her some good therapy couldn't fix. And maybe some meds. "I'm afraid the plan is changing. I can't go to DC tonight."

"Kala, I set up several meetings with big-time players at the Agency. These are serious people, and they won't like the schedule changing. I thought you wanted to work," Lena replied.

Kala put the phone on speaker as she walked through the bar. Should they get pizza and spend the night here, or go back to her place so she could get the lowdown on what happened with Ben? Scratch that. Definitely get the pizza delivered here because if they went home with it, TJ would almost certainly be hungry no matter what he'd had for dinner. She definitely wanted to know what happened with Ben. She wanted to make sure her heroic efforts did some good for her sister. Of course if they didn't, then she might be able to kill Ben. So it was a win-win either way. "I think I've got all the work I can handle with this team."

"You want to leave the team." Lena's tone had gone tight.

She should have known this would be a bit of a fight. Lena thought she was doing the right thing, but she hadn't been there in Colorado. She didn't know how much it changed her. "I've been persuaded otherwise."

"Did your father threaten you?" Lena asked. "You should know I've already filed an incident report with HR because your father told me not to talk to you any longer and that if I continued to interfere—his word, not mine—with his daughter, he will kill me."

So her father was already hard at work. "Lady, you got off easy. My dad can be very over the top when it comes to threats. I'm surprised he didn't detail the death he has planned. It usually involves viscera. Also, you should understand that it's not a threat. It's more of a promise. He's not like other dudes who say a bunch of shit but have no follow up. He's already planning on where to stuff your body." Maybe she and Coop should look for some land. A couple of acres. A bit off the beaten path. They had family traditions to uphold. "I'll talk to him. Once he understands I'm not leaving the team, he'll back off."

A low huff came over the line. "Oh, trust me. I'll handle your father. Kala, we've talked about this. We have been working through this, and I would hate to see you fall back into old patterns. You will do much better without the encumbrance of that team."

How had she even thought those words? Her team wasn't holding her back. This was what her dad meant. The dark voices and thoughts sometimes led her down dangerous paths. "They aren't an encumbrance. I've figured that out. They ground me."

"Yes, they ground you when you could fly. Have you forgotten the last few weeks of therapy? We worked through this. We have a plan. A plan to get you where you want to go, where you need to be."

Tears welled when she thought about some of the things she'd said in those therapy sessions. "I wanted to talk to you about the plan. And no, I haven't forgotten. I do appreciate the time and effort you put in, but I think I need someone else. I do think I should be in therapy, and I would like to talk to someone about whether or not some of what I'm going through is depression."

She'd thought so much about this when she was in Colorado. Even in her happiest, most content moments, she could still hear those dark voices. They were shadows that might always be there. They might simply be part of who she was, and if that was true, then she would get through it. But if it was some chemical imbalance, she wanted to know. Wanted a shot at quieting them so she could hear and feel the full extent of the amazing love she'd been given.

The line was silent for a moment. "Are you joking?"

"No." Did she sound like she was joking? Sometimes she could come off as joking even when she was serious. Cooper seemed to understand her. And her friends talked a lot about speaking Kala. Maybe Lena didn't yet, so she needed to be clear. "I think I should prioritize my mental health."

"Kala, if you start taking drugs, they'll very likely pull you from the field," Lena pointed out. "They won't allow a mentally unstable person to know some of the world's most important secrets."

She'd thought about it. Though it did seem unfair since she knew a lot of dudes who worked in intelligence who could use some help. And who used drugs like cocaine, but hey, the Lexapro was a bridge too far. "Then I'll work behind the scenes. Look, we talked about me doing what's best for myself. This is it. I want to be happy. I might never feel it like my sister does, but I'm going to do everything I can to be the best me. I have people I love who need me around, and if I keep going the way I'm going, I won't."

Starting with Devi, who should be here soon. This was her night to inspect the equipment and make sure the bar was stocked for play tomorrow, so she would be here with her bodyguard any minute now.

She was having such a talk with her cousin. If she had to kick her cousin's ass, she would. She and Aunt Erin could start setting up a secure room to hold her ass in if she had a problem with it. Ah, family time.

Damn, she loved her family. So fucking much.

"Are you serious? Who have you been talking to, Kala? You're not depressed. You're poison. You ruin the people around you. If you didn't have people watching you constantly, you would likely have become a criminal a long time ago. Is baby Kala trying to shut out the voices in her head with some drugs? Do you think you can? Those voices are right, and they're a part of your soul."

Holy shit. She kind of wanted to fist pump. The therapist was evil. Therapy sucked, and Lena proved it. She sighed. Or Lena was a plant. She could still hold it over her dad's head for all of time.

It had been a good day. She had something to hold over her sister's head, and now her dad had forced her to go to therapy with an evil minion. How bad was it? The worse it was, the more her dad would have to grovel. Also, she got to keep Coop for the rest of her life. That was the best part. But also the other stuff. She kind of bounced down the stairs. She needed a pizza. But first she would call her dad and tell him all the "Lena is evil" stuff. "Okay. So are you working for the shits in the Agency who want to take down my parents? Or someone else. Huisman plays a long game."

"You little bitch. I guess we have to do this the hard way."

Kala got to the bottom of the stairs and realized she wasn't alone. Her stomach dropped. Eve McKay stood there, tears shining in her eyes and one hand to her heart.

Fuck. It might not be a good day. Not if Eve was here to tell her to stay away from Cooper. She wasn't sure what the hard way was, but she had to deal with the situation at hand. "I'll have to kill you later. Bye." She hung up and straightened her shoulders. She'd told herself she didn't have to fight so much, didn't have to be defensive. But this was one fight she couldn't back down from. "Hello, Eve."

She was wearing her normal outfit. Eve was always stylish, with elegant lines. Where her mom wore a lot of trendy clothes, Eve stuck to the classics. Tailored slacks and a silk blouse with a Chanel necklace that Kala would absolutely use as a weapon if she had one. Those suckers were well made. Eve had blonde hair that reached her shoulders. The only thing that marred her perfect looks was the angry expression on her face. "Who were you talking to?"

"It doesn't matter." She wasn't sure why Eve would want to know about Lena. How much had she heard? Was she pissed she'd just found out about the possible depression? Maybe she thought she hadn't treated her therapist the way she should. She kind of felt like she was fifteen again and this woman thought she was going to wreck her perfect son's life.

"It matters. Was it the Agency woman?"

She needed to not get mad. Calm. She had to prove to Eve that she was working on her anger issues. "I'm not going to hurt her." A lie, but a necessary one. Lena's murder would happen off the books and only after she figured out why the woman had been placed there. "It was a joke. Look, this is Agency business. I think we should probably talk about why you're here. I can go wake up Cooper, if you like."

Eve ignored her. "She's had you in sessions for weeks, Kala. I want to know what she said to you."

"I thought that was supposed to be secret." It was kind of what they preached. What happened in therapy stayed in therapy. Though if Lena was working for someone bad, she probably didn't follow the rules.

"I heard what that bitch said. I want to know what she's been filling your head with, baby girl." Eve's voice cracked, and Kala realized the angry expression might not be directed at her. Eve walked right up to her, heels clicking on the stained-concrete floors. She got into Kala's space and cautiously brought her hands up, giving Kala plenty of time to step back if she wanted to. "You are not poison. There is nothing wrong with you. You are smart and bold and strong. You are resilient. You hold people accountable when they need it and you forgive when they deserve it, and I am so grateful you forgave my son."

Damn, she thought she'd cried it all out, but the world went watery again. "I think she's working for someone who wants to break up the team. Or maybe Huisman, though it feels more personal and Huisman doesn't have any ties to her. So if it was Huisman, she was probably doing it for the money and wouldn't have folded so fast. It sounded like she hates me. I've pissed off a lot of people at the Agency."

"So you didn't listen to her? You know the things she said were manipulative and wrong?"

Kala hesitated. "She sounded reasonable at the time. She didn't say the things she said on the phone just now. She told me how much better off I would be on my own."

Eve's head shook. "She is not supposed to have an opinion. She is supposed to ask questions so you figure out what your motivations are. She is supposed to lead you down a path, not make one up and put you on it."

"She said I was kind of evil." A rush of shame flowed over her even thinking about it. "Not in those words, but in a way that almost made it seem good to be evil. At least for my job. It's not the first time I've heard it."

"You are not evil," Eve said, her voice shaky. "You are good at your job. Every bit as good as your father. There are some people who have different impulses. You're a protector."

"I can be a killer." It was pure truth. She'd killed more than once and hadn't missed a wink of sleep over it.

Eve stepped back, frowning her way. "Name me one, Kala. One person who you killed who wasn't trying to kill you or someone else. One person who wasn't in the line of duty."

"Seth says I kill his soul sometimes." She was going to do something terrible to her brother who had betrayed her in the worst way. And she was also going to hug him because he was an asshole who deeply cared about her.

Eve chuckled but sobered quickly. "You are not what that woman said. I didn't like her from the beginning, and neither did your mother. Which I suspect is why you didn't tell her how deep in you were getting with her."

Kala shook her head. She was going to be honest with Cooper's mom and then maybe see how she handled that particular truth. "It was more than that. I was seriously considering leaving the team, and Lena was going to help me do it."

Eve paled. "Ian's going to kill her. Where are we going to put her? We're all full."

Yep, the family tradition. "I thought it would be a good way to gradually break the bonds between me and Cooper so he could find someone more suitable. Someone who wouldn't drag him down with her."

She went even paler, and her eyes closed. When they opened

again there was naked pain in her brown orbs. "I always wondered if he told you. We were good and then you would barely look at me and your mom said it was because of what happened during the kidnapping and the fact that Cooper broke your heart. But I knew different because you were fine around Alex. It was me you didn't want to be around."

"It's okay. I got over it." It was easy now to forgive Eve.

"No, you didn't," Eve insisted, "and you also didn't understand what I meant. I never thought you weren't good enough for Cooper. I worried he couldn't be enough for you. I worried he would do exactly what he did because at the time it was important to be popular and have the world see him as this perfect son. I know it's a common feeling among adopted children and it doesn't necessarily reflect on the parents, but it's hard to not wonder what we did wrong. What we did to make him think we loved him less."

"He knows now," Kala reassured her. "The question is how do you feel about me being with Cooper now?"

"He's a man," Eve replied with surety. "It's completely different now. He's not an insecure boy, but you have to know that he won't always do the right thing. He's human and he'll screw up sometimes, and he might not always know how to fix things."

"Oh, he has his ways." She let a smile cross her face and then frowned. "Unfortunately, my dad caught the end of that show."

Eve laughed. "Good. Then maybe I can talk him into being easier on Coop. You're his baby. No man is ever going to be good enough for you, but I think Cooper is, and I know you're good for him. But what Lena did, sweetheart, that wasn't therapy."

"No, it was apparently some form of black op," Kala grumbled, but she understood Eve's point. "I know. I'm actually a little hurt by it. I thought it was doing me some good."

"The talking part did you good, and she used it against you. Now we find someone who won't. Someone who will guide you in figuring out how to handle some of your more delicate emotions." Eve stopped for a moment as though trying to figure out how to move forward. "Were you serious about getting screened for depression?"

So she'd heard pretty much everything. Kala nodded. "Yes. I think we both know how that's going to go. My brain is all fucked up. I owe it to all the people I love to figure out if I can make it better."

Eve's head shook, and tears pooled in her eyes. "No. Your brain is perfect. It just needs some help so you can be happier. And you need to do it because you owe it to yourself. That's what therapy is about. You are worth the work, Kala Taggart. I'll do everything I can to help you."

So many emotions. She hugged the woman who was going to be her mother-in-law. That was one thing she didn't know. She should wait, but it was an impulse to tell her. "Cooper wants to get married next week."

She wanted to see if Eve would stiffen and change her mind if she knew they were serious. Eve stepped back, a big smile on her face. "I'm so happy. But, sweetie, your mother is never going to allow you to get married at a courthouse. I'm sure that's what he offered. Absolutely not. We'll put something together. I don't suppose we could have two weeks."

Nope. Her future MIL hadn't hesitated. "I'll talk to him."

The truth of the matter was she wanted her family there. She didn't want to wait too long, though, and she definitely wouldn't be having a full-on church wedding with twelve million flowers like Carys and Aidan tried to have. Though the exploding helicopter had been cool.

"Kala," a familiar voice said. "I'm so sorry."

Devi. Kala turned and there was her cousin. With Lena. Who—fuck it all—had a gun pointed to the back of Devi's head. Eve gasped and tried to move in front of Kala.

Yeah, it was a theme with the McKay family, and she was going to stop questioning if they loved her. She was sure if Alex had been here, he would be offering himself up, too. Unfortunately, it wouldn't help. She was the target, and she had to find a way to get out of this situation with everyone alive.

Well, at least now she knew what Lena had meant by doing it the hard way. Kala held her hands up and cursed the fact that she'd thought she would be safe in the club, so she hadn't walked around with her SIG. Rookie move. "Let Devi go and we can talk." That was when she noticed Lena had two friends with her. Big guys, and they hadn't made the same mistake she had. They were strapped and looked like they knew how to use them. She was sure they would have been waiting for her wherever Lena planned on taking her. "So we weren't going to DC?"

Lena had lost her super-professional look. The woman knew how to hide her crazy eyes. Kala would give her that. "It was the original plan, but earlier today my boss decided to change things up. I called these guys in because we're getting on a private jet. The doctor would like to see you."

Fuck. She was working for Huisman. Well, they'd known he'd been planning things for years and years. Was it so surprising he had a couple of long-term plants? "I'll go with you if you let Devi and Eve go."

"No, you won't," Eve said stubbornly.

"Dr. McKay, put the phone down," Lena warned. "I see your hand in your pocket. Toss it my way."

Kala heard the *thunk* of a phone hitting the hard floor. She prayed Eve had managed to get a call out and someone was listening in. She forced her panic down. It was there because losing his mother would devastate Cooper. And Devi… She couldn't stand the thought of losing her cousin. A thought hit her. How bad was it already? "Is Landon dead?"

Landon Vail, son of Eric and Deena Vail. Eric had been the head chef at Top Fort Worth for over a decade, and his wife Deena ran publicity and marketing for her Uncle Sean's restaurant group. They would… She couldn't even comprehend what they were going to go through if their only son was dead.

How bad would this get?

"Who the fuck is that?" Lena asked.

Kala felt her eyes narrow. "He's supposed to be her bodyguard, so now I have to figure out which of them I'm killing."

"I ditched him," Devi admitted. "I'm sorry. I'm so sorry. I didn't think it was this serious. Why is this happening?"

Lena might not know who she had. Devi had been convenient. Shit. Had she given up important intel? She hadn't called her *cousin*. Did Lena know the connection between Devi and Zach? "It's not anything that involves you. She needed a body to hide behind, and you came along at the wrong time."

"Yeah, I've been here before. Hoped I wouldn't again. This sucks, and it keeps happening," Devi complained. "It makes a girl think."

Lena's hold tightened. "Devon Taggart?"

Yep, she'd fucked that up. She was going to give Cooper a pass on his overly emotional reaction to thinking she was dead because here she was screwing up because she cared about the people around her.

"Oh, I think I can bring my boss a bonus. Maybe then he'll let me kill you myself for what your father did to mine," Lena said with a snarl. "I was pissed because this ruins everything I've worked for. I was almost close enough to kill your parents, but the truth is I'm afraid of Huisman. But when I present him with the perfect way to force Zach Reed to turn himself in, maybe he'll let me have you. He's obsessed with you, you see. He wants to experiment on you again. He dreams of your screams at night."

"Fun guy," she quipped, though her adrenaline was already up. She kind of wished Coop was. Up, that was. Shouldn't he have, like, felt the danger or something? Shouldn't all that great sex have given them a psychic connection? Romance novels had not properly prepared her. "Who the hell are you?"

She didn't have to ask what her parents had done. Probably killed someone. It didn't matter.

"Wouldn't you like to know."

Kala shook her head. "Yes, that's why I asked."

"I have no idea why people consider you dangerous," Lena shot back.

"I could show you," Kala offered. "But right now I want to know who you are."

"My father was a CIA operative," she announced. "Your parents killed him."

Eve gasped. "Eli Nelson was your father? He didn't have any children."

"He had me," Lena practically shouted. "He just didn't know it. And I didn't get the chance to meet him because your father murdered him."

"Oh, for fuck's sake." She was here for this? This? "First off, my father didn't kill yours. That was my mother, and she blew his lying, murderous ass all over the Arabian sea and..."

She'd been ready to explain the world to Lena when the woman nodded to one of the men and a shot blasted through the space. Devi went white and started toward the floor, but the other guard caught her, so the ploy didn't work. It merely allowed Lena some freedom as she passed Devi off.

At first Kala thought she was dead. She'd been shot before, and sometimes adrenaline played tricks on a mind.

Then Eve fell, her body twisting toward the floor as blood stained her silk shirt.

Kala dropped to her knees, unable to stop the panic now. Her chest. How close was the bullet to her heart? Eve's eyes were still open, but she was a pasty white.

"I can finish the bitch off or you can come with me," Lena offered.

"Don't," Eve whispered. "Fight. She'll kill me anyway."

"I won't." Lena stayed out of range of Kala's hands, which twitched to strike. "I think Cooper is here somewhere, and it'll slow him down if he has to save his mother. I like some chaos, too, you know. I missed her heart. Looks like I nicked a lung. She'll survive for a while yet. Likely just long enough for us to make it to the airfield and get out of here. If you want to fight, I can do that, too. But the first thing my men are going to do is kill your cousin. You might take a couple of us out, but she'll die and so will Eve. Though I suppose it would fit the Taggart way to choose the selfish path."

"Kala," Devi began.

Kala looked down at Eve. "Tell Cooper I love him."

The rest went without saying. If Lena wasn't lying and Eve could survive, she would tell them everything. Her parents would come for her.

Cooper would come for her.

And hey, maybe the bad guys wouldn't look in her butt cheek for the tracker. Probably not.

She squeezed Eve's hand. "And I love you, too."

Tears slipped from Eve's eyes. "I love you, sweet girl."

She hadn't been a sweet girl for a very long time. Maybe never, but then perhaps the people who loved her saw her differently. She stood. "Let's do this then."

Lena chuckled, a nasty sound. "Like I would let you walk out of here. I never intended to do that. I was going to slip this into your drink, but this will do."

She reached into her pocket and pulled out a syringe, setting it on the floor and rolling it Kala's way. Like she was too dangerous to get close to. It was the one smart thing the woman had done all day because simply laying hands on Devi had signed her death warrant. Much less shooting Eve. It might not be Kala who did it, but she had no doubt her family would take the trash out. She reached down and picked up the syringe. Ah, here she was. Full circle. Except this time she had to choose. Once she was out, they could do anything they wanted with her body.

And Cooper would still love her. Her parents would still love her. Her family would put her back together if they tore her apart.

It was oddly simple, this thing that had haunted her most of her life. She had to choose to go back to hell or watch her cousin and mother-in-law die.

Hell it was. She'd been through it once. If Satan wanted to dance again, he'd learn how good she'd gotten at it.

She stared at Lena as she shoved the syringe into her arm and pushed the plunger. "See you soon, Doc."

The world went dark as she felt herself falling to the floor.

## Chapter Seventeen

Where the hell had she gone? A dude takes one little nap and his soon-to-be wife slips away. Cooper yawned and rolled out of bed, stretching. How long had he been out? She couldn't blame him. He'd performed valiantly. He'd fucked her at least four times. Maybe five. It was a lot of sex.

He felt a grin split his face. He had her now. This time was forever.

He wasn't even worried that she'd gotten out of bed. She'd likely gone to get a drink or take a shower or…talk to Devi, who was probably here by now. The clock read a bit past seven.

They'd talked about her cousin in between bouts of extremely athletic sex. She was worried about Devi and what Zach might do if she kept up her recklessness.

He pulled on his jeans. He kind of wanted to see what his brother would do since if Zach showed up, he could catch the fucker and have the talk they so obviously needed to have.

Shit. He'd thought of Zach as his brother. He wasn't. Not the way Hunter was. Zach had kept secrets, but if Kala was willing to forgive him and thought he had his reasons, he was going to listen. He'd had a great relationship with Zach before. Zach had sought him out. If he'd done it because he wanted to know him, then maybe he should talk to his mom and figure out if this was a relationship he should explore. His mother always gave sound advice, likely because she was a psychologist.

His biological mom was an infamous bombmaker. He had to let that sit a little while longer.

He opened the door to the privacy room and listened for a moment. The privacy rooms were soundproofed, for obvious reasons, so he wouldn't have heard Devi and the bodyguard coming in. He listened to see if he could hear the dulcet tones of his soon-to-be bride giving her cousin the business.

He heard nothing.

They were probably in the locker room. He should go down and hang out with Landon so he wasn't bored while Kala argued with her stubbornest cousin. He grabbed two beers out of the lounge and then made for the stairs.

And dropped both when he looked down. For a split second he couldn't process what he was seeing.

His mom. She lay on her back on the floor of the lobby, her chest covered in blood.

The world sped up again and he took the stairs two at a time, desperate to get to her. He hit his knees. Phone. He left his phone somewhere down here. He reached for her hand.

Her eyes opened suddenly, and she struggled to breathe. "Kala. Lena Gallagher took Kala and Devi. You have to find them. Kala…they knocked her out, but Devi was still conscious."

What the hell? Who would take Kala? He shook his head. That was naïve. Any number of assholes she'd pissed off would love to kill her, but there wasn't a body. Nausea rolled through him. Huisman. Huisman wanted her once. Phone. He had to call 911.

His mom squeezed his hand. "You have to find her."

He did, but first he had to call an ambulance. And then Big Tag.

The door slammed open and Cooper stood, trying to protect his mom.

"Devi Taggart, you are in so much fucking trouble," a deep voice called out from the front hall. "The alarm isn't even on. I'm talking to your moth…" Landon stopped, his eyes going wide. "Coop?"

"Call 911." Thank god, he wasn't alone. "And then call Tag. He's probably at Sanctum, so he's not far. Tell him to turn on Kala's tracker." He leaned back over, taking his mother's hand again. She'd been shot but she was holding on. He heard Landon call. "Mom, I need you to stay with me."

"I'm fine," she said, her eyes tightening and proving her words wrong. "Kala and Devi aren't. That terrible woman. Tell Ian she's Eli Nelson's daughter and she's working with Huisman."

Fuck. If she was working with Huisman, then she probably had access to his tech, including whatever he did last time to overload the tracker. His gut tightened. "Did she say anything? Give you any indication about where she was taking them?"

His mom's head shook slightly, and it seemed to cause her pain. "No. I don't know. I'm just…"

"Shhhh," he said. "Save your strength." This couldn't be the end. He couldn't lose her. Couldn't lose Kala now that they were finally on solid ground.

He held his mother's hand while Landon called in the troops. His father made it mere seconds before the ambulance got there, and Cooper would never forget the look on his face. His father had been the one to hop in the ambulance after the EMTs stabilized her.

The sirens were still wailing as Big Tag and Charlotte ran in.

"What the fuck happened, Cooper?" Tag stared down at the pool of blood. "Eve?"

"The EMTs said she needs surgery, but she is in good shape." A weird numbness settled over him. If he let himself feel the horror of the last thirty minutes, he wouldn't be able to move, and he had to. Kala didn't need emotional reactions right now. She needed him focused on one thing. Getting her back. "What does the tracker say?"

*Please let her tracker work.*

Ian's head shook. "I tried and the software says it's offline. So it's Huisman. I find it very interesting that Ben Parker is in town and Huisman shows up."

"Ian, Ben is at Top with Kenzie right now," Charlotte pointed out. "He has no idea, and neither does Kenzie." She looked to Cooper. "We decided to leave her out for the time being. I'm worried she'll give herself away, and I don't know how we explain to Parker that the girl he's on a date with got kidnapped. While she's sitting there with him. But the rest of the team is on the way. Tris is already looking into private airfields around the area. I want to see the security tapes."

He'd already thought about that. When Landon had finished making his calls, Cooper had ordered him to go into the security office and pull everything they had. It wouldn't show what happened inside, but they had cameras covering all around the building and in the parking lot. "Landon is doing that right now."

"Yeah, I'll be having a talk with him," Big Tag said grimly.

Cooper's hands were trembling. He forced them to stop. Cool. Calm. He needed to stay that way. "Don't be hard on him. Devi's been acting up lately. She ditched him, and he came after her. He was too late. I think we have to bet she took Devi as a way to draw Zach out. Huisman wants the bombmaker, after all."

"Then why take Kala?" Charlotte asked, her face pale.

"Because Huisman wants to hurt me," Big Tag said with grim surety. "I've already got word into Drake that his super-psychologist was a plant. Between Zach and now Lena, we've got some real problems with the Agency's vetting process. I have to wonder where the hell Huisman found her and how much he paid her."

His mom had said something he hadn't truly understood. "Mom said Lena is someone's daughter. Do you know a guy named Nelson?" What was the first name? "Evan, maybe."

For the first time in his life, he watched Ian Taggart's jaw drop. "Eli fucking Nelson? He didn't have kids. He wasn't married."

"And I blew up the boat he was on. Technically, he blew it up himself. He didn't know I'd transferred the bomb to his ship," Charlotte explained.

Ian ran a hand over his sandy hair, a look of complete shock on his face. "He said it to Kala. *The sins of your father will be visited upon you.* He's been planning this for a fucking decade. He found Lena, brought her in, placed her where she could work her way close to the target. Us."

"I knew she was up to something. I think she's been using those so-called therapy sessions against Kala." Charlotte paced. "She's been trying to isolate her so she could do exactly this."

"And when it didn't work, she used Devi and Eve to get Kala to comply," Cooper explained. "That's what my mom said."

"You should go to the hospital and be with your dad," Charlotte offered.

Big Tag's head shook. "He's not going anywhere except to work. He's not going to be able to do or think about anything else right now. I called Hunter. He's on his way. And Vivi's trying to find a flight from London. Sean and Grace are on their way, too. Alex is going to have support."

A huge relief. In so many ways. Not only realizing his dad wasn't alone, but that Big Tag knew his heart. "I'm on this team. I won't lose it the way I did last time. She would be pissed if I did, and she already makes fun of me, so I'm going in stoic this time."

"See that you do." Big Tag reached for his wife's hand, drawing her close. "We're going to find her."

Charlotte wrapped her arms around her husband and held on.

The door came open, and Tristan strode through. He already had his laptop in hand. He looked like he'd come from the gym, dressed in sweats and a T-shirt. "Aidan dropped me off. He's heading to the hospital but wants you to know he'll come along if we figure out where they are. Or Carys. He wants a doctor there."

"We'll take Aidan. His specialty is…" Cooper had to take a long breath. "Trauma. God, hasn't she had enough damn trauma? At least I think he'll keep Devi halfway healthy because Zach won't come in otherwise, but he'll torture Kala. Again."

Tris moved in, giving him a big hug. "It's going to be okay. She's the toughest woman I know. And you should understand that I've already put the word out to Zach. There are some places I know he used to frequent on the Internet. I have to hope he still checks those addresses."

"We can't count on him," Cooper said, stepping back, but he was in control again. "The last time I saw him he was… Well, the last time Kala saw him he was walking through the Rocky Mountains. I was kind of drugged."

"He'll have a way," Charlotte said, wiping her eyes. "I'm going to look at those security cams."

Landon stepped out of the office. "She took them offline somehow. They're blank from five minutes after Eve walked in the door to right before I showed up. I have to assume they had something that took the wireless offline."

"Okay, we need to think. Where would they take her?" Charlotte asked. "She said she was flying to DC. Is there any way they would take her somewhere close? She wouldn't get on a plane without knowing where they were heading."

"No, but we have to assume using drugs to knock her out was always the plan," Big Tag replied. "We need a list of small planes that took off in the last hour. I know we can't be certain whatever flight plan they put in place is the real one, but we can call in the big guns and use satellites to track it."

"To track what?" Lou was breathless as she ran in. She had her laptop bag over her shoulder. She was in pajama bottoms and a hoodie. TJ was behind her wearing roughly the same. It looked like they'd been having a chill night at home.

"The plane they've got Kala and Devi on." Tris walked toward the conference room, opening his laptop.

TJ looked Landon's way, his eyes narrowing. "You…"

Cooper shook his head. "He did his job. Devi's been making it hard on him."

"She said she was going to the bathroom," Landon argued. "I can't go in there with her. Well, I did after she stayed there for fifteen minutes. She kept texting that she was having…girl problems. What am I supposed to do with that? By the time I went in and scared the crap out of a couple of elderly ladies, she'd gone through the window."

"I'm going to kill my sister," TJ muttered. "I need to call my mom and dad. They're supposed to be on vacation for their anniversary. I get to tell them once again one of their children is in trouble."

"Why do we need to track the plane?" Lou asked as TJ walked outside.

Cooper followed Ian and Charlotte as they entered the conference room. "Because we won't be able to use her tracker. It's Huisman. He killed it before."

Lou was hot on his heels. "Yes, I know. It's why I gave her a new one. Why hasn't Uncle Ian pulled it up?"

"I tried." Ian stood, looking over Tristan's shoulder. "It's showing offline. You know he has tech that can kill our trackers. It's how he got her the first time. Tris is going to give us a list of planes that could be Lena's. What I need from you is to hop on traffic cams around this building and see if we can ID what vehicle they used. If we can follow them via the camera feed, we'll have a better idea of what airport they flew out of."

"That's a good idea." Charlotte looked happy to have something to do. "I'll help you, Lou."

Lou's eyes closed, and she sighed. "No one ever listens to me."

What was going on with Lou? She wasn't as freaked out as she should be. Almost like she knew something the rest of them didn't.

"Ian couldn't find her tracker."

Lou looked up at him. "Did he use the new login I gave him or did he forget and go back to the old one?"

Ian's head came up. "There's a new login?"

A frustrated sigh came from Lou's mouth, and she pulled out her laptop. "I gave everyone the rundown on the new trackers and what they can do. And what can't be done to them. No one listens. I'm sure you were all doodling or thinking about what we were going to do in the club later that night." Her fingers moved across the keys, typing with precision and a little irritation. "Seriously, I invented a whole new technology that protects our trackers from mild EMPs, which is what he used last time. He won't even be able to tell it's still online, and do I get a cookie?" She turned her laptop screen around. "She's in the air."

Sure enough, there was a blip on the screen moving over North Texas to the east.

Cooper walked to Lou and wrapped her up in a big hug. "You are a freaking genius, Louisa Ward."

"That's why they hired me." She laid her head on Cooper's shoulder. "We're going to get her back. We'll get them both back. They'll be okay."

"Lou, I swear I'll listen to every lecture about science you ever try to give again." Big Tag came in behind her and kissed the top of her head. "I'll get the jet ready. Cooper, I need you to make an educated guess about where they're going. We're following."

"Hey, did everyone figure out Lou already solved the problem?" TJ joined in, wrapping his arms around Lou from behind. "I didn't know why everyone was so grim. I mean besides your mom nearly dying and my sister and Kala being in the clutches of a madman. But Lou will get us there and we'll fix it."

Such confidence.

And suddenly he had it, too.

"Did Lou find her?" Tasha was in the doorway, and Cooper saw a sight he hadn't counted on. Kenzie. She was still in the dress she'd worn when she met Ben Parker.

"Of course she did," Kenz said. She moved in and joined what was now a big bear hug, mostly around Lou. "She invented a whole new tech so she wouldn't lose Kala again. She gave us a lecture about it."

At least one of them listened. "We'll get her back."

With this team around him, they would make it happen.

\* \* \* \*

Kala came awake in darkness, nausea rolling through her.

"There's a bucket to your right," a familiar voice said. "The drug you took, the side effects include vomiting. Usually after the subject wakes."

His voice made her sick, too. She wanted to prove him wrong, but her stomach wasn't in compliance. She rolled to her right and found the bucket just before the contents of her stomach came up. Chocolate croissants weren't as good the second time around, but at least she hadn't eaten the pizza she'd wanted to order. "Where's my cousin?"

She hated being in the dark. Where the hell was Devi and what had she already gone through?

"She's safe," Huisman said, his deep voice accented lightly. French. He was born in Montreal, though he'd spent his formative years in Toronto. Still, that French accent was there in every word of English he spoke. "For now. I wanted to talk to you. What do you know about the bombmaker?"

She got to her feet. She needed to figure out where the hell she was and how much rope he'd given her. There was zero way she wasn't in a cage. She held her hands out, trying to find the bars or walls or whatever he had planned for her. "She's Shannon Reed."

"Very good," he said, sounding almost proud. "And you know Zach is your boyfriend's biological brother. He's boring, you know. *Fastideux*. Perhaps he would have been more interesting had he been raised by his true mother."

"I assure you Eve McKay is his true mother."

"We will agree to disagree," he said with a sniff. He was somewhere to her right, probably ten or twelve feet away. "I don't understand why an interesting woman such as you would have anything to do with him. He has no style. No real intelligence. Now your sister fits with him."

"I assure you my sister is intelligent." She hoped so because this fucker had almost certainly fried her tracker at this point. Kenzie and Lou and Tris would do anything they could to find her. And Devi. "I want to see my cousin."

"She's with Lena. They're talking through all of her problems. So many issues with that girl. One would almost think something's wrong with your family."

"Yeah, she was a great therapist. Top notch, Doc."

"She was actually top of her class. Completely delusional, though. I think her mother screwed her up with all those stories about the father who was taken away from them. The dumb bitch actually thought the rogue CIA agent she had a brief affair with would have come back to her."

The evil doc had a real problem with women. She moved as quietly as she could. There seemed to be some kind of cot. That was what she'd been laid out on. Roughly six feet away there was another cot on the opposite side. So she might be getting a roommate. Hopefully her cousin. "Yeah, dumb bitches. It's ridiculous to think the dude she's screwing would be interested in the fact that they had a child together. So how'd you find her? Did you put out a post on the Internet asking for anyone who my parents killed in the line of duty to join your extraordinary league of supervillains?"

If she kept him talking, then he wasn't torturing her. Although now that she thought about it, the worst would be him talking *while* he was torturing her.

He chuckled as though she'd amused him mightily. "League of Supervillains. I like this. It sounds strangely American. The rest of the world understands that these villains you look for are always close to the heroes. Personally, I think Americans don't know either definition deep down."

She reached out and found the bars. Yup. She was in a cage, but she didn't panic. She'd known. She was pretty sure the bucket she'd thrown up in would also be her brand-new toilet. Fun. "Let's move it along. I really would like to know how you found some random chick who thinks my father screwed her over. Is there, like, a Facebook group?"

He sighed as though disappointed. "Fine. You're not being much fun, but I do like to explain my methodology. It's probably the doctor in me. A very long time ago, my grandfather set up… Let's call it a surveillance system. He wanted to keep track of the family that ruined his life."

"Yes, the family that wasn't even in the room when someone

who wasn't a member of the family killed your dad. You know Levi Green killed him, right?"

"Oh, see, that's where you think the only people responsible for a tragedy are the direct actors. Such an American viewpoint. It tends to keep you from thinking of yourselves as, to use your word, villains. There's more to any act. There are forces behind it, things that shaped and moved pieces into place. Who is more important? The pawn who unknowingly does the king's work? Or the king himself."

She would get no information from arguing with a delusional individual. She gently let her hands move from bar to bar until she found a corner. "You were telling me how you found Lena Crazy Eyes."

Another chuckle. "See, when you talk like that, I find you amusing. So different from most women of my acquaintance." She heard him shifting. He was probably watching her through night vision goggles. The creep. "Like I said, my grandfather watched your family closely. He was rather weak, though. He wanted a way to hurt your father financially, but he never found it. I knew there were better ways to have revenge on a man like him. I was only eighteen when I started seriously looking for allies. I found Lena when she requested several Freedom of Information Act documents. She was looking for her father. He was connected to yours, so I had people tracking anyone who asked about him."

The cage was a square, and to her left there was the smell of…loam. Earth. Were they underground? "And she thought 'hey, I'll screw up my whole life to help this dude I've never met before?'"

"She hated anyone connected with her father's death. She couldn't actually find out what happened, but she knew her father was on a classified mission and that Ian Taggart was somehow involved. I might have fudged a little there. You see, my father had managed to get the reports on Taggart's missions. It's surprising what millions of dollars will make an employee do. I didn't tell her that Lena's father was being hunted by the Agency for his treason. I let her believe it was Taggart who caused him to go underground and abandon her mother. From what I can tell, Nelson was a bastard who likely wouldn't have cared even if he knew he had a child. But I find giving a person what they want helps make them far easier to manipulate."

"So you find Lena, convince her to use her powers for evil, and manipulate your way to get around all the Agency guardrails?"

"That's easier than you think, though I will admit I had a lot to work with when it comes to her. Despite her delusions about her father, she's quite smart when it comes to her job. She's a gifted therapist and a truly excellent profiler."

All right. So she was in a roughly eight by ten cell. The door was in front of her, and she'd felt a box that was likely the lock. Probably some high-tech biometric system. The room outside felt bigger since she was almost certain Huisman was at least twelve feet away from her. Maybe a basement. Perhaps that loamy smell was actually mold. "Well, I was one of her clients, so I'll have to disagree."

"Do you? I thought she handled you perfectly."

She should have known. "She recorded the sessions?"

"Yes. It's why I waited so long. I've known for a while I would take you back. But when Lena managed to get herself assigned to profile Zachary Reed and assess your team, I knew I would wait. I've listened to those sessions several times now. They're fascinating."

He was giving her some serious ick. "Great. I'm thrilled you managed to violate me on another level."

"I haven't, you know. Your body was safe the whole time. I wouldn't do such a thing to you."

"No, you wouldn't. You would want me awake."

"Exactly," he practically purred. "I want you to be with me every minute of the way, so you can be assured no one touched you this time."

"You're just a peach." She hated him. She'd thought she hated people before, but this one…this one truly threatened to turn her into what Lena thought she was.

Her eyes were starting to adjust. It wasn't completely dark. There was something humming in the room, and it had a few buttons or switches that were lit.

"I am fascinated by how the experience—or non-experience—affected the rest of your life. I wonder if it hadn't happened, would you be so fierce? Lena thinks so. Lena believes you were born a predator. She believes the only reason you don't kill with abandon is the family around you."

Lena was an idiot. She wasn't a predator. She was a protector. When she managed to ignore the voices in her head, she knew exactly who she was. She was a woman who cared enough to kick some ass, willing to risk not being liked to help the people around her. Though she could give the man some reassurance. "I promise I'll have total abandon when I kill you."

Another laugh, though this one closer. He was moving toward her. She went still, trying to focus. Maybe she could see his shadow hovering.

"And that is why you fascinate me. I find it hard to believe Benjamin has feelings for you."

"I think Ben's feelings concerning me can be defined as confusion," she replied.

"Yes, I agree. He's more attracted to your twin. Your light half. Does it hurt to know she got all the light?"

She hadn't. It was just Kala's own light didn't always shine as brightly. And the darkness didn't always mean something bad. "She's the sun. I'm more like moonlight."

The sun could burn, but the moon was silvery and illuminated the darkness. Not as showy, but every bit as important.

He hesitated. "That might be the first naivety I've heard from you. I don't think I like it."

"I don't care what you like or don't like," Kala admitted. "I don't care what you think of me."

"Which is perversely why I find you fascinating. I've been wondering if it wouldn't hurt your father more if you were dead or if you were trapped here with me. Like my own tiger to train. I wonder how much pain it will take to turn you into what you could truly be."

She had questions, too. "I wonder how much force it will take to kick your dick back into your body cavity."

The lights came on suddenly and Kala blinked, the brilliance overwhelming her. He was right. It made her feel sick again. It was far, far too much, but then that was his point. She tried to look at him, but he was still a hazy shadow as her eyes desperately attempted to adjust.

"You know I like to be a bit dramatic. This place came on the market a few years ago. I know what happened here, so I bought it out of sheer sentimentality. Another place where the Taggarts ended lives, though I think in this case her brother was on your side. So sad. I didn't know when I bought it how much it meant to you." His voice was low and soothing.

The world was becoming clearer now. Where the hell...

She was in the house Julia Ennis had brought her to, in the cell she'd shared with Kyle.

Emmanuel Huisman stood in front of her wearing slacks and a white button-down and expensive loafers. She saw what she hadn't been able to before. They weren't alone. Two large guards with big guns stood by the two ways in—the door that led up to the house and the one to her left that led to the tunnels her parents had saved her through the first time she'd been here.

She'd been right. She was back in Hell.

"Couldn't even come up with something new, could you, Doc? You lack imagination."

"And you lack respect. I need some information from you. I need to know how to communicate with Captain Reed," he said quietly, and she realized he had something in his hand.

"Can't help you, asshole." She couldn't. He was supposed to contact her, but she wasn't going to let him know that. And hey, she couldn't unless Lena had stopped and picked up her cell. So Zach was fucking safe, but she and Devi had real problems. She had a thought. It worked once. "I don't suppose you would order a pizza for me. I'm very hungry."

The first time she'd been held here, she'd managed to convince her captor to order pizza. Like most things in life, she was a weirdo when it came to pizza. No sauce double anchovies. It grossed most people out, but her cousin's wife had used that order to pinpoint where she was being held.

Not that anyone would look here this time.

"Starving you will be one of the fun activities we can share." The man sounded positively chipper. "We'll see how long you hold out. You see, while I'll enjoy raping you, I would also find it amusing to turn you into a pet."

She felt a nasty smile cross her face. "Oh, I can be your pet right now."

The door came open, and Lena's heels clicked down the stairs. She was back to her normal perfection, but she couldn't quite hide the crazy in her eyes. "Oh, look, you're up. I was kind of hoping you would die."

It was always good to make friends. She didn't reply, merely offered up her middle finger.

Devi was brought down after Lena, her hands in zip ties and an armed guard at her back. She'd obviously been crying but she didn't seem physically harmed.

"You okay?" Kala asked.

Devi nodded. "Apparently they want me all pretty and whole. They didn't do anything while you were asleep. Although listening to that one talk was torture. She thinks she's intelligent, but she's one more narcissistic asshole. Why is the world filled with them?"

Kala stepped back, allowing them to open the cage door. She watched the hand movements of the guard. It was how she'd gotten out of here the first time.

But they'd changed the locks. Now they used biometrics, so she would need someone's thumbprint. The good news? It didn't have to be attached to a living hand.

Devi was shoved in.

"I'm saving Devon for later," Huisman explained. "I think Zach is going to want proof of life, and he'll be far more reasonable if she's as perfectly pretty as she is right now. She's the bait. Though if it doesn't work, one can also make the bait bleed. Chum the waters a bit. However, I thought I would start with you."

Excellent. If they were going to let her out, she had a shot. Adrenaline started to pump through her, and she took a long breath, centering herself. She would have to be careful because the room was tight, and if they started firing it could hit Devi. But she could do this. There were only four of them, and Lena didn't count. Lena would run the first chance she got. Huisman might, too. He tended to run rather than fight. Coward. She would take him down, and he wouldn't get back up this time.

And then the dart hit her. Taser. Straight to her chest. She heard Devi's startled scream and then she was falling to the floor, every muscle in her body seizing and shaking. Her head hit hard, and her vision started to fade again.

"You idiot. I didn't give you the order," Huisman was saying.

Someone pulled the dart out but her body kept shaking.

"It doesn't matter," Lena replied. "You would be better off putting her down. She's nothing but an animal. She'll turn on you in the end. If you ask me, she should have been put down as a child. There are some animals that can't be tamed."

As the world started to go dark, she heard the most terrifying words come from Huisman's mouth.

"That sounds like a challenge."

## Chapter Eighteen

"You're sure she's there?" Drake looked through binoculars at the big house located on the outskirts of Winchester, Virginia. The small, sleepy town was peaceful at this time of the night. The moon was out but it was in a half phase, and the woods around him were dark.

Cooper was sure there was no peace tonight for his future wife. Did Kala even know she was back at the place of her original trauma? Had she woken up and looked around and screamed in despair?

Check that. His baby wouldn't freak out. She would wake up and plan how to slaughter her enemies.

He hoped she knew he was coming for her. Well, he hoped she knew they would do anything to find her. She slept through meetings. He was pretty sure she had no idea what Lou had created.

"Her tracker places her there, and I have zero doubt it does everything Lou says it does." Big Tag had been quiet on the plane. They hadn't even used their own plane. Big Tag was worried that Huisman had people watching the team, so they'd all gone into the MT building as though headed in for a long meeting, and he'd slowly gotten them all out undercover. A few years back, he'd found a tunnel that led from their building to one two blocks over. No idea why it was there, but they used it when they needed to.

They'd gone to an executive airfield where a Bond Aeronautics jet was waiting. It was owned by Big Tag's brother and sister-in-law and wouldn't show any of them as passengers. Cooper had flown the jet with quiet precision, happy he had something to focus on during those hours.

"She's in there," Lou insisted. She'd changed into all black, while TJ was in dark fatigues. "They moved her from one side of the house to another."

"Well, at least we know where they'll keep her," Charlotte said. She sat in the back of the van Drake had picked them up in, checking her guns.

"We have a go from Langley if you're sure," Drake informed them.

"I wish you hadn't told them." Big Tag sounded irritated. Drake had met them at the DC airfield with two vans and all the equipment they would need.

"You know I have to," Drake argued. "This is an op on American soil. If something goes down, we'll need an umbrella. The good news is this place is isolated. The nearest neighbor is two miles away."

Drake should know since it used to be his house. Or rather his mother's. At least some of this was the boss's fault. "Well, I kind of wished you hadn't decided to sell it. Or maybe you could have checked and seen who the buyer was."

"Coop," Kenzie began.

He wasn't having any of it. "Nope. I'm kind of done with the older generation telling me I should be more careful. I have a brother I didn't know I had and a bio mom who likes to blow shit up because they thought my father was close enough to the Taggarts to protect me. No one vetted them because apparently I was a cute baby and they didn't want to ask questions. And now Kala's in a place where she's already been tortured once because Drake here couldn't be bothered to read a contract."

"In my defense, my mother sold the place." Drake was in the passenger seat, staring at the house down the hill. "We couldn't go back after what happened. We held on to it for almost ten years before she retired and decided it was time to find a new place. I've never even taken my children here."

"And technically it's not Big Tag's fault you have a weapons forward bio mom and a brother who should be more open emotionally and informationally," Tris quipped from behind his laptop. "Technically that's your bio dad's fault because of the way semen works. See, this is why Big Tag is such an advocate for condoms. Should we be looking for him? Is this all going to be some weird family reunion?"

He might punch Tristan. They were getting nowhere. "If we have a go, why aren't we going yet? Tell me we're not waiting for Theo and Erin."

Devi's parents were on their way back from their trip, but it would take them hours to get there, and those hours would likely cost Kala an enormous amount of pain. He wouldn't allow it.

"We have to have a plan, Rambo," Big Tag said with a long sigh. "Unfortunately, we don't think we can move in the same way we did last time. Last time we used a set of tunnels that lead from about a half a mile away to the basement. Huisman has to know about the tunnels."

"Well, he's definitely got some security up and running." Tristan's face was ghostly behind the lights coming from his laptop. His partner, Aidan, was in the van waiting a half a mile down the road. Tasha was driving a backup van in case things went bad.

"Can we cut the electricity from here?" Lou was supposed to be in the van with Tasha, but she'd shut down the notion of being support in this case. She was going in to save her best friend and wouldn't be talked out of it. TJ hadn't even argued with her, merely told her she would be by his side the whole way.

"We can, but then he'll know we're coming," Tris argued. "I kind of wish we had Parker with us. No one knows this asshole better, and quite frankly, he's proven good in a fight."

"I wish we had Ben here, too, but he might have questions about how we're rescuing me." Kenzie had her hair hidden under the balaclava she would soon pull down to mask her face. "Believe me. I wish I hadn't been forced to leave him. We were really talking. And now he's talking to Dare."

It had been the plan to extricate Kenz without making it too obvious to Ben that something was going on. Dare had joined them and asked to speak to Ben. The good news was that Dare had definitely softened on his former friend and was actually ready to talk to him. Kenzie had set them up in a private room at Top with expensive Scotch and cigars, and according to Tash they'd stayed until about thirty minutes before.

Kenzie had told him she'd meet him for a late lunch tomorrow.

If she was still alive and not in mourning. If they lost Kala, all bets were off, and it wouldn't matter anymore if Parker or everyone else figured out they were twins. "We should think about letting him in on the secret. I don't know that it's fair that Huisman knows and he doesn't. It gives Huisman a weapon to use against Parker and us."

"I'll think about it," Ian returned.

Kenzie let out a deep breath. "Good. We'll talk about it when we get my sister and Devi back."

"I still think we should have brought Daisy," TJ said in a hushed tone. "I know y'all think bringing a civvie in is wrong, but she foils bad-guy plans all the time. We would just have to have her, like, walk by the house and it might fall down."

Cooper wasn't sure that TJ was joking. After all, the last time Devi found herself in a shitty situation, Daisy had handled it, and she hadn't even needed a gun. Not that she would have been able to hide a weapon since she'd walked out and distracted the bad guys with her nudity.

Cooper was absolutely sure it wouldn't work on Huisman. Nothing would except the element of surprise. "What's going on with the cameras? Can we take them over?"

"I can patch on to them, but it's going to be a while before I get control," Tris said with a frustrated growl. "This software is very complex. It's almost like he knew someone would try to take over."

This guy was always prepared. He was always one step ahead. "Do we have any idea how many people he has with him?"

"I'm going through the feeds." Lou had a laptop open as well. "I've got ten armed guards, I think. They're all dressed alike, so I might be off by one or two. He's got them patrolling a half a mile area around the house, and he's got one on the tunnels."

"Can you see the basement?" Charlotte asked. "It's almost surely where Kala will be when they're not..."

Torturing her. Charlotte might not be able to say the words out loud, but it didn't change what was likely happening to the woman he loved.

"The basement is one of the rooms they have blacked out," Tris admitted. "I can see there's a camera there, but it's offline. Same for a couple of the rooms upstairs."

"That's where she'll be," Ian said firmly. "We need to access those rooms. The ones with cameras on aren't important beyond letting us know where the bad guys are. But you have to consider that the blacked-out rooms will have potential threats in them."

"Like more guards?" TJ asked.

"Or traps," Charlotte replied. "Don't trust anything in that house at this point."

"My wife found a bunch of medical equipment being shipped to this address within the last three weeks," Drake said, staring down at his tablet. He was in touch with his wife, Taylor, who also worked for the Agency. "It appears they're trying to show this as some sort of clinic on paper. That's disturbing. He's done a good job. He had the whole area rezoned as a mental health center. Like a rehab for wealthy people. It allows him to legally ship drugs in without gaining the eye of law enforcement."

"He did all of this for her," Kenzie said, not quite able to hide the horror in her tone. "He bought the house because it was attached in a way to our family, but he prepped it after he took her the first time. We have to think he's got some kind of fascination with Kala. What's happening to her? I wish we had that twin thing where we can feel each other."

"He won't kill her right away." Ian's tone had gone stony. It was how he talked when he was in focus mode. No sarcasm. No emotion.

But the emotion was there. It simply didn't control him. Like Cooper was learning to do with his own. Kala didn't shut down because she couldn't feel. She did it so she could focus on the problem at hand and not give the enemy information they didn't need to know. He felt a steely resolve harden in his gut. "She'll survive. No matter what he throws at her, she'll survive it, and we'll all be there for her."

"I don't know if my sister can," TJ said, for the first time sounding a little on edge. He'd been a soldier for a long time and he'd had to fight for his teammates, but Devi was his baby sister. And she didn't have the training the rest of the family had. "Survive, that is."

"Kala will do everything she can to make them look at her instead of Devi," Cooper promised. He knew his girl. She would take the pain so her cousin didn't have to.

And she thought she was some kind of villain?

"Devi's tougher than you think," Kenzie added. "She's got a core of strength inside her. She won't break."

"We have movement to our left," Drake said. "About a hundred feet away. There's someone out here moving through the trees." He pulled his comms unit. "Tash, are you seeing what I'm seeing?"

The radio crackled and then Tasha's voice was heard. "Yes. I see him. He's roughly six and a half feet, and he's wearing fatigues but not the ones the guards wear. He seems...familiar to me. It's something about the way he... I think it's Zach. Don't shoot. He's making his way to the van. Are you out of camera range?"

It was precisely why they were parked where they were. Cooper stared out the window and then opened the door.

"Hey," Ian began.

"He's here to talk to me," Cooper replied, hopping out of the van. In the moonlight he could see the shadowy figure moving toward them. Every few seconds he would stop and ensure the guards weren't on their rounds to his left and then he would move again, gaining ground.

It was definitely Zach. Tasha was right. The man moved with predatory grace, clinging to the trees like a shadow. And then he was simply striding toward the van.

TJ had gotten out and stood behind Cooper, obviously lending his support. His hand was on the M16 on his chest.

Zach's hands came up. "Hey, brother. I'm not here to hurt anyone on this team."

Big Tag now stood at the front of the car, his eyes staring out at Zach. "I'll decide that."

Charlotte had other thoughts. She got out of the van and walked right up to the man, throwing her arms around him. "Are you okay?"

"Charlie," Ian barked out.

"You know damn well he's not here to hurt us." Charlotte stared up at Zach and gave him a maternal once-over. "Are you all right?"

Zach's eyes closed, and Cooper thought he was trying hard to not get emotional. He was dressed for battle, but Cooper noticed he didn't have a holster on him. If he was carrying, Cooper couldn't tell. Zach opened his eyes again and gazed down on Charlotte. "I'm as best as can be expected. I miss you. I miss everyone."

"Then why don't you come back in?" Big Tag offered.

"I'm going to pretend like I see nothing." Drake kept his head down. Probably because he was supposed to arrest Zach on sight. "I know nothing. You were never here."

"I appreciate that," Zach replied before looking to Ian. "And you know why I don't come in. Until I have something solid the Agency wants, they'll toss me in a cell somewhere. Or worse. They'll get rid of the problem. The problem being me. I'm close. When I have some leverage, you'll be the first to know. Hey, Lou."

Lou gave him a wave. "Hey. Do you know anything that could help us save Kala?"

"I might have a plan," Zach said mysteriously.

"How do you know she's here?" TJ asked.

Cooper rather thought he knew. "He had someone watching Devi. He told Kala he was worried about her. I didn't actually hear that convo because he shot me, but it's in Kala's report."

Zach had the grace to wince. "I'm sorry, but you were a little heated, and I was worried we were going to throw down."

Yeah, he was working on it. He was willing to do anything if he could get Kala and Devi out of that house alive. "What's your plan and I'll tell you if I'm going to talk to you the next time I see you or take your head off."

A ghost of a smile played at Zach's lips. "Good to know." He got serious. "I do have someone watching Devi, but he's one guy, and he didn't realize what was going on until they were taking her and Kala out. He's a friend of mine. A mercenary who's worked with my mother from time to time."

"And he followed her here?" Big Tag asked. "Because I'm unsure of how you figured out where she is. Unless someone on this team is talking."

Well, that wasn't even vaguely disguised as non-threatening. "No one on the team is talking to him behind your back. Kala talked to him and immediately reported what happened. You're pissed Charlotte hugged him and is acting like she's twelve kinds of fine with him showing up, but I'm pretty sure she was checking him for weapons."

"He doesn't have any," Charlotte agreed. "But he is carrying something. I don't know what it is, but it's taped to his waist. Small. It might be a detonator. If they don't carefully inspect him, he might get in with it."

Yep, Kala had come by her suspicion honestly.

"It is a detonator, and it's taped to my body with specifically colored adhesive that blends with my skin," Zach admitted.

Ian's lips curled up. "I should have known, but don't tell me you weren't worried about him."

"I was. I am. And so are you. Let Drake be the angry boss right now," Charlotte advised. "Zach should understand we're ready to talk when he is, and we'll withhold judgment until we know the full story."

"What she said, but none of that explains how he knew where we were," Ian agreed. "If he's got eyes on us, we have to know."

"No eyes." Cooper knew what happened. "Zach didn't know the tracker didn't work last time. He was on the run before we figured it out. He would have looked for her tracker. Now, I don't know how he got the new login, but that's how he wasn't confused."

"I couldn't get into Tris or Lou's system, but all operatives are also tracked by the Agency." Zach put his hands on his hips, staring out over the road that led to the house. "I know some people who still let me in, and no, I won't give them up. But I will give myself up when it's safe to. I promise. Everything I've done since the day Tristan found out I was involved with the bombmaker has been about protecting the people I love and hunting down Huisman. Now the person I love the most is in his hands, and I'm not going to leave her there. He wants me, he can have me."

Cooper didn't want the well of feeling that rose inside him. He wanted to stay pissed at Zach so he didn't have to examine all the shit between them. He got the feeling that wasn't going to happen. "You can't go in alone."

"Fuck, yes I can." Zach's shoulders went back, his spine lengthening. "I'm not handing him someone else I care about. I'll put you out again if I have to, little brother. You're not bait. You're going to focus on getting Kala to safety. You get your girl and I'll get mine."

"Or you can do the bait thing and I'll get my sister," TJ countered.

"I would if I thought for a second that you can handle her." Zach stared down TJ. "You've all proven you can't. She's been in danger, and no one has tried once to rein her in."

"Do you think I haven't talked to her?" TJ sounded flustered. "We got her a bodyguard."

"Who she ditched," Zach replied.

"I think Cooper should go in," Big Tag said suddenly.

"What?" Zach asked.

"Yes," Cooper said at the same time.

Big Tag looked them over and then seemed to focus on Zach. "What's the detonator attached to?"

Zach's shoulders slumped. "Some bombs out here on the grounds. The places I could hit without setting off the alarms or getting caught on camera. I had to be careful. I don't have a team behind me."

"You do now," Lou offered.

"Babe," TJ began.

Lou shook her head. "No. He's our best shot at getting our people back, and I don't give a crap what the Agency thinks about him. I'm going to help him get Kala and Devi back, and then I'm going to help him get away. If anyone wants to fire me over it, do it later. I'll face whatever consequences I have to in order to get my best friend and your sister back."

"Me, too," Kenzie said. "One of us needs to go in with Zach so we have two people on the inside when he blows the bombs. It's a distraction since it won't actually hit anyone inside the house."

"Oh, I wouldn't say that," Zach hedged. "When my mother makes a bomb, she really makes a bomb."

"Are you in touch with her?" Ian asked.

"Not exactly, but she proved today she knows how to find me. She left me the bombs and the detonator a few hours ago. I rented an Airbnb under an assumed name so I would have a small base of operations. She found me. At least I know I've got a shot at reaching her if she still cares," Zach said. He shook his head. "Anyway, the bombs should take out most of the windows at the front of the house, might even take out the front walls. But then Kala's going to be in the basement. I would assume that's where he'll keep her. I read the reports."

"Yep, those reports are classified." Drake started to hum as though he couldn't stand to hear anymore.

It wouldn't matter. Zach had been careful. Zach had wanted all the knowledge he could get.

"I'll go," Ian said finally.

Everyone erupted. Tasha started arguing over the walkie. Kenzie pointed out her father was the ultimate prize, and that Huisman would kill him then and there. Charlotte offered to take his place.

Cooper looked at the man who shared his DNA. Zach was

standing stoically as they all argued, Drake getting in on the scene.

There was no way he was letting Ian do his job. Ian had risked everything for his woman. It was time for Cooper McKay to do the same. "You ready?"

He kept his voice down.

Drake decided he had to call in if he might lose such an important asset as Ian Taggart, which caused Big Tag to threaten some medieval torture methods.

Lou walked up to Cooper, and he expected her to plead for him to stop the arguing. Instead, she put a finger to his shirt, pressing in on the fabric. "It's an ultra-thin camera. I brought a couple in case we managed to get someone on the inside. Thank god everyone wears black. It should work because he doesn't have a jammer on. He thinks he's safe here. Let's prove he's not."

Damn, but he loved Lou. Kala's best friend had been a little nerd girl when he met her, shy and so smart but awkward. She was still awkward and weird and one of the best humans he'd ever met. "Will do, Lou. Get them to stay out of the line of fire until the bombs are done, and then send in everyone. I'll get our people. You get the bad guys."

Lou nodded. "Yes."

"Guys, this isn't helping Kala or Devi," TJ was arguing. "I'll go."

Everyone wanted to sacrifice. Too bad. This was his place.

Big Tag started to turn toward them.

Kenzie got in her dad's face, like she knew he needed the distraction. "I'm going. I'm going to save my sister."

"Like hell you are," Ian started in on his daughter.

"They're totally dysfunctional at times," Zach said, watching them. There was the slightest grin on his face.

He did miss them. Coop was going to have to give his…brother…some slack. "Ready?"

Zach sighed. "I can't talk you out of it. It was stupid to try. Let's get our girls."

They turned and jogged into the darkness.

\* \* \* \*

Kala knew she was dreaming, knew that somewhere outside this quiet place inside her own brain, her body was going through torment. He'd strapped her down again, forced an IV into her arm, and asked her over and over where Zachary Reed was.

After a while she knew he didn't care about the answer. It was all just play to him. A means to deliver his torture. Perhaps a way to pretend she deserved it.

Didn't she deserve it?

At some point she'd passed out, and her brain hadn't done a great job of disassociating since she found herself in the kitchen again. The same one where she'd faced down Julia Ennis all those years ago. Where Julia had told her how much she reminded her of herself at a young age.

She'd carried those words for so damn long.

She'd also had this dream about a million times.

The door came open and Julia entered wearing the same slacks and blouse she'd been wearing the day she'd found Kala with her head in the refrigerator, hiding the knife she'd stolen.

In the dream, Kala was always fifteen again, vulnerable and aching at the thought she was like the monster who'd tried to kill her cousin Kyle and his awesome wife, MaeBe. In the dream she was scared and stubborn, and she listened to what Julia had to say.

"Hello, Kala. It's been a while," Julia said.

Oh, Lena would have a field day with this. She knew she was dreaming, and now dead Julia understood the passage of time from the afterlife.

Or perhaps these were all parts of her soul she had to mend so she could be the best Kala she could be. The best person, best friend, best lover, best mother someday. It was odd but she got a bit misty as she sat down at the kitchen table. "Hello, Julia."

Dream Julia stared at her. "You're not a child."

"No, I'm not. It's funny because at fifteen I would have told you the same, but time and experience changes our perspectives. I've started to wonder why you're the one who haunts my dreams. When I think about it, you weren't violent toward me. I've started to suspect nothing happened to me on the plane."

Julia stared at her. "I told you I wouldn't hurt you in that fashion."

She had. Kala simply hadn't believed her. "Oh, you violated my person. You wrecked me for years. Don't expect me to thank you for not raping me."

Julia's eyes narrowed. "You know you wouldn't be the first. You should be grateful."

"I'm going to stop you there. No. I am not grateful I wasn't raped. I'm mad that other women are. You don't get brownie points for sparing me something absolutely no one should ever be forced to endure. And don't give me the whole my generation had to deal with it shit. If I go through something terrible, I'm going to try to make sure no one has to suffer through it again. I'm not looking at women younger than me and turning a blind eye when they're harmed because I had to, so they should too." She was getting emotional in a dream. So weird what could happen when she asked the right questions and was honest about the answers. So many doors opened.

"Well, you won't have to endure. You're a predator."

Kala's eyes rolled. "Shut up. You're mostly meaningless here. I think I've found out what I'm truly afraid of. You see, it's hard when you're a twin. You wonder at times if you share a soul, and if you do, how did it split? I suppose I saw you as something of a shadow version of my mother. When I was fifteen, I heard all the stories. She loved Dad so much she did everything she could to get him back. I thought it was romantic."

"Yes, I rather know that story myself." Julia took the seat across from her, intelligent eyes studying her. "I did what I did for love."

"You killed a lot of people. Screwed a lot of people over. Fucked up lives. Betrayed your country," Kala pointed out. "All for a man who never really loved you."

For a moment it looked like Julia was going to argue. Then her face twisted and changed, and it became Lena sitting in front of her. "Like you did. Have you considered that your fascination with Cooper McKay is about trying to save yourself from your own worst instincts?"

She stared at Dream Lena for a moment and knew she would follow through with those therapy sessions. With a real therapist this time and not one who took on the face of all the dark voices in her head. "My instincts aren't wrong. They're quite good. The more violent impulses I shut down."

Lena leaned forward, and Kala would swear her normally perfect teeth had cutting edges now. Like a piranha about to feast. Her eyes seemed darker, too. "Do you? How many have you killed? Maimed? Destroyed? Do you ever wonder why Kenzie got the cutesy, sweet name and you are an acronym for kick a little ass? Your father did that to you. He saw what you were from the very beginning. He knew Kenzie was light and you were dark."

This was something important she'd learned. "We need the darkness, too. We need it to find rest and peace and sleep. The dark can be a beautiful thing. Just like too much light kills."

She shook her head. "You're not that darkness. You're evil. There's something wrong with you. Cursed. It's why bad things happen to you."

Yes, there were the voices. Intrusive and invasive. Sometimes they shouted. Sometimes they started as whispers of good that slowly turned into self-hate and anxiety. Sometimes she couldn't shut them off, but she was going to find a way. She deserved to find a way. "I am not you."

"No," Lena replied. "You're her."

And she was Julia again, except this time Julia was in an elegant dress. The kind her mom favored. She wore her hair in a very Charlotte Taggart style.

Darkness to her mother's light.

"We're the same, you and I," Julia insisted. "I'm the other side of your mother's coin, the same way you are with your twin. She's your mother."

How long had this idea dragged on her soul? Now that she was facing it, she could see how silly it was. Her mother wasn't some beacon of light. She had darkness, too. Everyone did. Kenzie had her own. She was more like her mom, but Kala wasn't Julia.

"No, I have my father's soul and many of his problems." He'd told her about them, how he needed a checkup every now and then. How stubborn he'd been as a young person, and it had almost cost him everything. How he didn't want it to do the same to her. Her father had those dark voices. The ones people sometimes called depression and anxiety, and he'd found a way to be happy. And so would she.

If she lived through this. Damn, but part of the problem with figuring out she didn't hate herself was kind of wanting to live. Completely wanting to live.

"Your father is evil, too," Julia insisted.

Her father was the awesomest asshole to ever exist. Tears filled her eyes as she felt a hand on her shoulder and knew without a doubt who it was. Another smaller hand grasped her other shoulder. Her parents. Always behind her even in her nightmares. "I don't need you anymore. I never did, but now I'm ready to let you go."

Julia stood, looking wilder now, like she was ready to strike.

But this wasn't a war she would win with a knife or a gun. It wasn't a war where she could slaughter her enemies to claim victory because this was a war inside her. These were pieces of her soul she needed to tame, and she'd learned she couldn't do it with anger. She couldn't fix it with discipline and being the best at what she did.

No, this war wouldn't be won with bombs but with the decision to lean into the love she'd been given.

Kala shifted back against those hands on her knowing there were so many more, but these hands were there from the very beginning. "Leave now."

She would always be difficult. Stubborness was her middle name, and it would stay that way. She wasn't going to eschew violence, become a vegan, and live off the grid for the sake of the earth. No. Her change was far gentler.

She would be kind to herself. She would give herself grace. She would accept that she deserved the love and affection she'd been given and take her place in her family without another question.

"I'm not about..." Dream Julia began...but she was already fading, her voice so soft against the other Kala now heard.

*I love you. It's you and me.* Cooper.

*You're my best friend.* Lou.

*I've got your back.* Kenzie.

*I am so glad to have you as my sister.* Tasha when she'd still had that Russian accent. When she'd been young and scared.

*You are the best mistress a sub could have.* Really, that was a lot of voices when she thought about it. She was good. So much better at topping than the boys.

*It'll all be alright.* She was pretty sure that was Kacey Musgraves because there was some music behind that one.

*I'm here if you want to talk. Or I could play a song for you if you're sad.* Seth was a weirdo. She loved him.

*You're going to be the best aunt. He's going to love you.* Travis.

Those voices meshed together, and she suddenly couldn't hear the others anymore, like a grand symphony of love taking over. The dark voices were still there. Would always be, but she could silence them with help. She could be stronger.

*Stay alive,* Cooper whispered. *I'm coming.*

She didn't need to see him. Didn't need to hold him to know he loved her. They all loved her.

And she would survive.

A blast of pain went through her system, and she was suddenly awake again. The world was filled with harsh light and jagged edges.

She couldn't move. Ah, yes, the paralytic. He used an experimental paralytic drug. It kept her still, but she could feel everything the man did to her.

"I thought you were better than this." Huisman was a shadowy figure beyond the lights. Surgical lights.

Fun times. "I'll try to be more focused, Doc."

"Why are you smiling?" Huisman sounded a bit disturbed.

Was she? Maybe she was perverse. Or maybe she'd figured out something so big that the torture didn't seem as bad as it had before. "I guess it's because you hurt so good, Doc."

She wasn't giving him a damn thing.

Huisman stepped in, his dark eyes hovering over her. "I haven't truly begun. This is all merely for fun. A warm-up. I haven't even given you the real drugs yet. Just a new concoction that elevates the pain of basic wounds. I've been using a violet wand on an extremely high setting. It should feel like I'm cutting you deep. You're covered with beautiful burns now, but I think we'll go more old school. Bring me the torch."

If she'd been able to move, she was sure her body would have stiffened. This was going to hurt.

And she would take it. She had a family to get back to, after all.

"Tell me where Zach Reed is," Huisman demanded.

"Fuck right the fuck off," she replied. If she passed out again and did the conscious dreaming thing, she was going to top Cooper in so many nasty ways. So many.

"He's in the hallway, sir," another voice said.

Huisman stopped and turned. "What?"

"Reed is in the hallway with some other dude. Says it's his brother."

Kala tried to lift her head. He wouldn't be this stupid. Couldn't be. Cooper wouldn't walk in and try to exchange himself for her.

If he died, she was going to kill him.

Although he did seem to have spared her the torch. For now.

"What an interesting surprise. I suppose my network is up to date since he found his way here so quickly. Send another patrol out. Tell them to expand the radius and get those cameras focused on anyone coming near the house. Also, get the helicopter ready in case. Let's go see what's happening," Huisman said. "Take her back and throw her in with the other."

"Uhm, sir, the paralytic is still in effect. She should be monitored. We know it can cause heart trouble," another voice said. It was good to know he had helpers.

"She's strong. I'm sure she'll be fine." Huisman turned and walked away.

And Kala prayed she got to see her love one more time.

## Chapter Nineteen

Cooper followed Zach down the road, adrenaline starting to pour through his system. "You know Drake's going to try to take you in. He kind of has to."

"I'm not going in," Zach replied. "I'm not ready yet. I promise you when the time is right and I've got all my work done, I'll turn myself in and I won't be a problem anymore."

"You'll go to prison?" He didn't like the sound of that. Even if he was still angry at Zach.

Zach shrugged as they turned the corner, and the house came into full view. "Hey, I'm carrying on the family tradition, I suppose. Stay close to me if you can. I'm hoping this asshole will monologue awhile before I need to set off the bombs. I want to give Big Tag some time to get everyone into place."

"You didn't tell him what places needed covering," Coop pointed out.

"Don't have to," Zach replied. "That's the great thing about Big Tag and Charlotte. They'll know what to do. I'm going to need you to pretend you've been with me all along. You've known we're brothers for the two years we've been working together."

Subterfuge. He could handle that.

He glanced off to the side of the house and saw a chopper sitting on a launch pad. "I wonder how long that's been there. And how long it's going to be there."

"I couldn't get close enough," Zach admitted. "I hope Big Tag knows about it because if Huisman wants to run, that's how he'll do it. I need you to understand that if it comes down to it, you leave me behind and get the ladies out of here. I think he's got a thing for Kala now, and Huisman likes to break his toys, if you know what I mean."

The words threatened to make him sick, but he was shoving down all emotion at this point. Up ahead he saw the porch light to the big house come on.

"They see us," Coop noted.

"Don't forget. You left the team this afternoon when I called you. He knows about your relationship with Kala. Assume he knows almost everything," Zach said, his voice tight. "And what happens if you can't get me out."

That was easy. "Oh, I'll leave your lying ass behind." He wasn't thrilled with Zach, but he also was already softening and would kind of like to know the story. His parents were his parents, and his brother and sister were his siblings. But there was always room for more. "Brother."

Zach stopped, his eyes on Cooper. "I hope we can sit down with our ladies and have a beer one day. If we can't, know that I loved you from the minute I knew you existed. I know you have a family, but I don't have much anymore. Thank you for sharing yours. Even for a little while."

Damn it. He didn't want the surge of sympathy that rolled over him. Or the curiosity about the man who was technically his big brother. He'd always been the big brother to Hunter and Vivian. There had definitely been times in his life when he could have used a guiding hand. Maybe if Zach had been around, he and Kala wouldn't have wasted so much time. "Zach, don't fucking die."

Up ahead he could see two armed guards coming out of the house, rifles pointed their way.

"It's show time, little brother," Zach said and put his hands up. He dropped to his knees. "When the time comes, a punch to the kidneys might be called for."

Cooper did the same. He'd disarmed back at the van with the exception of the camera Lou had given him. It was a weapon of sorts. It would definitely send intel back to the team about what was happening. "Who am I punching?"

He hoped it was Huisman. The guards yelled some guard-like things. Hands up. We'll shoot. Shit like that, but Coop was watching Zach. He had a grim look on his face as the guards approached.

"Me, if you have to," Zach said under his breath.

"Both of you stand up," one of the guards said. Now there were four of them. "Who the hell are you? This is private property."

"This is Dr. Emmanuel Huisman's property, and I think you'll find I was invited," Zach said. "Tell him Captain Reed is here to discuss a very important matter with him. You'll find I'm unarmed and hoping we can deal with the issue like gentlemen. My brother is here to ensure the negotiations go smoothly."

"Hey," Cooper said, giving the big guy a nod. "Nice place you have here. Do you know if they're hiring?"

Sarcasm. He'd gotten it from his woman.

The guard ignored him, pulling his radio out and talking in French.

"He's calling his boss, who's going to talk to Huisman," Zach said quietly, his arms still behind his head, but no one was tying them up yet. Zach was counting on Huisman's curiosity and his arrogance. "The boss says Huisman is with one of the prisoners."

He should have learned French. He was fluent in Spanish, German, and Russian, but only because he liked to know what the Taggart girls said about him. He'd learned Russian early since they spoke it around him all the time. Even when he was a kid he hadn't wanted to be left out of any group.

Now he only needed one. "Kala. He'll be with Kala."

He hoped he would be escorted to where she was. Huisman could be cruel and might think seeing her being tortured would wreck him. It would, but it would also mean he was in the room with her. The closer he could get, the more easily he could snatch her up and run like hell.

Nothing mattered but getting her and Devi out of here.

"Well, well. Look what the cat dragged in," a familiar voice said. Lena Gallagher stood not ten feet away from them. Her head tilted, features shadowy in the dim light from the moon. "I expected the captain. You're a surprise, McKay. Where's your boss and how did he find us?"

Cooper tilted his head slightly Zach's way. "Boss is right there, lady. He's in charge of this insane op."

She frowned, arms crossing over her chest. "I meant Ian Taggart."

"He's back in Texas. He doesn't know I'm here," Cooper replied. "When Zach found out you have Devi, he called me. You have Kala, too. You have to know she's mine, and we're willing to do what it takes to get them back. Bringing the team in means bringing the Agency in, and we don't want that."

She studied him for a moment as the guard waited for orders. "I'm supposed to believe you ditched your team? She's his daughter. You don't think Taggart would move heaven and earth for his precious girl? I call bullshit."

"Call it whatever you like," Cooper replied. "I have other family, and I have loyalty to them, too. I didn't want Kala hurt in the inevitable gunfight that would happen if I brought her parents in. Zach wants the same for Devi. Look, I'm only here so Zach has backup, and I can take the women with me when Zach turns himself in. He's my brother. I owe him."

"Ah, but he's not just turning himself in, is he?" Lena asked. "It's your biological mother Huisman wants. No loyalty to her?"

This had seemed so simple half a day ago, but now he had questions. He also had a part to play. "She's not my mom, so no. My loyalty is to my brother. He's the one who came and found me. And to her. My loyalty is always to Kala."

"To that psychopath?" Lena asked the question with a roll of her eyes. "That's what she is. She has sociopathic tendencies. All it would take for her to become a true monster is a loss. Do you have any idea what she's capable of?"

He did. Love. She was capable of loving deeply, of sacrifice. She was capable of making him laugh and feel safe. She was capable of being anything she wanted to be. He wasn't about to explain any of that to this woman who'd abused her trust so mightily. He was easily as angry with her as he was with Huisman. One tortured her body and the other her soul. Lena made her feel less, and he hated her for it. But he had to play a long game. "The heart wants what the heart wants."

She sneered down at him. "Well, what your heart wants is currently being experimented on. Like the animal she is. Honestly, I hope Manny kills her. He's treating her like some exotic animal he wants to tame, but she's feral. She'll always kill. Like her parents."

Zach growled a low warning.

Cooper needed it because his instinct was to get to his feet and make a run for the house. She was in pain, and the idea of it nearly floored him.

He took a long breath, checking his emotions. Getting his ass shot wouldn't help anyone at this point. But he could fuck around with Lena since now he knew the whole story. Big Tag had opened the files and let him read everything he had on the very dead Eli Nelson. "Like Charlotte took out your asshole father?"

Lena gasped and backhanded him, smacking him right across his jaw.

It tickled. Now if his baby had done it, she would have used her fist and he would be seeing stars. But Lena didn't spend the same time in the gym.

Zach snorted. "You okay, brother?"

Cooper shrugged. "I'll forego the tears. I find it interesting that the doctor here is more than willing to give up her career and likely her freedom to get revenge for a dude who knocked up her mom and left. You do understand those stories your mother told you were so you wouldn't know what a shit stain your dad actually was. He was a traitor to his country."

"At least I had a mother." Lena seemed to want to take the mean-girl route.

"My mother is doing well, no thanks to you." Cooper wasn't about to back down now. If she wanted to slap him again, he could use the massage. Huisman needed to find more terrifying minions. "And the woman who gave birth to me cared enough to spare me what could have been a difficult childhood. My biological aunt cared enough to find the best family she could."

When he thought about it, it didn't seem like a cold, calculated move. It felt like a loving sacrifice.

And one he was deeply grateful for.

"Well, Mommy's going to be in a world of hurt soon," Lena said with obvious superiority. "And I'm giving up nothing. I'm taking my place in the new world order Dr. Huisman is going to bring about. I'm going to have a special position in the organization."

"I bet you will," Zach agreed. "He respects you."

Cooper snorted. "Huisman hates women. He'll use her and toss her on the garbage heap, likely as a corpse."

"You know nothing," Lena practically snarled.

His brother's narrowed eyes spoke volumes about his irritation. "There's a reason you're usually behind the scenes. Dude, when we're dealing with a delusional person who also has a bunch of armed guards at her side, we agree with everything they say. She wants to believe she's going to be a queen? Here's to your crown, girl. See. It's simple. We both know Huisman's killing her tonight because her usefulness is over. Can't you give her a couple of good hours?"

Oh, his brother was a dick. Cooper liked this side of Zach. He looked back at Lena. "You're going to look great in a crown."

"My usefulness is not over," she said with a huff.

Now he saw what his brother was trying to do. Sow discord. Take a page out of Huisman's book and create chaos. "You were his insider at the Agency. Maybe not the only one, but you were his eyes and ears, at least in your department. You won't be able to go back. You have to know we have video footage of you taking Devi Taggart. You missed a camera. We have a few in the trees on the walk up to the club." He was lying, but it was a good idea he intended to bring up at the next meeting of the board of The Hideout. "It's been sent to Drake Radcliffe, who's probably already talked to his bosses."

"I took out the cameras." She'd paled slightly. Even in the low light he could see it.

"Not the ones you couldn't see," he replied.

"Hey, you brought him two important assets," Zach argued. "He'll be thrilled when it's your work that brings him the bombmaker."

This was kind of fun. He watched Lena's shoulders go back, pride on her face again. And then he went in for the kill. "And he won't need you anymore. I'm sure he'll still want you around. You won't be a liability or anything. He'll probably give you a pension or something. Maybe a good letter of recommendation to the next evil asshole looking for minions."

Her hand came back again, and Cooper simply smiled. She might do better this time.

The guard walked in and gestured for them to stand, getting in between Cooper and Lena. "Dr. Gallagher, maybe you should go inside. I don't think he wants anyone out here. Despite how far we are from the town, there could still be eyes on us."

Lena turned and started walking back in.

The guard watched her. "Did you have to wind her up like that?" He sighed. "Get up. Dr. Huisman will see you now."

Like they were being invited in for tea. He stood beside Zach as the guard took their places around them. Two in front and two on the sides. How many did that leave for the team?

They were given a cursory pat down. Exactly what Zach had been counting on. No one touched his waist except at his hips. When they were satisfied, the guard nodded.

Lena walked in front of them, her boots pounding against the porch boards, an agitated sound. She pushed through the double doors. "Manny, are you insane? We should leave right now. I don't buy this bullshit for a second."

Huisman stood at the top of the stairs, two guards flanking him. "Lena, do you think I don't know what I'm doing? Do you think I don't have eyes on Taggart? Even now he's huddled up in his office building with the rest of the team. They entered the building six hours ago. I do believe they're trying to figure out where to go. I know their jet is on standby. They haven't filed a flight plan yet because they can't figure out where to look."

Lena pointed his way. "Yeah, but their pilot is here. Have you thought about that?"

"I snuck him out," Zach claimed. "I was in Dallas today meeting with someone my mother works with. When I received your message, I knew I needed backup I could count on, and that's my brother. You can't possibly expect me to turn myself over without a guard to escort the women out of here. He's part of the deal."

"Ah, so he knows now." Huisman started down the stairs.

This was where he hoped he was a better liar than Kala thought he was. "I've known since he joined the team."

Huisman stopped, his expression shuttering. "No, you have not."

Either he had someone on the inside—and by inside it would have to be an actual member of the team—or he was guessing. The good news about his team? The only one who wasn't solid was standing beside him. "Zach told me when he joined the team."

Huisman's eyes narrowed. "I don't believe you."

Huisman was really arrogant. The man hadn't even restrained them. He was counting on his guards and their fear for the women. One of those things did keep Cooper on a leash, and it sure wasn't the guards. "It doesn't matter in the end. I'd like to see Kala and Devi. I'll take them off your hands. I have a car waiting at the road. Should I bring it down?"

Huisman's mask slipped back on, and he seemed jovial again. "Oh, I think we should negotiate first. I am completely willing to part with Devon Taggart in exchange for your brother selling out his mother." He walked to the small bar. It was a neatly kept tray in what appeared to be the front lounge. "Kala is another story. Kala is… Well, she's a personal project of mine."

Zach's hand reached out, stilling Cooper. "There's no deal without Kala."

Huisman's smile was vaguely reptilian. "Then I'm afraid we won't have a deal. Perhaps you will change your mind when I start cutting off pieces of young Miss Taggart. Or perhaps I'll get creative and take her eyes. She's some sort of designer. Well, she'll find other work. Guard, go down to the basement and shove your thumbs into Miss Taggart's eyes. Bring them to me." He held up a hand. "The redhead. Don't touch the pink-haired one. She's mine. But she's a bit of a feral animal at this point, so you might give her a shock or knock her out before you open the cage."

If they opened the cage, Kala would have a shot. Even if they used a Taser on her. She handled that pretty well. And Devi knew a bit about self-defense. If they set off the bombs after the cage was open, they had a fighting chance. Though he didn't know what they'd already taken from Kala.

"No," Zach practically shouted. "I'll do it. I'll get my mother here. Let Devi go with my brother. I'll call her as soon as Devi's gone."

He looked to his brother. "I'm not leaving Kala here."

The guard turned to Huisman. "You want me to stick my fingers in her eyes?"

While Huisman stared at his guard, Zach winked his way, and his hand came up to his waist as though highlighting the detonator he had there.

It was almost time. He wasn't going to leave Kala, but a fight between them would be a distraction.

"And I'm not letting them blind my girlfriend," Zach said. "You take her out of here. I'll deal with Kala."

"I think you should send Kala away," Lena argued. "If you send her out, Taggart might stop looking. We need to regroup. I don't like the fact that McKay is here. I think Taggart is here, too. He's hiding."

A crack bounced through the room, and Cooper realized it had been the sound of Huisman's hand hitting Lena's face. The psychologist put a palm to her cheek.

"I don't need your voice, woman," Huisman snarled, every word a dark threat. "As for you, you will do what I asked or I'll be the one taking your eyes. Am I clear?"

The guard nodded and started to walk away.

"Follow him," Huisman ordered another guard. "If he doesn't do it, kill him."

Now they were down to four guards. But they were running out of time.

Zach seemed ready to panic. "If you hurt her, all bets are off."

"But she'll be alive," Huisman argued, pouring himself a glass of what looked like whiskey or bourbon. "Isn't that the important thing? The poor girl. She'll be upset to find out your love only extends to her eyes. However, it's probably a better way to go. She'll be utterly useless, like most women."

"How dare you." Lena had been frozen, but she started to move now. "After everything I did for you. You know what? Let's see how you feel when I put that bitch out of her misery."

She started after the guards.

Now he needed to get moving.

Huisman waved it all off. "The guards won't let her. They have strict instructions to keep Kala Taggart alive. They'll take care of Lena. I won't call her a doctor. The amount of people trying to aggrandize themselves shocks me. Shall we have a drink while we wait for our prize?"

Zach looked Cooper's way and nodded. His hand went to his waist. "Or I can show you what my mother can do."

He pushed against his torso and the world started to explode. Light and heat blasted from behind them, the windows shattering in the rooms around them. He heard one of the guards scream, but Huisman stood there, glass in hand, perfectly comfortable with the chaos.

And the fucker smiled as though this all amused him.

"Get the women," Zach yelled his way. "I'll take care of this guy."

Huisman reached into his pocket. "Oh, Captain Reed, did you

think I wouldn't have a backup plan? Though this was spectacular. I thank you. I assume now that this is to distract me while Taggart rides in. What a fun way to end this day." He pressed down. "I have just begun a fire in the basement. Good luck getting them out. Or you can try to take me in. What will you choose?"

They didn't have guns and there were still guards moving around. He had seconds, and he already knew what his choice was.

Cooper ran for the kitchen and hoped he got there in time.

* * * *

Every inch of her body ached as the guard slammed the door shut behind her.

At least the lights were on and she'd gotten a halfway decent look at the locking mechanism. It was one she'd dealt with before, and if she had the right tools and enough time, she might be able to get them out of here.

"Kala, I'm so sorry." Devi knelt to help her up.

The guard stood on the other side of the door, staring down at them, a bank of monitors behind him. The security system had gotten an upgrade.

"You should behave now," the guard said. "I'm taking a leak. Make yourselves comfy, ladies. You're going to be here for a while."

Not if Kala could help it. Of course, she had to get her arms functioning first. "You're sorry? What are you sorry for, Devi? For ignoring my very reasonable advice and ditching the guard who could have avoided this for you? For probably getting Landon fired? For getting Eve shot? How about getting me tortured?"

Devi's eyes closed briefly. "You do not hold back, cousin."

"I never have." Her teeth chattered, and she forced her jaw to close. She flexed her hands.

"I'm sorry for all of it," Devi whispered. "Let me help you up."

She shook her head. "I need a minute, and that's probably all we have. Although I noticed he didn't use the bathroom down here."

"You know there's a bathroom down here?"

"This is where Julia Ennis took me and Kyle."

Devi's eyes widened. "I'm so sorry. What did he do to you?"

"Gave me a paralytic and sent a couple thousand watts through me," she replied. "Trust me, he's done worse. I didn't nearly break a rib from this. He's working his way up, though. What can you see on the monitors?"

"They rotate through the cameras." Devi glanced up. "There are a lot of cameras."

"I need to know if you see Cooper," Kala managed to get out. She could wiggle her toes again. It was starting to come back. "Can you sit me up? I'm pretty much going to need you to pose me like a doll."

Devi's brows rose, but she did as Kala asked, getting her into a seated position, her back against the concrete wall. She managed to hold her head up but she couldn't point. "See. There. He's walking through the damn door. Idiot. How the hell did he find me? If he's here…"

A brilliant smile broke over Devi's face. "Then Uncle Ian's here."

She tried to shake her head. "That's not possible. How would they know?"

"The tracker," Devi said as though it should be obvious.

"I assure you they disabled my tracker before they ever tossed my body in the car," Kala replied with no small amount of bitterness. Had Zach convinced Cooper to come with him? They were stepping into the foyer.

Devi stood, looking down at her with a quizzical expression on her face. "They already figured a way around the new system Lou designed? Damn. That's disappointing."

The new system… Lou talked about it. Holy shit. Kala hated to admit it but the science stuff Lou could spout from time to time almost always made her fall asleep. She'd slept through the big lecture on why they all needed new trackers. Now she kind of wished she'd listened in. "Lou designed trackers that get around the tech that Huisman uses to disable them?"

"Uh, yeah," Devi said as though she should know—which she should. "Sorry. She was talking to Kenz about it in the locker room one night and Bri made me be quiet because she wants to use it in a book. She listens in way too much."

They would have a talk about that, but for now hope surged through her. Somewhere out there her parents were waiting for their shot. Cooper was here, risking everything. Her team had come for her. Lena could fuck right the fuck off. Her bestie was getting a big old hug. After they got out of here. Huisman seemed to be doing that annoying thing where he talked forever. "Devi, I need you to find something we can dismantle that lock with."

"Like what? I don't think it comes apart. It looks solid."

"I assure you it comes apart. I know that system. My father makes us study all the new systems to ensure we know how to use them and how to best break them if we have to." She was never again going to complain about those long sessions they spent in the conference room at the MT building. "But we need something to spring out the back cover. It only looks solid state. It requires batteries, hence we can get in, but I need something like a pen or a paperclip."

"Sorry. I don't have office supplies on me," Devi replied.

They might be spending some time in the ring when they got back. Female Fight Club was how some of the women of The Hideout handled their issues. She stared at her cousin, who had her hair in a high ponytail. Devi was incredibly careful about her appearance. She didn't like flyaways messing up the line of her hairdo. "How about the bobby pins holding your hair up?"

Devi's jaw dropped, and her hands went to her hair. "I do have one. Two, actually." She pulled one out. "What are you going to do with it?"

Oh, if only it was so simple. "Well, I sit here and try to stay upright and you're going to slide it underneath until you feel the slightest indentation. You won't be able to see it, but you'll be able to feel it."

"You want me to do it?" Devi asked and then seemed to get the message Kala was sending. "I'll do it."

She got to her knees and straightened out the pin. Kala kept her eyes on the monitors. Huisman was talking. She could guess. Chaos. Blah, blah. New world order. Blah, blah, blah. Women bad. Yeah, Huisman thought he was, like, bringing something new to the world. That dude was obviously not on social media or he would know how tired his takes were.

"I'm not feeling anything."

"It's the smallest indentation." Kala tried to be patient. It had taken her hours to break this one. "Close your eyes and take a deep breath. Bring all your senses down to this one thing. It only seems solid. It's got a very small place where you can press down and the battery slides open. From there we've got roughly thirty seconds when the locking mechanism is open to use the factory setting code."

"Well, we have a problem unless you memorized the… You know it," Devi said with a sigh. "Do you know all of them?"

"All of the major ones," Kala admitted. "The best way to get away from any bad guy is to break out before the fight ever starts. When the lock comes open, you're going to run. To our left is a secret door that leads to tunnels. They'll take you roughly half a mile from here, but I need you to be ready because there's likely a guard on the other side. I'm hoping Zach is about to create some chaos and my team is going to swoop in. That should mean the guard leaves his post in an attempt to help his fellow guards, or the fucker flees when he realizes it's going bad. Whatever happens, you keep running. My parents will find you."

"I'm not leaving you here."

Such a pain in her ass. "I can't run, Dev. I can't walk. The paralytic he gave me is strong, and I'll probably be like this for at least another hour. We don't have time. The guard could be back any second. Do it."

"I'll carry you out if I have to," Devi muttered but got back to the task.

Kala looked to the monitors. She was starting to get some control over her extremities. She could wiggle her fingers and toes and keep her neck level. She hated this, hated feeling useless. How did she explain to Devi that being forced to sit here and watch her get hurt was far worse than having it happen to herself? How was she going to get her cousin to leave without her? "You know I think you're a bitch, right? I don't like you. I think you're stupid and you're the reason we're here."

"Not going to work." Devi didn't look back, merely knelt there, her fingers moving over and over the small base of the locking mechanism. "You love me. Though the *stupid* part I might agree with you over, and I'll use the whole 'you're the reason we're here' against you for the rest of our lives. Other people might think you're some heartless bitch, but I'm your cousin. I know exactly who you are, Kala Taggart." She turned suddenly, and a smile was on her face. She looked so much like her mother, but that smile was all Theo Taggart. "Hey, now I don't have to let you punch me in Female Fight Club. You already punched me. You punched my feelings."

Damn it. Why had she listened to Lena? Lena had her believing the world was afraid of her, and no one was. It was kind of insulting but also true. And a problem. "You have to leave. Zach will have more options if he knows you got away."

"Why is he here?" Devi asked.

"Because he loves you," Kala replied.

"He does no…" Devi stopped. "I have it."

Kala steeled herself. She could see the guard on the camera. He was moving through the kitchen, but he stopped to talk to another guard. Out in the foyer, Huisman seemed to be saying something to Lena. "Ease the pin under it and find the indentation. You need to push the pin inside and with enough force that the battery pack on the side slides out."

"Can I pull the battery?" Devi asked.

"No. After thirty seconds the lock will shut down, and then you need the owner code. I'm counting on the fact that almost no one understands they have to change both codes. The lock code is easy to change. The battery and manufacturer reset code can be changed, but it takes some work. So we're hoping whoever set this up isn't as good as McKay-Taggart guys."

"So I push this and have thirty seconds and I can't actually see the keypad since it's on the other side." Devi neatly summed up the problem.

"Yes. You have to do it backward. I can visualize it. When the battery pack comes out, put your finger on the bottom row, center. That's the zero. I'll guide you through the rest, but you have to be careful. If you hit the wrong key, reset is bottom right, and we'll try again. We might get three shots at this."

"I'll get it right," Devi promised. There was a slight whirring sound. "I'm ready."

Kala began telling her the code, though not in numbers but in key positions. All the while she watched the monitors.

That was when Lena threw her hands up and followed two guards who Huisman had just obviously given orders to.

Cooper's eyes had flared. Zach had gone stiff. Something was wrong.

They were coming.

"I'm sorry," Devi said. "I must have done something wrong. I reset the keypad."

Kala began again, her mouth moving while her eyes watched the slow-rolling tragedy that was coming their way. Huisman was playing hardball, and that meant someone was going to be in pain or worse. He'd threatened to take Carys's fingers off one by one the last time he had the team in this position.

"I've got it." Devi stood and looked back, relief plain in her eyes. "It's open. We did it."

The ground shook, and there was no way to miss the sound of glass exploding around the property. Kala shifted, trying to see the monitor, and it sent her sliding to the ground, her head slapping against the concrete.

"Hey, I got you." Her cousin started trying to get her up.

"It won't work," Kala said. She needed more time, and they didn't have it.

"No, it won't," a nasty voice said. Lena stood at the top of the stairs. "None of this will work."

Devi got Kala into a position where she could at least see what was coming for them. She could move a leg now. One. Fat lot of good that was going to do. And an arm. She had one leg and one arm. Lena didn't need to know that.

"Whatever those boys of yours are trying to do, it won't work," Lena said, stalking down the stairs, a gun in her hand. "Manny is too well prepared. He has plans you can't imagine. But for now, these nice gentlemen have orders to bring back Miss Taggart's eyes. We'll see if that loosens up Captain Reed's tongue."

Devi had an arm around Kala, propping her up, though she was holding almost all of Kala's weight. Thankfully Devi was a gym girl, not that it would help her in a couple of minutes. Her muscles wouldn't stop bullets.

"Okay, ewww," Devi said, her nose wrinkling. "I think I will keep my eyes, thank you. You're weird and super gross, lady."

She would give it to her cousin. Devi was cool under pressure. She wasn't wilting. She also probably noticed that the guards behind Lena had taken off when the explosion happened. They'd been flanking Lena but hadn't gotten down the stairs. Now she couldn't see them.

Lena's expression turned to a resentful sneer. "Do you know what's gross? The amount of families your family has destroyed."

"Lady, I don't care," Devi replied. "I get it. Daddy hurt you by walking away. Get the fuck over it. Do what the rest of us do and suck it up. Find a fucking hobby. I would say get some therapy, but it obviously doesn't work on you. Now are you going to put out the fire that just started or shall we all cook together?"

Kala could smell it, but she couldn't get her head to turn. There was a fire? The monitors had fritzed out. Damn it. "He's going to blow the whole place. Like he did in Toronto. He knows the team is here. He's going to get away, and he'll burn the house down to make sure he can."

"Guards, take them," Lena announced.

Dumbass. "They left. So you can shoot us, though you're holding the gun wrong and the safety's on."

Lena looked back. "Fuckers."

"Drop me and use the door," Kala whispered.

Lena turned her attention to the gun in her hand, and that was when Devi proved she could follow orders. She might be a fashion designer, but she was still a Taggart. She let Kala fall as she kicked out, slamming the door right into Lena, who fell back and sent the gun clattering to the floor.

Kala tried to hold her head up. Devi was pushing against Lena, who obviously had some training. It was a chaotic mess, and smoke was starting to pour through the basement. She could feel the heat from the flames that were currently engulfing the computer equipment Huisman kept down here.

She managed to force herself up enough to see a ghostly image of a helo taking off before the last monitor fritzed out.

Devi was fighting, but Lena was better trained. She had Devi against the wall, a hand around her cousin's throat.

Kala used her left foot to push herself forward. It took every bit of energy she had.

"I'm not about to go down alone," Lena was saying. "Let's see how well Taggarts burn."

There was a thud as Lena smashed Devi's head against the brick wall, and Devi slumped to the floor.

How was she going to get Devi to safety? Kala pushed the thought from her brain as she got her hand around the gun while Lena actually took the time to straighten her damn clothes out and kick a now unconscious Devi. It gave Kala a moment to force her fingers around the gun. Her arm was starting to work so she lifted, getting a line of sight on the woman who was going to try to kill her.

"As for you," Lena said, turning.

Kala fired. And then fired again. And again.

Lena put a hand to her gut and then her chest. Not Kala's best work, but she was giving herself some grace.

She fired one more time, and Lena hit her knees.

"I just wanted to know my dad," she said, blood on her lips.

The world didn't always give us what we wanted, but how we dealt with those tragedies made or broke souls. Lena's was done.

She had to find a way to make sure Devi's wasn't. She crawled or at least pushed herself toward her cousin. She needed to wake up. "Devi. Devon fucking Taggart, wake up."

She was almost to her when a set of boots came into view. She glanced up and Zach stood there, a grim look on his face. He knelt down and put two fingers to Devi's wrist, and a sigh of obvious relief went through him.

"Coop's on his way," Zach said as he leaned over and picked Devi up. "He got into a fight with one of the guards, but I think TJ is helping him. You tell Theo and Erin I'll take care of her."

"What?" Kala tried to turn because Zach stepped over her paralyzed body and was going for the tunnel. "Where the hell are you going?"

"Can't tell you, sister," he replied through the smoke. "But I'll call when I know something. Take care of him for me. When I'm done, I'll turn myself in."

"Then you should leave my cousin behind," Kala called out. "She's going to be pissed."

"Then she should have taken care of herself." Zach started to disappear behind the door. "Good-bye, Kala."

"Zach," she yelled out.

The flames seemed to find some fuel, and she could feel the heat on her skin. Naturally Huisman's paralytic merely meant she couldn't move. She could still feel.

But she was starting to not be able to breathe.

"Thank god." Cooper stood over her. He bent down and lifted her up as she coughed. "Where's Devi?"

TJ was behind him. "Where's my sister?"

"Zach took her through the tunnels," she managed to hack out.

TJ started toward them, but Cooper stopped him. "You can't. It's too much."

Kala managed to get a glimpse of the door. It was now engulfed in flames. They couldn't leave that way. Cooper started for the stairs, but Kala could feel her heart twisting inside her body. Like last time.

"Hey, I love you," she whispered. "I'm sorry. I love you so much."

A pain started in her chest, and the world went black.

## Chapter Twenty

Kala blinked as she woke, the world still hazy. She'd been in the house again. The one that haunted her dreams sometimes. But this time Cooper had been there. This time Lou had reached out across time and space and wouldn't let her go. This time she wouldn't hide and shove what happened deep inside.

She coughed and winced.

Everything hurt. Especially her chest.

Damn it. She'd had another heart attack. Huisman's drugs sucked. 0 out of 5. Would not recommend.

"Hey, kid."

Her father stood over her. He looked haggard, his dark clothes wrinkled and a long scrape on his cheek. It appeared someone had stitched him up in the field.

"You're in a hospital in Virginia," he said quietly. "You've been out for roughly six hours. The doctors say you'll be fine in the short term, but they want someone to watch you for a while. Aidan is talking about setting you up with a portable monitor for a couple of months. They don't know what the experimental drugs did. What kind of damage."

Probably a lot, but she was already feeling better because she glanced to her left and Cooper was asleep in a chair beside her bed.

Beyond Coop, Lou and TJ were curled up on what appeared to be the world's most uncomfortable cot. TJ's legs hung off.

"Is everyone okay? You look worse for the wear." She glanced around the room. "Mom and Kenz? What happened with Eve? Devi told me she was alive when Lena took us."

"Eve is recuperating nicely. I talked to Alex about an hour ago, and they're going to send her home tomorrow. The first thing she did when she came out of surgery was ask about you. Now I can tell her good news. Your mom and Kenzie are grabbing some coffee," her dad explained. "Tasha is with Tristan, trying to track the cars in case one of them contains Zach and Devi. As for the team, everyone's fine. I got into it with one of the guards. It's nothing. By the time we got in, they were mostly fleeing, so we didn't even get to fight much. It's you we're worried about. We were lucky to have Aidan with us."

"I'll be okay," she whispered back to her dad. How much had this job of hers cost her parents? "The last time he worked me over for way longer, and I was fine a couple of days later. But I think I should come out of the field for a while. Maybe a long while."

A long breath huffed out of her dad, and his shoulders slumped. He reached for her hand. "I thought…"

"You thought you would have to fight me," she surmised, squeezing her dad's hand. She'd learned this lesson. "You thought I would do anything I had to do to keep my job. I'm more than my job, and I don't want to find that bullet with my name on it. I think one day I'd like to actually work at McKay-Taggart, and I want to start learning how to run the place. I'm pretty sure Coop will be there with me, and we'll keep the name going strong. But it'll have to wait a couple of years. Dad, we have to see this one through. After we catch Huisman, we can all decide what we want to do, but we have to deal with him."

Or the world would burn. She knew that. She'd known for a long time. But it didn't look like she would be the one to take him down. She would be relegated to being behind the scenes.

And she was okay with that. Her sister could finish this job, and Kala would be cheering her on all the way.

"I promise we won't let him get away with it." Her father brought her hand up to his lips, kissing it. "I thought I lost you."

She gave him a smile. A weak smile, but a smile. "I'm tougher than that." She glanced over and Coop was still asleep, looking adorably rumpled. "Did he lose his shit? Did someone take video this time because I would like to see it."

Her father's eyes rolled. "No. He did not. He got you out of the house and then started CPR. Aidan took over as soon as he could. He had adrenaline in his pack and got your heart restarted, and here we are."

"And in the chaos Huisman escaped." But he wasn't the only one. One of the last things she remembered was watching her cousin being carried out like she was Persephone being dragged to the underworld. "How did Zach get away?"

Her father growled a little. "From what I can tell, he had someone waiting for him. He's in the wind. Do you think he plans to hurt your cousin?"

She managed to slightly shake her head. She was going to talk to Cooper about his CPR techniques. Or Aidan. One of them had nearly cracked her ribs, it felt like. Otherwise, she seemed to be in decent condition. "He's in love with her. I think he knows his time is limited, and he wants to protect her while he can. And probably sleep with her. A lot."

"Too much information. I'm going to kill that kid when we catch him," her father grumbled. "I could help him. I'm not going to turn him over to the damn Agency. Your mother wouldn't let me."

Her mom had a soft spot for Zach, but then she also knew what it meant to be beholden to a criminal parent. Although she was pretty sure Shannon Reed wasn't like her grandfather, the hard-core syndicate boss. She was about to do a lot of research into Cooper's biological mother. "He needs to do this. I think Devi will prove harder to deal with than he imagines."

The door opened, and she heard a soft gasp. "You're awake."

"Thank god you're awake."

Her mom and Kenzie. They rushed in, cups of coffee in hand.

Cooper stirred, and then his eyes went wide as he sat straight up. "Kala."

Her guy looked so relieved. He scrambled up, reaching for her hand. Her dad stepped back, an oddly wistful look on his face.

Then Cooper had all of her attention. He stared down at her like she was some sort of miracle.

"I'm okay." She needed to calm him down. She could only imagine how she would feel if he was the one lying in this bed. Hell, she might be overly dramatic and cause a massive scene. He was worth it. "I'm not going into the field again anytime soon, but I'm okay."

She heard a gasp, knew what she'd said was going to be a shock to her twin, but it was the right thing to do. For her future. For Cooper.

Cooper leaned over and kissed her forehead. "I can't tell you how happy that makes me."

Lou had rolled out of bed and joined Cooper. "You scared us."

It was no surprise to her that TJ was still sleeping. "Sorry. Also, you should know that I intend to listen to every lecture you give from now until the end of time."

Lou's grin kicked up. "Glad to know because I have some thoughts on our comms unit."

"We're going to let you get some sleep," her mother said. "We'll be back in a couple of hours. I think they'll release you and let you go home because we have Aidan with us. He's been a godsend dealing with the doctors here."

She was ready to be home. "Good because we have a wedding to plan."

Cooper settled in beside her. "We do, though I'm willing to give my mom an extra week. She got shot, after all."

Her mom frowned. "We need six months."

Cooper yawned and gently wrapped an arm around her. "Nope. We're getting married in a couple of weeks. If you and Mom want to plan a big old reception in six months we can talk, but I'm locking her down. I've waited way too long and seen her almost die too many times. We're getting married at the courthouse."

"We'll see about that," her mother vowed, a steely look in her eyes.

"Good luck," her dad said and frowned Cooper's way. "But no one is calling me Grumpa."

Kenzie reached out and squeezed her hand. "I'll call Travis, and we'll start teaching Colton immediately. It fits. And we'll talk later."

Her twin was going to be a problem, but she knew what she had to do. Take care of herself because Cooper deserved a partner who did.

Because she deserved to be loved. Even by herself.

Cooper laid his head on her shoulder. "Can I get you anything?"

She shook her head. She had everything she could possibly need. They all settled down for a couple more hours of sleep before taking the journey home.

There would be more missions, more danger to come. Probably a shit ton more drama.

And she was ready for it all.

"I need ketchup," TJ mumbled as Lou snuggled close.

Kala yawned and fell asleep to the steady sound of her cousin snoring.

All was right with her world.

\* \* \* \*

*Three Weeks Later*

"I can't believe they did it," Charlotte said, looking over at the dinner reception playing out at Top. The whole restaurant was decorated for a party and filled with family. "I thought I would be able to talk Cooper out of the whole three-week wedding thing. I knew I wouldn't be able to convince Kala, but I thought I could guilt Coop into it."

Eve McKay was just happy to be upright. Getting shot sucked. It was why she was really more of a behind-the-desk employee. Of course, having all her kids home made up for some of the pain. Vivian had come home from England, where she shared a flat with Sophy Weston. Both had hopped the first plane they could find, and they'd stayed for the wedding. Having her baby girl home for a while was lovely. Since Vivi was home, Hunter and Cooper had been coming over most days. Being with her family was the best thing in the world.

And all she had to do was take a bullet.

"You should be grateful," Eve told her friend. "You have plenty to do with Tasha's wedding, and don't bring up the double-wedding thing. You know Kala would die before sitting around picking flowers and DJs. Tash is more than happy to have a big to-do."

Tasha's wedding to Dare Nash was coming up in a few months, and Charlotte was deeply invested.

Charlotte whined a little because she was deeply invested in all of her kids. Even the ones who wouldn't like a big wedding. "But I could have done it for her."

Eve looked out over the gathering. Top was closed for the

evening, the entire restaurant filled with friends and family celebrating a wedding that felt like it would never happen. They had managed to convince the bride and groom that they could do a pared-down service here at Top. The ceremony itself had been brief and beautiful, with Kala surprising everyone she knew by giving her vows in the form of a poem.

And she let her brother play guitar, so it was almost like a song.

It had been a beautiful, romantic gesture from a woman who didn't make them. Except for her husband. Cooper had found a rare treasure in his wife. "It was what they wanted. They didn't want to wait, didn't need anything more than this."

Charlotte sniffled. "I suppose. I just wish her cousin could have been here."

Devi was still missing. The team had been trying to track Zach but had come up with nothing. They'd had a bit more luck with Huisman, who seemed to be in Asia. They were working with other intelligence agencies. Specifically in Nepal. She would have to watch her son and new daughter-in-law go back into danger, and way sooner than she would like. Which was never.

As long as Huisman was out there, no one in their world was safe. Maybe no one in *the* world was safe. But she had faith. If anyone could save the world, it was their kids.

So proud. She was so damn proud of them all.

"Well, she's not here because she's a dumbass," Erin said, walking up to join them. She was accompanied by Serena Dean-Miles. There was a glass of champagne in her hand and a frown on her face. "I still can't believe she ditched her guard. I told Zach he should spank her ass good. I hope they're holed up in a club and she gets acquainted with a spanking bench. I knew timeouts didn't work. Especially when her father would sit there with her. I blame Theo."

"He wasn't much of a disciplinarian," Serena noted. "Which is why all the kids adored him."

Eve felt her eyes go wide because Serena was missing the point. "You talked to him?"

"Of course," Erin replied. "He keeps us up to date, and Devi complains bitterly. Do you seriously think I would be calmly hanging out here if I didn't know she was safe?"

Serena nodded. "I've talked to her, too. Devi is Brianna's best friend. She was planning some crazy stuff. Those girls do not leave each other behind."

Erin stared at Serena. "Yeah, it was all about Bri. Tell me you're not plotting the book right now."

Serena was a romance writer. A grin crossed her face. "It's going to be fabulous. The kids are really giving me vibes. I think I'm even more prolific now."

"He contacted us two days after he took her," Charlotte explained, eyeing her sister-in-law. "Though that's supposed to be confidential."

Erin waved it off. "I'm not Agency. I don't have to keep their secrets. Besides, that boy is good with technology. Tristan's been trying to catch his signal when he calls, but he can't do it. We're pretty sure they're in the States. Or Europe. Or we don't know and my daughter has a mouth on her. I'm proud of her for that. Less proud that she was a dumbass and got Eve shot."

"I don't blame her for that. It wasn't like she pulled the trigger," Eve argued.

"She didn't understand the situation, and she thought Zach dumped her," Charlotte tried to explain.

"She was acting out, but it's understandable," Serena agreed. "She didn't think Zach cared enough about her that his enemies would think she was a good target."

"Well, she's aware now that he was always interested," Erin quipped. "It's a weird life, my friends. I feel like I have couples sessions with my daughter and her kidnapper, and I often come out on the kidnapper's side."

Eve gave her a half hug, leaning into Erin. "If it helps, I think he's desperately in love with her."

Erin sighed. "And I know she loves him, but I worry this is going to end in tragedy. I'm not worried about her being in danger. Zach is very competent, and I believe him when he tells me if he needs to, he'll bring her home. I think Zach is trying to spend what he thinks are his last days with her. It makes my heart ache." She took a long breath. "But I'm so happy for Kala and Cooper. And you guys didn't even have to do the whole wedding-plan thing. Daphne is serious about wedding planning. Lou is too busy working. TJ only cares about what food is going to be served, so someone had to step up and wedding plan with our future in-laws."

Charlotte grinned. "Theo's doing a great job. The peonies he selected are going to be lovely at the church."

"Oh, and I've seen his color scheme for the reception." Grace walked up with Avery O'Donnell. "Their venue is going to be gorgeous, and it will be Theo's doing. Daphne, for all her enthusiasm, is more about the cake and trying to force Lou into a wedding dress. Theo could go into wedding planning."

"I know I talked to him about the outdoor wedding Daisy and Nate are planning, and he had so many helpful hints," Avery added and then frowned. "He also told me I should be prepared for any number of weird weather things to happen. We are talking about Daisy, so it'll probably be a tornado, but Theo has thoughts on how to plan around it."

Erin laughed. "That's my guy. Eve's the only one who's getting out of this easy. We've all had to plan weddings lately. The good news is we'll be experts by the time Vivi and Hunter are ready to settle down."

"Hunter will be a while," Eve mused. "He's having too much fun. Vivi, on the other hand, well, I'm pretty sure she's got someone she's either seeing in London or wants to be seeing. She's very mysterious about it. I hope it's Archie and not his brother. She's working for Damon Knight, and she talks about his kids a lot. Archie is very normal. Oliver thinks he's James Bond and acts accordingly."

She really, really hoped it was Archie. Oliver Knight hit on every woman he found even vaguely attractive. Including her. And all the women standing near her.

Charlotte shook her head. "Oliver. How that kid came out of Penny's womb I have no idea. I mean I do. He got his dad's height and his mom's hair and eyes, but he got neither of their personalities. It's a shame."

It was fine because Vivi just had a crush, and she would likely get over it the next time a hot bodyguard got hired on.

Her daughter was smart and kind, and she would figure it out.

The way her baby boy had.

"Oh, no. She's got mama tears," Avery said with a grin. She moved in and gave Eve a hug.

Once she'd felt so apart from everyone in her life. She'd survived something unimaginable and told herself simply existing was enough. She'd held herself apart until these women had shown her a different way.

First Grace had come into her life. Her resilience and determination had sparked something in Eve. Serena's zest for life, her deep belief in happily ever afters, had been the first time Eve considered that maybe her story with Alex didn't have to be over. Avery had taught her the greatest gift she could have was to forgive herself. Charlotte was a force of nature who moved them all forward. And Erin was proof that second chances could be the best thing life could offer.

These women had changed her in so many ways, and now she got to go through life with them, got to share these moments. All the good was made more special because she was a part of them. All the bad was easier because they carried her through.

She reached out and hands were suddenly in hers, these magnificent women surrounding her with love.

"I think they're happy tears," Charlotte said with a few of her own in her blue eyes.

"Very happy," Eve agreed. "I'm so blessed to be here with you guys. Thank you for helping create this amazing family of ours. Thanks for being the best sisters I could have had."

"Well, fuck, now I want to cry," Erin complained, but she leaned into Serena.

"We're kind of the best," Avery said with a big smile. "And pretty soon we're going to have babies around again."

Babies. She might have grandbabies to love soon. She couldn't wait.

"I hear we're calling Ian Grumpa from now on," Serena said.

Charlotte groaned.

"Hey, if the shoe fits," Erin countered.

"Ladies, can I steal my wife for a moment? I'd love a dance with the most beautiful woman in the world," a deep voice said.

Her husband. Alex looked gorgeous in his suit. He held out a hand as Seth began to play a slow song.

Ian was with him, holding his hand out to Charlotte. "They want the parents to show off our moves. How about it, baby?"

Eve joined her husband and moved toward the dance floor.

This night and all the nights with him were perfect.

Zach, Devi, and all the New Recruits will return in *Spy With Me* coming September 16th, 2025.

# Acknowledgments

I would like to thank all the amazing people who helped make *No More Spies* such a great experience for me. As always my wonderful team—Kim Guidroz/Chloe Vale, Maria Monroy. Thanks so much to my beta readers—Stormy and Riane. Thanks to Kori Smith for giving me a way to really torture Cooper in the book and for being the best social media admin an author can have. Thanks to everyone at Valentine PR. And to my cover artist Frauke of Croco Designs who so many years ago designed the cover of *The Dom Who Loved Me* and is still with me today. Thanks to my son, Dylan, who formats every book without complaint. At least not in earshot.

As always thanks to my husband, Richard, who reminds me every day what it means to be loved.

# Author's Note

I'm often asked by generous readers how they can help get the word out about a book they enjoyed. There are so many ways to help an author you like. Leave a review. If your e-reader allows you to lend a book to a friend, please share it. Go to Goodreads and connect with others. Recommend the books you love because stories are meant to be shared. Thank you so much for reading this book and for supporting all the authors you love!

# Spy With Me
Masters and Mercenaries: New Recruits, Book 5
By Lexi Blake
Coming September 16, 2025

Zach Reed had two objectives when he joined the CIA team led by Ian and Charlotte Taggart. First, he needed to get close to Cooper McKay. Second, he needed to sideline or dismantle their operation. Getting to know Cooper was even better than he expected, but amongst the team he discovered a family he'd always dreamed of and a woman he wanted to spend his life with. Caught between his mission and his friends, his secrets are exposed, and his only choice is to run. He hopes someday he can make it up to the team and the young woman he's fallen hopelessly in love with.

Devi Taggart thought she finally found the man of her dreams. Spending a long weekend with Zach filled her soul and satisfied all her deepest desires. But dreams turned to nightmares when she discovered he betrayed his team, including her brother. When Zach disappears, Devi swears to turn her back on the man forever. Unfortunately, the real bad guys have figured out she is Zach's weak spot, which makes her a major target.

With Devi in real danger, Zach takes the situation into his own hands and offers her a place to stay with him. An offer he's not about to let her refuse. As they navigate a criminal underworld, Zach is committed to showing Devi he's the right man for her. If only they can survive his family.

# About Lexi Blake

*New York Times* bestselling author Lexi Blake lives in North Texas with her husband and three kids. Since starting her publishing journey in 2010, she's sold over three million copies of her books. She began writing at a young age, concentrating on plays and journalism. It wasn't until she started writing romance that she found success. She likes to find humor in the strangest places and believes in happy endings.

Connect with Lexi online:

Facebook: Lexi Blake
Twitter: authorlexiblake
Website: www.LexiBlake.net
Instagram: authorlexiblake

Sign up for Lexi's free newsletter at www.LexiBlake.net!

Made in United States
North Haven, CT
10 March 2025